Roswell 1947

Written by Zachary Fry

ISBN-13 (Paperback): **978-1-7364104-0-0**

Cover design by: Velcro Design

Contents

I would like to thank my friends and family for encouraging me to pursue my dreams of publishing my first novel. I would also like to thank Velcro Design for designing a badass cover, and I want to thank Jessie Raymond for editing Roswell 1947. The creation of this novel would not have been possible without the support and encouragement from the people in my life. Thank you all.

Chapter 1

---✦---

Will

Bzzzz... bzzzz... The rhythmic buzzing of the cicadas in the cottonwood trees signaled a brutally hot day. It was July 8th, 1947, a day as ordinary as any other day. William Brakel had been tending to the Heartley's farm animals on their property, located just outside Roswell, New Mexico. The sun was getting ready to set over the western horizon when Will noticed Buddy, the Heartley's family dog, a meaty German Shepherd, behaving strangely.

"Hey, what the hell are you looking at, boy?" Will croaked. Buddy was staring off into the desert beyond the chicken coop he stood next to. His shoulders were hunched, and brown and black tufts of hair stood straight up and down the length of his spine. His mouth was in a quiet snarl; eyes transfixed on nothing. "Hey, Buddy, come on," Will said, clapping loudly.

Buddy remained undeterred, statuesque against the orange-red background. Will cautiously approached closer to Buddy and looked in the direction of his gaze. Nothing but dirt and a cloudless sky. He reached his hand down to pat Buddy on the head, but as he touched him, Buddy violently turned his head and nipped Will's hand.

"Goddamn dog!" Will shouted while shaking his hand in pain. Buddy knew better. After biting Will, Buddy quickly relaxed, put his head down, and started to lick Will's leg, as if it was an apology for acting up. He walked in a circle and ended up plopping himself in between Will's legs. Buddy was clearly spooked because his tail was tucked between his hind legs, and he was shivering softly, something Will had rarely seen.

"It's okay, Buddy, you're fine," Will said as he moved again to pat his head. This time Buddy willingly accepted the head pat. "Huh, I wonder what he saw," Will said, perplexed. He scanned the area again to make sure he didn't miss something, but he couldn't see anything. Maybe Buddy was smelling nearby coyotes or some other predatory animal, but it was still unusual behavior. When Buddy saw coyotes or deer, or any other animal, he usually would bark wildly and wag his tail. This behavior was different.

Will still had plenty of work to do before sundown, so he thought it was best to put Buddy back in the Heartley's house for the night. He led Buddy to the house, observing him as he slowly walked up the porch steps and into the house, turning around to stare out at the farm. The house was of an old red brick design. There were two stories; the bottom story started with a concrete porch, surrounded by mesh to keep the bugs out. On the porch was a wooden bench swing, with a pale-yellow blanket resting on top. The porch led to the Heartley's front door, a stained wooden door with squares carved into it. Inside the house, a single central hallway connected the kitchen, dining room, a large bathroom, and two bedrooms. Towards the back of the house was a staircase that led to the second story attic, used mostly for storage, and a guest bedroom. Will lived in the guest bedroom when he worked for the Heartleys during the summer.

He looked at Buddy for a moment, then started his evening tasks. He cleaned the chicken coop and all the shit inside it. He repaired a hole in the metal fencing separating the chickens and pigs. He checked the horse stable, cleaned up the poop, and gave the horses fresh water. The stable held the Heartley's two horses, Prancer and Comet. Both Prancer and Comet were American quarter horses. Prancer was white with a few black patches, and Comet was a light brown color with a black mane. Will could usually finish work in time to watch the sunset, his favorite thing to do whilst he toiled on the Heartley farm.

When he was finally done with his evening tasks, he sat on the porch swing and lit up a Marlboro red. He inhaled deeply and blew the smoke out slowly. Long workdays deserved a cigarette. As he was smoking, his eye caught a flicker of light in the sky that disappeared. He was not quite sure what it was, but he thought he had seen the tail of a meteor in the sky for a brief moment. He blinked and rubbed his eyes, but he only saw the pink horizon stretching out across the sky. "I'm seein shit, it's time to go to sleep," Will said to himself while he put out his cigarette.

As he put out his cigarette, the Heartley family pulled off from the main road Santa Fe Trail that converged with the dirt road leading to the farm. It was flat enough that you could see cars on the highway a half-mile away. The family had been out for the day running errands that Tom

Heartley said needed to be done. First, they went to church, then they got more food for the animals, bought groceries, and bought more metal fencing so Will could fix the deteriorating remainder. The red pickup truck Tom was driving creaked to a halt as the truck parked several feet in front of the porch.

Tom hopped out of the driver's side first and greeted Will with a "Howdy!"

Tom was a small man, 5'6 and 130 pounds, but he was strong as hell for a 60-year-old. He had been doing farm work his whole life, which was why he was still able to chuck 100-pound hay bales with ease. He always wore overalls and a dirty cowboy hat, and today was no exception. In the driver's seat was his wife, Macey. She was slightly taller than Tom, with wide hips and a curvy figure. She had the curliest hair you had ever seen and a dark brown skin tone. Their daughter Daisy was a thin girl of 16, even taller than her mother. She had curly hair like her mom but had the complexion of her European father. Daisy and her mom were wearing matching yellow dresses. They walked into the house as Tom planted himself next to Will.

"How were all the animals today?" Tom asked as he sat down.

"Good and healthy. One of the hens laid four eggs. I put them by the fridge," Will replied. Tom nodded and closed his eyes.

"We're going to have to fix the horse stable soon too. Been leakin right above Comet's pen when it rains."

"I saw that and patched it up, but we need a new roof for the stable. A patch is only a temporary fix. I also fixed the fencing in most of the chicken coop. Oh yeah, and uh, that reminds me, Buddy was acting a little strange today. He was just starin off inta nothin. I tried to pet him, and the bastard nipped at me. He's never done nothin like that before."

"Yeah, I've noticed a change in him too. I reckon I started seeing it a couple of days back. One time just last week, I saw him barking at nothin, then suddenly he shit himself and came runnin in the house. It's like he's sensing something out there, or he's just going senile, haha," Tom chuckled.

Will let out a laugh in response. Tom was right. Buddy was getting up there in age and could just be getting paranoid over nothing. The sun was now completely set, and Will needed to sleep. He said goodnight to Tom and headed up the stairs to his bedroom in the dusty attic. He had a cot he always slept on, stuffed away in one corner of the attic. A tiny bathroom in the attic with a toilet and sink was where he got ready for bed. He washed his face with some cold water, brushed his teeth, and hit the cot. It took him all of five minutes to fall asleep. He awoke suddenly to Buddy's violent barking.

"Jesus Christ, what time is it?"

Will looked at the small owl clock in the room. It read 10:30 P.M. As he rolled out of bed, he noticed a faint glow of light coming from his window. He couldn't see much from his window, but whatever was producing the light was close to the horse stable. Frightened by the thought of thieves, he ran downstairs. He saw Tom at the front door, dreary eyed and naked except for his tidy whiteys, with his revolver drawn.

"Prolly them damn coyotes again. Shut your ass up, Buddy!" Tom snarled. Buddy looked up and whimpered, then went silent. Tom opened the front door and let in the blackness of the night. Will was surprised Daisy and Macey had not woken up from the noise.

Tom opened up the porch screen door, and Buddy started howling again. As soon as he opened the door, Buddy shot out of the porch at a dead sprint towards the horse stable. The farm was big enough that Buddy disappeared from eyesight within seconds, and Will could only faintly hear his barking as he ran. The horse stable was on the far side of the yard, about a quarter-mile away. Will and Tom stood on the porch for a second, shared a look, and then bolted after Buddy.

The property was around five acres in size, and the stable was in the northwest corner of the yard. Beyond the farm on the other side of the dirt road was a cornfield their neighbors owned. As Will and Tom ran past the horse stable, Will was almost blinded by a blue sphere of light. The horses were neighing and moving about in their stable, clearly spooked by something. Will covered his eyes, hearing Buddy only a few yards away, barking loudly. Will's eyes adjusted, and what he saw was both interesting and terrifying. Will rubbed his eyes and looked at Tom, who stood open-mouthed and wide-eyed at the light source.

"What the fuck is that thing?" Tom blurted out as he dropped the revolver. Will was looking at a large silvery metallic disc of some sort. The blue light was emanating from the bottom of the disc in a circle. He had heard reports in the local newspaper about U.F.O sightings in the area, but he didn't believe that shit. This had to be some military airplane that accidentally crashed, but he had never seen a plane or helicopter that looked like this.

As Will and Tom walked closer to the metallic disc, he got a better look at it. The blue light was actually individual blue lights that formed a small circle on the underside of the disc. The texture of the disc looked smooth like wax; he couldn't see any bolts or screws on the surface. Everything on the disc appeared to be smooth and seamless, as if it was constructed in one instant with no imperfections. It was roughly 25 feet in diameter. The center of the disc was the thickest part, maybe 10 feet in height, and as it spread towards its edges, it grew paper-thin. A small window could be seen near the middle of the disc, but Will could not see anybody inside of it. Will guessed that someone would have to sit in the middle to pilot the disc, but it was too dark to see seats inside of it. As Will examined the exterior, he noticed that the metal was unlike anything he had ever seen. It didn't appear to be steel or aluminum. It almost looked ceramic and shiny at the same time. The spaceship itself was grayish-silver in color with a bright sheen to it.

Will could see his reflection on the side of it. Pale skin, brown hair, long gangly legs. He looked tired. "What should we do?" Will asked Tom, who stood with his mouth open, staring. By now, at least Buddy was calm and had started sniffing around the disc.

"I'll tell you what, Will, this sure as hell ain't no coyotes," Tom said nervously.

"Think this is some military bullshit?" Will asked, too scared to walk all the way around the disc. Will looked at the path that it had made in the dirt as it crashed. He had been too frazzled to see the disc was sitting in a miniature crater it had created as it slid to a halt. He estimated the disc landed 50 feet away from the southeast and slid to its current location. He could see a trail of debris the spaceship had left in its wake. There were bits and pieces of the strange material scattered in the trail, but he couldn't tell what they were. The pieces didn't look like normal nuts or bolts, or engine parts, for that matter.

"This ain't no damn coyotes I can tell you that much," Tom shakily said again.

"Should we call the cops?" Will asked.

"I reckon we should."

Will could see Buddy's posture change. He sensed something. As Buddy made his way around to the backside of the disc, he started barking wildly again.

"Quit your barking dog," Tom shouted, "it's 10 o'clock in the damn night." Buddy was unrelenting in his clamor. Tom followed behind him cautiously.

"What the fuck? Wha- wha… Will, get the fuck over here!" Tom finally managed to shout.

Will ran to where Tom was standing and followed his gaze to the ground. By the backside of the disc, sprawled like roadkill, were two mangled bodies. At first glance, Will thought he was looking at two children, but a closer look revealed something otherworldly. The two small bodies had two legs, two arms, hands with five fingers and opposable thumbs, massive heads, and large black eyes. Their skin was grayish-green and looked slimy, almost reptilian. One of the bodies had its left arm torn completely off, and blood was dripping onto the ground. There was a large ovular patch of skin on its neck that looked like it had been burned badly. Will couldn't tell if it was alive or not. The other body lay halfway out of the disc like a limp ragdoll, from what appeared to be a small opening to get into the interior of the disc. This one had a large bump on the side of its head, and it was breathing rapidly and shallowly.

"Is-is-is it alive?" Will stammered, pointing to the body halfway in the disc.

"He's breathing, a'int he?" Tom said, hand on his revolver.

"Should we give it water or something?"

"Hell no, don't touch that thing. I'm gonna call the cops and pray to God this is all a bad dream." Tom started running back to the house, revolver in hand. Will saw the almost naked old man running as fast as his legs would carry him. He was scared.

Will was trying to wrap his head around the night's events, when suddenly Buddy bolted off to the north. Too terrified to stand there alone, Will went after him.

Buddy was running towards the cornfield across the street. Will had to walk slowly, too scared to venture off on his own. It was almost a full moon with no clouds in the sky, so Will could see relatively easily a few feet in front of him, but no farther. He was following the sound of Buddy's barks. He walked for two minutes to the north until he was nearly at the property line that separated the Heartleys from the Lovells, when Buddy suddenly went silent.

"Buddy, Buddy, are you there?" Will said to the darkness. He could hear him breathing, so he knew he was close. As Will walked towards Buddy's breathing, he spotted him. The hair on his back was standing up, and he was showing his teeth in a snarl, growling in a low guttural tone. Will couldn't see what Buddy was looking at, but he heard a quiet scratching noise. Terrified, he inched closer to Buddy to see what he was snarling at.

There on the ground was another one of those beings. Same green skin, same oversized eyes, same large head. This one was fully awake but injured. The little creature was pushing itself backwards with its hands as it sat on the ground. Its right ankle was badly broken. The ankle lay at a very unnatural angle as it anxiously crawled away. When the creature noticed Will staring at it, it turned its head to meet his gaze.

The creature slowly lifted its hand and pointed at Buddy. Buddy's posture changed again; his gums covered his teeth, his tail started wagging, and he looked up at Will. Will stood there astonished; it was as if the creature did something to Buddy to change his demeanor. Just then, Tom came bursting through the front door, running over to where the disc was.

"Will, where the hell are you?" Tom howled.

Will couldn't speak. He was mesmerized and petrified by the little creature on the ground. What he was looking at left him speechless. This creature was not from Earth. It was some kind of organism that had an energy he could not comprehend.

The creature was slowly moving away from Buddy and Will as Will stood there motionless. Finally, Will summed up the courage to speak, "Oh-over here. One of them is alive!"

"It's dark as hell Will, and I can't see a damn thing. Keeping saying here."

"Here... here. Here." Tom ran the several hundred yards towards Will's voice. When he got to Will, he stopped to look at him, then Buddy, then finally at the creature on the ground. He turned back to Will.

"We got to kill this son of a bitch," Tom said, aiming his revolver at the creature.

"No-no, don't shoot it! It ain't done nothin to you!"

The creature stopped moving and fixed its gaze on Tom. It was like it could sense what was about to happen. Tom raised the revolver, aimed it, and fired. A loud "BANG" was heard, and Will watched the creature fall to the ground. The bullet hit the creature right in its little chest, and the hole left by the bullet began swelling with dark red blood.

"The fuck did you do that for?" Will asked Tom angrily. If the creature didn't die from the crash, it would surely die from a gunshot wound to the chest. It lay motionless on the ground, its chest moving up and down rapidly.

"We have no fuckin clue what that thing is, and you expect me to let it live? The son of a bitch crashed a spaceship on my property, for God's sake. He could have killed one of my animals! As far as I'm concerned, that's another damn coyote."

"So now, what do we do? Did you call the cops? Was Macey or Daisy awake when you went back inside?"

"Yup, the cops said they would be a while. Daisy was awake when I went back into the house, but I told her to go back to sleep and to not worry about anything."

Hours later, after Will and Tom smoked through two packs of cigarettes and exchanged fewer than 20 words, Will saw red and blue lights in the distance. He watched for several minutes as the lights came closer to the house from the highway and peeled off from the highway down Santa Fe Trail, and then down the dirt road. Will saw six cop cars, two big black vans behind them, and a long half semi-truck with a large flatbed. The cars drove down the driveway and parked in front of the house. Will and Tom were waiting on the porch when the cops arrived.

Police in uniform hopped out of their squad cars, followed by four unidentified men in all black suits wearing sunglasses, and a very tall man in a heavily decorated military uniform walking in front of them. The man in the military uniform led the entourage and walked up to the porch first. He seemed to be getting taller with every step. As he approached the porch, Will could make out his features better. He was broad-shouldered with a square jaw and thick black eyebrows. His skin was a golden brown. Towering over Tom, he put out his hand and said, "I'm General Ramses Meddiah the III. You must be the ones who phoned in."

"Yes, sir, I did. My name is Tom Heartley. Thank you for coming out so late at night. I know it's late as shit."

"If you would be so kind to lead my friends and me to the crash site, we would greatly appreciate it," Ramses said, signaling to the police and the men in black standing behind him.

Tom shook his massive hand and started to lead Ramses to where the spaceship had crashed. Everybody behind Ramses was deathly quiet, which Will found strange. As Tom was leading the group to the crash site, the front door to the house swung open. Macey stood in the doorway in a nightgown, squinting at the large group of men and vehicles parked in her front yard.

She stomped out of the house angry faced. "What in the sam hell is going on here? It's two o'clock in the fucking morning." Her hands were on her hips, and she was staring straight at Tom.

"Babe, I'll tell you what's going on once all these nice folks leave," Tom said, trying to calm her down.

"To hell you will. Why are there ten cops in my front yard Tom? Huh?" Macey said, growing more agitated by the second.

"I, " Tom started to say before Ramses interrupted him.

"Ma'am, if you could step inside for a moment while we take care of this, that would make this easier. It's for your own safety." On cue, two of the cops exchanged a look and walked up the porch towards where Macey was standing. They were telling her something in hushed tones. After several moments Macey shook her head and walked back inside, slamming the door behind her.

After Macey left, the group headed to the horse stable, where the flying disc had crashed. All the police and the four men in black had flashlights, pointing them in every which direction. Several minutes later, they arrived at the spaceship, its blue lights still glowing on the underside. Every time Will looked at the spaceship, he understood it less. Where did this thing come from? Who made it? And why did the cops show up with a high-ranking military official? It was all so confusing.

As the group descended on the spaceship, gasps were heard. Will heard one cop quietly say "Holy fuck," under his breath while he followed his companions. The men in black suits began inspecting the spaceship and the two occupants who were slumped next to it. One of the men in black took the pulse of the creature that was halfway in and halfway out of the opening to the spaceship. Another began examining the disfigured creature that lay motionless on the ground beside its crew member. The other two men in black began walking back towards the house. The cops were picking up debris and putting it into labeled plastic bags.

As this was happening, Tom and Ramses exchanged a few words, and then they headed towards the creature Tom had shot. Except for the initial "Holy fuck," Will hadn't heard a single word spoken from any of the cops or the men in black. How bizarre of a scene it must have been to an outside observer to see an old man in overalls and a skinny farm boy, surrounded by cops and men in black suits working silently at three in the morning. Will approached one of the men in black who appeared to be taking a skin sample from one of the creatures. He had a small knife that he used to cut away a patch of the creature's skin.

"What's going on here? What are these things? Have you seen something like this before?" Will asked the man.

The man was white and bald. Come to think of it, all of the men in black suits were bald. He looked up from his work at Will. He had big bags under his eyes, visible from underneath the sunglasses. He held his gaze with Will for a moment, then returned to his work without saying anything. Will tried to ask him again, but this time the man didn't even look up. He just kept working. Will got the message; this was not to be talked about openly.

After a couple of minutes, the two men in black who had initially walked back to the house appeared, driving the large truck with the flatbed. "We need some cuffs over here. This one is still alive," Will heard Ramses shout hoarsely. One overweight white cop ran over to where Ramses and Tom were standing. Will could hear the cop fumbling with his handcuffs. "Give me the damn things, Jesus," Ramses said to him, snatching the cuffs from the cop's hands. The cop walked back into Will's view, pale-faced and scared.

The men in black were expressionless while they were going about their work. It was like they were seasoned veterans when it came to dealing with this kind of stuff. The cops all looked scared and uncertain, like kids who knew they shouldn't be out after dark. One of the cops vomited; it was the same guy Will saw who tried to cuff the creature. Differences between the two groups couldn't be more obvious.

Will guessed this was not the first time the men in black had encountered something otherworldly, based on the way they were handling the situation. Tom walked back over to where Will was standing, and they watched the group of men throw ropes over the spaceship. When it was safely tied, they lifted it with a series of pulleys and muscle power. The large spaceship hit the metal bed of the truck with a loud thud. Once the spaceship was on the bed of the truck, they removed all the ropes and covered it with a large black tarp that completely hid the spaceship underneath. All three of the creatures were wrapped in shiny silver bags and placed into one of the black vans. General Ramses walked over to where Tom and Will stood, solemn-faced and silent.

"A word with you two gents," the General said, motioning toward the darkness. Tom and Will followed Ramses until they were well out of earshot of the cops and men in black.

"Now I want you two to know you did the right thing calling the police. However, neither one of you can speak about any of the events you both witnessed tonight. Not even your families and loved ones can know about what happened tonight. These conditions are not optional. They are mandatory. Failure to abide by the conditions may result in your disappearance. Any questions? Good," the General finally concluded before Will or Tom could object to the terms.

"To hell, I ain't tellin no one. Goddamn aliens crash in my yard, and I can't tell no one?" Tom responded with fiery eyes. Ramses walked straight in front of Tom, his full stature looming over him, like an adult to a child. Tom only came up to his nipple. With his head pointing straight down, he looked at Tom squarely. He stayed staring at Tom for a couple of seconds, and Will watched the courage and strength Tom always had seep out of his body. Tom's head slumped down, and he nodded. "Alright, I won't tell nobody."

Will stood there, thinking silently. Did Tom say that aliens crashed on their property? Will had been praying that it wasn't aliens he had seen. He did not want to believe it. Maybe they were just little men from the Army... no. Fuck no. He was pretty damn sure when he first saw the bodies of the aliens next to the silvery disc that they were aliens, but part of him didn't want to believe it. Now, after hearing Tom call them aliens, he was more confident that they truly were beings from another world.

General Ramses turned and glared at Will, a long hard stare, then walked towards the vehicles. Ramses hopped into one of the black vans without saying a word. All six of the cop cars pulled out in front of the group then turned on their lights. They led the group and were followed by the two vans, and finally by the large truck with the flying disc in the back. As the group drove onto the dirt road and onto Santa Fe Trail, they looked like a miniature parade moving through the night, police lights flashing.

Will and Tom stood there for a second, silent. After a moment, Will said, "Well, it's nearly five in the mornin. I'm a get going to bed." Tom shook his head in acknowledgment.

"Take the day off tomorrow. We both gon need it," Tom replied. Will walked up the concrete porch steps and opened the door. Buddy was sleeping right beside the door, noisily snoring. Will turned to look at Tom one more time before he went to the attic. Tom was taking deep long puffs of his cigarette, staring at the sky. Will wondered if Tom was alright. Shit, he wondered if he was alright.

Will walked up to the attic and flew straight to his cot. Exhausted, he lay there thinking. What had he seen? Why was nobody talking during that retrieval mission? Would he really die if he talked about it? No answers. Will thought about God and wondered if God knew about aliens. Will fiddled with the golden cross hanging on one of the bedposts before he drifted off to sleep.

He awoke to sunlight beaming in his eyes. He guessed it was noon. He walked downstairs and saw Tom in his tidy whiteys with a bowl of cheerios in front of him. Macey and Daisy were cooking grilled cheese sandwiches.

"Goooodddd morning Will! Do you want a grilled cheese?" Daisy asked as she saw him enter the kitchen.

"Sure, thank you," Will said as he took a seat at the square table Tom was sitting at. Tom sat there, staring at his bowl, not taking a bite.

"Mornin," Will said to Tom. Tom looked up and grunted, then looked back down into his bowl.

"You haven't even touched your bowl, Tom," Macey said, walking over to Tom.

"Told you I ain't hungry," Tom replied. In all his years working on the Heartley farm, Will had never seen Tom turn down a breakfast. Clearly, Tom was distraught, and Macey picked up on it.

"Well, if you're not going to eat, then you have to tell me what happened last night," Macey said, now intensely staring at Tom.

"I can't!" Tom boomed, pushing the bowl away from him. Will could see the gears turning in his head.

"Damn it, Tom! Twenty police officers and a General of the Air Force show up at our house in the middle of the night, and you can't tell me what happened? Well, fine, cook your own damn lunch. I'm going into town for the day," Macey said angrily. She took off the red kitchen apron she was wearing, bagged up one of the grilled cheese sandwiches, kissed Daisy, and left the room.

"Well, this uh, grilled cheese sure is good. Thank you, Daisy," Will said, trying to break the awkward silence of the room. Tom sat silent, moving his spoon around the bowl but not eating.

"Thank you, Will."

"So... how did you sleep last night, Daisy? Did the commotion wake you?" Will asked.

"Yeah. I slept okay, but I had the strangest dream last night."

"Oh, what happened in your dream?" Will asked, pretending to be interested.

"Well, first off, I thought I was awake because it felt so real. I woke up to a really bright light coming from my window. What color was the light?" Daisy asked herself. "Oh yeah, it was a blue light, and when I opened the curtains, I saw the light floating in our yard. After a couple of seconds, it was really far away, then it suddenly reappeared and slammed into our yard and crashed, making a really loud noise. Once it hit the ground, the lights became dimmer, and I couldn't tell where it was cause it was too dark. It felt so real though. I even heard Buddy barking in the dream. Weird stuff, right?" Daisy concluded while biting into her sandwich.

"Oh my god," Will said in shock. Will looked at Tom, who sat wide-eyed, staring at his daughter, dropping his metal spoon to the floor. "Daddy, you dropped your spoon!"

Chapter 2

---※---

Ramses

Beep.. beeeep… beeep screeched the alarm clock next to Ramses' bed. 04:00, not a second more or a second less. It was July 8th, 1947. Ramses shot out of bed and began robotically making it. "Just like they taught me at boot camp," he said to himself. He had gotten up every day at 04:00 since he enlisted into the U.S. Army Signal Corps at 18 years old, in 1907. He was now 58, but had the physical health of a 25 five-year-old. He was fit both mentally and physically, a specimen of a man. 6'6 and 250 pounds, he was a force to be reckoned with.

Ramses joined the military partially to avenge his father, and partially to get his life back on track. His father, Rammad Meddiah the II, was an Egyptian immigrant who joined the U.S. Navy after he became a citizen in 1876. Fierce and intelligent, Ramses idolized his father. Ramses' mother, Samira Meddiah, met Rammad at Naval Station New Port in Rhode Island. The two fell in love and got married, and had Ramses in 1889. When Ramses was 10, his father died in an "unexplained" shipping accident over the Gulf of Mexico. Ever since, Ramses vowed to follow in his father's footsteps and join a branch of the military to avenge his death.

As a youth, he got in trouble a lot because he was depressed and confused after his father died. His family had never been given a proper explanation for what happened, and it haunted Ramses and his mother. He got into fights at school, refused to do his homework, and would even bully kids who were smaller than him. By 16, his mother had had enough and decided to put him in the New Mexico Military Institute in Roswell. Those two years changed Ramses completely, and after he graduated at 18, he went straight to the local recruiting office to join the U.S. Army Signal Corps.

His father had died a lieutenant in the Navy. Ramses was now a five-star General. He knew his father would be proud of him if he could see him today. After his father died, his mother was lonely and bitter the rest of her life, until she died ten years later, when Ramses was 20. Ramses spent the next 38 years of his life ranking up, eventually landing in the position he was currently at, as General of the Air Force. His current assignment was to oversee advanced nuclear weapons tests at Los Alamos National Laboratories. He sat in attendance during the first live atomic bomb test and had seen others since then.

The sheer scale of the explosions was the most numbing part of the experiences. An observer had to sit miles away to even see the explosion without being vaporized. Grenades and mortar shells on the battlefield hailed in comparison. He had participated in World War 2 and saw firsthand how weapons, especially weapons of mass destruction, could mean victory or complete failure.

As a General in the military, he was frequently involved in top-secret briefings. He had the highest level of clearance in the military: top-secret Q clearance. This meant if the president or other high ranking military officials needed to debrief him about high-level threats, they could do so without going through mountains of paperwork. The night before, on July 7th, 1947, he received a call from the N.S.A., telling him to report to Kirtland Air Force Base at 06:00 sharp the next day. He lived in the subsidized housing directly across from Kirtland Air Force Base, on Gibson Boulevard, so it was easy for him to make it on base by 06:00.

At 05:45 July 8th, 1947, he sat down in a debriefing room, ready to be debriefed on a top-secret development the pentagon had discovered. The room was small and dimly lit, with only a metal table, a few chairs, and a light bulb hanging overhead that was the only source of illumination in the room. He was led into the room by a young Sergeant. "Thank you, sir," Ramses said while the door between the room and the rest of the building closed. "It's just me," Ramses said to himself as he sat in the room quietly. After a minute or so, the door opened again, and Colonel Garcia walked through the door, followed by a short, plump man with a weaselly face, whom Ramses did not recognize. The Colonel was an old acquaintance of Ramses.

"General," Colonel Garcia said while shaking Ramses' hand.

"Pleasure seeing you again, Colonel," Ramses responded.

"Likewise, sir."

"Hi General, I am Dr. Barry," the plump man said, announcing himself to Ramses.

"General Ramses, pleased to meet you. Now, why have I been summoned today?"

"We uh- got some pictures you need to take a look at General," Barry said nervously, opening up a black briefcase he had been holding. He pulled out a manilla colored folder stamped "Top-secret" in bright red letters across the front of it. He handed the folder to Ramses.

He opened it up and started pulling out its contents. The first sheet appeared to show a small metallic object approximately 100 miles west of Florida, hovering in the Gulf of Mexico. The picture was dated July 3rd, 1947, 09:01. It had been taken by a pilot flying overhead during test flights the navy was conducting. A comment on the bottom of the photograph read, "I ain't never seen nothin like it. One second it'd be still; the next, it was like miles away. I tried to take several pictures, but only one came out good." Dennis Smith, Airman Basic.

"So, some lowly airman doesn't know what he saw, what's the big deal?" Ramses asked.

"Keep looking, General," Colonel Garcia urged.

Ramses started looking at the next sheet, which was another photograph. There was a cuboid metallic object floating about 50 feet above the ground, based on a nearby light-post it hovered over. The photograph was black and white, the cuboid appearing a dark gray against the lighter background. The observer was approximately 100 yards away, addressed in comments at the bottom of the photograph. The picture was blurry, but you could still make out a definitive square shape and the color of the object.

The sheet behind the photograph described the scenario in which the photograph was taken. Air Force recruits were doing their morning jog on Holloman Air Force Base when the base's radar system detected an unidentified flying object in their airspace. They tried to contact the plane, but it would not respond to any communications. The base went into red alert, and personnel manned their battle stations, preparing for a suspected Japanese attack.

As the group of jogging recruits made its way inside, the commanding officer saw the object appear "out of nowhere" and started trying to take pictures of it with his camera. Moments after the photograph had been taken, the object disappeared completely. The base could not pick it up on the radar, and nobody else observed it further. All of the men who were jogging saw the object and verified the account the commanding officer had given.

Strange. Ramses had never seen an airplane like that before. There were airplanes and helicopters, and pretty much nothing else. Squares had no way to gain speed or lift off the ground; the government had tried that. The United States military had built prototypes of some cuboids in 1940 but eventually scrapped the program altogether. This one was floating in the picture, clear as day. "We have reason to believe those two photographs show the same object," Colonel Garcia said quietly.

Ramses looked down at the time stamp on the second photograph: July 3rd, 1947, 09:01.

"Do you expect me to believe the object was in 2 different places at once?" Ramses asked.

"Well, you see, General, that is nothing but an illusion. The timestamp does not record time down to the second. So technically, the object could be going fast - very fast," Barry said while wiping his glasses on his lab coat.

"Listen here, Barry. I've worked in the military for 40 years, and I have never seen something that can move anywhere close to that fast. If a human being was in that object, he would die immediately. The G-forces would kill him. You are either incompetent or a dumbass," Ramses smirked. Barry blushed and put his head down.

"General, look at the radar reports. Same exact signal twice. One from Holloman Air Force Base, and one from the pilot in the gulf," Colonel Garcia said firmly.

Ramses sifted through the rest of the documents until he found both radar reports. One sheet from Holloman Air Force Base and one from the pilot in the gulf. The long list of data matched exactly on both documents. This was no coincidence. A real object was detected, an object moving exponentially faster than anything the United States military could create.

"Have there been any more sightings?" Ramses asked the room.

"One possibly. Unconfirmed, no photographs," Barry squeaked.

"Details of the report?" Ramses said while pointing to his watch.

"An old lady in Roswell, New Mexico called the cops and said she had seen a flying saucer," Colonel Garcia replied.

"Could have been something, or just a crazy old lady off her meds," Ramses retorted.

Ramses was contemplating what all this meant. The radar signal indicated the same object was in two different places, virtually at once. Multiple credible witnesses photographed and described similar phenomena.

"Keep the base on code yellow. If anything suspicious shows up on the radar, I will order the base to code red. I'm giving you the authority to use lethal force with your squadrons. I do not know what these airplanes are, but we need to be prepared if they attack," Ramses said while standing.

The Colonel nodded and shook the General's hand. Ramses looked down at his watch, 06:30. He would still have plenty of time to see the morning bomb test at Los Alamos National Laboratory. This was an important mock nuclear bomb test. The physicists and engineers would be testing a very small nuclear weapon deep below the ground and measuring its effects on the surface. He could not miss it.

"We will be in contact, Colonel. Keep your phone on at your home. I hate to do that to you, but you know the drill. I will not report this to any other General since no violence has occurred as of yet." Ramses stood up and shook the Colonel's hand.

"Yes, sir," the Colonel responded, returning the hand shake.

"Barry. Sorry about insulting you. I didn't mean any harm. I'm sure you're a great scientist."

"It's okay, General. Nice to meet you."

The three men left the small dark room one by one. Ramses left to go to a private helicopter pad, where he would be helicoptered into Los Alamos. He walked out to the airfield, the crisp wind escorting him in all his military significance. The mountains were looming tall to the east as he approached the helicopter. A young Captain was waiting for him at the pad. The blades were spinning loudly overhead as the pilot saluted Ramses, who returned the salute.

He flew by the desert, watching cactus and dirt appear and reappear out of the back window. Today was an important test. Scientists at Los Alamos were perfecting the hydrogen bomb, but it was so powerful that it was becoming hard to find places to test it at. Digging underground and exploding them down deep in the Earth became the best solution.

The helicopter made it to Los Alamos in a few hours and landed on a concrete landing strip next to the main Los Alamos facility. The helicopter came slowly to the ground, hitting it with a dull thud. Ramses waited for the blades to stop spinning, then opened up the cabin. He hopped out alongside the pilot who saluted him as he left the cabin.

Ramses was greeted by other high-ranking military personnel and scientists who were waiting for his arrival. They led him to their viewing station of the bomb test several kilometers away. The labs were surrounded by dirt and open space, perfect for blowing up bombs.

"Five, four, three, two, one," Ramses heard a man behind him say. He heard a small click, then on the western horizon, he saw a rumble in the Earth. Dirt and debris erupted from the ground, blasting high into the sky, creating a miniature mushroom cloud around 100 feet high. The shock wave could be seen traveling through the dust in the air, and then it hit. BOOM. Ramses felt his medals shaking on his uniform. There was a collective sigh of relief from the scientists that everything happened the way it was supposed to.

"Magnificent, is it not?" Ramses asked the group.

"Truly. The power is remarkable. We are nearly 5 kilometers away from the blast, yet we are affected by it. Not to mention it was buried underground," one of the physicists watching the blast said.

No matter how many times Ramses watched a bomb test, he felt uneasy about it. The capacity for destruction was immense. A small error could result in countless causalities. Ramses personally knew four people who died trying to build nuclear bombs or harness nuclear energy in some capacity. All four succumbed to different types of cancer; bone, liver, and brain cancer, to name a few. It was dangerous work, but a dark side of Ramses liked it. He liked the feeling of power. He liked having weapons and abilities that other nations didn't possess.

After some lengthy goodbyes, Ramses was flown back to Kirtland Air Force Base. It was nearly 17:00 when he got back. Once back, he spent the rest of his day preparing for the week ahead. He wrote his schedule out down to the minute for the whole week. He could still make Tuesday night mass at the local Christian church on Gibson.

Ramses thought about the objects that were detected that evening in church. He was positive the Russians did not have a plane that could travel that fast. The Germans certainly didn't either, because Ramses personally had seen every document related to the German military the United States possessed, and none showed a plane capable of that speed. Japan, more than likely, did not have the capability of the object either. Was it aliens? No, that's dumb talk. God created humans in the image of Himself. Ramses knew it. There were no such things as aliens.

The military was always coming up with reports on unidentified flying objects. Sometimes they were large birds, sometimes military prototype vehicles a civilian had spotted, and sometimes it was poor visibility. Ramses did not take any of the sightings very seriously, but these latest sightings were different and troublesome.

Ramses needed to sleep. Getting up at 04:00 every day meant he had to be disciplined about going to bed early. With the sun low in the sky, he closed the blinds and prepared for bed. He lived by himself in a small apartment the military paid for. He had no kids, no wife, and no animals. His life was work. Working was his sole purpose; he worked seven days a week and rarely took a day off. He had a golden crucifix with Jesus hanging on it, on one of his four bedposts. He prayed to it like he did every night. "Thank you, Lord, our Father, for your mercy. May you watch over me with your blessed hands, amen." He kissed the cross then put it back in its place. Next to his bed was a nightstand with an old electronic clock on it. He set his alarm for 04:00 and fell asleep.

He was awakened at 23:00 by his telephone ringing. He rolled out of bed and walked over to the ringing phone on his desk.

"General, it's Colonel Garcia. Sorry to wake you at this hour, but this is urgent. An unidentified flying object has crash-landed near Roswell, New Mexico. A farmer called the police 15 minutes ago, and the police called me," he said.

"Okay, thank you, Colonel. I'll put on my uniform and head to the base. Make sure we have a truck big enough to transport a large object. I will call the head of the N.S.A. myself for backup personnel. Meet me at the Gibson gate in 15 minutes with the N.S.A. guys."

"Will do, sir. Over and out," the Colonel said while hanging up the phone.

Ramses made his bed, then dawned his military uniform, dotted with ribbons and medals he had earned. The ribbons and medals clung to the jacket as a reminder of the importance of the man who was wearing them. After putting on his uniform and straightening out his tie, he called the head of the N.S.A.

"…. What, what time is it?" a groggy sounding voice answered.

"It's 23:00, sir, sorry for the bother. This is General Ramses of the United States Air Force. I have an urgent request. An unidentified flying object has crashed near Roswell, New Mexico, and I need Albuquerque's secret service agents to assist me in investigating the crash site."

"…Ahh.. uh, what? An unidentified flying object, you said? Sure, sure, General. Use my men how you see fit."

"Thank you, sir, and goodnight." And with that, Ramses hung up the phone.

Ramses then phoned the Operations Command Center at Kirtland Air Force Base and ordered four N.S.A. agents to meet him and Colonel Garcia at the Gibson gate in 15 minutes. He also ordered that there be two large, unmarked vehicles to meet them there as well, along with a flatbed truck.

Could this really be happening? Ramses' heart was racing. In all his years of military service, he never had encountered one of these objects firsthand. Who was operating this mysterious airplane, and why was it in Roswell, New Mexico? So many questions, no answers. His heart rate was steadily increasing as he made his way to the Gibson gate in anticipation. Depending on the seriousness of the situation, he would maybe have to order the base to go on code red until more information was deduced. For now, he had to focus on getting to Roswell in a timely manner.

Upon arriving at the Gibson gate, Ramses was greeted by a small entourage of men. Colonel Garcia was standing outside in his full uniform, with a large truck and two unidentified black vans behind him. Four men wearing black suits and sunglasses hopped out of one of the vehicles and greeted the General. Those were the N.S.A. agents. Colonel Garcia briefed him and told him the Roswell Chief of Police, along with 15 other officers, would meet Ramses and the N.S.A. men a few miles outside of the property. They had reportedly closed the highway so Ramses could get there faster. Ramses thanked the Colonel, who saluted him as the   squad of two vans and the truck barreled to the southeast, towards Roswell. Ramses rode with one of the N.S.A. men in a black van. They said nothing to each other for the 2.75-hour drive to Roswell. Upon entering the city limits of Roswell, they were greeted by a large squad of police cars.

The driver of their vehicle along with Ramses hopped out to talk to the waiting police officers.

"Hello everybody, my name is Ramses, and I am here on behalf of the United States military. I want to thank you all for coming out tonight; I know it's late, and some of you are working overtime. Now I want to make this clear. You are not to tell anybody what you see tonight, not loved ones, not friends, no one. If you do, you will be disappeared. Your houses will be monitored closely for the next 90 days to make sure you adhere to this policy. Any questions?" Ramses said, towering over the group of officers. Some of the officers shifted uneasily. There was silence, then a feeble hand was raised up but quickly lowered.

"Good. Now we need to have some officers stay back and continue to block the interstate, should we need it," Ramses decreed.

It was decided that five cars stay behind, while another six go to the scene of the crash. The caravan departed to the Heartley farm, quietly through the night. Ramses' heart rate was picking up again as they approached the outskirts of Roswell, near the farm. It felt like someone had trapped a thousand butterflies in a jar, shook them up, then released them into his stomach. He felt like something was different about this, a feeling that was hard to pin down.

On his way to the farm, he read over the reports of the recent anomalies detected by the military. He closely checked the data and the eyewitness accounts. There was an unmistakable object that had traveled thousands of miles in less than a minute and appeared in the United States' airspace days before. Were they about to stumble upon that very object?

The president had been notified of the incident, and all eyes were on Ramses and his team. This was top-secret, and the fewer people who knew about it, the better. Ramses was instructed to tell only the people he deemed necessary to know about the crash.

The caravan headed down the dusty dirt road that led to the Heartley house. As they approached it, Ramses saw several figures. Two men were sitting on the porch smoking cigarettes; no doubt one of them had phoned the local police. One was short and lean, naked - except for a pair of pants he wore. The other was taller with ripped jeans and a tee-shirt. Ramses got out of the van and approached the short half-naked man. He stuck his hand out and said, "I'm General Ramses Meddiah the III. You must be the ones who phoned in."

"Yes, sir, I did. My name is Tom Heartley. Thank you for coming out so late at night. I know it's late as shit."

"If you could be so kind to lead my friends and me to the crash site, we would greatly appreciate it," Ramses said, signaling to the police and the N.S.A. agents standing behind him. Tom nodded and started to lead them to the crash site when the front door suddenly burst open. A distraught woman was standing in the doorway in her nightgown.

"What in the sam hell is going on here? It's two o'clock in the fucking morning," the woman shouted, staring straight at Tom.

"Babe, I'll tell you what's going on once all these nice folks leave," Tom said, trying to calm her down.

"To hell you will. Why are there ten cops in my front yard Tom? Huh?" she said, growing more agitated by the second.

"I, " Tom started to say before Ramses interrupted him.

"Ma'am, if you could step inside for a moment while we take care of this, that would make this easier. It's for your own safety." Ramses signaled for the police to take care of her.

Two cops approached her from behind him. They talked to her, and after a moment, she reluctantly closed the door and went back inside.

The group followed Tom, who was walking northwest into the darkness. It was 02:30, and the first hint of light was still several hours away. The family dog was running between the men and sniffing their feet.

After two minutes, Ramses saw a glowing blue circle of lights near the ground. He saw the lights before he saw the spaceship. It was small, maybe 25 feet in diameter and 10 feet tall. It was made out of metal that was dark gray and silvery in color, with a little sheen to it. Ramses did not recognize what the metal was. The spaceship was constructed like a flat disc, with a bulge towards the middle where a pilot would sit. There were no visible nuts or bolts, or even any indication that this thing had flown before. No chipping paint, no scratch marks, nothing: Ramses had never seen an airplane like this in his life.

Ramses walked around the spaceship and saw a small opening where two mangled bodies were lying. At first, he thought they were children from the small size of them, but a closer look revealed something not human. They had five fingers, greenish-gray skin, and large black eyes that appeared to have no eyelids. Their heads were massive in comparison to their little bodies. One was halfway in the spaceship, still breathing. The other had its arm torn off and a massive burn on its neck.

"Holy fuck," a cop muttered behind Ramses, seeing the creatures. The cop leaned in closer and almost threw up, turning around in terror.

What the hell was he looking at? Even though he saw it, it was hard to believe. Clearly, no children would be flying a thing like this around at 23:00 in the desert. He stood frozen for a second, unable to think about what to do next. He had to walk away from the group to gain his composure. He took a few deep breaths then walked back to the group. He pulled Tom aside.

"Did you see any other creatures besides these two?" Ramses asked, pointing to the bodies near the spaceship.

"Yeah. I shot one that was alive right over there," Tom responded, pointing to the darkness.

"Take me to it."

Tom nodded and walked towards where he pointed. Ramses followed close behind, not sure what to expect. After a minute, Tom stopped and pointed to the ground. Ramses followed his finger and saw another body on the ground. He could hear it wheezing softly.

Ramses turned on his flashlight and moved it over to the body. On the ground was another one of the creatures, bleeding from a bullet wound in its chest. *At least it bleeds*, thought Ramses, somewhat relieved they could be hurt by human-made weapons.

Ramses knew he needed to keep the two surviving aliens alive at all costs. Their knowledge would be key to helping them reverse-engineer the spaceship. He also wanted to question them and ask what they were doing on Earth in the first place. Ramses walked back to where the men were standing and called all the N.S.A. agents together in a huddle, away from everyone.

"I want you all to bag up these bodies and monitor them closely. One is dead for certain, and the other two are alive but in serious condition. Keep those two alive at all costs. We have medical bags in the vans, so patch up their wounds, give them water, do whatever you have to do to keep them alive until we get back to Kirtland Air Force Base. In case they die, blast the air conditioner in the vans so we can preserve them as much as possible."

They all nodded in unison. Two of them went to get the truck, and the other two back to the spaceship. The cops were bagging up the pieces of the crash debris and handing them to the agents. For such a forceful crash, there were surprisingly little pieces that had fallen off—just some pieces of metal here and there, but nothing that looked like engine parts. The agents bagged up the aliens in silver bags, keeping the face open for the two that were alive. They carefully loaded them up into one of the vans, just as the truck with the flatbed pulled up close to the spaceship.

At the same time, the agents and the police helped lift the spaceship onto the flatbed of the large truck, using muscle, ropes, and pulleys. They tied it down securely with a rope cord, making sure it would not fall out of the bed of the truck during transport. When it was firmly secured, they threw a large black tarp over the spaceship and tied it down with rope. The whole endeavor took several hours, and it was nearly 04:00 before they were ready to leave. Before they left, Ramses walked around the entire site, aided by the dawn light slowly creeping up from the eastern horizon. He wanted to leave no stone unturned. Satisfied with the job, he walked over to the exhausted-looking Tom and his farm hand Will, who introduced himself to Ramses a few hours earlier.

With the vans packed and the flying disc loaded, Ramses was ready to bid a farewell to Tom and Will. "Tom, Will, a word with you two gents," Ramses said, ushering them out of earshot of the group.

"Now I want you two to know you did the right thing tonight calling the police. This could have been a real mess had you decided not to do that. With that being said, neither of you can speak about any of the events that have taken place tonight. Not even with your families and loved ones. These conditions are not optional. They are mandatory. Failure to abide by the conditions may result in your disappearance. Any questions? Good," Ramses finished.

"To hell I ain't tellin no one. Goddamn aliens crash in my yard, and I can't tell no one?!" Tom argued.

Ramses walked uncomfortably close to Tom and stared straight down at him. He was over a foot taller than he was, and he wanted Tom to feel it. Tom's posture changed, and he slinked away, saying, "Alright, I won't tell nobody." Ramses was going to make sure someone would monitor Tom closely.

He turned to look at Will, tall and lean. Will shared his gaze for a moment but didn't put up a fight. Ramses was sure he wouldn't tell anybody. Ramses walked back to the group of cops and agents who were waiting for him to leave. He gave them the thumbs up and thanked the police chief who was in charge of the squadron. He then ordered the chief to close the highway for several hours that morning so they could make it back to Kirtland without any interruptions. He hopped into the van with the bodies and observed Will and Tom staring at the group as they left the property.

Ramses and the other two men in the van were silent as they drove down I-40 west. Driving down the highway, Ramses didn't see another car; the blockade had worked. When they got to the I-25, I-40 crossing point, civilian cars were driving on the highway, indicating they were now out of the blockade. The truck, the police cars, and the two vans drove in line; one van in the front, another in the back of the truck, and police cars in the front and back of the vans. The vans had police lights they turned on, as well as the police cars, so everyone knew to get out of the way. As they drove toward Albuquerque, Ramses thought about the events of the night.

The vehicle he and his team had retrieved could be more valuable than all the military equipment the United States possessed combined. This looked like advanced technology, even though he had retrieved it from a crash. Discovering alien bodies was crazy and unbelievable at the same time, but Ramses was really after the technology. Assuming these beings were not of Earth meant they had traveled an incredible distance to get here. This technology could be deadly if it fell into the wrong hands. The public could not know about this, not even the slightest detail. A huge part of that depended on all of the police, and Will and Tom keeping their mouths shut. Silencing a group of people was easier said than done, and Ramses knew it would be an ongoing challenge.

If the Russians or the Germans ever got wind of this, all hell could break loose. It was now Ramses' top priority to keep a lid on this, this monumental, Earth-shattering discovery. Ramses looked behind him at the face of the beings poking through the openings of the silver bags. Their mouths were small and delicate, their noses only two small holes in the face. Looking at the creatures made Ramses feel uneasy, and goosebumps pricked his flesh before he turned around.

Ramses had never seen an object move anywhere near the speed of light, not even 1% the speed of light. If these creatures came from a distant planet, surely they had to travel as fast as the speed of light, if not faster. After all, they were living organisms. The more he thought about it, the more worrisome the thought became. If these ships could disappear from radar and then suddenly reappear thousands of miles away, they could attack any spot on U.S. soil with impunity. Ramses needed to phone the president again so they could map out a plan if more of these objects showed up on the radar, but he would have to wait until they were safely back at Kirtland Air Force Base.

After several hours, the vans, police cars, and the truck pulled up to the gate of Kirtland Air Force Base on the north side. The sun was high in the sky when they arrived. Two armed military personnel were standing in front of the entrance gate. Ramses got out of the van and signaled for the agents to do the same. As the guards recognized him, they saluted.

One by one, the police officers and agents streamed out of their vehicles. When they were all out of their vehicles, Ramses spoke. "Thank you for the help you gentlemen provided tonight, superb job. Nobody here is to speak of what was seen tonight. Don't let your tongues slip. We will be listening. Officers, you are free to go." Nobody moved for a second. The cops looked around at each other wide-eyed and silent, no doubt replaying the ominous words Ramses had told them. The agents stood stoic as ever, expressionless. After a pause, the officers slowly got back into their cars and drove away. They knew who Ramses was. They wouldn't fuck with a General.

The guards opened up the gates to the base, and the vans pulled through the entrance, followed by the truck. Ramses wanted to take the bodies to the most secure location on the base, the underground facility under the Sandias to the southeast. Only a select number of individuals had access to the facility, most of them being civilian scientists. The facility was where top-secret weapons research was being conducted, so the Air Force closely guarded who had access to it and who didn't. Some personnel on the base knew the facility existed, but few knew what its true purpose was.

Dirt and cactus dotted the road to the facility. Weeds were growing on every inch of dirt they possibly could. This part of the base was basically wilderness, except for the missile silos and the underground facility. The military owned this stretch of land for dozens of miles until an arbitrary line separated it from the Indian reservation. As the vehicles headed toward the facility, they were faced with a large barbed wire fence and another gate at which more armed personnel were waiting. They were at the base of the Sandias. Beyond the gate were large metal doors that led to the interior of the mountain.

Ramses hopped out of the van, and the men guarding the gate saluted him. He walked up to them and showed them his badge. They scanned it under an ultraviolet light, and one of them said, "All clear," to someone on a walkie talkie on the inside of the doors. They unlocked the gate guarding the metal doors, and Ramses got back into the van he was sitting in.

The group of vehicles started driving through the gate towards a set of metal doors which swung open, inviting them into the mountain. Ramses eyed the two men who stood at the position of attention watching the vans and truck drive through. As they entered into the darkness of the mountain, the doors closed behind the truck, separating them from the outside world. Light began to flicker on overhead as the motion sensor lights detected the movement of the vehicles. The light revealed a dimly lit tunnel, with the lights forming a spinal cord guiding the way to the brain, the laboratory. Ramses had been here before, but only on special occasions.

"Drive straight until you hit the next set of doors," Ramses instructed the secret service man driving him. The man nodded and hit the gas. Ramses signaled for the other vehicles to follow behind them. They drove for 20 minutes slowly down the dank tunnel before they arrived at the final bend. As they made a slight right turn, Ramses saw the door. It was 30 feet tall and 50 feet wide and painted bright red, as if it was hard to miss in the first place. In the middle was a large wheel mechanism that could be turned to unlock the door. Through the middle of the wheel was a large metal bar that indicated if it was in the locked position or the unlocked position. Horizontal was locked, vertical was open; it was currently in the locked position.

At this door, there were two more armed guards with dogs by their feet. Ramses jumped out of the van again and was greeted by the same salute. He showed the guards his badge. One of the young men took it from his hand and scanned it again under an ultraviolet light. The light revealed a bald eagle, which meant Ramses had access to the facility. The N.S.A. agents got out of the vehicles and proceeded to show the guards their IDs as well. Down here, where it was almost impossible to break into the lab, your ID was checked every time, even if you were a General of the Air Force. The United States military took no chances, and everything had to follow a specific protocol.

The guard saw the eagle then saluted Ramses again. "All clear," he radioed to another individual on a walkie talkie, who was on the inside of the facility. The other guard turned the mechanism in the door to the unlocked position with a definitive click.

The door creaked open, and before them was the blinding white of the underground laboratory. There were two men waiting immediately on the other side of the door as the vehicles drove through, both in military uniform and armed. Next to them were two scientists wearing white lab coats. One Ramses recognized as Barry, the scientist who had briefed him about the objects several days earlier. The other scientist was a tall and lanky young man, with pale skin and blue eyes.

"Barry," Ramses said with a nod while sticking out his hand.

"General, a pleasure to see you again."

"And you are?" Ramses asked the young scientist next to Barry.

"Nicolai, sir, pleased to meet you."

"How old are you, Nicolai?"

"I'm 28, sir."

"You got a degree?"

"Yes, sir. I have a doctorate in Astrophysics and an undergraduate degree in Advanced Propulsion Systems."

Ramses nodded. Such a young kid. He would have him monitored closely. Ramses turned around and waved the two black vans and the large truck through the open door. As they entered, the giant red door closed behind them.

The laboratory facility was huge, approximately 330,000 square feet. It was divided into many smaller labs that hugged the far wall of the facility. Everything was white and perfectly clean. Each lab had separate access, and very few people had access to more than one lab. There was a hot side where all the labs were located, and a cold side where people could use the bathroom, eat, and make coffee. Each lab room had its own ceiling, but the facility as a whole did not; the ceiling of the cold side was the mountain rock. The overall shape of the laboratory facility was a giant cube, with smaller cubes forming the individual laboratory rooms.

The hot and cold sides were separated by a long wall that ran from the floor to the 50-foot ceiling. Entrances to the hot side were near lab 2 and lab 100. On the hot side, there were 100 labs in all, lab 100 being the largest. Each lab had a red number painted on the door for distinction, because they all looked identical except for lab 100, which was much larger than the rest, in order to house large objects such as an airplane.

Ramses ordered the N.S.A. agents to zip up the bags that housed the creatures for transport. He didn't want any peeping scientist to see what they were transferring. Nicolai looked puzzled as the agents pulled the silver bags out of one of the vans and loaded them onto gurneys that were stashed in the back of the van. "Specimens," Ramses said, wheeling past Nicolai.

"Oh yes, right this way," Nicolai said, guiding them to lab 7. They walked through the dividing wall, pushing open the glass door that separated the hot from the cold side. A long hallway stretched from one end of the lab to the other. They walked down the hallway towards lab 7. They stopped in front of lab number 7, and Nicolai took out a key on his key ring. He inserted the key and opened the door. He then turned on the lights, revealing a lab with four metal tables in the middle and a wall on the far side of the lab that contained countless drawers with labels on each one. The side closest to the door had a long workbench with several stools standing up below it. Scientific instruments lay atop the bench. An eyewash station was in the far corner of the room, close to the tool drawers.

Ramses and the agents moved the bodies of the specimens onto three of the metal tables, still zipped up in the silver bags. Nicolai scrunched his face.

"Thank you, two of you are dismissed. The other two agents need to stay and help me move the spaceship to lab 100," Ramses ordered the N.S.A. agents as the bodies were lifted onto the tables. They nodded, and two of them walked out of lab 7 silently, while the other two remained.

"Something wrong young man?" Ramses asked Nicolai forcefully, noticing his expression.

"No... it's just..., why are the bodies so small? Are these children?" Nicolai asked worriedly.

Ramses didn't say a word as he unzipped the body bags of the two living specimens, revealing the aliens beneath. Nicolai gasped and stood transfixed, staring at the aliens.

"These two are alive. I want it to stay that way, understood? You and Barry will be their primary caregivers. If anything happens to them, you two will bear the full responsibility." Ramses could tell by Nicolai's expression that he had never seen anything like this. Shit, Ramses had never seen anything like this until 6 hours ago. Nicolai remained silent, still staring at the faces of the aliens.

"I said, do you understand?"

"Yuh.. yes, I understand."

Ramses walked out of the lab and shut the door, the remaining two N.S.A. agents in tow. Now the other issue. Where to put the spaceship? He knew lab 100 was the largest room in the facility, but he didn't know if it was being used for another purpose at this moment.

"Hey, Barry. What's in lab 100 right now?" Ramses asked, walking back to Barry, who was waiting outside of the lab.

"Nothing as far as I know."

"Okay. We'll put the spaceship in lab 100 then."

Ramses had access to lab 100, but he had never been inside of it. This would be his first time. He ordered the agents to drive the truck down to lab 100. There was a bigger door on that side of the divider, similar to a garage door that would allow large vehicles to pass into the hot zone and into lab 100. Ramses walked out of lab 7 and signaled the men driving the truck to follow him to the very back of the laboratory. The cold side space was so big and open that a large truck could drive on the cold side with ease, even with a 25-foot-wide spaceship on its bed. As he approached the garage looking door, he scanned his ID on a sensor near the bottom of the door. The sensor produced a green light, indicating the door could be opened. Ramses pushed the red button on the control pad to open the garage door. Behind this door was another large red garage door with the number 100 painted on it. This was one of two doors to get into lab 100 on the hot side. It was wide enough for the truck to get through with the spaceship.

Lab 100 had two doors on the hot side. One was a smaller door that could be accessed by personnel via key, which was not directly behind the metal garage door separating the hot and cold sides of the facility. The other larger door leading into the lab was directly behind the garage type door that led to the hot side. It was opened at the push of a button, and it slid up and back to reveal the cavernous laboratory room. The same scan tool used by the garage door entrance to access the hot side was used on the alternative door entrance to get into lab 100. Ramses placed his ID on the scanner, and a light on the tool turned green, indicating he could open the alternative door to lab 100. He pushed the red button on the control pad, and the door slid up and back on rollers, revealing the huge lab 100. There was nothing in the middle of the lab except for a large flat circular pillar that could be lifted up or down to raise an object off the ground. An assortment of tools hung off all the walls; drills, wrenches, screwdrivers, and everything else a mechanic could think of.

Ramses ushered the truck through the large openings. The truck drove through, and Ramses directed it to turn around, with the bed of the truck facing the large circular pillar on the floor. They needed to get the spaceship safely onto the platform. When Ramses signaled to stop, he and the two agents unbuckled the tarp and the spaceship, getting ready to transfer it. Ramses directed the driver to lower the bed of the truck, so it was level with the platform.

"We are going to slide the spaceship into place on the count of three. Sir, I need you to tilt the bed of the truck when I say so. On the count of three, you will raise the bed of the truck," Ramses said to the driver, "while you help slow the descent with me," Ramses directed the agent next to him. "One, two, three," Ramses said as the truck bed lifted, tilting one side higher than the other. The spaceship started slowly sliding down as Ramses and another agent pushed back against it to slow the descent. The spaceship was unbelievably light. It felt like they were pushing against a small beetle as it slid into place. Ramses guessed it only weighed 1,000 pounds. The spaceship slid on to the large platform with a scrapping noise. Success. Ramses felt a wave of relief as the spaceship was lifted safely in place.

"Wonderful job. You two are free to go now. Remember, speak of this to no one." The men acknowledged Ramses and hopped into the truck, driving out of the large laboratory door and the garage door that separated the cold from the hot side. Ramses shut both doors as he left lab 100 and walked back down to lab 7, where Nicolai and Barry were examining the alien specimens.

"Nicolai, you need to perform emergency surgery on the alien who was shot. It has a chance of surviving if you can remove the bullet."

"Call me if anything interesting happens," Ramses said to the scientists without looking at the pair.

"I will right away, sir," Barry replied. Nicolai had a look of worry on his face, which had grown paler since he had seen the aliens.

Ramses walked out of lab 7 and saw the agents driving the truck and the van through the red door as he walked towards the exit. He approached one of the armed guards and said, "Call me a ride back, please, sir," and the guard nodded.

"General Ramses is ready to depart. Requesting a transport vehicle back to the surface," he said while speaking in a walkie talkie to a guard on the outside.

After a few minutes, the guard was radioed, "Transport vehicle outside and ready." The guard looked at Ramses and saluted him. Ramses saluted him back as the large red door was opened, swinging outwards. An unmarked black van was waiting for him on the other side in the dimly lit tunnel.

Before entering the van, Ramses fiddled with the golden cross that hung around his neck. His heart was still beating fast, even hours after he came to grips with what he had seen. "Let this be a dream, God. Please, I beg you, let this be some sick dream," he thought to himself as he approached the van. His world had been turned upside down in a matter of hours, but he was still clinging to his faith. He let out a silent prayer as he hopped into the vehicle. Nothing made sense anymore.

Chapter 3

🜊

Nicolai

Nicolai was in lab 7 with the alien specimens by himself while Barry was busy examining the spaceship in lab 100. He was frightened by the aliens, even though both of them were incapacitated. They lay there motionless on the metal tables as he hooked them up to IVs that had electrolytes in them. He wasn't sure how to treat them, but he thought giving them electrolytes seemed like a sensible thing to do.

Did these creatures even need water, or sodium, or potassium? Only time would tell. Nicolai worked quickly to wipe the bump on one of the alien's head with antibiotic wipes, and then he tied an ice pack around it once he finished wiping. He administered a mild tranquilizer just in case the alien suddenly woke up; he didn't want any surprises while working on the other alien's wounds.

He turned to the other alien, looking at the bullet hole in its chest. Its skin was paler than the other, and it looked to be dying. Nicolai needed to perform emergency surgery to get the bullet out of its chest. The alien had suffered a less severe leg injury, an obvious broken bone in the ankle, but Nicolai would worry about that later. He took another antibiotic wipe and wiped it around the bullet hole. He administered a heavy tranquilizer dose to make sure the alien was asleep while he cut open its chest. Nicolai was no surgeon, but he had experience cutting open cadavers when he worked at a mortuary as a teen. He knew where most of the internal organs were and how to cut a human body properly. Because of this experience, Ramses tasked him with performing the alien's surgery, despite Nicolai objecting. So here he was about to perform emergency surgery on a non-human species.

Nicolai dawned medical-grade scrubs, covered his face with a mask, and slipped on nitrile gloves. He wasn't sure if these aliens contained any blood pathogens that could be lethal to humans, so he needed to take every precaution. He walked over to the lab's far side, where all the tools were, including medical grade scalpels, scissors, and stitching kits. He opened a drawer labeled "Medical Instruments" and reached for a red box that contained a 24-piece set with every shape and size of blade imaginable. He grabbed the box and walked back to the metal table. He set up a metal stand and put a cloth over it before laying out the instruments.

After carefully opening the box, he looked for a scalpel to make an incision. He also needed a rib spreader to break open the sternum and rib cage to access the heart. The blade he picked up was about 6 inches long, with a very sharp edge. The alien laying below him had a bloody hole in its chest where the bullet had gone through. It was thin enough that Nicolai could see a rib cage beneath its skin, moving up and down with each inhale and exhale. He took a deep breath and dug the knife into the hole. He needed to cut it a little wider to see precisely where the bullet was.

The skin was tougher than human skin; it was almost like cutting leather. Nicolai had to put a decent amount of force into the blade before it sunk into the alien's flesh. He felt the blade travel through the layers of skin, then the muscle. The incision he made was roughly four inches long, covering most of the creature's little chest. When he hit one of the creature's rib bones, he knew he had to open up the chest. The bullet was deep in the alien's chest cavity, possibly in its heart, but he couldn't tell exactly where it was yet.

He carefully placed the rib spreader over the little green chest of the alien. The rib spreader was quite large because it was designed for an adult human, so Nicolai had to put it on the smallest setting and open it from there. He inserted the rib spreader's blade firmly under the skin and started turning the handle, slowly widening the incision he had made. He turned the handle a few times until he heard a loud "crack," indicating the sternum was broken. He turned it a few more times until he could see the heart, next to two lungs. It was amazing how similar the anatomy was to a human.

The heart was four-chambered, similar to a human heart. It had two atria and two ventricles. Lodged in the left atria was the bullet. Nicolai could see a silvery sheen in the otherwise red and blue mess of muscle and nerves. The heart appeared to be beating erratically, and blood was oozing out of the bullet wound. It might die instantly with the bullet removed, but he had to remove the shell quickly. He had no choice. Removing the bullet was the only chance this alien had at surviving. He grabbed the forceps from the box and started slowly towards the bullet.

His hand began shaking as he descended into the creature's chest cavity. He was looking straight into the creature's face; it looked so foreign and unnatural. His brain was having trouble comprehending what he was looking at. He felt his insides turn as the gravity of the situation hit him. He was operating on an alien from another world, perhaps one of the only aliens that had ever visited Earth.

He was surely the first person to ever operate on a live alien. He didn't have any understanding of the chemical processes that dictated the life of this being. Maybe he was doing the wrong thing. The alien might wake up randomly and kill him or run away, or even control his mind. He just didn't know what it was capable of. If he told anyone about what he was doing, Ramses would have him killed. He gulped down his fear.

"Holy shit. Phewww. Deep breaths. You're okay," he whispered to himself while placing the forceps off to the side. He was pacing back and forth by the table, not fully ready to try to pull the bullet out. His heart was beating fast, and his palms were sweaty. He needed to calm down so he could save this thing's life. That was his task.

He composed himself, then walked back towards the operating table. He picked up the forceps again and aimed at the gaping hole in its chest. The forceps tips touched the metal surface of the bullet. Nicolai could feel the hardness of the metal through the tool. He squeezed the forceps together to get a better grip, and blood started welling up around the forceps as he applied the pressure. "One, two, three!" he exclaimed as he ripped the bullet free. Blood started squirting out of the wound onto his scrubs. He began to panic, dropping the bloody bullet on the ground.

He frantically looked in the box for something to stop the bleeding. He found a small stapler and decided the best thing to do was to staple the wound. It was his only hope. He picked it up and aimed it at the wall of the heart that was squirting blood. He grabbed a piece of the heart in his hand and stapled it to itself several times. It looked like something an 18-year-old Army medic would have done on the battlefield. The blood stopped squirting out, but the heart was still beating erratically. He didn't know if the creature would survive.

He set aside the forceps and grabbed a package of medical-grade wire, used to help hold the sternum closed while it healed. Nicolai turned the rib spreader's handle in the opposite direction, slowly closing the chasm in the creature's chest. When the two halves of the sternum were as close together as they would get, he removed the rib spreader. He unwound about five feet of the metal wire and tied it around the sternum, setting it back into its rightful place. After tying the tightest knot he could, he cut the excess wire and set it off to the side. The flap of skin he originally cut was now ready to be stitched. He grabbed a small needle and strung the blue stitching through it. In, out, in, out. He slowly made his way down the entire incision until the stitching sewed up the hole completely. He cut the excess stitching and threw it to the side. He picked up some more antibiotic wipes and wiped the freshly stitched incision for several minutes until he was satisfied with how the incision looked.

Exhausted and emotionally drained, Nicolai slumped back in his chair. The chances of either one surviving were slim. One had lost a large amount of blood and had a badly broken leg, and Nicolai was worried it would die by the end of the night. The other was completely unconscious, possibly in a coma from a bad head wound. Nicolai would see if the alien survived the heart surgery, then he would try to set the leg in the correct orientation with a cast. The third alien was dead as a doornail. All Nicolai could do was pray for the best.

He walked to the body bag with the dead alien. He unzipped the bag and looked at the mangled corpse. It looked like a sickly child with its greenish skin and small stature. He closed the bag up again and walked toward bigger drawers near the bottom of the tool wall. They were 8 feet long, 3 feet wide, and 3 feet tall; they were designed for storing corpses. The small body of the alien would easily fit inside. Before he opened up the drawer, he pulled out a large scale from a nearby drawer. He turned it on and tared it. When he saw the scale read 0.0, he lifted the alien corpse onto it, carefully lowering the body onto the scale. It read 50.6 lbs. The weight was not surprising, considering the creature was only 3.5 feet tall with a slim build. Nicolai transcribed the weight on a piece of paper and opened the drawer. He slid the corpse onto the long metal tray and rolled it back into its metal sarcophagus.

Nicolai started taking off all his protective equipment when he heard the door to lab 7 open. Barry burst into the room nearly out of breath. Nicolai thought something bad had happened.

"Nicolai, you must come to lab 100 at once. I discovered something very important about the spaceship's engine, and I want you to look at it!"

Barry stared at the two aliens laying on the metal tables, IVs hooked up to their wrists, and a machine monitoring their resting heart rates and blood pressure.

"Are they stable?"

"As stable as they can be. Both are in serious condition, and death is likely."

Barry nodded, then walked towards the door and out of the lab. Nicolai finished taking off his protective equipment and threw it in a biohazard trash can near the door. He grabbed the tools he used and put them in a sink in the lab with bleach and water. Nicolai then grabbed a mop bucket and filled it with bleach and water. He scrubbed the area surrounding the metal table he performed the surgery on. After he finished cleaning the lab and the tools, he glanced at the aliens shallowly breathing on the metal tables. They looked like patients in an insane asylum, surrounded by all-white walls, strapped down to the tables. They appeared to be human, almost.

The thought unnerved Nicolai. Did these beings sexually reproduce? Did they have feelings and emotions similar to humans? He was both intrigued and terrified at the unknown. There was so much he wanted to ask the little creatures.

The aliens were similar anatomically to humans; that much was obvious. They had two eyes, a nose, and a mouth. The most noticeable difference between them and humans was the huge heads and eyes, the greenish skin color, and the lack of body hair. They had a four-chambered heart as humans did, and they were clearly able to breathe oxygen, or else they would have already died. Nicolai had not seen them walk, but based on their body structure and leg limb length, they were bipedal. Like humans, they had five fingers and five toes on both hands and feet. Human bones looked very similar to the alien bones; the aliens did not have any extra bones that Nicolai did not immediately recognize, as well as any that served a different mechanical purpose. Their heads were abnormally large, hence bigger brains, so Nicolai assumed they were more intelligent than humans.

These beings were not humans; no matter how human-like they appeared, Nicolai was sure of it. They were also certainly not any creature Nicolai had ever seen on Earth. They were aliens, visitors from another world.

Nicolai turned off the lights and locked lab 7 after double-checking both the live specimens' wrist and ankle shackles. He walked down the long hallway to lab 100, where Barry was waiting for him. He unlocked the door to lab 100 and saw Barry working on a spaceship piece on a lab bench.

"What is that?" Nicolai asked as he looked more closely at what Barry was holding.

"This is the engine that powers the ship." Barry held a metal disc that fit perfectly around a metallic sphere. The disc and sphere could be separated. It made no sense. There was no intake manifold, no exhaust port, no cylinders, no camshaft.

"What do you mean this is the engine? How can this thing possibly fly an ant, let alone a spaceship? It's a sphere, for God's sakes."

"I do not know. I was tinkering around the middle and lower levels of the spaceship and discovered this object in the direct center. When I removed it, the blue lights on the bottom of the spaceship turned off, so I presume it is some type of power source for the ship. I tried to put it back in place, but the ship didn't automatically turn on when I did. However, when the sphere was removed, the ship could still extend a ladder from the main cabin down to the floor, allowing me to get out. When I walked away from the ship, the ladder shortened back up into the ship and closed up again. So now I'm stuck, and that is why I summoned you."

Nicolai picked up the metal sphere in his hands. It was about the size of a soccer ball, but it felt like it weighed 100 pounds. Stunned, he put the sphere down with some effort and examined it again. It looked like mercury, but Nicolai knew that was impossible. At 25°C, mercury would be liquid. He ran his hand along the surface and could detect no imperfection. The sphere was perfectly smooth except for a small lump in one spot. Nicolai turned the sphere, so the lump was facing up towards the light. It looked like a small lever.

Nicolai pulled down on the lump, and it moved downwards in his hands. He felt the metal sphere changing. The metal began to turn into liquid, and it seeped between his fingers like water. It was expanding from the center of the sphere in all directions. The liquid held its position in the air, revealing a small black rod pocking out of a smaller jet-black, golf ball-sized sphere that now rested in Nicolai's palms.

"That must be the core. The fuel to the reactor," Barry said while reaching for it. His hand slid through silver liquid shimmering in the lab light. His fingers gripped the smaller black sphere, and he removed the rod from inside. The rod was smaller than a pinky finger. Nicolai was trying to make sense of what he was experiencing, but all his hours spent studying physics had not prepared him for this.

"Be careful, Barry. It could be radioactive," Nicolai said, trying to pull the rod out of Barry's hands. Barry's grip didn't fail him as he stood transfixed. He shrugged Nicolai off and marveled at the little black rod. The liquid metal in the air began to condense around the sphere in Nicolai's hands until it returned to the original shape and hardness.

Nicolai was speechless. The sphere changing from a metal to a liquid was trifling. This metallic material was unlike anything Nicolai knew existed on Earth. No known metal on Earth could change from a solid to a liquid at the same temperature. There were no visible wires or opening mechanisms, so it was hard to explain how the sphere would open in the first place.

"Looks like we have our work cut out for us," Barry said with a grin on his face.

Nicolai wasn't sure if he was enjoying this as much as Barry. He was thinking about the implications of the past 12 hours, and it made him noxious. He was frightened and unsure, but he had to keep all of this bottled up to himself. Nicolai and Barry were the only two scientists who knew about what was going on. The commanding officer under General Ramses named Colonel Garcia had debriefed them earlier.

"You two are the only individuals assigned directly to this project at Kirtland Air Force Base. Tell nobody in the cafeteria when you eat lunch, and do not tell anybody outside of Kirtland about your work. I know Ramses told you the same thing, but take his warning seriously. For the time being, your security clearance is majestic. Ramses will be expecting regular updates from you two. Understood?"

Majestic. Nicolai had never heard of that clearance before, but he guessed few had it.

"How do you think it works?" Barry asked, still examining the rod.

"I don't have the slightest clue. Where did you find the metallic sphere exactly?"

Barry gently placed the rod in a zip lock bag on a nearby lab bench. He walked over to the spaceship in the center of the room and motioned Nicolai. Barry tore off the massive cloth covering the spaceship, revealing the disc-shaped object beneath. A small door opened into the interior of the spaceship. Barry pulled out a flashlight so they could see the dark inside of the spaceship. The interior was the same color as the outside. Dark gray, and it was all smooth. Both Barry and Nicolai had to be crouched to fit inside the middle level, which was no doubt made for beings much smaller than adult humans. No nuts, no bolts, no screws, everything was completely smooth. There were three levels to the spaceship. The middle level had a small pillar with a depressed curve on top, and there were three small chairs faced in front of a large window. Below the window was a blank panel at wrist height. There were no buttons on the panel, just a smooth flat surface the same color as the rest of the spaceship. Nicolai guessed the pillar was where the sphere went.

Barry walked over to the pillar and pointed. Nicolai nodded at him as he confirmed his guess. He looked closer and noticed small inscriptions on all four sides of the pillar. So, the aliens had a written language; Nicolai made a mental note. Unlike any writing Nicolai had seen, it was almost a cross between Chinese and Egyptian hieroglyphics: indecipherable.

Nicolai's eyes scanned the ceiling of the spaceship. In the center of the ceiling, directly above the pillar, was a black square-shaped box sitting on top of clear plastic-like material. The black box was the top level of the ship, the smallest of the three levels. You couldn't tell it was there from the outside, the top just looked like the top of a Hershey kiss, but inside you could see there was an object in that space. Nicolai wondered what the object was and what purpose it had on the spaceship. It was the only part of the spaceship that was a different color from the rest of the spaceship.

Immediately adjacent to the pillar was a hatch that led down to the lower level. It was honeycomb-shaped and gray, except for a white handle. Nicolai grabbed the handle, and the hatch door flung open, revealing the lower level beneath.

A little ladder hung from the top to the bottom of the lower level. Nicolai estimated it was a 7-foot drop to the bottom. Already crouched, maneuvering himself onto the ladder proved difficult. Each rung was too small, so he had to be extra careful while he was lowering himself. Once safely on the ground, he could fully stand up on this lower level. The lower level contained nothing, except three poles running from the ceiling to the floor, directly below the sphere on the middle level. On each of the three poles was a large rectangular object that looked like an upside-down trash can hanging in the middle of them. Even on this level, there were no wires, screws, nuts, or bolts.

"Did you find anything?" Barry asked from above him, peeking his head through the hatch.

"Just a couple of trash cans on some poles. I have no clue as to what function they would serve."

He was still scared to touch anything; he didn't know what was toxic or what would blow up if he pressed it. He and Barry would need to put on full radiation suits and scan the whole ship. But he was exhausted.

"Well, I don't know how much I can figure out while I'm half awake. I'm going to check on the aliens one more time, then head out. I'll be back tomorrow by 15:00," Nicolai said while climbing back up the ladder to the main cabin. He and Barry crawl-hopped out of the opening and into the lab light. The opening closed behind them automatically as the ladder shortened into the side of the ship.

Barry went back to the lab bench and started fiddling with the rod in his plump fingers. "Okay, I will see you then."

Nicolai left lab 100 and walked back down the hallway to lab 7. It was now mid-afternoon, and the cafeteria was buzzing with the talk of scientists. He ignored them as he thought about the metal sphere.

Was it possible the spaceship had no direct fuel source? Every single engine on Earth was a combustion engine that used up large quantities of material, but this spaceship had no such engine. If the spaceship had no combustible fuel, how could it fly about and leave a planet's gravity? Were the sphere and the rod composed of elements found on Earth, or of completely alien origin? So many questions, but little hope in finding the answers.

Nicolai found his way back to lab 7 and took a deep breath. The report he had read immediately before seeing the aliens in real life was that William Brakel stated, "The creatures may or may not be able to control animals." This was an account given to one of the police officers at the scene of the crash. Humans were considered animals, right? Nicolai was fearful the aliens would wake up and control his mind to release them, or worse, to make him kill himself. All of these thoughts were running through his mind as he opened the door, making sure nobody was lurking nearby in the hallway on the hot side.

The creature with the head injury shot its head straight up at the noise and looked at Nicolai with big black pits of eyes. Goosebumps prickled his flesh as he struggled to move. It was awake and clearly looking at him. Nicolai's hand was shaking as he reached for the walkie talkie in his lab coat pocket. He pressed the button to start communications. "Ba-ba-B-Barry. Barry! One of them is- is awake," he finally managed to stammer.

The alien was now violently shaking the wrist and ankle shackles that held it in place. Nicolai ran towards a cabinet that had common tranquilizers in it. He frantically looked for the ketamine bottle. He found it and quickly removed it from a cabinet and grabbed a needle in a sterile package.

Barry ran through the door of lab 7 and looked at the alien, huffing and puffing. He slammed the door behind him, locking it. He walked toward it slowly, not taking his eyes off it.

"Did you find the ketamine?" Barry asked while rolling up his sleeves and putting on his gloves.

"Here," Nicolai responded, handing the bottle to Barry.

Barry used a long needle to suck up the ketamine liquid from inside the bottle. A few drops oozed out of the top of the needle. Ketamine was powerful stuff, enough to put a large beast to sleep. There was a possibility the dosage would kill the alien. Barry sucked up 1.0 milliliter of the fluid, flicked the needle, then jammed it into the alien's arm and pressed down on the plunger. The alien started hissing loudly, and a chill ran down Nicolai's spine.

Barry calmly watched as the hissing subsided, and the alien slumped its large head in submission to the ketamine. The fight was over. Nicolai relaxed a little bit. After a moment of silence, Nicolai said, "Are you sure that dosage is safe, Barry? What if the ketamine kills it? Ramses will have our asses."

Barry turned to look at him. "Do you want that thing hissing at you?" he retorted. Nicolai shook his head. He certainly did not want that. It was terrifying.

"You're right. I'm going to bed. I need to sleep. I've been up since 03:00, and it's 14:00 now."

Barry nodded, then went back to examining the alien. Did he ever sleep? Nicolai could not tell. He left lab 7 and subtly shut and locked the door behind him. He saw the giant red door in the distance, and he made his way to it.

Nicolai passed a scientist on his way toward the red door after exiting the laboratory complex's hot side. The man was roughly 5'8 and had a slouch to his posture. As he walked closer, Nicolai could see he was Asian. Black hair, brown eyes. The man walked by without even a blink.

"Scientists," Nicolai muttered while walking past the man. A guard was waiting on the inside of the laboratory, next to the red door.

"ID," the guard said with an outstretched hand as Nicolai approached the door. Nicolai reached into his lab coat pocket and produced an ID. The guard grabbed it and shined an ultraviolet light on to it. A bald eagle appeared on the card.

"All clear," the guard said over his walkie talkie while eyeing Nicolai.

Nicolai heard the ball and levers moving as the door turned into the unlocked position from the outside. The door slowly opened, revealing the cavernous mouth of the tunnel. A black van was at the entrance of the tunnel, waiting for his departure. A Colonel Nicolai did not recognize was standing by the driver's side of the vehicle. Upon seeing Nicolai, he motioned for him to get in.

"Thank you," Nicolai said, attempting to greet the driver as they turned around in the tunnel. He got no response, just a nod. The van drove through the winding tunnel to the entrance under the Sandia mountains. He made it through the barbed wire fence and into daylight. Sunlight shined into his eyes, and the heat of the afternoon hit him.

Finally, he could go home and get some sleep. The van drove him northwest towards the entrance at the Gibson gate. It escorted him into the subsidized military homes across the street, with their little complex. A high wooden fence surrounded it, and the overall shape was rectangular. Nicolai lived in one of the studio units, 200 square feet in size. The van pulled up to his little adobe house, identical to all the other houses in the complex. Yawning, Nicolai walked up to the front door and stopped. The Albuquerque Journal was on the front steps of his house. The paper's front page said, "U.F.O. Crashes on Farmer's Land in Roswell, New Mexico."

Chapter 4

---✦---

Oousma

"Oousma…. Oousma… OOUSMA!!"

Oousma woke up with a jolt. Oousma scanned the white room and saw Ishma lying on a metal table next to it. Ishma was trying to break free of the metal restraints that anchored it against the metal table.

"Oousma, we have to leave. We were supposed to be back on our home planet by now. Oousma, can you hear me? Oousma!"

Oousma cut the line of communication with Ishma. Its species had lost the ability to speak verbally 750,000 years before the present. Telepathic communication was the only form of communication that they could use now. Oousma had to silence Ishma's stream of consciousness in its mind so it could think.

Oousma became aware of the metal touching its body and inside its chest. There was metal in Oousma's heart. Oousma could feel it throbbing in pain. The pain felt like little ice picks jabbing into its heart every time it took a breath. Its sternum was also extremely sore, and it felt like a heavyweight was being pressed into its chest. Slowly, the events leading up to this moment came back to Oousma's memory.

Oousma, Ishma, and Mahisma had set out from their home world Nirubu, in the Alpha Centauri star system, an unknown number of days before. Oousma was not sure how long it had been unconscious. Oousma's species had visited Earth on three occasions: 12,500 years before the present, 1,947 years before the present, and the final visit was the most recent, in which they had crashed their spaceship, Sirius. The missions back then had far different purposes than the current task.

Oousma's species were concerned for the people of Earth. Over the past several years, their satellites orbiting Earth detected vast bursts of radiation. The scientists of Nirubu were perplexed as to what the cause of the radiation bursts were until it was theorized that the humans were building atom bombs. The theory gained momentum as their satellites beamed back images of massive explosions over North America and Russia. They had been intensely monitoring the Earth ever since, and they finally decided it was time to investigate what exactly was happening. Humans were the only other intelligent life the Annonaki had detected, and they were keen on preserving it, especially Oousma.

On their home planet Nirubu, a Council of Elders presided over all interstellar travel and international laws. Oousma was the Supreme Chancellor of the council for thousands of years until it decided to surrender the title to Bousnu. Oousma wanted to stay on Earth during its first visit 12,500 years before the present, so it had to give up the Supreme Chancellor position. There were 12 members on the council, including Oousma. The 12 members had more than 80,000 years of lived life and experience, Oousma being one of the oldest at 16,000 years old in the present day (1947). The people of Nirubu trusted their wisdom, and the council members were elected every 500 years by popular vote.

Visiting Earth required a tremendous amount of resources and power, so a journey as long as this was a hot button issue for the council. The Annonaki had visited Earth on three occasions with live Annonaki because they were limited in the amount of element 115 they could produce. They had sent autonomous probes to Earth many times in the past and the present to monitor the humans' progress and watch for impending disasters, but to bring live Annonaki to the surface was different. The probes were powered by solar energy, which was abundant and cheap, but it took them far longer to reach Earth. In the present day, they had several dozen autonomous probes and satellites flying around the Earth, looking for missile launches and radiation spikes. They could not move as the spaceships did, but they were still faster than any human-made object and allowed for the Earth's continued surveillance.

The spaceships that the Annonaki flew in made use of element 115 as a fuel source. Element 115 was rare and very time consuming to adjust on the atomic level to give it its ability to generate gravity waves. Element 115 was the only known element that could generate a repulsive gravity wave on its own. The ship amplified and used gravity waves to travel through the universe. Their spaceships created a gravity wave powerful enough to tear a hole in the universe, allowing faster than light travel. The council voted on the most recent mission to Earth to be necessary despite the expense of creating stable element 115, because the human species were advancing fast with weapons technology.

As the human race advanced technologically, the journey and entry into Earth became more dangerous. In the distant past, humans could merely watch the spaceships and drones the Annonaki sent in awe. But now, the humans had weapons capable of shooting down and destroying the Annonaki spaceships. It also appeared that they had recently discovered the ability to destroy themselves many times over.

Oousma proposed the departure to the Council of Elders, only to get mixed responses. Some of the members thought they were justified in sending a crew to Earth because the Annonaki needed to dismantle the bombs, if possible, to save the human race. Dismantling the bombs could only be done by live Annonaki, not robots or drones. Other members thought the Annonaki should stay out of human history as they always thought they should have. These members believed interfering with the evolution and life history of a planet and species could have devastating effects on the planet's longevity. In the end, it was put to a vote, and the vote was split 6-5. Oousma was the last to vote, breaking the potential tie. Oousma voted yes; the Annonaki should send a crew to Earth, which left the final vote at 7-5, in favor of going back to the Earth. The crew that left Nirubu was three strong, including Mahisma, Oousma, and Ishma.

Mahisma was very gifted in mathematics and physics. Mahisma was one of the designers of the new modern warp drive engine the Annonaki used on their ships. It was more efficient than previous versions, and required less element 115 to operate at its fullest capacity. Ishma was an engineering genius. It built the warp drives, the computers that tracked the stars, and the spaceships. Ishma also understood how to fix the spaceship should it break down for any reason. Oousma had no particular qualifications other than flight experience, but it had been twice before, on the other two live space missions to Earth. All three knew how to fly the spacecraft they were currently in, Sirius, but Oousma was the most experienced and the best pilot of the crew, having flown on dozens of missions before.

Where was Mahisma? Oousma was shackled to a metal table identical to Ishma's. Oousma couldn't move, so it searched for Mahisma's brain wave. Nothing. Oousma tried again: nothing. Oousma began to fear the worst.

Had Mahisma died during the crash? Oousma could not remember. As Oousma closed its eyes, the memories of the crash started flooding back into its mind.

Oousma, Mahisma, and Ishma were in Earth's gravitational pull when the first problem was detected.

"I see lower output power signatures from our engine." - Mahisma.

"Did you check the levels of element 115 before we left?" - Oousma.

"I did. The levels were reading at 99.9% before we departed from Nirubu. Our current level is 75%, and our power output is at 50%. We should not have lost that much element 115 in a four-lightyear journey."

Ishma was looking at the monitors worryingly, trying to diagnose the exact problem. The computer was saying there was a malfunction in the middle gravity amplifier.

"We have to land soon, so I can try to fix the problem. The power levels are lowering rapidly because our middle gravity amplifier is out, meaning the spaceship has to draw exponentially more power and element 115 to fly. The broken amplifier is resulting in element 115 being used up more quickly. I'll put in coordinates to an isolated part of the Earth to land and fix the spaceship. We cannot get stranded here; we need enough fuel to return home," Ishma said.

Oousma felt frightened. During the other visits to Earth, no ship malfunctions had occurred, but this time was different. The plan was to visit Earth, deduce the exact source of the big spikes in radiation, and if the radiation spikes were coming from bombs, disarm the bombs and leave. It was a difficult mission, but very possible. The Council of Elders suspected it would take them 168 Earth hours to complete the mission and return home.

"Prepare yourselves. I am about to turn on the warp drive. We will arrive at our destination in 0.00005 seconds," Ishma said while setting up the spaceship's interface.

Oousma braced for the jump. In front of the ship, the large blue marble melted away, and a desert landscape appeared before them through the viewing window. The spaceship shook slightly, then held still, floating in midair above the ground. Oousma looked at the ground more closely and saw trouble. Below them was a group of human men all dressed the same, in some kind of uniform. They were marching in a line when one of them shouted something and pointed at the spaceship.

"Ishma, we must leave now!" Oousma said worriedly.

"Warp drive enabled. Destination, Siberian forest."

The scenery melted away again, giving birth to an endless body of trees. They were in the middle of a forest, miles away from the nearest town or settlement.

"I need to check the power core. Power levels are at 40%, and element 115 is at 35%. Energy is leaking from one of the gravity amplifiers at a rapid rate," Ishma finished saying while Mahisma landed the spaceship amongst a small opening of the trees. With a gentle thud, the spaceship contacted the ground, and Ishma turned the primary operating system off.

Ishma got out of its seat and headed for the hatch that led down to the gravity amplifiers on the ship's bottom level. Before descending, Ishma pulled the power core off of the gravitational ring and disassembled it with a finger's push, revealing the element 115 core inside. It had taken Oousma's species 250,000 years to develop the first modern ship capable of faster than light travel. The current warp drive was built 13,000 years before the present. Trial and error were part of the search for answers, so inevitably, the designs became more efficient and better through time. The first warp drive ship ever built only traveled 2 kilometers before it stopped due to lack of fuel (element 115). Now here they were, traveling between stars.

"Ah yes, the middle amplifier is not running at full capacity as our software indicated. The atomic structure has been thrown off, creating an off-center gravitational wave. We will have to divert power away from it to the other two amplifiers while using the warp drive. It may not be safe to operate it at warp speeds, so we may take quite a bit longer on the return journey than we expected. I did not bring any tools to fix it, but we should be fine; we need to move closer to our target location and wait. We do not have the energy to spare flying around aimlessly," Ishma said from the bottom level.

Mahisma nodded, hearing Ishma's words. Mahisma looked at Oousma, "Now what?" Oousma sat in its chair, thinking about their next move.

"Mahisma, chart a course to put us near the epicenter of the blasts. Time is of the essence."

Mahisma started pressing a multitude of buttons on the control panel. Soon a screen appeared with coordinates on it. "I am charting a course for 33.3943°N, 104.5230°W. The coordinates should put us close to where the spikes of radiation were detected recently. Prepare for the warp drive jump."

By now, Ishma was back in its seat, waiting for Mahisma to enable the warp drive. The spaceship lifted off the ground, and the forest trees blurred, then turned into a desert landscape again. Oousma could see a highway with cars driving along it and several properties with animals and crops on them through the window. Farmland.

"Ishma, enable the invisibility cloak," Oousma said, nervous someone would spot them again.

"Invisibility cloak enabled," Ishma responded after pressing a series of buttons.

Around twenty yards in front of the spaceship stood a human and an animal. The animal had hair covering its entire body, and it walked on four legs—a dog. Oousma had interacted with dogs in the past on its previous two visits to Earth. They loved humans, and the humans loved them. It was a strange relationship between the species, but it was prevalent.

The dog slowly started to walk towards the spaceship. It stopped directly below the spacecraft, where it was out of view. "Turn on outside audio, Mahisma," Oousma said, still not sure if the dog could sense them. Mahisma turned on the outside audio, and they heard a low snarling coming from the dog. It knew they were there.

"What are you looking at, boy? There ain't nothing to see," they heard the human say to the dog.

"It can't see us, right, Oousma?" Ishma asked.

"No, but it can sense us. The human is not aware of our presence, but the dog is. On Earth, the animals can pick up on environmental cues much easier than humans."

"Move the spaceship slightly backward so we can see what they are doing," Oousma ordered.

Mahisma slowly piloted the spaceship backward, so they were not directly on top of the human and the dog anymore. The dog looked tense; it had hunched shoulders, and its tail was between its legs. The man tried to grab the dog, but the dog nipped his hand. "Damn dog!" the man yelled, pulling his hand back. Oousma focused the energy in its mind and bridged a connection to the consciousness of the dog. Oousma could smell what the dog was smelling and felt the anxiety welled up behind its shoulders. Oousma sent the dog feelings of happiness, compassion, and companionship. The dog relaxed, and Oousma pulled its consciousness out of the dog's. The dog looked up at its owner and licked his hand. Free will was impossible to control completely; Oousma could only guide it along in certain beings, ones that had simple minds.

The man bent down to pet the dog again, and this time the dog accepted the pets willingly. "It's okay, Buddy, you're fine," the man gently said to the dog.

"Turn outside audio off," Oousma ordered.

Mahisma turned off the microphone to the outside world and looked at Oousma. "Hmmm... well done, Oousma." Mahisma knew what Oousma had done without words.

The man and dog turned around to make their way back to the house, away from the cornfield. Ishma looked at a display on the part of the window indicating their power levels. "Power levels 35%, element 115 remaining, 30%. We are running dangerously low on energy and fuel. I estimate we will need 5% of our current supply of element 115 to move to the epicenter of the radiation bursts since we are still not at the exact location we need to be at."

"How much do we need to get back home?" Oousma asked Mahisma.

"Approximately 20% of our element 115 stores, given that our middle amplifier is out and not working properly."

"Understood. We will leave at nightfall. For now, we must remain still. Humans sleep at night and work during the day. There is less of a chance we will be seen if we wait until the night."

Mahisma and Ishma nodded in agreement. Oousma had visited Earth more than once and knew the human species well from its travels. Neither Ishma nor Mahisma had been to Earth before, so they only knew what they read in books about humans. But books didn't tell all there was to know. Oousma learned the general patterns humans followed, from their birth and death to how they slept and worked. Oousma visited Earth on three occasions, and each visit was thousands of years apart, but the same general patterns remained. Long ago, the human species were on a far less destructive path into the universe, but times were meant to change. When the moon was high in the sky, Oousma signaled Mahisma and Ishma. It was time to leave.

"Preparing the warp drive," Ishma said while inputting the settings into the computer system. The scenery in the front of the spaceship began to melt away, as it always did when they flew faster than the speed of light. Suddenly the spaceship flew backward with tremendous force. Oousma, Ishma, and Mahisma fell out of their seats as the spaceship plunged back towards the Earth.

It was all coming back to Oousma. The man, the dog, the crash. Oousma wondered how long it had been since the crash. It looked over at Ishma and felt Ishma trying to link their consciousnesses into one.

"Oousma, Oousma! Are you awake?!" Ishma asked frantically.

"I am hurt badly, but I am alive. How long have I been unconscious?"

"I am not sure. I have been awake for five Earth days. One of the humans keeps drugging me, so it is difficult to keep track of time. I estimate you have been unconscious for seven days, and I think we crashed eight days ago."

Seven days was an eternity. They were already supposed to be back on Nirubu. The Council of Elders would be worried. They had to make it off of Earth themselves. They flew the only ship with enough element 115 in it to make the journey to Earth.

"Any escape options available to us?" Oousma asked.

"None that I have detected. If we don't get any ultraviolet light, you and I will eventually die down here, Oousma; we can't move shackled to these tables like prisoners."

§

Oousma's species had changed the evolutionary trajectory of their species forever. Oousma's species, the Annonaki, arose in their anatomically modern form on Nirubu 5,000,000 years before the present day. After 3,000,000 years, the world government decided to mutate the DNA of every new fetus to make them autotrophic and photosynthetic. At the same time, all the Annonaki with the altered genome became unable to reproduce sexually, due to the new genetic mutations. New babies were born from stem cells in birthing facilities. Food stores were running extremely low due to the lack of environmental awareness on the Annonaki's part, so the decision was made to alter every newborn's DNA. They had stripped the land of almost all its natural resources, and they were desperate to find a new way of feeding the inhabitants. The two suns in the Alpha Centauri solar system provided an incredible amount of energy. Ultimately, those suns provided food energy to the Annonaki of Nirubu for millions of years up to the present day.

No longer would the Annonaki of Nirubu need to eat food to gain energy; they simply required ultraviolet radiation from the suns for sustenance. Mimicking plants, they spliced the DNA of over 1,000 different plant species on Nirubu with their genes; genes encoding stomach enzymes, liver enzymes, lung function, skin cell function, and small intestine growth and development. Their skin was a light greenish color because of all the chlorophyll it contained. The ramifications of the decision were significant and unfixable. Birth rates plummeted, Annonaki rioted and burned down government buildings in revolt. Class warfare broke out as the elites of the times tried to monopolize the newly spliced DNA for themselves and their offspring. After a few millennia, no individual with un-altered DNA remained on the planet.

§

"If we want to get out of here, we have to be nice to the humans. They are our key to survival."

"I will if they stop constantly drugging me. Until then, I cannot promise you peace Oousma," Ishma said defiantly.

The door to the big white room opened, and two men walked through. One of the men was tall, skinny, and young. He had brown hair and wore a white lab coat. The other was short and stout and older looking. He was balding on the top and sides of his head. He wore a pair of black-rimmed spectacles and a similar lab coat to the taller man.

"The other one just woke up," the taller man said while walking towards Oousma.

"Hopefully, he is a little nicer than his friend here," the fat one replied.

The short fat man walked closer to Oousma and touched its chest with cold fingers. Oousma flinched at the pain.

"Still sensitive. Remove the bandage and apply a new one. The leg seems to be stable; hopefully, the cast will heal the broken bone." Oousma had been in too much shock to realize its right leg was injured. It was at this realization that it felt a throbbing pain emanating from its ankle.

"My name is Barry, and I wish you no harm. Do you understand?" the short man said while staring at Oousma. Ishma hissed loudly.

Oousma looked into the scientist's eyes and nodded its head up and down. This was a human's way of saying yes, and Oousma had learned it at least 1,947 years ago. Barry looked at Oousma, then at the taller man.

"Hand me the keys. We will unchain this one's wrists after you dress the wound again. We need to probe it for information."

"But Barry, we don't know if it is violent or what it is capable of. What if it is many times stronger than we are?"

"Nicolai, you're 6'3 and 190 pounds. These little guys are a third of your size. They couldn't hurt you if they tried, now hand me the keys," Barry finished while motioning with one of his hands.

Nicolai and Barry. Oousma would remember their names. Nicolai started to put a finger up in protest, then he sighed and walked towards a set of drawers. He pulled out a jar of cotton swabs, a pair of scissors, and a cloth bandage. Oousma could sense a gentleness in Nicolai that was not present in the other human.

Nicolai carefully cut away the bloody bandage around Oousma's chest. He dipped several cotton swabs into a clear solution and rubbed it into the wound. The solution smelled like rubbing alcohol, a common antibacterial used by humans for many years. It stung badly, and Oousma winced in pain. Nicolai carefully wrapped new bandages around the wound and threw away the soiled bandages.

"What about it?" Nicolai said, pointing to Ishma.

"We must not unshackle that one for a while. We can work with this one once its wounds have healed up. For now, if this one acts up," Barry said, pointing to Ishma, "then we will knock it out again."

Nicolai pressed Barry, "I thought you said they were harmless?"

Barry chuckled then left the room, leaving Oousma alone with Nicolai.

"Oousma, we can use this boy to our advantage. I sense he is of a weaker mind and more malleable than the other one."

"Yes, yes, I agree. First, we have to build trust by acting peacefully. You heard Barry. If you keep hissing at them, then he will continue to drug you."

"Yes, well, I don't like the thought of being a human science experiment," Ishma growled.

"So, what now, Oousma?"

"For now, we have no choice but to wait. To escape back to our home world, we need to get back to Sirius and call the council to tell them what happened. We also need to find Mahisma. It is dead, but it must be honored in death by the Annonaki tradition."

Oousma could sense the frustration of Ishma. Here were two beings of an inferior intelligence holding Oousma and Ishma as prisoners. They were helpless in the hands of the humans. If only they knew how Oousma and the Annonaki had tried to help them in the past and the present, maybe they would let them go, but some things were better left undisturbed.

"Who knows how big this facility is. Finding our ship could be like finding a needle in a haystack," Ishma said.

"But look, we must, Ishma."

Oousma turned to Ishma. Ishma had light green skin, and very large eyes, even by Annonaki standards. Like humans, they varied slightly in their appearance. Ishma was smaller than Oousma. Ishma stood 3'2 while Oousma stood 3'6, a giant among the Annonaki. Against the large metal table Oousma was laying on, Oousma felt very small.

Physically the Annonaki had deteriorated since the time Oousma's species evolved into their anatomically modern forms. Millions of years ago, the Annonaki were much taller, around 4'6 on average, and they had much higher bone density than they currently did. Their stature shrunk as they became more reliant on tools and machines to do work instead of their bodies. Element 115 was discovered early on in their history to have beneficial properties for generating energy, and as a species, they became more reliant on it. It took them millions of years to discover and make the stable isotope that generated the gravity waves, but early on, they used it for energy through nuclear fission. It produced a tremendous amount of energy in its unstable form through nuclear fission, and thus powered the buildings and infrastructure of Nirubu. The stable isotope made atomically was only used for space travel because it was too time-consuming and costly to produce. Humans appeared to be on a similar trajectory of becoming reliant on machines to do their work, but they were a much younger species than the Annonaki were. They were significantly larger and more robust than the Annonaki. Escaping through force would be impossible; Oousma and Ishma were considerably weaker than the humans.

Barry came into the room again. This time he was wielding a large needle in his hand. He walked over to Ishma, who tried to jerk away, but couldn't because of the ankle and wrist shackles.

"It's okay; this is for your own good," Barry said, smiling. He jammed the needle into Ishma's right arm.

"Now go ahead and unshackle specimen 2's wrists, Nicolai. We have questions to ask."

"Oousma! Oousma! Hhh-eell…", Ishma tried to say before falling unconscious. Oousma was weary of Barry at first, but that weariness had turned to fear quickly. He saw a fire in his eyes that he did not like or trust. It might be a long time before they made it back home.

Chapter 5

---✦---

Will

It had been eight weeks since the crash, and Will and the Heartley family were living through hell daily. As General Ramses proclaimed, the Heartley property was under constant surveillance. Will could see black vans camped outside of the property every day and night, 24/7. The vans were at the property so frequently that one of the Heartley's neighbors inquired about it.

Patsy Lovell, a short, plump woman with big brown eyes, walked up to the front door one morning, wearing nothing but a bathrobe and hair net. "Mind tellin me what the hell is goin on, Will?" she asked as Will answered the door.

"What do you mean?"

"You know goddamn well what I'm talking about. These friggin blacked-out vans are always drivin by my damn house, and I know it's got something to do with you guys. Word around town is an alien ship crashed in your yard, and the feds are watchin."

Tom came to the front door, getting up from his favorite rocking chair in the living room. He looked gaunt and tired. "Ain't nothin happen over here, so go on your way, Patsy."

"You're gonna tell me what happened, or I'll tell my cousin Ricky to beat your ass."

"Tell your cousin, Ricky, I'll be waiting on my front porch with a shotgun and a jar to put his balls in after I chop them off," Tom replied with a cigarette in his mouth. Patsy huffed, then waddled back down the road to her house, several hundred meters away. As she made it to the end of the driveway, near the cornfield, she turned around and flipped off Will and Tom before disappearing around the corner.

"That old bitch. We ain't sayin nothin, understand?" Tom said while looking up at Will.

"I understand," Will replied. This was only one of many incidents they had dealt with since the crash. Another ongoing issue was the absurd number of plumbers, electricians, and inspectors coming to the property to perform "maintenance." It got so bad that Tom started to train Buddy to bark at anyone trying to get on the property, in hopes it would scare them off. As the days passed by, Daisy became more curious.

"Dad, what color were the aliens? Did they crash in our backyard? Are you lying to me? Are you lying to me? I know you're lying."

The bombardment of questions was endless. Will felt sorry for Tom. He couldn't tell his daughter the truth, but the evidence was right there. Even though the crash happened eight weeks prior, the cratered Earth was still visible. The cratered Earth became challenging to explain to Daisy and Macey because the ground had been disturbed by something large. Macey and Tom fought about it, and Tom eventually said Will had accidentally dug the hoe through the dirt. Macey didn't believe it.

Since the crash, Tom had lost at least 10 pounds of weight, and he was skinny to begin with. His pale blue eyes looked like they were sunken into his skull. His skin looked tight and dehydrated. Tom used to stand up straight with a bright smile; now, he slouched with a permanent frown.

Will had never seen Tom look so defeated, and it frightened him. The stress of the situation was overwhelming, Tom. Will started to notice Tom was graying at an exponentially fast rate. He had a full head of blonde hair two months ago. Now his hair was mostly white with a few pieces of blonde. The rest of the house was not faring much better. Everybody was on edge.

Will wanted to go back to working on the farm, tending to the animals and fixing broken things, but he found it nearly impossible. Whenever he looked at the cratered ground, he would get flashbacks to the night of the crash; the silver spaceship, the aliens' mangled bodies, the police officers, and the verbal warnings of Ramses. It was all too much; Will could not focus. It felt like he was living in a bad dream.

Will had gone into town on two occasions since the crash to buy food and other supplies they needed at the house. Both times, he was followed by black vans and spied on by the agents inside of the vans. Bald men in black suits with black sunglasses, who never seemed to be wearing any form of identification, would watch him. The first time he left the house was ten days after the crash.

Will needed to buy new wood to completely fix the horse stable, so he borrowed Tom's red Chevrolet truck and headed into town. Since the crash, the horse stable had gone into disarray due to lack of maintenance, and monsoon season brought in rain weekly. Will needed to put on a new wooden roof to protect the horses; the patch he had put on a few weeks before no longer sufficed. He drove north on Santa Fe Trail past the highway exit until it turned into Auburn Drive, at which point he noticed two vans following him in his rear-view mirror. At first, he tried to play it off as a coincidence, but as he drove to the lumber yard, it was clear he was being followed.

He had seen the black vans circling the property and keeping the Heartley family's vigilance, but he did not think they would follow him into town. He was wrong. As he pulled into the lumber yard's parking lot, the black vans followed and parked directly across from him in a vacant parking lot across the street.

"What the hell is goin on?" Will said to himself while walking to the entrance of the yard. The vans were Ramses' puppets, watching his every move like a hawk. They were not even secretive about it. They were following him in broad daylight and parking where Will could see them.

Will got out of his truck and walked towards the lumber yard, surrounded by a large steel fence. There was an entrance on the near side, and he walked through seeing the owner of the yard, Sherman. Sherman was old and wrinkly, dressed in a tie-dye shirt with a peace symbol in the middle. He was splitting a log with an ax when he saw Will.

"Hey there, Sherman. Can I get 15 two by fours, please?"

"Only if you tell me where the aliens are," Sherman replied with a grin on his face.

"Aliens? Ain't no aliens around here," Will replied while looking over his shoulder. He could never be too sure about who was listening.

"I'm just yankin your chain Will," Sherman chuckled, "you said 15, right?"

"Uh, yes. Yes. 15 two by fours. I got $20 cash on me," Will replied.

"That'll do. Say, would you mind helpin me load up the wood into the wheelbarrow? Ol pimp daddy Sherman is getting stiff."

"Yeah, sure thing," Will replied, walking behind Sherman to the wood storage area.

He helped Sherman load the 15 large pieces of wood into the wheelbarrow and wheeled them out to the truck's bed, where he laid them down. Will looked at the opposite side of the street when he finished loading the wood. The black vans were still there, watching him. Will noticed that two large antennas were sticking out of the top of each van now. He wondered what they were for.

Sherman was standing behind Will, looking at the vans. "Must be drug dealers. Probably sellin pot," Sherman chuckled as they walked back to the lumber yard.

"Haha, yeah, they must be," Will replied while trying to mask the fear in his voice.

Next to the lumber yard was a small wooden building where Sherman made the lumber sales. Sherman unlocked the door, and they walked inside. There were moose heads, deer heads, and other stuffed animals in the dusty little store. Miscellaneous scraps of wood hung on the shelves, and a small desk with a cash register sat lonely in one corner of the store.

"Thank you for your help Will, I appreciate it."

"You know Will, the talk of the townsfolk is that something fishy happened at the Heartley house in early July. I know people are probably hounding you for information, but if you ever need to talk to anyone, I'm here for you. My shop is a judgment-free zone. I can keep my ears open and my mouth shut," Sherman said.

The sentiment meant a lot to Will. Will knew Sherman well, and he trusted him. Still, he did not want to tell him anything, fearing he could put the old lumber yard owner in harm's way. "Thank you, Sherman. It is nice to hear that someone in this town still wants to conversate with me as a friend." Will grabbed the $20 dollar bill out of his jean pocket and handed it to Sherman. They shook hands, and Will walked out of the shop and into the yard.

The black vans were still waiting across the street as Will got into the truck and started the engine. If Will felt like he could not hold it in anymore, he would go to Sherman. He prayed he had the strength not to. Will turned out of the parking lot onto Auburn Drive and was surprised to see the black vans were not immediately following him. "Well, they know where I live anyway," he said to himself while driving back to the farm. It was still strange, though, and he left with an uneasy feeling in his gut.

That was the first time Will had left the property since the crash. Two days after Will visited Sherman's lumber yard, Sherman was found dead outside of his mobile home on July 20th, 1947. He had suffered from a broken neck, apparently falling off of a ladder. That was the official cause of death determined by a local medical examiner, but Will suspected foul play. The article said that homicide had been ruled out, and Sherman's death was deemed accidental. As Will read about the story in the paper, he could barely finish it. He felt responsible for the death of his longtime friend, just by visiting him two days before. He couldn't help but feel like the men in the black vans had something to do with his death.

Sherman had been building and fixing things his whole life. Even at 75, he was sure-footed and strong. He had lived by himself for 50 years in the same mobile home outside of Roswell. He had never hurt himself seriously before his death, despite cutting down large trees and using heavy machinery daily. That was why Will didn't believe the cause of death was accurate. Sherman knew how to use a ladder if nothing else, and the chances of him falling off on his own were slim to none.

Will could not sleep for three days after learning of his friend's death. He almost broke down and told Tom what he suspected had happened, but he didn't; Will might be killed if he said anything. Sherman died by simply offering Will an ear to listen. Well felt responsible for his death.

The second visit outside of the home since the crash was even more eventful. On July 25th, both Will and Tom had agreed they needed to get medicine for some of the pigs because they were ill. An influenza virus was spreading amongst them, and Tom could not afford for any of them to die this year. The sick animals were hacking up mucus and coughing, most likely from a bacterial lung infection caused by the flu. Tom was going to slaughter one of the older fatter pigs before they got sick, but now he did not want to. The meat tasted bad when the animal was sick, and he couldn't sell it at the same price.

"It ruins the meat," he said gruffly as they pulled out of the driveway.

Tom drove down the dirt road, and sure enough, two black vans were waiting on both sides of Santa Fe Trail. Antennae were sticking out of the top on one of the vans.

"Gets old, don't it?" Tom asked Will as they pulled onto the entrance of the highway.

"Yeah, it sure does," Will responded, staring at the tinted window of one of the vans.

Will felt uneasy. The last time he had left the property, somebody had died. Tom and Will could not address the elephant in the room; they were under constant surveillance. Neighbors kept complaining about the constant invasive presence. They would call their house phone daily and yell at them. Eventually, Macey stopped picking up because she got so annoyed with the neighbors yelling at her. People stopped coming by the house, excluding the many miscellaneous "handymen."

Tom and Will decided not to answer the door for any servicemen after one of them started peering through a side window. All guests were scared off the property by the violent barking of Buddy. Tom had seen an electricity meter reader planting some small device on the circuit box one afternoon while pulling weeds. Tom ran into the house to grab his shotgun, but the man was gone when he came outside again. After the fourth or fifth incident with these random people, Tom called the police.

"Uhh- sorry, Tom. We can't help you with this one. The uh-uh feds are investigating your house. I don't know why these people keep showing up at your house, but we can't do nothin if they are from the feds. We have no jurisdiction over your house," a police officer over the phone told him.

Will could tell Tom was deteriorating both mentally and physically. He had large black bags under both of his eyes, and he said little as they pulled into town. They drove to the small veterinary clinic at the south end of town. The vans followed them the whole way and parked close by in the same parking lot. Will and Tom shared a look, and then Will got out of the truck to get the medicine.

The clinic was a lime green building with an ever-green roof. Glass doors with a red cross stood in front of the building. A small sign showing the hours was glued below the red cross.

"Mornin. I'm here to pick up a prescription of antibiotics," Will said, walking into the clinic. The building consisted of three large rooms; the lobby where people could sit and wait, and two operating/ examination rooms down a narrow hall.

"Name please?" a woman working as secretary asked Will.

"Tom Heartley," Will responded.

"Great. I got your paperwork right here. Be back in one second." The woman behind the lobby desk walked back through the hallway into one of the rooms and emerged with three large bottles of pills.

"Instructions are in the bottle. I hope your animals feel better," the woman said, handing the brown paper bag to Will. "Thank you," Will said, giving the woman $10 in cash.

Will waved goodbye as he walked out of the store and into the parking lot. Tom was sitting in the big red truck talking to someone dressed in a black suit and pants, wearing sunglasses. Will could instantly tell that something was wrong by the facial expression of Tom. The hair on the back of his neck stood up as he realized it was one of the men in black. He hurried over to the truck, carrying the bag of medicine.

"I told you I ain't said nothin. Now stop bothering me. Mind your own damn business," Tom was saying as Will approached the truck.

The man turned and stared at Tom through his shades, then walked back over to one of the vans. Will hopped into the truck and looked at Tom.

"What was that about?"

"Nothin. He was just trying to scare me. Sayin' General Ramses is watching. One false move, and you're gone," Tom replied, lighting up a Marlboro red.

Will nodded in understanding. What could they do? They were being spied on constantly by their government, and the Roswell police would not help them. On top of that, their closest neighbors did not trust them and were now calling and harassing them. Whatever agency was watching their house had unlimited resources and time on their hands to monitor them as closely as they did.

"You know Will, I've been thinkin about tellin Macey and Daisy what happened on July 8th. I can't stand lying to them no more. They're my wife and daughter for Christ's sake!"

Will froze. His heart started pounding. He was not sure if the cars were bugged and the men in black could hear what Tom was saying, but he assumed they were bugged. If these mysterious men in black figures heard what Tom was saying, surely they would kill him, and maybe Will. He didn't want to say anything that could get him killed. He thought for a moment about what to say next. He answered carefully.

"I don't think it is wise to say anything to them. What happens if Macey and Daisy can't take the truth?" Will asked, trying to sound genuine.

Tom scratched his chin, "Yeah, you're right. I just hate looking them in the eye and lying through my teeth. Lyin ain't in my DNA."

As Will and Tom exited onto Santa Fe Trail from the highway, he noticed a car parked on the side of the road. It was a white, four-door Ford, with tinted windows. Tom's truck passed the vehicle, and Will looked behind them through the side-view mirror. The lights flashed, and the doors opened. Someone from the driver's side jumped out, holding a small object in his hand.

"What the," Will started to say before he heard a loud BANG, followed by the back window of the truck shattering.

Tom swerved violently as the glass fell onto the back seat, the tires making a screeching noise.

"The fuck was that?!" Tom shouted, hitting the gas.

BANG! BANG!

"Someone's trying to shoot us from behind! Tom, you gotta."

BANG!

The side view mirror Will was looking out of was shot off. Veins of wires and metal clung onto the outside of the truck.

"Jesus Christ, son of a bitch!" Tom yelled as their truck flew down the dirt road. Tom drifted into the final bend around Santa Fe Trail towards the long Heartley driveway. Dust and debris were flying everywhere. Tom's hands were trembling on the wheel. Will was looking back constantly.

The road seemed to last forever as Tom sped towards the house. Buddy, Macey, and Daisy were sitting on the porch when the truck came careening into view. Buddy started barking from the excitement. Tom slammed on the brakes just before running into the front porch. Tom and Will jumped out of the truck and ran towards the front door.

Woof, woof, woof!

"Hey dad," Macey started to say as Will and Tom threw open the front door.

"Inside, now!" Tom shouted, grabbing Macey and throwing her inside.

"Tom, what in the hell," Macey started to say.

"I'll explain later. In the house NOW! Both of you go hide in my room with Buddy. MOVEEE!" Tom boomed.

Macey and Daisy reluctantly followed the orders. Tom and Will entered the house, and Tom slammed the door shut and locked all the deadbolts, four in total. Tom had recently installed two more deadbolts in the door for extra protection.

"Will, we need to get my pistol and shotgun. If one of those sons of bitches comes to the door, you and I are gonna blow his head off," Tom said, gasping for air.

Will followed Tom into his and Macey's room.

"Tom what the hell is going on? I saw the back window. Were you driving drunk?" Macey asked as they came into the room.

The bedroom had a queen-sized bed with a navy-blue comforter and blue pillows. To the right of the bed was a walk-in closet with a large wooden cabinet in its middle. A lock and chain protected the inner contents of the gun safe.

"Not now. I'll talk later. Stay in here and don't say nothin," Tom croaked while unlocking the cabinet.

In the cabinet were the shotgun and the pistol. Tom passed the shotgun to Will and took the pistol for himself. Tom always had a better shot, so the decision made sense. Will and Tom loaded up their guns and ran down the hallway into the living room. Will peeked through the blinds, looking down the driveway.

"Think anyone is coming?" Will asked nervously.

"I hope so. It would be fun to kill one of those bastards," Tom replied while lighting up a Marlboro red cigarette.

Will only saw grass and corn stalks. Nothing moved. Occasionally Buddy would bark only to be hushed. Will and Tom watched and sat by the front door for two hours before they called it quits. Exhausted, they both slumped back into the soft leather couch in the living room.

"Who do you think was shooting at us?" Will asked, knowing the answer.

"Who do you think?" Tom growled.

"I'm sorry, I shouldn't get so mad, I just- I just," Tom stammered as he put his head in his hands and started to sob.

Will sat on the couch silently, observing Tom. In the twelve years Will had been working for Tom, he had never seen him cry. Not even after he shot his old dog, Junior. Will reached out a hand and patted Tom on the back.

"It'll be okay man, I promise. Couple more months and everyone will forget about it, including the feds," Will said, trying to console Tom.

"Yeah, yeah," Tom said, wiping his eyes. "I just can't take much more of this. I'm just an old, worn-out farmer."

Will looked at Tom's face. He indeed looked old and tired. This was all too much for both of them.

"You're still a young bastard to me," Will said, trying to cheer him up.

"Young enough to still whoop your ass," Tom replied, smiling and wiping away his tears.

Both visits outside the house were ordeals, and Will was scared to go out again. Around the farm, everything slowly began to deteriorate. The pig pen fence needed to be fixed, the chicken coop wiring needed to be replaced, and the horses needed new horseshoes. To make matters worse, Tom and Will were growing isolated from Macey.

Macey was not speaking to Tom unless she needed to. Daisy was still bombarding both Will and Tom with questions, ever curious. Daisy was sharp, and that concerned Will. It was becoming increasingly impossible to lie.

"What color were the aliens? Were they mean? Did they have superpowers? Why are those creepy vans always watching us?"

Will and Tom had long run out of excuses. At a certain point, they just stopped responding to the questions. Will could feel Tom's eagerness to tell the truth. The string of lies were taking a toll on his mind and body.

Approximately two and a half months after the initial crash, the Heartleys got a letter in the mail, dated 9-27-1947. It had the bank's wax seal on it. The envelope was addressed to Tom, the owner of the property. Tom broke the wax, pulling out a small piece of paper. He read through the letter and cursed.

"The bank is going to foreclose the property if we don't pay rent this next month," Tom said to a wide-eyed Daisy, Macey, and Will.

"So, what are we going to do?" Macey asked worriedly.

"Well, I need to go to the bank to sort this out. No way around it. The only problem is it ain't safe for me to go. Last time Will and I left the house, we nearly got blasted off the road."

"I'll go with you," Daisy said.

"No. You stay here with your mom. Will, you gotta come with me. Bring the shotgun."

Will looked at Macey, who shook her head. He turned to the pouting Daisy, "Your dad is right, Daisy. It has become too dangerous for us to leave the house, so only Tom and I should go."

Daisy nodded; she was not the type to argue. Daisy had barely been out of the house in the past three months and was undoubtedly missing her friends. Any mission Tom and Will went on, she eagerly wanted to tag along but was never allowed to come. Her life would never be the same after all this. Will was sure of that.

Will and Tom walked to Tom's bedroom and opened the wooden gun cabinet. They shared a look as Tom passed the gun to Will. Tom hugged

Daisy, then kissed Macey on the cheek. Will felt strange walking out of the house with a shotgun just to go to the bank. As soon as Will and Tom hopped into the red truck and started driving, Tom started talking.

"Will, I can't take this shit no more man. When we get back, I'm tellin Macey and Daisy everything. My wife ain't even kissing me back, my own fucking wife. Lying to them day in and day out is eating me alive. They deserve to know the truth," Tom said, fighting back the tears. He was white-knuckled, gripping the steering wheel.

Will's heart rate jumped up. Was Tom serious? Tom might put the whole family in danger if he said something. Yet, he understood where he was coming from. He had to lie to his wife and daughter every day for months, and now he couldn't anymore. He had reached his breaking point.

"What if the house is bugged and they hear you?"

"Then we prepare for a fight. I ain't gonna let these sons of a bitches control my life to ruin it. To hell with that. Are you with me or not?" Tom asked, glaring at Will.

Will gulped. "Yeah I'm with you. Fuck them cops. We gotta be prepared to make a run for it," Will replied while looking in the rear-view. Today only one van was waiting on Santa Fe Trail to follow them.

"You mean to abandon the farm? I can't do that. Put too much time and money into this place. Besides, what would we do with all the animals?"

"But Tom, you might----" Will got out before Tom interrupted him.

"What, I might die? Will, me and you almost fuckin died getting medicine for the damn pigs. You think hiding and pretendin these bastards will disappear is going to work? It's been three damn months!"

Will didn't know what to say. Tom had a point. They were not safe doing normal daily activities anymore; they couldn't keep pretending like the men in black would leave. They were there to stay.

"You're right," Will finally stammered, "We have to be careful though, Tom. And there's something I need to tell you."

"Remember Sherman, the shopkeeper?" Will asked as the pair pulled up to the bank.

"Oh yeah, the fella who fell off his roof and broke his neck. He sold good wood."

"Yes, him... Tom, I don't think he fell off his roof. I think the men in black killed him. They followed me the day I went to get wood, and they parked in the parking lot across the street. When I left, they stayed; nobody followed me home."

Tom looked at Will wide-eyed. "Do you have any proof?"

"No, but I know Sherman. He's been fixing things since he could shit in the toilet. I don't think he fell off his ladder. I reckon he was pushed off his roof."

Tom studied Will for a second then replied, "Well shit. We better prepare for a fight then, eh?" he said while grinning.

Will was scared. He didn't want to die; he was only 28 years old.

"Wait here while I figure out what to do inside the bank."

Tom hopped out of the truck and walked towards the building. The bank was a large white building with a pitched roof. Four large stone pillars held up the roof. A miniature staircase led to the entrance of the building. Double wooden doors with the lettering *Roswell City Bank* were painted in white on the doors. Tom pushed them open and walked through.

The parking lot was small and empty, except for the Heartley's truck and a black van parked 30 feet away. Will lit a cigarette as he watched the entrance of the building.

"Don't these fuckers ever go to sleep?" Will said while exhaling. He could not see into the black van; the windows were too tinted. It was an eerie feeling, being watched in broad daylight without knowing who was watching you. Will wondered if these men had families - surely they were not robots.

After 15 minutes, Tom reemerged from the bank looking sour-faced. He walked over to the truck and opened the door.

"Is everything all right?" Will asked.

"Well, for them. They're having a grand old time deciding what assets I need to sell to the state to save the property. I had an emergency account with $300, and they took all that. That should get us through to the new year, but after January 1st, 1948, nothing is certain."

"Damn, so that was the rest of the money you had?"

"Every last penny," Tom said while starting the truck.

That was the nail in the coffin. Tom was definitely not joking about staying put. Macey would throw two fits when they got back: one for not telling her and Daisy the truth initially, and the second for Tom spending all the savings on the property without her consent. Will could tell Tom was trying to cling on to the last bit of normalcy he had in an already chaotic life.

For the rest of the car ride back to the house, they were silent. They both knew what was coming. It was obvious: all they had to do was look into the rear-view mirror. Their problem followed them everywhere. As they pulled into the last turn on Santa Fe trail, Will turned to Tom.

"How should we tell them?"

"Well, I figure we walk straight into the house, sit em down and let loose."

"What if they handle it badly?"

"Well, that's what I'm expectin. We have to tell them regardless of how we think they will react."

Will agreed. He looked at Tom's overalls and his brown work boots. An honest man can only lie for so long.

"You're right. You're right. Okay, we can do this," Will said, taking a deep breath.

They pulled into the long dirt driveway. Nobody was waiting on the porch for them. Tom turned off the truck, and they walked through the screen door and into the house. Buddy was standing at the door, ready for his visitors. He looked happy as ever, wagging his tail. Will envied Buddy at that moment. How nice it must be to live care-free like that.

Tom and Will walked into the living room where Macey and Daisy were sitting on the old leather couch. Tom looked Macey straight in the face and said, "Macey, Daisy, Will and I got to tell y'all something you both need to hear."

Chapter 6

---※---

Ramses

"Yes, Mr. President. I have ensured nobody will talk about the incident."

"Good. It is your top priority to ensure the information about this unidentified flying object stays in the hands of those with majestic clearance. Nobody else must know what we have discovered. Also, I need you to keep track of the other unidentified flying objects we have detected. They seem to be active mostly over military installations and bomb testing sites."

"Understood, Mr. President."

"Oh, and one more thing Ramses. Call me Harry. You know me well enough to refer to me on a first-name basis. We will be in touch. Bye-bye."

Ramses hung up the phone in his room. The military had detected other objects similar to the one in Roswell. Vehicles that were either flying in the exosphere or thermosphere that the United States did not build. The Russians were developing a satellite; an object capable of orbiting the Earth, but as of yet, they had not launched one. Some of these mysterious objects had been detected flying down to the troposphere, only to pop back up into the exosphere in a few seconds. The objects' origins were a mystery. Keeping a lid on the phenomena as it grew would be hard, especially since they were spotted near military installations. Alternative tactics would need to be employed. These objects never showed any hostility, but the military did not want to take such aerial feats lightly. The spaceship currently at Kirtland Air Force Base was unlike any other airplane made on Earth, and Ramses suspected these objects were made by the same group of aliens.

Barry and Nicolai discovered the spaceship did not have a reactionary propulsion system; it used gravity waves to move. Every airplane that had been built on Earth used a reactionary propulsion system. Barry and Nicolai could not yet figure out how the fuel core's mysterious element was interacting with gravity, so they were stuck. The progress had been slow since the initial discovery of how to disassemble the core and turn the ship on. The technology used to make the spaceship was far beyond what any government agency was currently capable of on Earth. Barry hypothesized the aliens were tens of thousands, possibly even millions of years more advanced than the humans on Earth currently were.

In the weeks since the crash, Ramses made sure the N.S.A. agents monitored the Heartley property 24/7. He was talking to them every week; there would be no slip-ups. Ramses was not worried about Will. He had scared him right and good on the night of the crash - that he was sure of. Tom was the wild card Ramses worried about. Ramses hoped for Tom's own good that he did not tell the rest of his family what happened on July 8th, 1947.

Tom was defiant enough to raise suspicion at the time of the crash, and Ramses knew he needed to pay special attention to him and monitor him closely. Ramses ordered the N.S.A. agents to follow the truck every time it left the Heartley property, even in broad daylight. The men would rotate surveillance of the property in week-long shifts. Ramses had a pool of 20 agents at his disposal, and four would be on shift at once. After the week was up, they would get three weeks off, then go back to monitoring the property. Their period of employment was indefinite.

In addition to assigning a surveillance team, Ramses paid off the entire Roswell police department to not further investigate the incident. He also paid them not to respond to any calls from the Heartley family or do weekly patrols in their neighborhood. Ramses still remembered the call with police chief Gordon.

"Hello, this is the Roswell police department, Sergeant Lucero speaking."

"Hello, Sergeant Lucero. My name is Ramses Meddiah the III. I am a five-star General of the United States Air Force. May I speak with your chief of police?"

"Yes, sir, right away." In the background, Ramses could hear the policeman shouting, "Hey Gordon, we got a General Ramses on the line!"

"One-second, sir."

"Thank you."

"Police Chief Gordon White speaking. How can I help you, General?"

"Gordon, I have an offer for you and your police department."

"Go ahead, sir, I'm listening."

"I'll pay you $20,000 and every man you have under you $10,000 to not investigate any incidents or complaints filed by the Heartley family, including William Brakel."

Ramses heard the phone drop, then Gordon picked it up again.

"Uh, did I hear you correctly? Did you say $20,000?"

"Yes, that is correct."

"Wait a minute. Are you bribing me? Isn't that illegal?"

Ramses shuffled through a few documents laying out in front of him on his work desk at Kirtland. They were the names of all the Roswell police officers and their immediate family members. He looked for Gordon White. Bingo. He found it. He picked up the phone again.

"Now, Gordon, you would not want to disappoint your wife Caren or your son Thomas would you?"

There was silence on the line then, "How, how did you get the names of my family? That is confidential."

"Gordon, I'm running out of time and patience. I could have you or your family disappear by the end of the hour if I wanted to. Do you understand me? Now, do we have a deal?"

"Ye-yes, sir. I will make sure none of my officers investigate the property further. We will also not respond to any civilian calls from their residence."

"Very good. One of my men will bring briefcases of the money to your headquarters. You are not going to tell your men about this conversation. You will tell them the money is from a private donor to thank you for your service to the community. If I find out you or one of the other officers is running their mouths about the crash, they will be disappeared. Understood?"

Ramses hung up the phone before Gordon could respond. Gordon had been at the scene of the crash along with most of the local officers in Roswell. Ramses needed to make sure they didn't say anything. Submission through fear was always a good option. The N.S.A. agents knew they had to swear secrecy as well, but Ramses was not concerned about them. They were airtight.

Six weeks after the crash on August 15th, 1947, Ramses was sitting in his bedroom looking up at a box labeled "Top-secret" on a wooden shelf, hovering above his desk. He opened it, exposing two manilla folders: one was a report about what Nicolai and Barry had done over the previous two weeks, titled *Work on Advanced Aerospace Design 7-21-1947 to 8-7-1947.* The other manilla folder was a final report from Los Alamos National Laboratory concerning the last nuclear bomb test.

Ramses opened the report about the nuclear bomb test first. The document inside was 150 pages, mostly graphs describing the energy distribution of the small-scale atomic explosion. The physicists set up sensors to monitor the explosion's impact, and the data was taken from those sensors and put into the report. Ramses was no scientist, so he skipped to the summary at the end of the report.

The summary read: "The 100-kiloton nuclear detonation on 7-8-1947 at 13:00 was observed by ten individuals, from approximately 2 miles away. Observers viewed the mushroom cloud rising for approximately 3 minutes before it started to dissipate into the atmosphere. Radiation levels were high, even 2 miles away from the blast at the observation post. If dropped on a major city, the estimated death toll would be between 250,000-500,000, depending on where and how it hit. The warhead detonated was FB-1376."

The Air Force never released the exact time of the detonation until the day before it was scheduled. This was so spies could not disseminate the information to Russia or Germany easily. It was in the best interest of the United States to keep prying eyes out of their business. Ramses believed that it was a necessary precaution. He had witnessed espionage from his own squadron of men at one point in time. He took no chances.

Ramses shivered as he put the report into a shredding machine. Nuclear bombs were powerful, immensely powerful. Powerful enough to change the face of an entire nation in an instant. Information of this sort was lethal in the wrong hands. After they had been read, shredding top-secret documents was standard practice in the Air Force, especially with material this sensitive. Now he moved to the folder from Kirtland Air Force Base.

The document inside was much larger than the report from Los Alamos. It was nearly 300 pages in length. Ramses looked around his bland, neat room for a cigarette. He would need one for this. He looked at his black nightstand next to his bed and opened the top drawer. There was a little altoid can next to a worn-out picture of his parents' faces. He flicked up the can, revealing a hidden stash of Marlboro reds.

"Only when I need it," he told himself while lighting the cigarette. He walked back over to his desk and let out a long puff of smoke. Smoke danced around the document, teasing Ramses to read it. Secretly he did not want to read it. His belief in God and Jesus had defined life. He felt like the past six weeks had changed that: the case for God was dying.

The document's first page was a cover page with the Air Force logo printed on it; Arnold wings splayed out from a star. He flipped to the next page, which contained a table of contents. The table of contents read:

1. Health Status of Two Living Specimens
30. Anatomy of the Two Living Specimens
35. Propulsion System: Possible Mechanisms
210: Materials from the Spaceship: Properties
240. Conclusions
250. Appendix 1: Specimen in Depth Anatomy Chart
270. Appendix 2: Known Spaceship Components

Ramses cared little for the creatures themselves. All he cared about was them living and helping them fix the spaceship, to learn more about it in the long run. Ramses was truly after their technology. He skipped to page 35 and began reading.

In the weeks since the United States obtained the spaceship, Barry and Nicolai had learned some startling things about the spaceship's propulsion system. First, the spaceship did not move by reactionary propulsion, it warped the gravitational field around it to fly through a separate pocket of spacetime, or so Barry thought. The technology was so advanced that Barry and Nicolai had no way of proving it operated through gravitational waves, because they had no device to detect changes in gravitational waves. Still, through trial and error, they came down to this conclusion and eventually hypothesized how the core and the ship interacted to fly.

The reactor core was a small metallic sphere that sat in a metallic disc. The core was positioned in the exact center of the spaceship, and the spaceship could only be activated if the reactor core was set on the disc in the middle of the spaceship. According to the written account of Nicolai on page 175, "The sphere behaves like no metal I have ever seen. If the sphere is manipulated in a special way once it is taken outside of the metal disc, it disassembles itself and turns into a liquid, revealing a smaller sphere inside made of a super-heavy element, and this sphere houses a rod of the same element. Barry and I believe the rod could be the fuel source. Isotopic readings from our instruments indicate the inner sphere and the rod are made out of element 115. It is unclear at this time how element 115 can generate gravity waves." Nicolai hypothesized in the next paragraph that the element in the inner core was artificially made. Stable element 115 had not been detected on Earth, and Nicolai hypothesized it was too large to occur naturally in a stable isotope.

Ramses was intrigued by the discovery of element 115. That was definitive progress in the right direction. The report made it seem like the element was manufactured on a different planet entirely, a planet with different properties from Earth's. No human scientific team had ever created element 115 for a single second, let alone used it to power a spaceship. There was no goddamn chance the Russians or the Germans were behind all this in some crazy way. What was also clear about the report was that neither Nicolai nor Barry had a good working hypothesis about how element 115 was able to power the spaceship. They knew it used gravity waves, but didn't know how it generated those waves or how they were used to manipulate 4-D spacetime.

Reverse-engineering the spaceship would be impossible if element 115 could not be created on Earth, and Ramses doubted it could be. President Truman expected weekly briefings from Ramses about the team's progress. Ramses needed to be making steady progress in the federal government's eyes for him to keep his job as leading supervisor of the Roswell Project. The government was paying Barry and Nicolai $40,000 a year each, in addition to $5,000 a week for the ongoing surveillance of the Heartley home. Time was ticking.

On September 1st, 1947, Ramses had a conversation with the president as part of the weekly briefings he was ordered to give. The call from Truman was anything but peachy.

"Ramses, when will we be able to fly the spaceship ourselves?"

"Well, sir, we do not understand the physics of how the spaceship flies yet. I am not comfortable releasing it for a test flight. It could break down at any moment and become useless, if it is not already."

"It has been two months since the crash, Ramses. How complicated can an airplane be? The Air Force has been flying planes for years."

"Sir, this spaceship is unlike anything the United States Air Force has ever seen or developed. If we fly it and crash it, we may never be able to reverse-engineer the technology. This technology would be a game-changer if we can figure out how to build it ourselves. The spaceship is priceless."

"And what of the aliens? Are they alive? Has anyone at the facility seen them other than Barry and Nicolai?"

"No, sir. Only Barry and Nicolai have access to the spaceship and to the room where the aliens are being kept."

"Good, make sure it stays that way. One last thing, Ramses."

"What is it, sir?"

"I received an intelligence report from our men at the N.S.A. in Roswell saying they eliminated a Sherman Dunley in Roswell on July 19th. Did you know about this?"

"Yes, sir, I authorized the hit. My men reported to me that Sherman talked to William Brakel one day, saying Will could tell him anything about the crash and that he could be trusted. Our research indicates they have had extensive contact. Several cashier checks from Will's bank had been made out to Sherman Dunley over the past ten years. I felt like he posed a sufficient threat to security based on this exchange. I instructed our men to do the hit, but make it look like an accidental death so nobody would be suspicious."

There was a long pause before the president spoke. "I trust you. Make sure you keep fatalities to a minimum in the near future. We do not need to bring any more unwanted attention to Roswell. Keep me posted with new information."

"Roger that, sir," Ramses said before hanging up his phone. The past two weeks wore him down. Nicolai and Barry made no significant discoveries at the end of August. Now September was beginning to look much the same. He sighed and looked at himself in a mirror above his desk. He looked tired. His dark skin and square jaw looked as menacing as ever. He turned to the bible, resting on his nightstand. "Please, God, tell me these little green aliens are a part of your creation. Please," he finished, almost in tears.

His dad was a Christian, and his mother converted to Christianity to marry him. Both of Ramses' parents believed strongly in God, in Jesus Christ. The eternal Creator who put man above all other creatures. Those values heavily influenced his way of thinking and doing. Ramses was trying to figure out where the aliens fit into the equation. They were so far advanced that Ramses thought they might as well be little 3-foot-tall gods. Assuming they had traveled from a world very far away, they could traverse the universe as a God would. Compared to the aliens, humans were mindless cockroaches: useless.

Ramses went to visit the facility five days later, on September 6th, 1947. He was going in to check on the aliens and Nicolai and Barry. The visit was to see if Ramses could increase the efficiency or cut down the project's costs, but in the end, the visit did little. Truman authorized Ramses to make in-person visits to the lab whenever he deemed it necessary. After the lack of progress in two months, Truman wanted Ramses to hire more men to work on the spaceship to expedite the research. Ramses disagreed with him, citing national security concerns. This led to a heated debate with the president.

"Fine. We will not hire any more men for now. But Ramses, I need some progress. Our time is running out. Congress is on my ass about the money we are spending on the Roswell Project. $100 million dollars of taxpayer money is on the line."

Truman wanted to awe the world into submission with the technology. He called this the "aggressive socialist" approach. Ramses knew they were not anywhere close to utilizing the technology in any capacity, much less show it off to the world. He had been considering releasing the aliens from their restraints with armed guards present, which would allow the aliens to aid them in their research efforts, but that was a long shot. The aliens were unpredictable, and their intelligence was still unmeasured on any formal test. Barry and Nicolai had reported that the aliens had not eaten anything given to them in the two months since they found them, but they did drink water. Ramses guessed they either did not need food in the same way humans did, or they were on some form of hunger strike in protest of captivity. Either way, the two live specimens could not be trusted to be released.

On September 28th, 1947, Ramses got a call from his agents stationed in Roswell. "Hello, sir, this is agent 1175-B speaking. We have important information you may want to hear."

"Go ahead, agent. I'm listening."

"One of our agents was listening to audio recordings coming from the Heartley house, and it appears William Brakel and Tom Heartley have told the other occupants in the house the details of the crash."

Fuck - that was not supposed to happen. Ramses knew he had to be decisive, or the story could get released and blow up quickly. Surely Macey and Daisy would tell other people what happened, or they already had. It was the nature of women to talk.

"This is dangerous news, agent 1175-B. Are you certain of what you are saying?"

"Yes, sir. I have listened to the audio recordings myself and have typed them out. You can hear Tom and William talking clear as day. I can have the tape sent to you."

"That will not be necessary," Ramses interrupted. "Stay close to the phone. I will give you orders within the hour, agent."

"Roger that."

Ramses quickly dialed the number of the oval office. He heard one ring before a response. "Mr. Acheson speaking. May I ask who is calling?"

"General Ramses, sir. I need to speak to the president. This is urgent."

"Yes, I will get him right away."

A second later, the president picked up the phone, "Ramses, what's the news?"

"I received a briefing from agent 1175-B. He has an audio recording of William Brakel and Tom Heartley talking to Macey and Daisy Heartley about the crash. The agent said they described the crash in full detail."

"Well, shit... what do you think is the best course of action?"

"We tried to scare them before, and that didn't work. It is time to take things a little more seriously."

"What do you mean by that?"

"Since they are the only four civilians other than the officers who arrived at the crash, we can assume they have not disseminated the information to anybody else yet. My agent listened to the recording of Tom and Will speaking about the crash and called me immediately afterward. We need to detain them and question them. All of them."

"Ramses, we cannot arrest United States citizens without probable cause or a warrant."

"Don't worry about a warrant. I'll talk to Police Chief Gordon and see if we can work something out under the table. If he does not cooperate, we will have to take matters into our own hands."

"What do you mean by taking matters into our own hands?"

"Macey, Daisy, William, and Tom are all threats to national security at this point. Congress is spending $100,000,000 of taxpayer money to keep this program secret. We must try to dampen the threat through fear and intimidation."

"Jesus Ramses, you can't be serious. I bet nobody will listen to their story; they will go down as crazies. We changed the press release the day after the incident to say we found a weather balloon, so I doubt many people in the American public care anymore."

"And what if the Russians or the Germans or the Chinese figure out what we have? What will you be saying when they are questioning you about the technology?"

There was a long pause.

"You're right. I know you're right. Having this information get out could be deadly. I only want you to use your tactics as a last resort. Try to coax them into a meeting and peacefully explain the government's terms, and if that fails, then you can use force."

"Understood, sir, I will let you know how everything pans out. Good day to you," Ramses said, hanging up the phone.

When did he become so cold? Probably in the war. Ramses was responsible for the deaths of thousands in World War 2. He tried to empathize with the Heartley family, but he could not. A cold lump of flesh occupied the place where his heart should have been. Life was easier when you didn't care about other people. Ramses lit up a Marlboro red cigarette and then dialed Police Chief Gordon in Roswell.

Gordon answered the phone on the second ring, "Hello, this is Police Chief Gordon of the Roswell Police Department speaking. May I ask who is calling?"

"General Ramses here. I have another request."

"Wh-what is it?" Gordon asked nervously.

"I need you to arrest Tom, William, Macey, and Daisy on the grounds of conspiring against the United States government."

"We can't do that without evidence and a signed warrant from a judge."

Ramses cut him off and said, "You love your son Thomas, right? It would be a shame if something unfortunate happened to your only boy."

Ramses heard Gordon gulp. "I'll bring them in for you."

"Good, I will let my men know as well. Thank you for your cooperation," Ramses said, hanging up the phone.

It had been weeks since Ramses had spoken to Police Chief Gordon White: he was still scared of Ramses. Ramses needed it to stay that way. He needed the police in Roswell to cooperate with him fully, no questions asked. Fear was the cement that held the delicate hierarchy in place.

After calling the president and the police chief, Ramses needed to call his agents out in Roswell to let them know of the plan. He dialed the number for agent-1175B.

"Hello, agent. I want you and three more agents to contact Police Chief Gordon. Tell him you are working for me, and you will be aiding in the arrest of Tom, William, Macey, and Daisy. I give you full permission to use force if one of them tries to escape. In the event there is a fatality, you must report it to me immediately. Try to keep the suspects alive; it will be less messy. Understood?"

"Yes, sir, understood. I will contact the other agents in our unit. Do you want me to call you again before the actual arrest?"

"No need. I'm not exactly sure when Gordon wants to make the arrests, but push for it in the next couple of days. Call me after the arrest has been made and the suspects have been questioned," Ramses said and then promptly hung up the phone.

The gentle sunrise announcing the dawn of day crept through Ramses' blinds. He looked at the electronic clock on his nightstand; it read 07:00 November 1st, 1947. Next to the clock was a picture of him, his mom, and his dad standing by a model rocket he had built. His dad always encouraged his interest in guns and explosives. He served in the United States military for eighteen years before he had his fatal accident. Ramses wondered if his dad had seen anything otherworldly during his time in the military. How would his dad handle the situation Ramses was in right now? Would he lose his faith and his hope? Would he be intrigued? Ramses did not know.

His whole day consisted of reading reports and talking on the phone with military personnel. A few Japanese warships were spotted 2,000 miles off the pacific coast, near Hawaii, which raised alarms for the morning. Several hours after he was notified of the fleet, they headed back to Japan. It was all a practice exercise. He had to write his report on the incident and mail it off to the General commanding the Pearl Harbor naval station. He also ordered 15 bombers to fly from California to Hawaii, just in case the

Japanese decided to attack for real. He didn't want another Pearl Harbor incident on his hands. After finishing all his paperwork for the Air Force, he focused on his other task at hand - the Roswell Project.

Ramses planned on making another visit to the underground facility the next day, on November 2nd, so he prepared a list of questions he needed to ask Barry and Nicolai. The alien who was shot in the chest was making a speedy recovery, while the other alien got worse. Ramses had not visited the facility in person for weeks, and he was eager to test the abilities of the alien who was conscious and healthier. The mystery behind the aliens and the spaceship was alluring, and he heavily anticipated its unraveling.

Chapter 7

Nicolai

Since late September, Nicolai and Barry had been working 70-hour workweeks. They were constantly testing new theories and experiments on the spaceship and the aliens. By design, the spaceship made little sense to the scientists. It had no wings, no tail, and no thrusters. The shape was not aerodynamic at all; in fact, the United States military had tried to build a flying saucer-shaped object in the past to no avail. Every prototype failed because it could not lift off the ground with enough speed and lift.

They could turn on the reactor core and start the ship itself. That much, Barry and Nicolai had figured out. While they were examining the spaceship from the inside, Colonel Garcia appeared in lab 100 and told the pair that the Air Force wanted to do a live flight test with the spaceship. He showed them a written order from Ramses stating they had made enough progress to do a test flight. The order was dated November 4th, 1947, and Ramses signed it.

"That's preposterous! We have no idea how to turn on the computer interface to the ship itself. This is how the spaceship controls its movements, and without knowing the controls or buttons to press, we cannot safely fly it," Barry said, sounding flabbergasted.

"We do not have to know how everything works. Ramses gave us the all-clear to release one of the aliens to help fly the spaceship," Colonel Garcia responded coolly.

Barry gasped at the Colonel's words, and Nicolai almost pissed himself. Both Nicolai and Barry were scared of the aliens, but they did not want to admit it. On top of being scared, they were given specific orders by Ramses on August 8th, 1947, not to release the aliens for any reason, even during an emergency evacuation. This new order came as a surprise to both of them. It was unlike Ramses to fall back on a decision he had made previously, especially after visiting the lab days before, on November 2nd, and not saying anything then.

Barry and Nicolai had not released either of the aliens completely yet. The alien who had the heart surgery was getting better, and quickly, but Nicolai was unsure of its abilities when healthy. Despite the alien recovering quickly, Nicolai could tell it was still weakened because of the way it moved and breathed. The other alien was hissing every time it woke up from the drugs and would lash out if Barry or Nicolai walked near it. Because the aliens were shackled down onto a metal bed, Nicolai assumed they were angry and ready to escape at any cost, but they could not verbally communicate with the aliens. Releasing them was risky.

"Which one are we going to release? Specimen 1 is violent and unpredictable, and specimen 2 is still weak," Nicolai asked.

"Specimen 2," the Colonel responded coldly.

Nicolai looked at the Colonel in his military garb first, and then around at the giant white laboratory they were standing in. Nicolai was working in a top-secret military facility on Kirtland Air Force Base. Even though he was oddly concerned for the wellbeing of the aliens, his opinion mattered little here. Everything was done by the military bureaucracy. He did as he was told, which was the end of it: all rebels were silenced.

"Yes, sir. I will prepare specimen 2 the best way I can before the test flight."

"Good. We fly tonight at 22:00. I will be sending in armed men to protect you while the specimen is being released. Expect my men here at the facility at 21:00."

With that, the Colonel exited the room and shut the door behind him. Barry and Nicolai stood in the laboratory, the spaceship looming behind them. Nicolai looked at Barry for an answer, and he only shrugged. Nicolai wondered if the pressure of the president had gotten to Ramses since his last visit. The test flight would be a chilly one. It was November 5th, 1947, and the predicted temperature at 22:00 was 15°F.

Several weeks before his most recent visit, Ramses had come to the facility in person to see what progress had been made on researching the spaceship. Nicolai and Barry were able to show him how the power core worked and how the ship turned on. When Nicolai had taken the metal sphere out and disassembled it, Ramses watched in awe as the metal turned to liquid. "Impressive," was all Ramses could say. However, he became less impressed as the visit went on and eventually stormed out of the facility calling Nicolai and Barry idiots because all they could do was turn the ship on.

In the days leading up to November 5th, Barry and Nicolai ran several different iterations of experiments a day. Nicolai was the one who was mainly studying the aliens, and Barry was the main one studying the spaceship. Nicolai had compiled an extensive medical journal about the aliens. Most of the information was from an autopsy he performed on the dead alien. He learned the aliens had a breathing system similar to humans; they needed oxygen to survive, and they had two lungs with alveoli inside them. They had brains that were approximately 1700 cubic centimeters - much larger than the average human brain, despite their small size. They did have eyelids, but the eyelids were almost a translucent green color, different from the surrounding skin. They had eight pairs of ribs instead of twelve like humans, and they had similar forearm bones, leg bones, and vertebrae compared to humans. They had one kidney and several organs near the kidneys that Nicolai could not identify. However, their digestive system was completely different from humans.

Their stomachs were tiny, almost nonexistent. Instead, they had what appeared to be an intestine with millions of cilia attaching to veins on the outside of the intestine, which in turn were directly attached to skin cells. The cilia network was so extensive that Nicolai mistook it for cancer, until he realized the cilia could be synonymous with the villi in the small intestine of humans. Nicolai was not certain, but he suspected the aliens got their energy from the sun. In other words, they were photosynthetic, but how this worked biologically was a complete mystery.

Another puzzling difference between the aliens and humans was the lack of reproductive organs in the aliens. Nicolai searched the dead alien body meticulously, but found no fallopian tubes, no uterus, no testes, and no penis. Somehow the aliens were able to reproduce without having sex. Nicolai could not guess the sexes of the aliens and concluded they were all of the same sex. The body contained only a small opening near their glutes, where he assumed they pooped out of, but since the aliens had been in his presence, no fecal matter was detected on the metal tables. He reported all this to Ramses, who was less than amused. He only cared about the spaceship.

Shortly after that visit, Colonel Garcia stormed into lab 100 and demanded, "Pick up the pace because Ramses needed to see tangible progress."

Now here they were on the night of November 5th, 1947, about to release one of the aliens for the first time. The hours of the day were dragging by; Nicolai was nervous. He and Barry had checked the vitals of specimen 2, and everything looked normal: 160/120 mmHg blood pressure and a resting heart rate of 115 beats per minute. The aliens had extremely high blood pressure and resting heart rates compared to humans, most likely so that their bodies could get enough oxygenated blood to their massive heads.

Finally, when 21:00 came around, Nicolai and Barry heard a pounding on the door to lab 7. Nicolai looked through the small peephole and saw two men dressed in all black standing right outside the door. The two men looked like omens of death in a sea of white—Ramses' men. As Nicolai opened the door and the two men walked in, he peered into the hot side's empty hallway. They were the only ones left on the hot side this late at night.

"I'm excited," Barry whispered to Nicolai as they shut the door. Excited was not the word Nicolai would use right now. One of the agents stuck out his hand to Nicolai, "I'm agent 1168-A."

"Nicolai, nice to meet you," Nicolai responded.

"And I am agent 1172-C. We are both here to assist you with specimen transport."

Agent 1168-A was short and muscular with a bald head. Agent 1172-C was the taller, skinnier version of 1168-A, bald head and all.

"Yes, right this way. Our specimens are being held over here," Barry said, directing them to the metal tables.

The men in black approached the tables slowly. Specimen 1 started hissing as the men approached. The hissing grew louder as they came closer. The men in black stood there, observing the specimen unapologetically.

"Nicolai, go get the shackle keys," Barry said while opening up a medicine drawer on the far side of the lab. Nicolai walked toward the near side of the lab, closer to the entrance. All the security keys were kept in a box hanging close to the entrance of the lab. He opened up the box and grabbed the shackle key. A triangular head sat atop a metal shaft and base, forming the shackle key. As he walked back across the room toward the specimens, the agents suddenly drew their weapons.

"Can't take any chances. Orders from the boss," agent 1168-A said.

Specimen 1 was hissing so loudly that Nicolai could barely think. He was astonished such a small organism could make this loud of a noise. Nicolai looked over to specimen 2. It turned its head and looked straight at Nicolai. His flesh turned to goosebumps, and his hair stood straight up. Tension hung heavy in the air; nobody knew what would happen next.

Nicolai slid the key into the first wrist shackle on the right arm, barely noticing Barry drugging specimen 1 with a tranquilizer. The first shackle slid off, and Nicolai stopped. The alien did not move or turn away from Nicolai. After a moment, he went for the other wrist. Another tense moment passed. Still, the alien remained calm. Nicolai finished with the ankles and walked a few steps back. The alien propped itself up and rubbed its wrists. It no longer had the cast on its leg; the leg healed back extraordinarily fast. The bandage covering its heart was still present and visible, a reminder of the violence it had endured. It looked around at the two men in black and the two scientists staring at it. The alien pointed to its unconscious friend and made an unlocking motion with its hands.

"Sorry, buddy, we can't release your friend. He is too dangerous," Barry said before Nicolai could say anything. "Can you understand us?" Barry asked the alien.

The alien nodded its head up and down. Nicolai found it odd that the creature would be nodding. Maybe it had observed Barry or Nicolai nodding when they agreed about something. It was also unclear how it knew English, but it did.

"Good. We want you to help us fly the spaceship tonight."

The alien stood motionless for a second then nodded again.

"Our friends here will accompany us on the test flight," Barry said while pointing to the men in black.

One of the men in black radioed to someone outside of the facility, "Bring the transport truck to the outside of lab 100, please."

"Yes, sir. Opening door Gamma-3 now." Nicolai heard the massive red door to the lab opening.

"Stay here while I drive the truck to lab 100. We will need some help loading the spaceship, but four of us should be able to do it," agent 1172-C directed Nicolai and Barry. Nicolai and Barry shared a look as the agent left the room, leaving agent 1168-A with the scientists. Nicolai wondered how the creature felt trapped here in this facility, having to cater to the whim of the humans keeping it prisoner. The alien was still clearly physically weak from the open-heart surgery, four months after the crash. It appeared to be in a slouched, tired posture, with its head looking at the ground as they waited for the other agent to come back.

A few minutes later, Nicolai heard knocking on the door to lab 7. Barry opened it, and there stood the taller agent with a heavy cloth sack in his hands.

"Put this on while we walk to lab 100. We cannot have your identity exposed on the cameras here," he instructed the alien while handing it the sack. The alien shifted the sack in its little hands for a moment, then draped itself under the sack, sagging from the weight of it. It was a sad sight, watching a creature so intelligent being diminished to a prisoner. The men in black grabbed each arm of the alien and walked out into the hot side hallway.

Nicolai and Barry followed the men in black, shutting and locking the door behind them. Down the long large hallway, they could see a big flatbed truck waiting by the garage door of lab 100. The large cavernous facility was silent except for the echoes of their footsteps. As they approached the door to lab 100, Nicolai could see the truck was painted Army green and was a two-seater with 30 wheels. There was a large tarp strapped down onto the truck, no doubt to conceal the spaceship for transport outside the facility. To Nicolai and Barry's surprise, Ramses was waiting inside lab 100 when they opened the door. Usually, Ramses would tell them when he planned on coming in. This was an impromptu visit.

The spaceship was waiting in the middle of the large room, sitting on the circular raising platform. The men in black greeted Ramses, and he greeted them back. "Welcome, gentlemen. I hope everything is prepared for the test," Ramses said. One of the men in black went back out to the truck, while the other opened up the garage door using his ID, so the first one could back the truck close to the spaceship. After the truck was backed inside and the garage door was shut, Ramses gave the order to remove the sackcloth covering the alien. The alien rubbed its eyes and blinked in a human-like manner. Maybe they were not so different from humans, after all.

"So how do we fly this spaceship?" Barry asked the alien.

The alien looked around the room and spotted the power core laying out on a lab bench. It walked over to the sphere, closely followed by the men in black. The alien picked up the sphere and the metal disc it was resting on and looked back at the group. It pointed to the spaceship.

"Go ahead. Let it go into the ship. But you go first agent 1172-C," Ramses said to one of the men in black. The agent nodded and walked over to the ship. The ship detected him and opened a door with a small ladder to climb to the main cabin. Agent 1172-C was tall and had to slowly go up the ladder, making sure not to bang his head on the metal exterior as he ascended. Agent 1168-A went in after, ascending the small ladder quickly. Next came the alien carrying the power core and disc.

"Go ahead, Nicolai, I want you and Barry to go up now. I will not be joining you on the flight; I will be staying behind," Ramses said to the scientists. Nicolai nodded, then walked up the ladder, with Barry following behind.

Once everybody was squeezed tight into the spaceship except for Ramses, the alien walked over to the pillar in the center and placed the disc on top. It immediately placed the sphere on top of the metal disc, and the spaceship came to life. The interior and exterior lights came on, and a low humming noise could be heard. An array of lights appeared below the viewing window, lighting up a previously hidden control panel with hundreds of buttons.

Nicolai and Barry had gotten this far before - the problem was that they did not know what any of the buttons did, and there were hundreds of them.

"Why are you turning the spaceship on in here? We cannot fly out of this facility; we have no open space or runway," agent 1172-C asked the alien. The alien ignored him and started pressing buttons.

"Hey, stop that! Stop pressing those buttons!" agent 1168-A shouted, drawing his gun.

"What the fuck is going on in there?" Ramses bellowed from outside the spaceship.

"Easy, agent 1168-A," Barry said while moving his hands in a downward motion, "this spaceship operates through gravitational waves. It is unimpeded by matter, or the physical universe as we know it."

The two agents looked at each other, then agent 1172-C shouted, "Boss, the alien wants to start the ship in here. One of your scientists thinks it can fly through the walls."

There was a brief silence.

"Let the alien fly the ship. I trust the scientist's analysis. It is consistent with the data." The men in black shrugged then looked at the alien.

During the chaos, the alien was pressing and sliding away at the control panel. Nicolai was looking over the alien's shoulder, trying to get an idea of the button sequence. The buttons were changing colors and moving around as the alien went about its business. After a few minutes, the spaceship made a different noise. It sounded deep, and it was coming from the power core. The control panel changed to only three buttons, one blue button, one purple button, and one red button. The ladder extending to the ground below shortened and retracted back into the cabin, closing the panel in the ship it originated from. They were now separated from the outside world. The alien turned to look at Barry and Nicolai and pointed at the viewing window of the spaceship.

The window's glass became a screen that projected three different images. The first image showed a rocky planet with a blue dot next to it. The second image showed a spiral galaxy next to a purple dot, and the final image showed a cluster of galaxies with space in between the galaxies and a red dot next to it.

Nicolai guessed these were the three speeds the spaceship could operate at. Interplanetary speed, intragalactic speed, and intergalactic speed. "Fascinating," Barry said while looking up at the images.

"What's going on? Is anything happening?" Ramses asked from outside the spaceship.

"No, sir, not yet. A screen which appears to show the different speeds of the craft has popped up, but that's about it," agent 1172-C yelled back.

The alien waved its hand in front of the group. It looked straight at Nicolai and made a motion with its hand like it wanted to write.

"Hey, I think it wants to write something for us," Nicolai said to Barry.

Nicolai had a small pen and pad he was taking notes with inside his lab coat pocket. He pulled them out and handed them to the alien. This was a monumental moment. The alien had not been given a chance to write or move its hands freely since coming to the lab, so this was the first chance Nicolai or Barry had to directly communicate with the alien in any meaningful way.

The alien reached for the pad and pen and started writing. Swift and accurate strokes. It took Nicolai a second to realize what he was seeing. The alien was writing in English! He couldn't believe it. Barry was equally amazed as he too, realized what the alien was doing. After a few moments, the alien handed the pad back to Nicolai, who grabbed it, stunned. Nicolai was speechless. In near-perfect handwriting, the note read: "The spaceship is very low on fuel, and only travel within Earth is safe. In addition to being low on fuel, one of the main gravity amplifiers of the spaceship is malfunctioning. The spaceship needs exact coordinates on a planet to fly to. Where do you want to fly?"

The short, muscular agent 1168-A was reading the note from beside Nicolai. "Holy shit. The little bastard knows English! Hey boss, the alien knows how to write in English!"

Ramses' only reply was, "That's interesting. Very Interesting."

"Let me see that," the taller agent 1172-C said, grabbing the note pad from Nicolai's hand. "I'll be damned," he said quietly, handing the note pad back to Nicolai.

Nicolai was not sure how to respond. It was shocking that the alien could understand verbal language, but it was more astonishing that it could also write in that language. Nicolai wondered where it had learned English and how it knew what to write. It did not make any sense. Surely the alien had not learned the entire English language since waking up from its surgery. Unable to move or respond, Nicolai turned to Barry, who was now holding the note pad and reading it.

"Incredible," Barry said while scratching his chin and adjusting his spectacles.

"How does the middle of the Pacific Ocean sound to you, Ramses?" Barry bellowed towards the entrance port.

"There is no fucking way that spaceship can fly that far right now. It will take 5 hours to get to the ocean. You are out of your damn mind."

Barry blushed, then started writing numbers down onto the note pad. "What are you doing, Barry?" Nicolai whispered as he watched.

"Writing down the coordinates to the Pacific Ocean." Nicolai saw the numbers 8.7832° S, 124.5085° W written on the paper. "Ramses, I know it can fly that far. Trust me," Barry said while handing the note to the alien.

"Alright, alright. Don't fucking break it, or I will have your ass for it," Ramses growled from outside.

The alien looked at the note and nodded. It pressed a large blue button on the control panel. A new image appeared on the window, and all the other images disappeared. It was an image of the Earth as if taken from space. The alien pressed more buttons, and then the Earth rotated on the screen. Earth became magnified as the camera zoomed in on the Pacific Ocean. A blinking red dot appeared in the middle of the ocean.

"Jesus Christ, it's going to take us 8 hours to get there," agent 1172-C said.

Before Barry could respond, the spaceship shifted slightly. It felt like the spaceship was lifting off the platform. Frightened, Nicolai took a big breath and held on to the seat in front of him.

The spaceship stopped ascending and hovered midair in the white lab. Nicolai could see the background of the lab behind the image of the ocean. He saw some papers and tools laid out on one of the benches and Ramses standing there staring up at the spaceship. He didn't know what was about to happen, but he could sense it was going to be incredible.

The alien pressed the blue button on the panel again, and the spaceship was moving. The world appeared to be moving around them and curved around the spaceship from Nicolai's perspective. Flying through material like this was against the laws of physics; it shouldn't be happening, even if Barry thought it was possible. They were flying through solid rock for one second, and then suddenly, they were zipping by the countryside. Nicolai could not even estimate how fast they were going because within 10 seconds; they were already at the Pacific Ocean. At 22:01, the spaceship reached its destination, approximately 10 seconds after it left Kirtland Air Force Base in Albuquerque, New Mexico.

The spaceship hovered above the ocean surface, and Nicolai could hear a faint whooshing noise coming from below. The world in front of the spaceship was completely different from the laboratory. A crescent moon sat high in the sky, blanketed by a field of stars. The view was amazing. It was pitch black, except for the light from the moon, and not a single boat in sight.

"I'll be damned," agent 1168-A said in amazement.

Barry reached for the notepad Nicolai was carrying in his right hand and started writing something down. He passed the notepad to the alien, who took it with little green hands. It read the message then wrote a response. Barry grabbed the note pad and read the response.

"What's it saying?" the tall agent 1172-C asked, hunched over in a corner.

"I asked if it could repair the gravity amplifier once we get back to the lab."

"What did it say?"

"It said that its friend who is back at the lab could. It just needs us to free its friend first. Then they can help us fix it."

"We are under strict orders from Ramses not to release the other alien," Nicolai protested.

"I am not saying we do it now, but I believe this spaceship can travel between solar systems and even galaxies when it is at its full capability. I estimate we were traveling at roughly 1/10th the speed of light just now. To unlock the full potential of this technology, we might need to employ both of the aliens, by free will or by force, but ultimately it is Ramses' decision," Barry responded coldly.

Barry scribbled down coordinates on the note pad again and handed it to the alien. "We are going back to the lab. As soon as we get back, we need to report our findings to Ramses and try to convince him that the other alien should be released during these experiments."

Nicolai nodded. He needed time to digest everything he had seen in the last 2 minutes. His degree in astrophysics seemed useless to him now. There was much more to learn about the universe than what his books had taught him.

The technology from this spaceship was priceless. The United States military airplanes paled in comparison to this spaceship. Nicolai felt like one of these spaceships could take out the entire United States military infrastructure if it was armed. This spaceship could fly anywhere in the world in almost no time at all and disappear without a trace. This could be the offensive weapon that separated the United States from the Germans and the Russians once and for all. He hoped it would not come to that.

The alien pressed a series of buttons again, and soon the image of the Earth appeared on the window before them. It rotated and magnified to a view of the United States, then to New Mexico, then to Albuquerque, and then finally to Kirtland Air Force Base. A red blinking dot appeared in the base's southeast corner, right where the underground facility was located.

"Can we fly straight back into the lab? It was easy to fly to the ocean because we have nothing to hit. If we fly into the lab and hit something, the spaceship could be damaged, or our expensive lab equipment could be broken."

The alien looked at Nicolai, hearing his words. It blinked several times, then motioned for the note pad, which Barry passed to it. Nicolai read the message it wrote: "It is safe. Barry has the exact coordinates for the lab, even the room where the spaceship is stored itself."

Nicolai obliged as the alien pressed the large blue button on the control panel. Soon the world was changing at a rapid rate again, melting from one scene into another. Nicolai now believed that the spaceship did not simply use gravitational waves to propel itself through the universe; the spaceship created its own pocket of space, while the waves around it moved space-time. Technically if the space around the spaceship was moving, and not the spaceship itself, it would not experience any gravitational forces or drag or gain in mass as its velocity increased. The energy source had to be immense to create such a space, but the tiny rod Nicolai and Barry discovered did not seem sufficient to power the spaceship. While the spaceship moved, there was no noise or detectable exhaust. The only way Nicolai could tell they were moving was by watching the Earth flyby below them. There were so many questions Nicolai had for the alien.

The world became desert again, and soon they were back into the bright whiteness of the lab. It was like they were being birthed into the lab from the outside world. Papers flew about as the spaceship came to a stop in the middle of the room, directly above the circular raising platform, exactly where it started its journey only minutes before. Ramses was waiting in the room, looking at his watch, scribbling down notes. They had traveled thousands of miles and were back in less than 5 minutes; a world record, to say the least.

"I don't fucking believe it," agent 1172-C said as he looked around the lab through the window. "We were just flying over the ocean minutes ago. This is magic."

Nicolai thought it was magic too, and he had a doctorate studying this stuff. No fuel burned. No exhaust or plumage came out of the back of the spaceship, and no forces were felt as the spaceship was moving. Thousands of miles were covered in an incredibly short time, and the spaceship was not running at its fullest capacity. There were no visible screws, bolts, wires, or electronic devices allowing the spaceship to fly. Magic.

The alien slid a button that appeared across the control panel, and the entire panel turned a bright red color. Slowly the spaceship lowered itself on the circular platform, and Nicolai heard a noise like air escaping. He felt a slight thud, then stillness. The alien pressed one more button, and the control panel turned off, with the entrance to the spaceship opening. The interior lights dimmed.

"It's too damn crowded in here," agent 1168-A said as he descended the ladder outside of the spaceship. The alien got up from its seat and started to walk towards the metallic sphere when agent 1172-C grabbed its shoulder with a large hand.

"Not so fast. The scientists can handle it from here. You go out of the spaceship now. I will follow behind you," the tall agent said to the alien. For a moment, the alien did not move, its eyes staring at the sphere. Then it turned and walked towards the ladder without making a noise. Nicolai walked over to the sphere and took it off the metal disc, and the interior lights turned off completely. The sphere was dense and heavy but oddly smooth, like water.

Barry picked up the metal disc and followed Nicolai on his way down the ladder. The spaceship closed the entrance and turned its exterior lights off when no presence was detected. Nicolai saw Ramses standing there looking at the alien, listening to agent 1172-C talk to him. The other agent was looking around the lab, hand on his gun. An uneasy feeling settled over Nicolai. The nature of this discovery and experiment process was taking a dark turn.

"Nicolai, Barry," Ramses said as they all assembled in the group.

"Yes, sir, I know what I saw. I am telling you that this spaceship can fly faster than any man-made object by an incredible margin," agent 1168-A said to Ramses.

"From my perspective, the ship flew straight through the wall. I saw a bright blue light for a split second; then, the ship was gone. Now we know what capabilities the spaceship has, we can start conducting more regular test flights. Our little friend here is being cooperative," Ramses said, looming large over the small alien.

"Ramses, the alien told us its friend could fully repair the spaceship, and I believe we should release it on our next test flight to see if it can fix the ship," Barry said to Ramses.

Ramses turned to look at Barry. "Don't ever tell me how to run this project again, Barry. We will not be releasing the other specimen until I decide it is necessary. For all we know, the alien could be lying and might be able to fix the spaceship itself. Get out of my sight before I hear another idiotic word from your mouth," Ramses beamed at Barry. Barry dropped his head and walked to a lab bench where Nicolai had placed the metallic sphere and started fiddling with it in his hands.

"Nicolai, you will go with my men and place specimen 2 back in lab 7. They will provide the security escort."

"Yes, sir," Nicolai responded, too afraid to defend Barry. The men in black grabbed the heavy burlap sack and gently threw it over the alien, concealing its identity. It shifted under the weight of the heavy sack. Agent 1172-C opened the smaller side door of lab 100 that led directly into the main hot side hallway. Agent 1168-A placed his hand on the alien's shoulder, guiding it down to lab 7. When they approached the lab door, Nicolai reached into a lower lab coat pocket, took out the key to the lab, and unlocked the deadbolt. He turned the knob, revealing the cavernous darkness. He fumbled around for a light switch, found one, then turned it on.

Nicolai walked in first and saw specimen 1 picking its head up and looking at the entering party. The hair on Nicolai's neck stood up. Both agents walked in after Nicolai, shutting the door firmly behind them. With the door secured, agent 1168-A took the burlap sack off of specimen 2. The alien on the table looked at its friend, then started hissing in a low steady tone.

"I'll quiet that son of a bitch right now," agent 1172-C boomed, walking over to the table where specimen 1 was lying.

"Easy, easy. We need both specimens alive. You heard the boss," agent 1168-A said.

Agent 1172-C shrugged and sat down in a chair. Nicolai motioned specimen 2 to the vacant metal table. Specimen 2 was looking at its companion on the other metal table, barely noticing Nicolai. The alien turned its head and looked up at Nicolai with big black eyes. Thoughts sprouted into his mind, "Please free us. We seek peace. We are here to help." Nicolai felt like the thoughts did not originate from him entirely. A dreadful fear crept over him, one that he had never experienced before. He was scared to touch the alien. Instead, he walked over to the empty table and pointed. Specimen 2 put its head down and walked over to the table reluctantly.

Nicolai never liked shackling the aliens. They were intelligent beings, not animals in a biomedical facility. It felt wrong, especially after Nicolai had those thoughts. Watching the alien operate the spaceship was an experience he would never forget. An alien being who effortlessly piloted the most advanced spaceship he had ever seen, and here it was being strapped down to a metal table. Inner feelings of guilt were repressed as he shackled the alien's wrists and ankles one by one.

The men in the black did not leave the lab until they double-checked all the shackles on both specimens 1 and 2. Satisfied with the work, they shook Nicolai's hand and left him by himself in lab 7, with one alien hissing and the other quiet as a mouse. An eerie feeling crept over the room. Nicolai headed for the door, not wanting to be in there alone with the aliens. Before turning off the lights, he turned around and saw the aliens with their heads tilted up, staring directly at him. Nicolai felt bad for them. These were two of the smartest creatures to ever walk the face of the Earth, and they were shackled to metal tables like lunatics. Nicolai hit the lights and shut the door. He locked the deadbolt and tested the door, making sure it was locked. It would be easier if they were animals, but they were not animals; they were beings far more advanced than humans, an entity so incredible Nicolai could not comprehend what lay in the lab behind him.

Chapter 8

Oousma

Ishma's condition was worsening. Oousma could barely understand what Ishma was trying to tell it most of the time. Words became incoherent, and random thoughts would flood into Oousma's consciousness. Oousma believed the head wound Ishma had suffered during the crash was far more serious than it had originally thought. Like humans, the Annonaki were heavily reliant on their brainpower to function normally. As Ishma's condition grew worse by the day, Oousma felt increasingly alone inside the laboratory.

It had been four months since the crash, and they were now in mid-November. The only way Oousma could tell how long it had been was by listening to the conversations Barry and Nicolai had with each other and Ramses. Recently, Oousma overheard Barry talking to Ramses, saying it had been approximately 130 days since the crash, and the president was expecting a progress report in two weeks. It was almost impossible to tell how much time had passed any way else because Oousma was locked inside the laboratory 24/7, with no view of the outside world. The days were long and numbing.

They were kept shackled to the tables nearly every second of every day. Oousma had been set free briefly on three occasions since waking up from its heart surgery. The first time Oousma was called upon, Ramses wanted Oousma to pilot the spaceship to a specific location to test its abilities. Even with the ship malfunctioning due to the broken gravity amplifier, its ability to fly surpassed every other Earth plane. Within the gravitational pull of the Earth, and with the gravitational amplifier broken, the ship could only go about 1/10th the speed of light. Each test flight made an escape more improbable as the amount of element 115 slowly dwindled. Luckily, the ship used very little element 115 when flying so slowly, so unless the military tested the spaceship every day for years, there would still be enough to get back to Nirubu. The ship could use a planet's gravity to help conserve element 115, but flying the ship between planets and solar systems was different.

When the ship generated a powerful enough gravity wave to move itself through space at speeds higher than the speed of light, it used much more element 115. The greater the distance traveled, the more element 115 had to be used. The energy usage was so great at astronomical distances that the Annonaki had never traveled outside their local solar system cluster. Mathematicians and astrophysicists on Nirubu predicted the ship could cross the entire galaxy and possibly make it into another galaxy, but they would run out of element 115 and be stuck at the location they arrived at. There was no way around it; the universe was simply too big to explore it all. With a gravity amplifier malfunctioning, the spaceship had to use more element 115 to compensate for the loss of gravity wave amplification, which was why they had lost so much fuel entering Earth's atmosphere.

The second and third time Oousma had been summoned, the scientists did not want to fly the spaceship; they only wanted Oousma to help them work on the spaceship in lab 100. Both times Oousma was directed to fix the amplifier, but it couldn't. Oousma had the basic knowledge to fly the spaceship and operate the software, but fixing it was different. It required special tools not on Earth to fix, and expertise in gravitational wave mechanics. Ishma was an expert on gravitational wave mechanics and was trained to fix spaceships. Ishma would know how to fix the spaceship with the available materials if it was possible at all.

Oousma never let an opportunity go to waste when it was let free for a bit. All three times, Oousma had been freed; it had access to the spaceship's interface. Oousma knew that Barry and Nicolai did not understand the basics of the software, so it could get away with things right in front of their faces. What the scientists had seen when Oousma flew the spaceship the first time, and when it was working on it the second and third times was mostly fluff. It only took a sequence of seven buttons to initiate the launching sequence of the ship. The minutes' long process the scientists observed when Oousma first started the spaceship was Oousma sending the Council of Elders on Nirubu a desperate message.

The messages were all identical. They read: "This is Oousma. I am in dire need of help. I am stranded on Earth with Ishma, lead engineer of gravity wave propulsion at the Nirubu School of Astrophysics. Our middle gravity amplifier went out, and we crashed, and the military later detained us. We are being held captive inside a military compound in the southwestern United States. Sirius is broken and unable to fly to Nirubu promptly, and Ishma's health condition is critical. I send this message hoping I will be back before it reaches you in four years. If you receive this, send us help."

Because the middle gravity amplifier was broken, Oousma could not send the signals faster than the speed of light, so it would take the messages four years to reach Nirubu. The satellites and autonomous probes were specifically designed to be untraceable, so Oousma couldn't ping them from the spaceship. They could only be maneuvered and operated from a secure location on Nirubu.

Oousma knew the humans would not understand the symbols that appeared on the screen in front of them. Had they known what Oousma was doing, they might have killed it. Writing messages to the Annonaki council was dangerous and hopeful. More than likely, Oousma and Ishma would either die or be killed before the messages reached Nirubu, four lightyears away. Oousma tried to tell Ishma it was sending the emergency messages, but Ishma did not understand.

"What do you mean you sent a message to the council? What council?"

"I sent three messages to the council on Nirubu, asking for help. We are stuck on planet Earth right now, Ishma."

"Nirubu… that name is so familiar. Oousma! Oousma? Oousma?"

§

Ishma could no longer remember the name of its home planet, where it had spent nearly 1,000 years of its life. The Annonaki had altered their genes 500,000 years before the present to allow them to live longer than evolution had intended. The average life span after the genetic alteration was 18,000 years, so Oousma was an older adult in a sense. Before the genetic alteration lengthening their life span, Annonaki lived to be around 150 years old on average. A scientist of the time named Koousmi had discovered a way to stop telomeres from shortening by deleting a codon that coded for a protein which shortened telomeres throughout life. The initial scientific breakthrough led to chaos as the elites of 500,000 years before the present tried to monopolize the treatment for themselves. World war on Nirubu broke out between the elitist class and the common folk that lasted nearly 50 years. In the end, 7 billion of the 10 billion living Annonaki were killed in the war.

A new world order was established in the aftermath of the great war. A single governmental entity called the Kuhan Empire rose to power and established a world government that forced every new Annonaki child to have the telomere shortening protein removed. The result was a change in the lifespan of every new Annonaki. This was relatively easy for the Kuhan Empire to accomplish, since all Annonaki were born in artificial birthing facilities before the hostile takeover. The birthing facilities were created hundreds of thousands of years before when the Annonaki stopped reproducing sexually and became autotrophic. The Kuhan Empire took control of the birthing facilities and changed the genetic makeup of all the Annonaki babies in vitro at the time. In one of these birthing facilities controlled by the Kuhan Empire, Oousma was born 16,000 years before the present.

Oousma was one of the first Annonaki to visit Earth. Thousands of years before Oousma's birth, around 150,000 years before the present, the Annonaki were able to study Earth with satellites and probes that took decades to reach the Earth for the first time. At the time, warp drives were still in their infancy, so the probes used solar energy to fly instead of gravitational waves, slowing down their speed to 1/20th the speed of light. The first images to come back from their autonomous probes showed that Earth was filled with an abundant array of life, including intelligent, mysterious beings that walked on two legs. During this period, the Annonaki became increasingly interested in studying the Earth because they had discovered the first intelligent species other than themselves, capable of producing art and constructing small enclosures and buildings.

The finds excited the Annonaki on Nirubu, and when Oousma was 3,500 years old, the decision was made by the council to build a ship that could fly to the Earth and back within a small amount of time. Warp drive technology had been perfected over the 250,000 years the Annonaki had been working on it, and they were finally ready to make the leap and send live Annonaki to the planet Earth, 12,500 years before the present day.

Oousma was present on the first live mission to Earth, and the main objective was to study the two-legged creatures that were building things.

Oousma was the Supreme Chancellor of the Council of Elders at the time, being voted into the position after leading the historic rebellion that toppled the Kuhan Empire 2,500 years before. Oousma was selected to lead the mission, and Oousma went with four other members of the council. Star Seed 1 was the name of the first mission.

The year of the first departure was 12,500 years before the present. At the time of their arrival, human beings occupied nearly every corner of the Earth. They were the most dominant organism and one of the most numerous mammalian species. Finding them was easy. As soon as they flew closer to the surface of the Earth, they saw thousands of them. Settlements, villages, and ruins were spotted throughout the various landmasses. When their ship first saw a group of humans in the valley below going about their work, the group debated whether they should leave the humans alone. The humans could not see them or sense them since the ship had its invisibility shield enabled. Oousma remembered the argument like it was yesterday.

"We must let them live in peace. We cannot influence another species' evolution, especially an intelligent species, on their own path. It is not ethical."

"I disagree. Right now, humans are on the cusp of becoming incredible. They just need a push in the right direction."

"You pompous fool! We have already changed our species forever; we cannot change another!"

"Fool?! Who are you calling a fool?"

"You are a fool for wishing to change their genetic course. We all know what happened when the Kuhan Empire forced every Annonaki to change its genome."

"I'm not suggesting altering their genome. I just want to help move them along in mathematics and science."

For days before the five members of the crew on Star Seed 1 decided what to do, the debates went on up to the point of them consulting the remaining council members for guidance. The Council of Elders on Nirubu was contacted, and it was decided to put the matter to a vote. All council members were required to cast an anonymous ballot and send it to the council server. The ballot was a simple yes or no, with only one question: "Should the Annonaki help/shape/teach or otherwise interact with humans now or in the future?" Tensions escalated in the confined ship as the members of Star Seed 1 anxiously awaited the results from the council members on Nirubu. Crew members on the spaceship made it obvious what their decisions were, and Oousma had to break up several altercations between them.

Finally, after several long waiting days, a transmission appeared on the window panel of the spaceship. It was from the Council of Elders. One of the Annonaki on the Star Seed 1 crew named Zahmu opened up the message. All that lay between the humans and the Annonaki of Star Seed 1 was the electronic file deciding their fate. The total tally of the results on the vote was in, and the oldest member of the council at that time, Olma the Great, appeared on the window panel. Oousma anxiously awaited Zahmu to start the recording of Olma, anticipating that the council would unanimously vote not to interact with the humans.

"Greetings, Star Seed 1. The results of the vote are in. Eight votes in favor of interacting with humans, and four votes against interacting with the humans." An uproar in the spaceship ensued.

"This cannot be correct! This is blasphemous!"

"Quiet down Issla. Your ignorance is hurting my ears. The vote is clear."

"Don't tell me to quiet down, Vahisma! I'm your superior!"

§

Oousma remembered it all, 12,500 years later in crystal clear detail. What a different time it was back then. The Annonaki came to visit Earth only two more times, the third mission being this most recent mission where they had crashed, and the mission before that, 1,947 years before the present day. Oousma saw the potential humans had to be a great species; they had a bountiful planet with abundant natural resources and a capacity to learn abstract concepts and arithmetic. Oousma had voted yes to interacting with the humans all those years ago. Oousma wanted humans to be the civilization the Annonaki never was.

This was all long ago, especially when compared to human life. Countless human generations had come and passed since the Annonaki's first visit. So much history had elapsed, and Oousma felt detached. It was strange being strapped down to a metal table by the humans. The same humans Oousma had been guiding for tens of thousands of years. This was not the civilization Oousma had hoped the humans would create. Humans of the modern-day were subject to corruption, violence, and deceit, much like the Annonaki of the past.

The hours turned into days, the days turned into weeks, and the weeks turned into months. Oousma could wait for only so long in this environment. Sunlight was essential for the Annonaki's health; without sunlight, the biological mechanisms the Annonaki had engineered that supported life in Oousma and Ishma would shut down. The chlorophyll pigment in their skin provided them their only way of getting energy. Oousma was born long after the Annonaki made the change to become autotrophic, so Oousma too was an autotroph. Light was life, and Oousma was running low on energy.

Nicolai was the only human Oousma liked and somewhat trusted. He would often give Oousma a note pad to write with, but he let only one of Oousma's hands free. Still, Oousma felt a warmness and kindness in his heart that none of the other humans had. Oousma had written him several notes explaining why it needed the sun. Nicolai understood and took the messages seriously and tried to convince Barry to let the aliens into the sunlight for a brief moment to regain the health and energy they desperately needed.

"No. We can't let them out, especially in broad daylight. Ramses will have our necks if he finds out we let them out without his authorization."

"They need the sun to live! Without it, both of them will die, Barry. The alien told me itself, and I believe it. Now it makes sense why their stomachs are so small. They do not need them! They get their energy from the sun."

"They are both still alive, aren't they?"

"One is alive, conscious, and slowly dying, and the other has a serious brain injury that is getting worse, and is also dying. This alien told me its friend is about to die within the next couple of weeks or months if it does not get any sunlight. What will we tell Ramses then?"

Since the days before the crash, Oousma and Ishma had not seen the sun. The clock was ticking. Even if Nirubu received Oousma's message, Oousma would be dead if it could not get any sunlight.

Earth was more dangerous than it had ever been. Humans were mastering the art of war through technology. This facility proved that. Oousma could not possibly escape under the current conditions. Oousma had to come up with a plan and quickly.

Somehow Oousma would need to convince Nicolai to let it and Ishma outside. All they needed was a few minutes of sunlight, and that could sustain them for many months. Oousma knew it could hold out for a while longer, but Ishma desperately needed the sun. Ishma's physical condition was bad, and no amount of human-made medicine would fix it.

Oousma was tired of waiting endlessly, but it was not Oousma's decision when it could leave lab 7. General Ramses issued all the direct orders about the movement and surveillance of Oousma and Ishma. Oousma did not trust Ramses one bit, and it was scared of him. He had a malevolent presence, mixed with a high degree of intelligence; a deadly combination. Ramses tried to communicate with Oousma by writing several times, but Oousma never responded. This was the man who had Oousma's and Ishma's life in his hands. Oousma had to tread very lightly when Ramses was around. On one occasion, Ramses had tried to get Oousma to write him for two hours before he finally quit in frustration.

"This fucking alien never writes anything. How do I know it's not you two writing these messages?" Ramses growled at Barry and Nicolai before storming out of the lab in disgust.

Oousma wanted to keep Ramses mad and unstable - that was the only way he might make a mistake or have a lapse in judgment, but it was a dangerous game to play. Ramses was like a titanium egg, impossible to crack. Oousma had to try to crack the egg; there was no other choice. Oousma needed to get back to Nirubu. Oousma was the elected leader of its species, the Annonaki, and without the guidance of Oousma, the Annonaki were fractured.

Oousma was elected the Supreme Chancellor of the Council of Elders after it saved the Annonaki from the Kuhan Empire that dominated the planet for 485,000 years. When Oousma was 1,000 years old, a massive rebellion against the Kuhan Empire started with the civilians of Nirubu, led by Oousma. Oousma was the main General for the civilian Army. After a long and bloody war, Oousma and the Annonaki who followed it arose victoriously and established a new world government that promoted peace and free will of the individual. The new world government, started by Oousma, created the Council of Elders, a board of 12 members that were elected every 500 years by the civilians of Nirubu in a popular election. Oousma was the first elected Supreme Chancellor and remained in that position for thousands of years, until it abdicated the position on its first visit to Earth, 12,500 years before the present. After abdicating its position to Bousnu 12,500 years before the present, Oousma was re-elected Supreme Chancellor of the Council of Elders 2,000 years before the present and had remained the Supreme Chancellor since.

Time moved slowly in the lab. Oousma stared at the same spot of the cavernous white ceiling most days, reflecting on the past. The memories would come flooding back into its mind as it tried not to go insane. Memories about past trips to Earth, memories about the Kuhan Empire, and memories about Oousma's friends back on Nirubu. Oousma was an old patient being, but any intelligent being would go insane being chained down to a table, staring at the same patch of the wall all day.

Oousma needed to wait for the opportunity to escape to present itself; first, Oousma had to convince Barry and Nicolai to release Ishma and take it to a patch of sun. They both required sunlight, but Ishma's physical state was an emergency. The same sun that humans had written about and prayed to, and depicted in hieroglyphics, was the lifeblood for Oousma and Ishma.

Chapter 9

———※———

Will

Tick-tock, tick-tock, tick-tock. Will was staring at the old stained cedar clock in his attic room. Sleep did not come as easy since the crash. After the crash, Will started having night terrors and frightening dreams. Alien abductions, mutilated livestock, being chased by men in black and getting murdered. The dreams were too much. Most nights, Will lay in bed, hand on his gun, ready for a firefight. After the police raid on the home several days before, Will was even more wired than usual.

It was late November, and the weather in Roswell was becoming cold and miserable. The cornfields of their neighbors were dead, leaving dead stalks flapping in the wind. Life on the farm was near a standstill. The whole family was cooped up in the house most of the time, and nobody talked about the always imposing men in black, or the dire situation they were in. It was an unspoken oath.

Will thought about his mom a lot. He missed her sweet honey-like voice and her calm eyes. He had not spoken to her since the crash, and he did not want to. The less the men in black knew about his family, the better. For all he knew, they had already gone to see her, but he hoped that they had not. The last thing he wanted to do was rope her into this whole mess.

After Tom and Will spilled the beans to Macey and Daisy, things took a turn for the worse. Will remembered Macey exploding on Tom, "You goddamned son of a bitch," she yelled, pointing at Tom. "You lied to your family for three months about the danger we're in! How dare you!"

The tension in the room could be cut with a knife. For several hours after the talk happened, Macey paced up and down the house, thinking madly. She eventually knelt down by the couch in the living room, sobbing.

"I'm sorry, Tom. I'm just scared as hell."

'Don't worry, honey, we'll be alright," Tom responded, holding her.

Several weeks later, when everybody was trying to sleep, the Roswell police raided their house. In the middle of the night, Will heard a thunderous knocking at the front door. Will immediately thought the men in black were back, so he ran down the stairs, prepared for a fight. Within seconds of the knocking, Tom met Will in the main hallway downstairs as they both shared a look. Tom passed him a shotgun, and he brandished his pistol. Buddy was violently barking right behind the front door, and Macey and Daisy were poking their heads out of their bedrooms, too scared to come into the hallway.

"Who the fuck is there? I'll blow your goddamn brains out if you don't get off my porch!" Tom shouted, cocking the pistol.

"This is the Roswell police. We have your house surrounded. Come out with your hands up!"

"To hell with that. I ain't leavin my house. Now be gone! Nobody called you over here!"

"We have a warrant for the arrest of Tom Heartley and William Brakel."

"A warrant for what?"

Will shook his head. He couldn't believe what he was hearing. How did the Roswell police have a warrant for his and Tom's arrest? They had not done anything wrong, and they cooperated to the fullest extent with law enforcement on the night of the crash. Something wasn't right.

"We have a warrant for conspiring against the United States government. Last chance! Come out with your hands up peacefully, or we will come in by force!"

Will looked around the house. Cop lights seemed like they were shining through the windows from every direction. They were not bluffing; they had the house surrounded.

"Tom, we have to surrender. They have the entire house surrounded. They'll kill us if we shoot at them."

Tom was silent for a second, then said, "Aye. We have to hide the guns first before we open up. I will stall them while you go put them away. If we ever make it back to the house, we still might need them. Here's mine."

Tom handed his pistol to Will. Will took the clip out and opened the chamber, taking out the cocked bullet.

"Alright, we are coming out. I have to tie my dog up first, or else he will chomp your balls off."

Will ran past Macey into Tom's room and opened the wooden gun cabinet, placing the guns inside. He locked it with the master lock before running back to the door. Tom dragged Buddy towards Macey, who was still barking loudly. Will watched Tom and Macey exchange a few words before she took Buddy and locked him in her room.

Will and Tom made their way to the door and shared a look before walking out with their hands up.

"Get down on the fucking ground!" an officer screamed as soon as they walked outside. Will was blinded by all of the lights shining on the front door. Tom and Will dropped to the ground, submitting to the arrest. A large hand shoved Will's head into the freezing cold porch. His arms were contorted behind him, and he felt handcuffs being tightly closed around his wrists. Several officers grabbed him by the collar and hoisted him up, where he saw 15 Roswell police cars and two unmarked black vans off in the distance behind them. It felt like every time he saw those black vans, something bad happened.

Will and Tom were being led into a cop car when they were confronted by two men in black. One was muscular and dark-skinned. The other was tall, skinny, and white. Both were shaved bald. The muscular one spoke first.

"Agent 1175-A here. We will be taking it from here, boys," he said, showing his badge to the officers who were arresting Will and Tom. The officer examined the badge, nodded, and then passed the pair off to the man in black, hands cuffed behind their backs. Tom and Will were led to one of the two black vans, which were now parked much closer to the rest of the police cars.

The inside of the van was covered with screens and electronic equipment, except for near the back. There were two metal seats behind a cage, separating the electronics from where detainees were kept. Below the metal seats were metal ankle cuffs that could be attached from below the seat, preventing the hope of any escape. The tall, skinny man in black ushered them to sit on the seats, and Will and Tom sat down, facing each other.

The muscular man in black fastened Will's ankles while the skinny man in black fastened Tom's ankles. When their ankles were secure, the agents shut the back doors and disappeared for a moment. The door swung open again, and they were each carrying a sackcloth of some sort. Will's heart started pounding. Why did they need those? Before Will got to ask, one of the sacks was over his head: a world filled with nothing but blackness.

"You ain't putting that on me," Tom protested. Will heard Tom's ankle chains rattle as he tried twisting away. Then he heard a loud bang against the inside of the van. Suddenly Tom was not moving, and there was an eerie silence. Unable to see what was happening, Will was worried. The back doors slammed shut with a definitive "thwap!"

"Tom! Tom!? Are you okay?" Will whispered into his covering. He got no response. He wasn't sure what the banging noise was, but he guessed it was Tom's head being slammed into the wall of the van. Will prayed Tom was still alive.

The drive seemed to last for an eternity. For a while, it felt like they were driving on straight paved roads, with only a few turns. Then suddenly, the drive became bumpy, and the van was making lots of turns. Will could hear the pebbles and dirt being ejected from the wheels as the van plowed towards an unknown destination. The road felt like a mountain road, but there was no way of knowing without being able to see. If they were being taken to the mountains, they would likely be killed. Nobody around, no witnesses - the location made sense. Finally, after a particularly winding turn, the van stopped. The air in the van hung heavy for a second as Will tried to anticipate their next move. Will waited to hear the front doors slam shut before speaking.

"Tom. Tom! Can you hear me?"

"Wha- what? Why is it so dark?"

The back doors of the van were thrust open, and a freezing gust of wind blew through the van. The air smelled of pine and sap; mountain air.

"Well, boys, we've arrived at your hotel, named You're Fucked hahaha," one of the men in black chuckled.

It was cold enough outside to chill your bones - too cold for the pajamas Will was wearing and the tidy whiteys Tom had on. Will felt his feet get unchained, and he seriously considered running for a second but decided it would be best to stay put. He felt a heavy hand grab his arm to guide him out of the van and onto the ground.

"Let's take a little walk, gentlemen," one of the men in black said.

Will and Tom were being led to some unknown spot away from the van, like a bunch of terrorist prisoners. After a brief walk, the guiding hand on Will's back shoved him to the ground. His knees hit dirt and rocks as he groaned in pain. Will heard Tom hit the ground right next to him. The poor old man did not deserve any of this. The sackcloth was ripped off of Will's head. Will blinked a couple of times to adjust to the new surroundings.

He was right. They were in a forest. Which forest, he did not know. He turned to Tom, who was blinking and looking around confused. Tom turned his head, and Will saw a bulging bump on the back of his head, even in the dark. That must have been the loud bang Will heard in the van before they started driving. Tom was shivering, his breath visible in the cold night air. Tom and Will slowly stood, staring at the two men in black across from them.

"Now listen here. Ramses instructed us to give you guys a firm warning. Shut your fucking mouths about the crash. We wouldn't be in this position if you guys had kept your mouths shut," the tall, white man in black said.

"Fuck you," Tom spat through shivers.

"Hear that?" the man in black said, turning to his shorter, more muscular partner, "looks like we outta teach him a lesson."

The muscular man in black walked over to Tom and reared his hand back like he was about to punch him. He swung with a closed fist and hit Tom square in the nose. Tom's head snapped back, and blood started dripping from his nose onto the dirt in front of him. Tom was breathing heavily from the cold, and from the blow he just suffered.

"That's all you got? You're a big old pussy!" Tom shouted at the man in black, spitting blood out in the process.

Will was scared. They might actually kill Tom if he didn't stop talking like this.

"Shut up, Tom! Let's give them what they want. " Will was interrupted by
the ripped black man kicking Tom hard in the stomach.

"It's always the old ones," the taller man in black said, shaking his head.

"Now, as I was saying, Ramses wanted us to have a little chat. We offered to just kill you two for your disobedience, but Ramses is a generous man. He wanted to pass on this message. 'Talk about the crash with anyone again, and both of you and everyone you love will be eliminated.' This includes Macey, Daisy, and Valerie."

The last name stung Will. How could they possibly know who his mother was? She had given birth to Will, so there was a birth certificate, but that was it. As far as Will knew, only his mother had a copy of the birth certificate, and only that copy existed. Will did not understand how they could trace his mother through him. He had not called her or spoken to her since before the crash, so there was no way they tapped into a conversation he had with her. His worst fear had been spoken into reality; the government knew who his mom was, and was willing to kill her for something Will had gotten her into.

"Alright, alright. We won't say nothin to nobody," Will said nervously, answering for Tom and him both.

"I want the old man to say it with you," the tall agent said.

Will looked over at Tom. He sat there shivering, lips turning blue, blood oozing from his face. He looked barely conscious. Tom rose his head to look at the agent in the eyes. After holding his gaze for a second, his eyes rolled back in his head, and he fell forward, hitting the Earth face first.

"Tom! Jesus Christ, he needs medical attention!"

The two men in black shared a glance, then the taller one said, "That should be good enough. That oughtta' scare the old bastard into silence."

Will couldn't do much to help. He had his wrists handcuffed behind his back, and two armed men with governmental impunity were standing in front of him. Tom looked bad; he had just sustained some heavy blows from a bodybuilder-looking jock, and he was already a frail old man. The men in black picked them both up off the ground and threw the sacks back over their heads. Will felt the familiar heavy hand on his back, guiding him through the darkness. Will could hear Tom being dragged behind him as the group made their way back to the van.

After a minute or so of walking, they stopped, and Will heard the van doors opening. He was pushed inside the van and seated on the metal chair again. His ankles were shackled, and he heard Tom's ankle shackles click shut. Then came the audible sound of the back doors closing. He heard Tom groan and move his body, a sign that he had regained consciousness. Will and Tom sat silently, too tired and too afraid to say anything.

The van ride felt longer on the way back. The mountainous part of the journey took ages; Will felt every bend and pebble in the road. Will had no idea where they were going, he suspected they would be dropped off at the Roswell police station and properly arrested, but he wasn't sure. After a while, Will realized they probably were not going to the police station. They would have been there by now if that's where they were being taken.

Will's mind raced to a thousand different locations. Maybe they were going to a different part of the mountains. Maybe they were going to some underground facility to be killed. Then Will smelled it. Poop. Cow manure, to be specific. One of the agents in the front had rolled down their window, so the smell came flooding into the van.

After a couple of minutes, the smell disappeared, and the van made a sharp left. A few seconds later, the van stopped, and the engine was turned off. The front doors slammed shut, and the back doors were opened, letting in cold air.

"Home sweet home," the tall man in black said from the front seat.

Will felt a hand working around his ankle shackle. He heard a click, and then he heard the chains drop to the ground. Next were his wrists. Before he could move, a hand grabbed him by the collar and threw him out of the van, and he hit the ground hard. A second later, the cloth sack was ripped off the top of his head, pulling some strands of hair with it.

Will saw Tom being hurled from the back of the van next, following a similar trajectory. He landed next to Will and had his sackcloth removed from his head. Will blinked a few times and looked around. They were at the edge of Tom Heartley's property, close to the cornfield of their neighbors. Will could see the painted white wooden fence that surrounded Tom's property and the brick house in the distance. Will was shocked they brought them back to the property; why kill them here?

Tom was equally surprised as he took in the surroundings, hacking up blood in the process.

"Well, gentlemen, it's been a pleasure. I'm sure we won't be needing to talk again. Adios!" the tall man in black said with a sarcastic wave.

The pair walked back to the van and drove away noisily. Will and Tom sat there watching the van drive down the dirt road and onto Santa Fe Trail. Neither one of them spoke for a second.

"We better go inside. It's fuckin freezing out here," Will said, grabbing Tom's hand.

Tom grunted in reply as they walked back to the house they had just been arrested at, tired and raggedy. It felt strange walking back to the house after everything that had happened. Will knocked on the door, not knowing if Macey or Daisy were still inside. Little eyes appeared in a window to the right of the door. Daisy.

She threw open the door and said, "Oh daddy, I was so scared. Dadd-what happened to your face?"

The rest of the night, Tom and Will told Macey and Daisy what happened to them. They asked few questions as they both sat there and listened intensely. After they were arrested, Macey said she and Daisy were questioned by the police about the events of July 8th, 1947. They asked if they had seen the crash, if they knew anybody else who saw it, and if they had told anybody what they knew. They had also asked about Will and Tom, wanting to know how much they said to Macey and Daisy about the crash. The conversation between all of them lasted until the morning.

After everybody had spoken their piece, they all sat silently on the old leather couch, absorbing the information. Will eventually broke the silence, "So what do we do now?"

They all looked at Tom. He motioned with his finger to be quiet then pointed to his ears. They were listening, and Tom didn't want to speak an ill-conceived thought. He left the room and came back with a pen and paper. He wrote down one word: escape.

The events of that night were burned into Will's memory for the next several weeks, as they came upon December. The Heartley family and Will needed to leave, and fast. Through the first week of December, they were silently planning their escape, writing down their plans and questions they had for each other. They only spoke when it was about something other than the crash or the surveillance they were under. Conversation was reduced to basic questions like, "Do you want eggs this morning? Have you cleaned the chicken coop yet?" Everything else was prohibited. It was like being in a verbal prison, one where the wrong word said would get you killed. Even Buddy seemed to sense that something was very wrong; he was following Tom around non-stop, never leaving his side.

The plan they had come up with was simple, simple so they did not mess anything up. On Christmas, a day when the entire town of Roswell was at rest, they would make their move. Tom and Will would drive their truck to the outskirts of town, hopefully attracting the two vans that were always watching the property. When the distraction had been set, and the vans had left the property, Macey and Daisy would move essential supplies (food, sleeping bags, medical kits) to the front porch and wait for Tom and Will to come back.

Tom and Will would bring their guns and Buddy with them on the distraction run. Tom knew of a road off the highway that led to a steep incline which turned and summited in a dead-end. He and Will would drive all the way up the road and park at the very top. From the top, the vantage point of the highway and the road below were good enough to launch a sneak attack if the vans and their drivers were unsuspecting. If you were driving up the road from the highway, you couldn't see the very top of the dead-end until you were nearly there. And that was the sketchy part of the plan.

Tom and Will would make it to the top and prepare for a firefight with the men in black. Being on top of the curved road would provide them with a tremendous advantage in a gunfight. The idea was to lure the vehicles to the road and open fire on them when they rounded the last bend. Tom thought this would work because the vans usually did not trail immediately behind them, so in the event that they were a few hundred yards behind them, they would have enough time to drive all the way up the hill and position the truck for the fight. If everything went according to plan, they would kill whoever was driving, take their vehicle, and rendezvous back at the Heartley house. There they would pick up Macey and Daisy and make their escape: the final destination was Mexico.

When Tom first hatched the plan with the help of Will, Macey had thrown a fit. She angrily said there were too many bugs in Mexico and it was too hot. She would not accept Mexico as her new home. Tom gradually convinced her that they didn't really have a choice. In the United States, nowhere was safe; the government had unlimited resources and the jurisdiction to do what they pleased. Escaping to another part of the United States would eventually lead to their capture, so they had to go out of the country. Mexico was chosen because it was much closer than Canada. In Mexico, the United States government had little to no jurisdiction, especially in the rural parts, so that was where they would go.

The plan was extremely risky and would possibly end in death, but the decision was made. Living life like a prisoner when no wrong had been committed had worn them all down. Stress and exhaustion pushed them to this point, and Will could see no other way out. Finally, after weeks of planning and preparation, the day was on them.

On the morning of December 25th, 1947, the day started like any other normal Christmas day. They ate a big breakfast, played some card games, and celebrated. When the morning festivities were over, the impending plan hung heavy in the air, knowing this was likely the last Christmas they would all spend together in peace. Will and Tom fetched their guns and placed them in the truck, observing one unmarked black van near the cornfield. Tom placed an extra pistol he had in the driver's side door, just in case more firepower was needed. Macey and Daisy had moved all the supplies near the front door. Suitcases filled with canned foods and other essentials were placed eerily on the ground near the door. Everything was set.

Will and Tom walked to the front door, where Tom kissed Macey on the forehead. "I love you," he said, zipping up his leather jacket. Daisy ran up to Tom and hugged him tightly. It felt like Tom and Will were walking purposefully into a death-trap. Daisy then hugged Will, looking up at him with big blue eyes.

Tom and Will lingered at the door for a second before heading out. As soon as they stepped outside, Will saw another black van next to the one he had seen a few minutes before. He felt his blood start to boil. Those fucking bastards. Just looking at them angered him more than it scared him now. They beat up an old man and threatened to kill his mom. For once, trepidation was replaced by courage. Will's life had come down to this moment.

Tom and Will made it to Tom's truck without being harassed. Tom hopped in the driver side with Buddy, Will on the passenger side. Tom tried to start the truck but couldn't; his hands were shaking uncontrollably. For an instant, Will thought he was having a stroke, but what he was actually seeing was fear. Suddenly, the tough old cowboy he knew was just a scared little boy.

"Take a deep breath, we're going to be alright," Will tried to reassure Tom as he successfully started the truck. Buddy moved to the back seat, wagging his tail, oblivious to the situation.

"I'm fuckin fine," Tom spat, staring blankly out the front window.

They drove toward the dirt road, separating themselves from the womb they had been surviving in. The unmarked vans were waiting for them on the far side of the dirt road near the cornfield. When the truck passed by them, the vans started their engines and began following their prey. Will's heart rate was rising as the truck drove off. The future was uncertain.

After driving on I-40 east for 20 minutes, they saw the mile marker they were looking for, 777. Hopefully, today would be their lucky day.

"Get ready," Tom muttered, barely audible, as they approached the off-ramp.

The ramp was coming up fast. The vans were trailing behind the truck, keeping just far enough away as not to raise any suspicion. Tom hit the gas when he saw the little side road, putting the vans out of the rear-view mirror. The road was dirty and full of large pebbles, a good sign that nobody had used it for quite some time.

Tom raced up the ramp, taking all the turns as fast as he could. Buddy was trying to keep his balance in the back seat, amidst all the fast turning. Will was looking out the back window, trying to spot the vans. After they were almost halfway up the ramp, Will saw the vans turn off onto the side road that led to the ramp. The vans approached the ramp fender to bumper. "I got eyes on the vans," Will said as Tom was staring intently at the road ahead of them.

The vans had now stopped and were parallel to each other. Will could see they had rolled down their windows like they were planning something. Why were they not following the truck anymore? Almost as fast as he had seen them stop, Will saw one of the vans turn around and drive back towards the highway. Maybe they had lost sight of them and were going back to the highway to locate the truck.

"Tom, something ain't right. They're not following us anymore."

They were now waiting at the top of the ramp, looking down at the van several stories below them. Will could see the highway from up here, but he didn't see the van that had left for the highway. Before Will could figure out where it was, the other van started driving towards the highway too. They had not planned for this. Both of the vans should have followed them up the off-ramp, but now they were going back to the highway. Will didn't see them until he saw the vans driving back west on I-40.

"What the hell are they doin, oh shit, Tom! Tom!" Tom turned to look at Will, perplexed by his tone of voice. "I think they're heading back to the house! They must suspect something is up. We have to beat them back there!"

Tom didn't need to hear anything else; he pressed the gas and flew down the ramp, drifting around the last turn, pebbles, and dirt spraying out behind the wheels. Where the hell had he learned to drive like that? Will would have to ask him later.

It was a race against the clock. By the time they had made it back onto the highway, the vans were nowhere to be seen. Tom drove through the dirt space between I-40 east and west, and headed west, hitting the gas. The old truck creaked as Tom shifted it into its highest gear. Still no sign of the vans. Worry started to settle into Will's mind.

"Tom, what if we don't make it back before they do?"

"Shut up. We will get there before they do," Tom interrupted Will.

Will sat in the passenger seat in silence. It wasn't until they reached the Roswell city limits that Will noticed the vans up ahead. They were gaining on them fast. If Tom kept up the speed he was driving at; they could beat them to the exit into the city.

"When we get close enough, start shooting those sons of bitches," Tom said, handing Will his Smith and Wesson pistol.

Will moved his hand over the 9mm Smith and Wesson, turning it in his hand and cocking it.

"Get ready," Tom growled as they neared the pair of black vans. The truck was roughly 20 yards behind the vans now, less than a half-mile from the highway exit. Everything seemed to move in slow motion, and Will barely noticed any of the other cars driving on the highway. Tom pulled right up next to one of the vans. The other one was driving slightly in front of it. Will looked through his passenger window and saw two white bald men, dressed in black suits and black sunglasses looking back at him through the driver side window of the van. Tom waved, then flipped them off.

"Now!" he screamed, swerving into the van.

Will started firing rounds into the driver side window of the van. Bullets flew through the window of the van, shattering it. Buddy started barking violently at the loud noises. One of the bullets hit the driver in the jaw, in an explosion of blood and gum. The driver lost control of the vehicle and swerved off the road.

The exit was upon them. The van in front of them seemed oblivious to the commotion behind it.

"Whooooah! You hit that son of a bitch right in the fuckin mouth!" Tom shouted wildly as he drove into the exit lane, right behind the other van. Will looked behind him to see the other van on the side of the road driving towards them again. Through the windshield, Will could see the man who hadn't been shot communicating on the radio and driving the vehicle towards them again. He moved the dead agent to the seat next to him.

"Tom, we got trouble. I only shot one of them in the other van, and the one that's alive is on the radio," Will said, looking at the pistol.

"Shit. Reload and try to get the other one. The less of them we have to deal with back at the house, the better!"

Will loaded the small metal bullets into the clip. His hands were shaking, and he dropped a couple before loading the full 15 round clip. He popped the clip into the gun. "Hold my belt!" he shouted at Tom. He half flopped out of the passenger window to get a better angle at the van behind them. Will steadied his hand as best he could, with Tom's hand halfway down his ass grabbing his belt. He fired four rounds into the windshield of the van, and two hit the driver. One in the chest and one in the arm. The van veered suddenly into the steel medium erected off the highway exit and slammed into it with a loud "Bang!" One down, one to go.

"Tom, I shot the other one!"

"Attaboy! Damn, this bastard in front of us is runnin red lights!"

Will's glory was short-lived. The van in front of them was plowing through a four-way intersection at full speed, not heeding the red lights. Buddy was whimpering in the back seat, scared by the erratic driving.

"Faster! Tom, we have to make it back to the house before the van does!" Will screamed as Tom's truck careened through the red light. Will heard honking from every direction as several cars had to slam on their brakes to avoid hitting the van and the truck.

There was no turning back; Will had just murdered two government agents. They were on the run now. The world moved by in a blur. Will focused on the road ahead, pushing out negative thoughts. He prayed to God silently as the cornfield came into view.

Tom rounded the last turn to get to the Heartley property, dust flying everywhere as he screeched around the corner. The van was only 30 feet in front of them when they entered the dirt road that led to the Heartley property. The van was heading straight for the house, and Tom was in hot pursuit. It accelerated as it entered the Heartley property and drove right up to the front porch, where Macey and Daisy were waiting, confused.

"Fuck," was all Tom could say as he came to the realization that the van had gotten there first. They drove up slowly and shined the truck lights on the van. Two men in black dressed identically to the ones in the other van hopped out and bolted for the porch. Will did not want to shoot at them, fearing he would accidentally hit Daisy or Macey.

Tom slammed on the brakes and jumped out of the truck, chasing the agents. Buddy hopped out of the car after Tom, but Will quickly forgot about him as he focused on the men in black. They got to the porch before Tom did. One grabbed Macey, and the other grabbed Daisy, guns in hand. They pushed Macey and Daisy out into the open where Will and Tom were standing in disbelief.

"I'll fuckin kill you both!" Tom screamed as he watched them lead their hostages off the porch. Will stood behind Tom, hiding the gun in his hands behind his back.

"Easy, buddy. We don't want anyone to get hurt. If you listen to us, everything will go smoothly," one of the men in black said, with his gun pointing at Daisy's head. Daisy was sobbing hysterically. Macey stood next to her daughter, stone-faced.

Tom walked back to the truck, and Will was unsure of what he was doing. Before he had the chance to stop him, Tom brought back another pistol he had hidden in the truck and cocked it right in front of the men in black.

"Don't shoot that gun, Tom. If you do, I will blow your wife and daughter's heads off," the agent holding Daisy said. Tom aimed the gun and fired. The man in black holding Daisy fell backward, blood and brain squirting out from his forehead. It was a perfect shot. Daisy screamed.

The man in black holding Macey gurgled something, then pulled the trigger. Macey's head exploded in the front as the bullet flew out and whizzed past Will. Her body went limp as she slumped to the ground. Tom dropped the pistol and ran toward her lifeless body. "Macee," was all Tom got out before he was shot in the head.

Will forced his body to move, cocking the gun and aiming at the man in black, who was now holding Daisy at gunpoint. For a second, the world stopped as Will tried to figure out his next move. He looked at the dead Tom wearing his jean overalls, leather jacket, and boots, and Macey wearing a red house dress and regained his composure. Will raised the gun, aiming at the man in black. "Don't shoot. I'll kill her," the man said, looking at Will through his sunglasses. Will hesitated for a second, then fired. The bullet missed the man's head by an inch, grazing his ear. The man in black winced in pain as he pulled the trigger. "Bang!" Daisy's head started gushing out blood, and half of her brain hung out from one side of her head. Rage and pain flooded into Will as he wildly let off the rest of the clip into the man in black. Bullets flew into his chest, abdomen, and legs. The man lay motionless on the ground oozing blood from everywhere. Will walked up to his corpse and shot him in the back of the head with his last bullet. "Fuck you. Fuck you!!!" he sobbed as he slumped to the ground, exhausted, amidst the carnage.

Will looked around at all the corpses. His entire second family lay dead on the ground, blood and brains splattered everywhere. What had they done to deserve this? All of them were innocent, especially Daisy and Macey. He started crying uncontrollably as the situation fully hit him. The adrenaline was wearing off and as he realized how horrible the situation was. What was he to do? All he could do was keep running and surviving.

After several minutes of sobbing, he wiped his eyes and searched both the men in black for keys. He found them in the front left pocket of one of the agents and headed towards their van. Buddy couldn't be found anywhere, and Will guessed he had run away from the sound of all the gunshots. He opened the driver side door of the van and sat there taking in the scene. He knew the police would be coming soon. Surely the Heartley's neighbors had heard all the gunshots and called them.

Will had to leave to protect his own life. If he was here when the police arrived, they could easily try to pin the whole thing on him. He had to go to Mexico and find a news outlet to break the story. That was the only way. The world needed to hear what happened in Roswell, New Mexico, on July 8th, 1947, and hear about the hell he and the Heartleys had endured ever since. Will stuck the keys into the ignition of the van, sending a prayer out to God. "Please, God, may their souls rest in heaven. They ain't did nothing wrong, God. Watch over their souls, and let me get revenge on these bastards who ruined our lives."

Chapter 10

------- ⚐ -------

Nicolai

"We don't even have the machines to test this energy source," Barry said.

"Yes, I know, but we know it is powered by gravity. How else can we explain the repulsive force that is not magnetic when we turn on the ship?" Nicolai responded.

"I agree with you, but we can't prove that. None of our machines can detect this gravitational field, but we can personally feel its effects. We have no hard data that can validate that claim. The fuel source is from an element we cannot make here on Earth. How are we supposed to reverse-engineer this spaceship when we can't create the fuel source? We can't even fly the ship without the help of the alien," Barry said, frustrated.

The words stung Nicolai. He was frustrated too. No significant progress had been made since the alien showed them how to fly the spaceship the first several flights. The sequence of buttons the alien was pressing was too confusing to follow exactly. Barry even questioned whether or not all the button pressing was necessary. There was no way of knowing if the alien was deceiving them or not. Nicolai believed all the button pressing had a purpose in turning on the spaceship because he was starting to trust the alien more.

"I'm sorry," Barry said, sitting his heavy frame on a metal chair in lab 100. "I'm just tired of failing. Ramses is breathing down our necks, and we have not been showing him anything new recently."

"We both are, don't worry about it. Hey, you know, I've been thinking, maybe we should secretly let the aliens fly the ship to an undisclosed location on Earth and get sunlight. We would obviously accompany them. I think it would be the right thing to do. The alien keeps telling me they both desperately need the sun to survive, and it is essential for their health. With both of them healthy, maybe they will be more willing to help us build our own spaceship and fix the one we have. The whole trip could take only 15 minutes if we let them get 10 minutes of sunlight. We would be back before anyone knew we even flew."

"And then what happens when Ramses finds out that we flew the ship without his orders? He has eyes everywhere. Do you think he will be kind enough to empathize with your reasoning? Ramses has no heart, and defying him would be foolish. I'm not in."

Nicolai had no answer for Barry. Barry was right; he was overly optimistic. There was no way they could do it secretly without Ramses finding out what happened. Nicolai and Barry were only allowed to come to the lab when they were ordered by Ramses, so there was no free access to fly when they pleased. Every lab visit had a specific purpose. Besides, there was no guarantee that both the aliens would cooperate if they were healthy and together.

The main objective of the Roswell Project was to reverse-engineer the spaceship so that the United States Air Force could fly it. Deciphering the alien technology was so difficult it was as if a nuclear reactor was given to Homo Erectus; none of them would know what they were looking at, but over time they would discover some novel things about it by default. Nicolai and Barry were the Homo Erectus trying to figure out how the nuclear reactor worked and how they could build it themselves. They were also running out of time and money from the congressional budget.

Nicolai had been contracted for two years to work on the project. The expectation was to have a feasible plan to engineer a spaceship for the military by the time the project expired. They had been working on the spaceship for six months. It was mid-December 1947, exactly one-fourth of the way through the deadline. The quarterly checkups from Ramses' contemporaries were exhausting. Experts in aerodynamics and physics, as well as aerospace propulsion, pored over every inch of data Nicolai and Barry collected and scrutinized it endlessly. Nicolai and Barry were told by numerous experts how dumb and pointless their tests were and how they needed to build different machines to test the propulsion system. A significant problem was that the experts were given the flight test data, but they were never allowed to see the spaceship directly. Their assessments were based entirely on the "prototype" Ramses told them they were building. Everything on the project was classified on the majestic level, meaning only Barry and Nicolai had the clearance to work directly with the spaceship or the aliens. The experts weighing in on their "prototype" progress was hard enough to deal with, and then there was Ramses.

Nicolai attempted to explain how difficult the task of reverse-engineering the spaceship would be, but Ramses would hear none of it. Results were what mattered to Ramses. It didn't help that the conscious alien refused to communicate with Ramses at all. Sometimes Ramses would sit there for hours trying to probe the alien for information to no avail. On one such occasion, Ramses became so angry with the alien's lack of cooperation that he started accusing Nicolai of fabricating the notes the alien was writing to him. "This is bullshit. Damn thing can't even understand me. Maybe you're the one writing these notes." He had made this accusation before, even though he knew it wasn't true. He just wanted somebody to blame for the lack of progress the Roswell Project was making.

Barry and Nicolai were present during all the live flights the spaceship performed. They documented the velocity as best they could, using their own equipment positioned on the ground outside of the mountain. Their equipment simply could not calculate the speed of the spaceship as it moved from one point in the sky to another. It only went up to 99,999 mph, so after that, it was anybody's guess how fast the spaceship was moving.

All the test flights were performed with extreme secrecy. All the tests were conducted at night, and Ramses would only tell Barry and Nicolai hours before the flight that they would be doing a live test. Often, they would fly to some random location over the ocean and then fly back into the lab, but sometimes they flew on Kirtland Air Force Base far out to the southeast where nobody could see them. It was there they tried to test the velocity of the spaceship in detail. Test after test concluded the spaceship was flying at incredible, impossible speeds. After the fourth or fifth test, no new insights were gained, so it was decided they should test the spaceship in the water. On December 17th, 1947, they were scheduled to do a test flight over the ocean in the south Pacific, and if they could, fly under the water.

Barry was certain the spaceship could move through any media unobstructed, because it created its own pocket of space to fly through. It could fly through the walls of the underground lab, but the water was a different medium. Thus far, all the test flights had been in the air; now, they were testing the spaceship's abilities in the sea. A vehicle that moved seamlessly from the air to the water was a game-changer. The United States could launch a missile from off the coast of a country, dive into the water, and then reemerge and fly to an airport all in a small span of time. Nicolai was eager to test this capability of the spaceship, mostly to give new useful information to Ramses so he would ease up on his hawk-like surveillance.

Barry was preparing the spaceship for the test, checking all the components he knew how to check, which included the lights, the power core, and the window display. Nicolai watched Barry filling out his paperwork, checking his watch to make sure he was in lab 7 when he needed to be. The test was scheduled for 02:00, so very few Albuquerque inhabitants would be up and watching the skies. During the day, the underground facility was a hub of activity and chatter, but this late at night, it was a ghost town. The only people in the facility were Nicolai and Barry, one agent, and the security guards at the laboratory entrance. Ramses would not be attending the test, so it was just Nicolai, Barry and the man in black for this one.

Nicolai entered lab 7 and saw the familiar sight of the two aliens strapped to metal tables. Upon entering, the conscious alien, specimen 2, picked up its head and looked at Nicolai. Goosebumps prickled the flesh of his neck; after all this time, Nicolai still was not used to the sight of them. His brain would not let him fully believe what he saw on a daily basis. He grabbed the notebook he wrote all of his messages addressed to the alien. It was a small black composition book, with 100 pages in it. More than half had been taken up by the back-and-forth conversations he had with the alien. He always started every message by asking the name of the alien, but as of yet, it would not give Nicolai its name. He unshackled the alien's wrists and stowed the key in his lab pocket.

Nicolai's message was simple. "Underwater test is scheduled for today. Can the spaceship be safely operated in the water?" Nicolai finished scribbling the note and passed it to the alien, who was now sitting up looking at the notebook with big black eyes. The alien's hand moved swiftly as it wrote the reply, then handed the notebook back to Nicolai.

"Yes. The spaceship can be operated in any medium, including liquid water. Can we land on dry land so my friend and I can get sunlight?"

Nicolai read the note while glancing at the alien strapped down on the table next to them, eyes closed and softly breathing. The creature did not look well; that much was obvious. The light green skin had taken on a more yellowish tone in the months since the crash. The alien's face looked gaunt compared to the one Nicolai was communicating with. There were varicose veins running up the right side of its large skull, coalescing on a tumor-like bump. The alien was close to death. Nicolai could sense it. He sighed and wrote back, "I'm sorry, we cannot release your friend at this time. I was ordered only to release you. Our mission is to test the spaceship's underwater capabilities. Any other side missions are strictly prohibited."

Nicolai passed the notebook back to the alien who read it over, then looked up at Nicolai. Big black intelligent eyes stared at Nicolai, and he immediately felt its sadness through the gaze. He had to avert his eyes; it was too much. This felt so wrong. He wanted to help the alien's friend badly, but he couldn't. He had begged Ramses to let the aliens out into the sun, but he was unwavering.

"He's near-death! According to the other alien, this one can fully fix the ship. We have to let them out and get sunlight. The worst that happens is they are lying about it, and then we don't let them out again," Nicolai remembered telling Ramses.

"No."

That was the only answer he had heard thus far. He would need to keep trying for the sake of the aliens. Nicolai had reason to believe the alien was telling him the truth, at least on this front. Their strange anatomy would explain it. The small stomach, the chlorophyll in the pigment of the skin - Nicolai believed they were photosynthetic. Ramses refused to see the intelligence in the aliens, the spirit inside of the creatures. To Ramses, the aliens were expendable, no different than a common lab chimpanzee. Still, it was in his best interest to keep the aliens alive, and he knew that.

Nicolai fetched the large burlap sack they had been using to transfer the aliens. He threw it over the small alien and moved it, so it was comfortably weighted on its shoulders. Nicolai unshackled the ankle restraints just as the man in black walked in. The alien stretched and hopped off the table, coming up to Nicolai's hip. The man in black nodded at Nicolai, then silently walked over to where he was. He grabbed the alien by the shoulder and escorted it and Nicolai down to lab 100, where Barry was waiting for them.

The intense white of the room momentarily blinded Nicolai as his eyes adjusted to the lab. The spaceship was fully lowered to ground level; a silvery-gray metallic disc that defied all known laws of physics. Nicolai took the burlap sack off the alien with the help of the man in black. It blinked a couple of times before scanning the room. It turned to Nicolai and pointed to the spaceship. The spaceship was turned on, evident from the blue lights shining beneath it. "Yes, but wait. Let us go in first."

Barry was the first one into the spaceship, ducking while climbing the ladder to the middle level. Nicolai followed close behind. When they were up, and tucked away into the main cabin, the alien came up, followed by the man in black. Three humans and a small alien made the spaceship feel really crowded. Barry wielded a clipboard with a blank sheet of paper to take notes on. He was watching the alien and writing about the buttons it was pressing and the display on the screen. Soon the Earth appeared on the window in the front of the spaceship. The alien turned to Barry, who had written a note with coordinates on it. The alien looked over the note, then pressed a series of buttons on the control panel. A blinking red dot drew the point of interest closer, zooming in on the Pacific.

Nicolai heard the audible click of the engine engaging, and the ladder folded up into the ship, sealing them off from the outside universe. The view through the display on the windows consisted of the white walls and drawers of lab 100. White melted into darkness as they were suddenly hovering above the ocean. A full blanket of stars could be seen on the clear, cold night.

The man in black was taken aback. All the briefings, all the documents they had gone over, could never have prepared them to experience their first flight on the spaceship. On one flight test, one of the men in black actually fainted when he realized how far they had flown. It was an unnerving experience. Nicolai was every bit as perplexed as they were, maybe even more so. He just never showed it.

"Alright, take us to the bottom of the ocean," Barry instructed the alien. The alien pressed a button on the control panel, changing the entire panel a purplish hue. It started pressing a series of buttons Nicolai had not seen before. The glass window changed to a display depicting the spaceship moving along three axes, the x, the y, and the z-axis. The panel of buttons changed again to show three large buttons, all different colors.

The alien pressed a button, and the y axis on the display lit up. The three buttons changed again into a larger button. A green down-pointing arrow appeared on the control panel. Nicolai felt a subtle movement under his feet as the spaceship began descending. The moonlight was visible on the horizon, casting a streak of silver on the water's surface.

The spaceship started to lower itself slowly and gently. Nicolai had never seen the spaceship move so slowly. Usually, it darted from point A to point B and nothing in between, but they were slowly lowered into the ocean as if they were on a conveyer belt to the bottom. Air turned to water as the spaceship submerged itself into the ocean.

During the descent, Barry watched the alien like a hawk, taking notes on every button pressed and every display diagram that appeared on the window. That was the best way Barry and Nicolai could gather information about the spaceship, watching the only being on Earth who could fly it and taking scrupulous notes. On each test, one of them was the recorder, while the other observed the environment around the spaceship for any unique phenomena they had not noticed before. On this test, Nicolai was the environmental observer.

Nicolai observed some fish curiously swimming up to the blue metallic object, then swimming away when they realized it was not food. Towards the bottom, he saw a lantern fish with its light sticking out in front of it. Slowly but surely, they made their way to the bottom of the Pacific Ocean. The spaceship hit the bottom with a dull thud, twenty minutes after starting its descent above the water's surface.

"Well, I'll be damned. We made it to the bottom of the ocean," the man in black said, looking out into the watery darkness through his sunglasses.

He was right. Nothing could be seen beyond ten feet from the ship, except the blue glow emanating from underneath the ship. Nicolai was amazed the spaceship could handle such immense pressure; typically, deep water submersion vessels were spheres, not discs. Everything about the spaceship was perplexing. A normal airplane couldn't get water into its fuel tank, but this spaceship had no fuel tank. Shit, a normal airplane couldn't even land on the water, let alone descend to the deepest part of the ocean.

"Alright, wonderful. I think we got what we needed. Let's go back to the lab," Barry said after they sat on the bottom of the ocean for a few minutes.

Nicolai knew by now that the tests were usually very short endeavors, less than 20 minutes. The spaceship could fly anywhere on Earth almost instantaneously and be back in the lab just as quickly. It could fly through the water, air, cement, and rock. Nicolai had pressed the creature for days after their first flight, asking endless questions about the propulsion system.

How fast can the spaceship move at top speed? How long does the fuel last? The alien only wrote vague answers in response to technical questions, giving nothing away.

The spaceship flew back into the pristine white lab, melting a deep blue sea scenery into the artificial lab. The control panel changed hue, and Nicolai watched the alien plan the landing sequence. The spaceship slowly lowered itself onto the center platform about 6 feet off the ground, and with a thud, made contact. The ladder opened up from the side of the ship, automatically detecting the height of the ground beneath it. Nicolai and Barry discovered one day that the ladder was able to open at an adjustable height. If the spaceship was closer to the ground, the ladder did not extend as far. It grew from seemingly nothing when it extended and shrunk back into the ship when it shortened.

The man in black walked down the ladder first, directing the alien to come after him. Nicolai and Barry exited the spaceship last. As they all made it outside, the ladder started to automatically close and fold itself into the ship, and the lights on the bottom turned off. Barry had removed the sphere and disc, placing them on a nearby lab bench. The man in black threw the burlap sack over the alien and said, "I'm taking it back to lab 7."

"I will go with you," Nicolai said, not fully trusting the mysterious agent.

Barry looked at Nicolai and pointed to his notes. "I need to analyze the data we collected on today's test. I will stay here," Barry added.

The man in black nodded and opened up the door to lab 100 with Nicolai trailing behind. Nicolai looked down the long hall and saw a large man standing in front of lab 7. As the man in black and Nicolai got closer, Nicolai could see it was Ramses, standing 6'6 in his military garb, waiting at the door and looking at his watch. Nicolai could recognize him from a mile away.

As they approached Ramses, he stuck out his hand and said, "Nicolai." Ramses shook his hand firmly. He then shook the man in black's hand, who took his hand off the alien for a second to shake back. Ramses looked at the man in black and said, "Thank you for your service, sir. You have completed your job for the night. Nicolai and I will take it from here." He nodded, then walked quietly towards the entrance to the coldside near lab 2.

Ramses motioned to the lab 7 door. Nicolai fumbled through the keys in his lab coat pocket before finding the one he was looking for. He slid it into the lock and unlocked the large deadbolt. He opened the door to the darkness and felt around for the light switch. He felt the plastic beneath his fingers and flicked them on. Bright white lights lit up the lab, showing the two metal tables with specimen 1 on one of the tables in the middle of the lab. Ramses ushered specimen 2 into the lab with his hands and followed close behind. Nicolai walked in after them, shutting and locking the door behind him.

Ramses took the sack off the alien's head and pointed the table, letting it know he wanted to put the ankle shackles on.

"Nicolai, me and you are going to play 20 questions with this little sack of shit. We'll start with simple questions: where are you from, how old are you? If the alien behaves, I don't shock it. If the alien doesn't behave, I will shock it more intensely until it learns to behave. You will be asking the questions, understood?" Ramses boomed, showing Nicolai a taser he had brought into the lab. The taser range was 50,000 volts all the way up to 85,000 volts.

Nicolai looked at Ramses nervously; he had a crazy look in his brown almond-shaped eyes that frightened him. His hands started sweating as he struggled to respond. "Yes, sir," was all he could manage to spit out. Nicolai fastened the ankle shackles around the small ankles of the alien and shook them to confirm that they were secure.

What was Ramses planning? Nicolai did not like where the situation was going. Ramses reached into his jacket pocket and pulled out a blank sheet of paper. He uncreased it and handed it to Nicolai.

"This is a paper for you to write my questions on. I will ask a question, and you will write that question down and pass it to the alien."

This was a new tactic. Ramses had written questions to the alien, but the alien never wrote a response. Ramses would get angry with the alien, and on several occasions, he hit the alien for not responding to his questions. If Nicolai wrote the question while Ramses was in the room, it might respond. Nicolai could tell the alien was scared of Ramses. Nicolai never explicitly asked the alien if it was afraid of Ramses, but he could sense that it was.

"Ask what star system it came from," Ramses said, staring intensely at the alien sitting up on the metal table.

Nicolai wrote down the question and handed the paper over to the alien. The alien examined the question, then shook its head and passed the paper back to Nicolai.

"Well then, looks like we got someone who doesn't want to talk," Ramses boomed, reaching for his taser. In one swift motion, Ramses zapped the alien in the stomach with the taser at 50,000 volts. The alien let out a shriek of pain that made Nicolai's skin crawl. Its hands violently vibrated as the electricity raced through its body. The alien laid back on the table, breathing heavily.

"Pick it up, and ask it again," Ramses ordered Nicolai.

Nicolai looked at the small helpless being in a heap on the metal table, with Ramses looming over it. This felt very wrong. The alien had always been peaceful; it never tried to hurt anyone or escape. Nicolai hated what Ramses was making him do.

"Don't make me repeat myself," Ramses growled, glaring at Nicolai.

Nicolai grabbed the alien's smooth hand. It felt like he was lifting up air. The alien looked at him with those big black eyes, and Nicolai had to turn away. He lifted the alien back into a sitting position. When Nicolai asked the alien again what star system it was from, it responded: Alpha Centauri. Nicolai was amazed by the response of the alien. It had never told Nicolai where it was from, despite him asking numerous times before. Fear was a powerful motivator.

Nicolai passed the note to Ramses, examining the alien who appeared very weak from the electric shock. "Very good, this is progress. Ask it what the source of fuel for the engine is."

Ramses knew the answer to the question; element 115. Nicolai could not figure out why Ramses was asking a question he already knew the answer to. Nicolai wrote down the second question. He had explained to Ramses numerous times it used element 115, as detected by their sample analysis of the fuel rod in the spectrometer. Again, to the surprise of Nicolai, the alien wrote a response and quickly passed back the sheet of paper. It read element 115. Nicolai and Barry had been right.

"Element 115. That is what you and Barry proposed," Ramses said, pointing to Nicolai. "Is it naturally found on Earth?"

"No, sir. Element 115 is not found naturally occurring on Earth. We still can't even make a single atom of it in a lab; it is not stable," Nicolai responded.

Nicolai felt vindicated that the alien had told them it was element 115 that powered the spaceship. He and Barry had conclusively shown that element 115 powered the spaceship through experimentation, but it was good to see the alien confirm it. Alpha Centauri was a binary star solar system, so it was surprising that the alien stated it as its home world location. Astronomers on Earth believed only solar systems with one star could harbor life. Theoretically, a planet in the habitable zone between the two stars could contain elements that occurred naturally on that planet and not on Earth. Alpha Centauri also happened to be the closest solar system to Earth. No wonder why the aliens came to visit Earth; Earth was the closest planet to the Alpha Centauri solar system that harbored intelligent life. It all started to make sense.

"Ask it what its name is," Ramses ordered Nicolai.

Nicolai knew the alien would most likely not answer. He had asked it its name secretly on many occasions, but the alien never told him. Why the alien would not reveal its name was a mystery to Nicolai. He obeyed Ramses' orders and wrote down the question. The alien looked down at the question and wrote a response. Nicolai felt butterflies in his stomach. He read the response, disappointed.

"It says they have no names where it is from," Nicolai said to Ramses, who was reading the note over his shoulder.

"Bullshit," Ramses said, walking over to a metal tray that stood in between the two metal examining tables. On the tray was an assortment of tools from needles to small scalpels. Nicolai used the instruments to do daily blood draws and skin samples. Ramses grabbed a sharp scalpel.

"What are you doing?"

"Shut the fuck up. Don't ask any questions, don't make any noises, don't even fucking breathe," Ramses told Nicolai coldly.

Ramses might actually be crazy enough to kill the alien, Nicolai thought to himself. He wanted to stop Ramses, but he couldn't. Ramses had supreme authority over the secret facility; if he wanted to kill the alien, he could do it.

Ramses was now lording over the alien, scalpel in his right hand. "Ask him again," he directed Nicolai. For a moment, Nicolai didn't move, then out of fear, he passed the paper back to the alien and pointed at the question. The alien shook its head and passed it back to Nicolai. "Restrain him," Ramses growled at Nicolai.

Nicolai looked at the alien and pointed to the table. It knew the drill; they had been through the procedure many times before. With the obedience of a dog, the supremely intelligent being slowly laid down, spreading out its arms to be shackled at the wrist. Nicolai nervously locked the wrist shackles that anchored into the metal table one by one.

"It's time to teach you a lesson. When I ask you a question, you answer it," Ramses said, putting the scalpel to the chest of the alien, right over the scar left by the heart surgery. Ramses started slicing horizontally across the alien's chest, drawing a small line of blood beneath its pectorals. The alien's face contorted in pain, scrunching its eyes, nose, and mouth, and squirming its body to get away from the blade. It was too awful to watch.

"Stop!" Nicolai finally burst out, unable to contain himself.

Ramses turned, glaring at Nicolai. "What did you say to me?" he asked, grabbing Nicolai's collar. Nicolai was 6'2, but at that moment, Ramses made him feel like a little boy.

"No-nothing, sir," Nicolai stammered.

"Good. Now get out. Leave the alien and me alone. We need some one-on-one bonding time."

Nicolai gulped down fear. He didn't want to leave the alien alone with Ramses; he was sure he would kill it. He sent out a silent prayer to God to spare the alien's life. He turned his back and walked out of lab 7, leaving the deranged military General alone with the alien. He wondered if he would see the little creature alive again. The thought caused him pain; he cared for the alien as he would care for a human, but he didn't know why.

There were still 10 hours left of his shift. Nicolai walked over to lab 100 and opened the door. Barry was looking at the spherical power core on a large lab bench that protruded from the wall. He was using different lasers to observe the reactor at various wavelengths of light, and writing what he observed in a lab notebook. Each laser corresponded to a different part of the visible light spectrum.

He was trying to figure out if the power core responded to different wavelengths of light. Thus far, neither Barry nor Nicolai detected any change of the power core in blue light versus red light. Barry was in deep thought and did not notice Nicolai hovering behind him. Nicolai wanted to tell Barry what Ramses was doing to the alien in lab 7. After a moment, he decided he would. "Hey Barry, we have to talk about something really important."

"Talk, I'm listening," Barry said, jotting down notes into his notebook.

"Barry, I think Ramses is going to badly injure the conscious alien. He made me restrain it, and then he started cutting its chest with a scalpel because it wouldn't tell Ramses its name. Barry, I'm scared Ramses has gone off the deep end." This kind of talk was treasonous in a laboratory of this secrecy.

Barry thought for a moment, then said, "Well, as long as it stays alive, we should be fine."

Nicolai took a step away from the scientist. Did Barry really care so little for the creature's wellbeing? Suddenly Nicolai felt more distant from Barry than he ever had. Barry saw a test subject and a mission, nothing else. Nicolai realized he could not confide in Barry anymore. He would have to be the only advocate for the health and safety of the aliens.

"Should be fine? That creature is the only living thing on Earth that can pilot that spaceship. Without it, we will never be able to fly it, let alone reproduce it. It is in our best interest to keep the aliens as healthy as possible for as long as possible, so we can keep obtaining useful help and information from them."

Barry turned from his work and looked up at Nicolai. He looked tired and old; his head was starting to bald extensively, and gray whiskers intermixed with orange hairs on his head and beard. Nicolai wondered if he ever left the lab. Barry was always in the lab before Nicolai and always left after him.

"It's not like we have a say in what happens around here. If we stand up to Ramses, he'll have our asses. He can do as he pleases; whatever he says goes."

Nicolai knew he was right, but it felt wrong to drop the subject. He thought it would be best to look at the notes Barry had taken to ease the tension. In his notes, Barry described how no observable visible wavelength of light affected the function or the properties of the sphere. He noted that the fuel rod did appear to block all forms of incoming light. When a laser was shined directly on the rod, light would bend around and over it and appear on the wall on the other side of it, but it would not pass through the rod. Somehow element 115 did not interact with the light all around it.

The notes above December 17th (today's date), dated to December 15th, talked about Barry's theories as to how element 115 worked. Barry hypothesized that element 115 worked by interacting with a mysterious type of energy he called *dark energy*. Dark energy only interacted with the observable universe through a repulsive gravity force. This spaceship could utilize the repulsive gravity and amplify the wave it generated to tear a hole in space-time and create its own pocket of space to ride in.

"Well, I guess we should be able to bomb the Germans right from their front porch without them noticing, right?" Nicolai said, trying to break the awkward silence.

Barry wasn't amused. The only reply Nicolai got was a grunt. Just then, three loud knocks came from the door. Nicolai already knew who it was. He opened the door, and Ramses walked through, his head almost hitting the top of the door frame.

"Go home early today, you two. We have a long week ahead of us." Ramses held eye contact with both scientists for a moment, then walked out of the lab, slamming the door behind him. Nicolai looked at Barry, who shrugged at him. In the six months since the crash, Nicolai and Barry had never gone home early. Something was off; Nicolai felt like he should check on the aliens one more time before he left. He needed to make sure Ramses hadn't killed them.

"I'm going to check the aliens before we leave," Nicolai said, walking towards the red door of lab 100. Barry eyed him suspiciously, then turned around and started cleaning up his work station.

Nicolai left lab 100 and walked out into the hallway, where he saw Ramses making his way to the cold side. When Ramses was out of sight, Nicolai walked down to lab 7 and unlocked the door, fearing the worst. Both aliens were restrained and breathing shallowly. Nicolai walked over to the alien who he always communicated with. Ramses had drugged him unconscious, evident by the ketamine drip it was attached to. The wounds of the encounter were visible.

Its left eye was swollen and pink, most likely from blunt force trauma. Bruised fingerprints lined the small neck of the alien, clearly a sign of strangulation. There was also dried blood on the cut Ramses had made on its chest. Nicolai's heart skipped a beat. He felt the creature's pain.

He looked around the lab for an antimicrobial paste to rub over its chest and an icepack to put near its eye. A small drawer on the wall nearest to the door contained medical supplies. He opened it with the master key and took out an ice pack and an antibiotic wipe. He shut the drawer and walked back over to the alien. He then gently placed the ice pack on the alien's eye and wiped the dried blood off its chest with the antimicrobial wipe.

Nicolai feared direct contact with humans could be dangerous for the aliens. A virus or microbial antigen could get into the alien and kill it. Having an unclean scalpel dug into your skin was an easy way to get an infection. Nicolai couldn't fathom why Ramses would go to such extreme lengths to probe the alien for answers. The alien was his most valuable asset, yet he was treating it like its life was worthless.

Nicolai did not know much about Ramses. He knew he was important, but he knew little about his personal life. Most Generals would make public appearances: Ramses never did. His aura was strange. There was something wild about it that Nicolai did not like.

After looking at the alien one last time, Nicolai sighed and walked out of the lab. What could he do? He didn't want them to suffer anymore, but he didn't want to be killed trying to save them. He convinced himself he was doing all he could do.

Nicolai barely noticed the guard on the inside of the facility radio the outside that the door needed to be opened. The massive red door's wheel and axle mechanism began turning, and Nicolai heard the locking bar click into the open position. On the other side of the door, more armed military men were waiting. "ID," one of the young military security forces personnel told him. Nicolai took out his ID and the man examined it with ultraviolet light. A bald eagle appeared. The soldier handed Nicolai his ID back after the all clear and motioned him to a black van waiting in the tunnel. The tunnel was dusty and stale. As Nicolai hopped into the truck, he thought about his dismal surroundings.

Down below the mountain, this deep into the tunnel, no sunlight broke through. If what the alien said was true, they would both die inside the laboratory. Nicolai knew what he had to do, what he was compelled to do: get the aliens into the sunlight. He didn't know how he was going to convince Ramses to let them out, but he would find a way. He might be fired for disagreeing or raising a ruckus, and if that was the case, that would be fine with him. He would do everything in his power to look after the wellbeing of the aliens.

Nicolai would have to convince Ramses alone; Barry would be no help. Worse, he might team up with Ramses and disagree with Nicolai just to do it. Nicolai knew time was of the essence. The aliens' lives depended on him.

Chapter 11

***

Ramses

Ramses was constantly reading the reports Nicolai and Barry generated about the spaceship and the aliens. The conscious alien could read and write in English, and it was now responding to Ramses, but it took a little coercion. Ramses had phoned Truman after a particularly frustrating night of getting no response from the alien. He asked Truman if he could use physical intervention techniques to force the alien's compliance. Truman hesitantly agreed.

Since he started implementing these techniques, Ramses had learned much about the alien. Where it came from, how long it had been alive, and why it had visited Earth. Ramses also asked the alien technical questions about the spaceship. How much it weighed, what it used for propulsion, how fast it could potentially fly, and if it would be possible to repair it. Ramses had been in the Air Force for 40 years and knew a great deal about planes and how they worked. The information the alien was giving him made little sense and, at times, seemed impossible. He was accustomed to reactionary propulsion systems that were wildly less efficient than the alien spaceship.

The alien and its friend were from a small planet in the Alpha Centauri solar system, just four lightyears from Earth. Their planet sat in between the two stars, right in the habitable zone. Nicolai had theorized element 115 could only exist in a solar system with many times the mass of their own solar system; Alpha Centauri was a binary solar system that contained an enormous amount of mass in a relatively small area, astronomically speaking. Ramses would not admit it, but this theory of Nicolai's was very plausible. The gravity on the alien's home planet allowed heavier elements to form, and element 115 was one of these elements. The alien said its home world had 1.25 times the gravity of Earth, and the composition of its atmosphere was nearly identical to Earth, with slightly more oxygen. The alien told Ramses element 115 was mined from deep in the ground, where the pressure was immense. It was then processed at a factory of some sort where its atomic structure was changed to give it the properties it had in the spaceship, mainly a repulsive gravity that generated a gravitational wave it could ride through 4-D space.

Day in and day out, Nicolai pleaded with Ramses to let the aliens outside of the laboratory to get sunlight. The alien requested the same from Ramses. He had learned that the aliens were photosynthetic organisms of sorts, and without the sun, they would die. They had been kept alive for almost seven months, so every time the alien or Nicolai made a request, he refused. The security risk was too high. He was already being questioned by an F.B.I. detective about the deaths of the Heartley family. He didn't need anybody else sniffing around trying to dig up dirt.

One of the agents from the N.S.A., agent 1104-C, had been assigned the task of watching the Heartley property in December. The agents suspected the family was plotting to escape and go off the radar. They heard bits and pieces of conversations the family had from their observation van, so they decided to contact Ramses. After learning of the plot, Ramses had authorized the agents to use lethal force if they deemed it necessary, but only in the event they were fired upon first.

Ramses received a call from the Roswell police department on December 25th, 1947, saying there was a deadly shoot-out between Tom Heartley, William Brakel, and the N.S.A. agents. The police department informed Ramses that the four men who were watching the house that week were killed by gunfire from guns legally purchased by Tom Heartley. Two of the agents were discovered shot dead in a van off of I-40 west, and the other two agents were killed at the Heartley property. They also told Ramses that Tom Heartley, Macey Heartley, and Daisy Heartley were killed by gunfire from the N.S.A. agents. On top of all that, William Brakel was missing, as was one of the surveillance vans the N.S.A. was using to conduct their missions. Ramses instructed the police department to destroy the evidence that proved the N.S.A. agents had killed the family, but it was still a disastrous mess he was dealing with. He then instructed them to pin the entire incident on William Brakel.

On the night of the shootings, one of the Heartley's neighbors heard all the gunshots coming from their property and called the local police department. The police arrived at a scene of blood and carnage, evident in the reports they generated. One policeman described it as "A satanic cult-like mass murder," and another described the scene as "A slaughterhouse." The local newspaper ran a front-page news story the next day detailing the incident, saying a tragic firefight with federal agents led to the deaths of Macey, Daisy, and Tom. Ramses was getting tips from the new agents he had patrolling the town that town folks in Roswell were suggesting their deaths had something to do with the flying saucer crash back in July.

That next night on December 26th, 1947, President Truman learned of the incident through one of his security briefings and phoned Ramses.

"I can't fucking believe it, Ramses; we are in deep shit. Why the hell did your agents think they could use lethal force on the mother and daughter, for Christ's sake? If Tom and Will were killed, we would not be in this mess, but instead, the whole fucking family is dead, and it's on you. I got the C.I.A. up my ass about the situation, and I got the F.B.I. trying to open an investigation into the incident. What the hell am I supposed to do, Ramses?"

"With all due respect, sir, something needed to be done. My agents had intel that suggested the Heartleys and William Brakel were planning an escape. We presume they were going to leak top-secret information about the crash to the public. The risk this posed was too great. I instructed my men to use lethal force if necessary, and by the Roswell police reports, it was necessary. The investigation they conducted showed that Tom and Will fired on my agents, and my agents returned fire, unfortunately hitting Macey and Daisy in the process."

"People died, Ramses. An innocent sixteen-year-old girl was killed. A mother and father were killed, and we still managed to lose one of the subjects."

"Sir, we can't let this information spread. This is the most top-secret information the United States government currently has, and if it leaks to the Germans or the Russians, we are fucked, sir. We simply cannot, under any circumstances, let this information out. I have planted misinformants in the city of Roswell to quell the civil unrest there. Right after the crash, I had to have several Air Force airplane engineers come forward and lie to the public that what actually crashed on July 8th, 1947, was a weather balloon and provide proof. We have been covering up the story from the beginning, and we will have to continue to do so under any and all circumstances."

"What does that have to do with the dead family and the dead girl?"

"If we can sway the public opinion into thinking a weather balloon crashed instead of an alien spaceship, then there is no case. If the public believes there was never a crashed alien ship, then we can make them believe that Tom and Will were to blame for the incident. I say we hold a public press conference about the issue. If I appear on a public broadcast and lay out all of the facts, the public's mind will be eased."

There was a moment of silence before the president spoke.

"I... I don't know Ramses. This is fucked up. My cabinet is encouraging me to go to Roswell and give a speech about the crash and the deaths of the Heartley family members. Your name has been tossed around in some of the news articles, so it might be better if I squashed the subject myself. I am the president of the United States, after all."

"I don't think that is wise, Mr. President. I am the only military General with the in on what is going on at Kirtland Air Force Base, so it should be me who does a press conference or a speech, not you. If my name is the papers, then let it be me."

Ramses heard Truman sigh then say, "Yes, you are right. I'm just worried that this is all getting out of hand very quickly, Ramses. Three civilians are dead, and four high-security clearance agents are dead. No more deaths. That is final."

"Yes, sir, I understand. I am not one for press conferences, but at this point, it has to be done. When you are ready to schedule one, call me."

"Will do. Get some rest, Ramses. You sound exhausted over the phone."

"Yes, sir. Have a good night, Mr. President," Ramses hung up the phone with a bitter taste in his mouth. He hated press conferences almost as much as he hated Airman Basics. Ramses was the quiet type; the type to build a makeshift bomb in the first grade and blow it up in a field without telling his parents type. Talking to reporters who knew next to nothing about nuclear weapons, airplanes, or the military was a waste of oxygen, but it needed to be done from time to time. This was one of those times.

Each second of the day was precious to Ramses. He spent months and months looking over Nicolai's and Barry's data, trying to figure out how to reproduce and replicate the spaceship. Fourteen hours a day, seven days a week, Ramses worked. Not only was he preoccupied with the secret reverse-engineering of the spaceship and the oversight of the nuclear weapons facility at Kirtland Air Force Base, but he also had to routinely meet with the chiefs of staff in Washington D.C. to discuss new and emerging threats to national security. He had a full plate, with no time to spare.

As December turned into January, ushering in a new year, Ramses was becoming increasingly focused on the reverse-engineering project and the aliens. Sometimes he would lash out at the alien just to show it who was dominant. Ramses needed the alien to fear him, as a child did an angry mother. He was not afraid to take the life of the aliens if they became utterly useless, but he suspected Nicolai cared for the aliens, particularly the alien that was conscious and well. Ramses was trying to use the relationship between Nicolai and the alien to his advantage.

If Nicolai cared for the alien, then the alien maybe cared for Nicolai in some weird unforeseen way. Ramses wanted to use Nicolai as an extraction point for information. The alien wrote things to Nicolai that it would never tell Ramses; he was sure of it. On one visit to the lab, Ramses caught Nicolai throwing away notes that he and the alien had written.

Ramses was walking through lab 100 and noticed papers in the trash can. He reached into the bin and pulled out notes of conversation Nicolai and the alien had earlier in the day. Ramses summoned Nicolai to lab 100 and questioned him about the notes. After pressing Nicolai for several minutes, Nicolai reluctantly admitted that the notes were a conversation he and the alien had. The conversation was about the sunlight the aliens needed and how Nicolai wanted to let the aliens out into the sunlight, but Ramses would not let them.

Despite the numerous attempts from the aliens and Nicolai to convince him to let the aliens out of the lab, Ramses would not budge. He was not entirely certain of the mental and physical capabilities of the aliens when they were out in the open. For all he knew, they could run 100 miles per hour. If an alien escaped, or worse, if both of the aliens somehow escaped, Ramses would never live it down. It would be the single worst mistake of his career. For now, he had to focus on making an outline for the press conference - one full of lies and deceit.

The president scheduled the press conference for January 15th, 1948. Ramses was to publicly address the incident of July 8th, 1947, in Roswell, New Mexico. He would also be talking about the grisly murders of the Heartleys that happened a month earlier. It all felt so long ago. Ramses remembered being driven to the crash site thinking some Army airplane had fallen out of the sky, or a meteorite had crash-landed into their yard. Boy, was he wrong.

The night of the crash changed Ramses' entire outlook on life. Since his youth, he was always very pious, believing strongly in God and Jesus Christ. He went to Sunday school every Sunday, and had read the Bible dozens of times over the course of his life. After seeing the spaceship and the aliens for the first time, he couldn't think about God and the bible the same. The aliens made Ramses realize how insignificant humans were in the grand scheme of the universe.

For the press conference, Ramses prepared a script he would say in front of the cameras and the reporters. The conference would be held on Kirtland Air Force Base to give Ramses home-field advantage. Since the press conference was to be held in a room on base, fewer media personnel would be granted access to the conference. Of those in the room, half would be military personnel Ramses placed there to make it seem like it was a room full of reporters. Ramses did not want to deal with too many tough questions; he had instructed the military personnel filling in the room to "not ask a damn thing."

On the day of the conference, Ramses dressed in his full military uniform, shaved his beard clean, and waxed his eyebrows. He wanted to look as presentable as possible while he lied to the United States general public. From his little military apartment, he was escorted by an unmarked car to the room where he would be giving his press conference. There were already reporters setting up in the room when he arrived. He was to be seated at a flat table, with microphones from various organizations broadcasting his voice to the different networks. When everyone was all set, he began the press conference.

"All right, we are going to be live in three, two, one!" a cameraman in the back shouted to Ramses.

"Hello and good evening America. My name is Ramses Meddiah the III, General of the United States Air Force. I am here to address two issues: the first is the reported crash of a weather balloon in Roswell, New Mexico on July 8th, 1947, and the second issue I will be discussing is the deaths of Tom, Macey, and Daisy Heartley on December 25th, 1947."

"At approximately 23:00 local time on July 8th, 1947, I received a call from the Chief of Roswell police, that an unknown object had crashed on the property of Tom Heartley. The Roswell police were contacted by

Tom Heartley shortly before they contacted me and were already in motion to respond to the crash. After I received the call, I assembled the 963rd Airborne Air Control Squadron to assist me in the recovery of the unknown object." This was the first lie. Ramses actually contacted the N.S.A., who wanted their agents to accompany him to the crash site.

"After assembling my team, I worked with the local Roswell police, and they escorted me from I-25 to 380, where we drove to the Heartley ranch, off Santa Fe Trail. I arrived with my men at the scene of the crash at approximately 02:00. It was discovered by myself and my team that the object that had crashed was a military weather balloon, monitoring the area for nuclear radiation from our nuclear bomb tests. That is all I have to say about the crash."

"As for the deaths of the Heartley family, let me start off with a moment of silence for the lost family members. I am going to ask everyone to pray for them before we dive into this subject."

Cameras flashed, and pens furiously scribbled down at the papers from the few reporters in the room who could ask questions. The military personnel were visibly static.

"I was made aware of the deaths right before many of you in here heard about them on the radio or from the newspapers."

"At 16:00 on December 25th, 1947, the local Roswell police were contacted by a neighbor who lived very close to the Heartleys. For confidentiality, I will not release the name of the individual who called the police. The neighbor told the police they heard gunfire coming from the Heartley property, so they decided to call."

"The Roswell police arrived at the Heartley property at 16:20 perplexed. Two unidentified men had been shot and killed, as well as Tom, Macey, and Daisy Heartley, and William Brakel was nowhere to be found." Ramses did not mention that two more unidentified men who had been doing surveillance of the Heartley house were also killed pursuing the suspects.

"The official report from the Roswell police department lists William Brakel as the prime suspect in the murders of the unidentified men who were shot. Forensics reports identified that the bullets in the bodies of the unidentified men were from a Smith and Wesson 9-millimeter that Tom Heartley legally purchased. It is believed that William Brakel was wielding the gun at the time of the fight and that he fired upon the unidentified men. It is also concluded in the report that either William or Tom opened fire on the men, who returned fire and accidentally hit Macey and Daisy with their return fire. William Brakel is now a wanted suspect and is armed and dangerous. His location is unknown, but if you have any information on his whereabouts, call 1-800-TIP-LINE. That is all the information available at this time. Now I will open up the conference for questions."

Ramses did not explain why the unidentified men were at the property in the first place, or why they were armed. He also lied about the forensics report. It was conclusive that his N.S.A. agents (which were the unidentified men) had shot both Macey and Daisy at point-blank range in the head, ruling out the possibility of accidentally hitting them with return fire.

Ramses saw hands immediately shoot up. As much as he wanted to walk out of the room and say nothing, he couldn't. He had to answer some questions the reporters were going to ask to appease the mind of the public. Despite the high number of seats filled with military personnel, there were still at least a dozen reporters from local and national news agencies who managed to get access to the press conference.

He scanned the raised hands for a submissive target. Men were more likely to challenge his statements; women were too afraid of his imposing physical stature to question him critically. He spotted a hand sprouting from a young female. She looked like she was in her mid-twenties and was probably starting her reporting career. She was wearing a tight blue skirt and black turtle glasses, with her hair pinned up in a bun.

"The woman in the blue shirt," Ramses said, pointing to the young woman.

"Thank you, General. I am Marisol Chavez from the Albuquerque Journal. I have a few questions about the crash. We have received several eyewitness reports from anonymous individuals who claimed that after the crash, men dressed in black suits began frequently appearing around Roswell. Do you have any knowledge of who these men are and why they started appearing after the crash?"

Ramses did not want to be associated with the men in black. Two of the men in black had been found at the house after the Heartley murders, and he specifically referred to them as unidentified men during his speech so he would not raise suspicion. If a link was ever made between the men in black and himself, he could bear the responsibility for the deaths of the family. He could not let that happen. Too much was at stake in his professional career. "The United States Air Force and the federal government have no knowledge of who these men are or why they were in Roswell."

"But, sir, there were tens of eyewitnesses. Some of those witnesses were Roswell police officers who responded to the call the night of the crash. They claimed the men in black were under your direct supervision."

That son of a bitch Gordon must have opened his mouth. Ramses would have his balls for this. He had to think of something quick; all eyes were on him. He forced all the police officers who responded to the crash to swear an oath of silence. Ramses paid them handsomely for their mandatory compliance. He was now regretting that decision.

"I was in charge of a special unit the night of the crash, which I named a few minutes ago. These police officers are either mistaken, or lying. I was not directing anybody the night of the crash except for the squadron I brought to the crash site. My men were in Roswell for that only and have not stayed around since. For the folks of the town and the police officers who claim to have seen these mysterious men in black, I have heard nothing or know nothing about them."

Ramses would need to call his N.S.A. agents out of Roswell immediately after the conference. The sooner they disappeared, the sooner they would be forgotten in the memories of the people who had seen them.

The reporter looked like she would keep pressing Ramses, but she sat silently. Maybe she hesitated because of Ramses' uniform, heavily decorated with emblems of various colors and medals. She was looking at the most decorated General of the United States Air Force. His magnitude pierced through her. He took the moment of silence to call on another reporter.

"And you in the back with the red shirt," Ramses said to another young female reporter.

"Thank you, General. Melinda Crawford of A.B.C. news. There were several eyewitness reports and a police report filed about a bad car accident on I-40 going westbound into Roswell. Two men dressed in black suits were killed, and according to the autopsy, they were killed from gunfire, not the crash itself. The crash occurred on December 25th, 1947, in the afternoon hours, the same day as the murders of Daisy, Tom, and Macey Heartley. The vehicle was an unlicensed black van, similar to the one eyewitnesses described seeing in town. Were you aware of this crash, and did your men have any involvement in it?"

Ramses did not like where this press conference was going. He would keep being attached to the men in black; that much was obvious. Too many people in Roswell had seen them for them to slip under the radar. He looked at his watch, and it read 13:00. He had been talking and answering questions for nearly twenty minutes, and the questions were getting increasingly impossible to evade. It was time to wrap it up.

"I have no comment about that car accident except that my men were not involved at all."

"Well, it looks like our time is up, ladies and gentlemen. I will not be taking any more questions at this time. Thank you for your time."

Ramses started to get up and heard cameras flashing and reporters shouting out questions who were too scared to speak up before.

"Were there any alien bodies discovered at the scene of the crash?"

"Who are the mysterious men in black?"

"When will the autopsy reports of the Heartley family be publicly released?"

"Is Roswell safe?"

"Why are the Roswell police saying you directed the men in black the night of the crash?"

Ramses slammed the door of the conference room behind him, leaving the endless banter of reporters and journalists. Lots of thoughts were racing through his head. He had to meet with Gordon in person to ask him what the fuck had happened. None of his police officers should have talked to reporters, and Ramses bet he could figure out which ones did. He needed to contact all of the agents currently stationed in Roswell and tell them to leave. He had to contact the president to relay all of his plans before executing them. And lastly, he had to find and eliminate William Brakel. If he was able to leak valuable information to a media outlet, Ramses would be fucked. So many things to do in such little time.

Chapter 12

✦

Will

Will had driven straight to Mexico after leaving the Heartley property. By nightfall, he was at the United States-Mexico border in Las Cruces, New Mexico. At the border, border patrol agents eyed his van suspiciously. There was no license plate, and the windows were completely tinted, but because he was going into Mexico, they didn't mind much. After a few questions, he was waved through the checkpoint. After crossing over the border, he stopped several miles in to relieve himself. The night air was cold and brisk, and he could make out all the stars in the night sky. This far south, there was nobody for miles and no artificial light sources. He wondered which star the aliens came from.

Before he hopped back into the van, he thought it would be best to check out what equipment the agents had in the van. Behind the front seats were a multitude of boxes and instruments; most of them for monitoring and surveillance purposes. He saw a device with headphones plugged into it, a large metal dish, a black toolbox with every standard tool you could think of, several televisions, and emergency medical kits. All of it was neatly packaged and stored, so there was enough space to sit in the back comfortably and use the equipment. In a small pouch next to a spare tire was a license plate that read G-0002A, a governmental license plate. He made a mental note to put it on before he departed again, so he would not be harassed or stopped in Mexico. There were also a couple of clips of ammunition for a 9mm in the glove box, along with a walkie talkie set and $1,000 in cash. After thoroughly looking through the van, he grabbed a screwdriver out of the toolbox and screwed in the license plate. With one final visual check, Will was ready to set off again.

He put the keys in the ignition and started the van. The van was pretty speedy, and he assumed it was turbocharged, but he had not looked under the hood to confirm his suspicion. As long as it drove, that was good enough for him.

From the moment Tom and Will had forged the escape plan, Will knew he would be a wanted man. Hell, he and the whole Heartley family were wanted; wanted for witnessing an extraordinary event on July 8th, 1947. They did nothing wrong. They just happened to live in the exact wrong spot in the universe that night. Now they were all dead except for Will. He had to tell their story to the world, to avenge their deaths.

Will drove through the night and through the next day and didn't stop until he got to Mexico City, hoping he could blend in with the millions of people living there. He stuck out like a sore thumb. He was tall, white, and could only speak a lick of Spanish. After arriving, he checked into a run-down local motel and slept for 12 hours straight. After waking up, he looked at a calendar in the lobby and realized it was December 28th, almost time for the New Year. He would not be celebrating the New Year, but instead would be hiding in his motel room, hoping the United States government did not catch his scent.

He spent the next couple of days in hiding and didn't leave his room except to eat the complimentary breakfast the motel provided. The room fee was 50 pesos a night, which was really cheap, especially considering he had found a $1,000 cash in United States' bills, stashed in the glove box of the van. When he arrived, the first thing Will did was exchange some of the American money for pesos at a local bank. He exchanged $200 American dollars into pesos, which was about 4,000 pesos.

During the day, he would read the local newspaper, seeing if he could locate a local radio station to report his story, but he never found anything useful. After the first week passed and he didn't see any United States government agents, he became more comfortable and started adventuring around the city.

One morning Will went to a local library to do research. He was looking for news stations close by that aired bizarre stories. He knew his chances of finding a reporter or news station in Mexico who would take his story seriously were slim to none because he didn't speak Spanish, and they most likely would not believe his story or understand what he was saying. Almost all of the books and newspapers in the library were in Spanish, making the research much more difficult. Outside of the library, some men would always sell copies of American newspapers that were in English. The newspapers were from the states closest to the border, such as New Mexico, Texas, and Nevada. Those newspapers were Will's only hope.

Will walked up to a small man with a cowboy hat on, standing over a wagon filled with the American newspapers.

"Que paso amigo? Como muchas por tres papeles?" Will stammered, pointing to the wagon full of newspapers.

"Cincuenta y seis."

Fifty-six pesos for each newspaper. That was a little expensive, but it was only a drop in the bucket of the $800 Will still had in cash. Will learned very quickly that people took advantage of his language handicap. He had to spend his money wisely, despite having a small fortune. He decided to fight back.

"Vente," he said to the man.

"Cuarenta," the man replied.

"Vente cinco," Will said back.

The man thought about it for a second, then nodded his head. Will reached into his pocket and pulled out 25 pesos. The man looked at the money carefully, examining the currency, making sure it was authentic. After a moment, the man said, "Which one?" in broken English.

"Nevada," Will said, pointing to a newspaper with a headline from Las Vegas, Nevada, on the front page. The man grabbed the paper out of the wagon and passed it to Will. It was almost two months old, dated November 16th, 1947. Will thanked the man, then walked back into the library. He flipped to the back, where the ads were.

He saw ads for landscaping companies, retail stores, Army recruiting stations, and everything in between. After scanning the ads pages, near the bottom of one of the pages, he found what he was looking for. A giant red advertisement for a radio station called the X-Files Radio Station drew his attention. The advertisement read: "Do you have a crazy story nobody would believe, but you know in your heart of hearts it is true? We are looking for ordinary people who have experienced the extraordinary. Saw bigfoot? Call us. Witnessed an anomaly you can't explain? Call us. Encountered a U.F.O. or aliens? Call us." The last part got Will's heart racing. Would they really listen to him if he told them his story? It was worth a shot.

The telephone number was listed below the advertisement, 1-702-255-4343. He scribbled down the number on a sheet of paper to ensure he had it in more than one place. Was this advertisement a sign from God? Will thought so. He ripped the advertisement out of the newspaper so ferociously that people around the library turned their heads to see where the noise had come from.

Will ran all the way back to his motel, panting and sweating as he approached the dull blue door to his motel room, number 6. Will had chosen that room specifically because it was the closest room to the parking lot. If the government managed to find him, he would at least have a fighting chance of escaping. He had already been in the same spot for too long. He could sense it.

Inside the motel room was a twin-sized bed, sporting blue sheets to match the exterior of the building. A tiny bathroom was tucked away in one corner of the room. It was a small room, but it was Will's new home. Will had a bag of pesos that he kept in the motel room lying in a corner discretely, so a maid wouldn't think about stealing it. Will reached into the bag and pulled out the 2 pesos required to place a 30-minute call from a nearby phone booth.

The phone booth was conveniently located close to room 6 where he was staying, so it was only a short walk across the motel parking lot before he made it there. As Will walked out of the motel room and shut the door, he saw a black van with tinted windows driving in the parking lot: he froze. He jumped behind the corner of the motel, fearing he had been spotted. Cautiously, he poked his head around the corner after a few seconds.

The van was moving slowly, ominously slowly. Right in the middle of the driving lane of the parking lot, the van stopped. Will's palms became sweaty, and his heart started beating faster. Will crouched a little lower, hoping the van would not see him. The driver's door opened, and out walked a massive man wearing a gray muscle tee shirt and blue jeans. He had slicked-back black hair and a thick mustache.

The large man looked around the parking lot, then walked to the passenger's side door and opened it. He helped a small man in a purple suit get out of the large van. Will breathed a sigh of relief, realizing these were not the men in black he had come to fear and hate. This was perhaps a boss and his henchman, evident from the different attire of the two men. Finally, after deciding it was safe, Will walked over to the phone booth to call the number of the advertisement he had seen.

Will walked into the old red phone booth and closed the glass door behind him. A black phone with a metal cord dangled from the phone case. Will dialed the number 1-702-255-4343, and the phone rang a couple of times. "X-Files Radio Station, please hold," a female voice said. An audible beep was heard, and Will heard *I'm Looking for a Four-Leaf Clover* playing in the background. Will hoped he would be lucky. He needed it. He turned inside the phone booth to see the large man in the muscle shirt and the man in the purple suit walking towards the phone booth. Will didn't think much of it and turned back to the phone case. The music was still playing in the background. After a minute, the operator came back on with an audible click.

"Hello, are you still there?"

"Yes, ma'am, I am."

"Great. Thank you for holding. How can I assist you today?"

"I read your ad in the Nevada newspaper, and I am interested in telling you uh, a story I have. It's about the U.F.O. incident in Roswell, New Mexico that happened on July 8th, 1947."

"Okay, and what is your name?"

Will hesitated as he thought about the consequences of the call, then he spoke. "I uh, can't give that to you right now, sorry. Please let me talk to your boss; I'm desperate. The world needs to hear my story."

"Sir, slow down. I have to get your name and a phone number I can reach you at, as well as a brief description of your story. I will pass along the information to our team of journalists. If one of them likes your story, they will pay you to come to Las Vegas and give an interview on our radio station. Now, your name please."

"Okay. Okay. I don't have much time. My name is William Bra," just as Will was about to say his last name; he heard three loud knocks on the phone booth that startled him. He dropped the phone and turned to see who was knocking. It was the large man in the muscle shirt, looming over him from outside the booth. He impatiently tapped his watch towards Will's face. Will knew he had to be quick or risk getting his ass whopped.

"My name is William Brakel. I worked as a farmhand at the Heartley ranch, and I was there on the night of July 8th, 1947. The story that the military released is not the truth. I want to tell the world what really happened that night."

"The truth. Okay, yeah. Where can we reach you should your story be selected for the interview?"

"I am currently staying in a different country, and you cannot reach me by mail or by phone. Can I come into your office in person and meet directly with one of your reporters?"

The woman on the line was silent for a second, stunned by the bluntness of the question. Will prayed she would accept the request.

"Well, you know what? I like your attitude, and I am intrigued by what you're saying. I read about the story myself, and I found it fascinating. I think I know just the reporter who would do great with your story. Can you come down this upcoming Monday, January 13th?"

"Yes, absolutely. What is the address?"

"Fantastic. Our office headquarters are located at 1108 Las Vegas Boulevard."

Will repeated the address silently in his head. He searched for a pen to write the address down on his hand, but he couldn't find one.

"Thank you so much. I must go now. I really cannot thank you enough." Will hung up the phone after hearing the final goodbye. He was surprised his plan had worked so well. Will turned around to see the large man standing with his back to the booth, talking with the smaller man in the purple suit.

"Gracias, amigo," the large man said, opening the door for Will as he stepped out of the phone booth, and the man in the purple suit walked in. Will heard the phone booth door close shut as he walked back across the parking lot to his room.

The phone conversation hung heavy in Will's mind as he contemplated his next move. Las Vegas was 1,800 miles away, and he only had four days to get there. He would have to drive 14-16 hours a day, but he could make it. The only potential issue would be crossing the border again, because this time, he would be entering into the United States, not leaving it. Will knew the federal government would be looking for him and probably the van he was driving too, but he didn't know how extensive their efforts would be.

Will felt like a wanted criminal whose only crime was innocently witnessing a classified event by accident. He wondered if he would be detained and arrested upon arriving at the border. He could almost picture the men in black waiting there, ready to take him away. He needed to leave immediately if he was going to make it in time. This was his only chance to tell his story: he might be a dead man after he spoke.

In the motel room, he quickly gathered his bag of pesos and the American money lying on top of the bed. All he had on him was the new clothes he bought at a thrift store in town, his money, and the van keys. He walked into the reception area of the motel complex, a square room with brown tile flooring, stained by dirt and dust. A crusty old lady smoking a cigarette was sitting in a chair behind the main desk area. Will gave her 150 pesos. She looked up at Will, confused, knowing he had given her a small fortune.

"No, it's fine. Keep the money. I really must be going now! Thank you!" Will left the motel reception lobby in a hurry, almost sprinting to the van.

He started the van and hit a nearby gas station, where he filled up his tank. He drove and drove, only stopping for the bathroom, gas, and to sleep. Within two days, he was at the United States and Mexico border. When he arrived, there were only two border patrol agents working at the port of entry. Both looked very young. They could not have been older than 21. Will drove up and rolled down the window. A small white kid with brown hair poked his head into the window. "ID, sir," he said to Will.

Will did not have his ID on him, so he pulled out $40 cash and handed it to the border patrol agent. "Here, take this in place of my ID. It'll be our little secret," Will said to the agent. The agent looked at him suspiciously before stuffing the money in his front pocket. "Go right ahead, sir, you have a good rest of your day," the young agent said, ushering Will into the United States. As Will drove through the gate, he breathed a sigh of relief. That was easy enough; money could get you anything.

After driving up I-40 west for several hours, Will started hearing an unfamiliar beeping noise coming from the back of the van. His heart started racing with his thoughts. He pulled over immediately, fearful the noise was some type of tracking device he had missed. Will slammed the driver's side door shut and ran to the back of the van, where he opened the back doors. He started searching around the van frantically.

He saw several black monitors displaying nothing; Will had unplugged all of them, fearing the government could use them to spy on him and track him. The beeping was not coming from any of the monitors. Will looked around at all the boxes of radio equipment and tools and tried to pinpoint the noise. He saw the red and white first aid bag and picked it up, the noise growing louder. Something in the first aid bag was beeping.

Will unzipped the zipper, ripping apart the white cross as he unzipped. He saw bandage kits, band-aids, antibiotic wipes, and scissors. On the bottom of the bag was an automatic defibrillator. A red indicator light was flashing, and the beeping noise indicated it was on a very low battery. Mystery solved. Will removed the battery, and the beeping stopped.

He was very on edge, paranoid the instant he crossed into the United States. He had been constantly monitored without his consent for months, and it felt like every device, and every noise could be someone spying on him. The thought of being constantly watched was maddening. Ever since the night of the crash, he became more and more worried, and the murder of the Heartley family kept him up at night. Will felt small; he was lonely and could not confide in anybody about his situation.

After the massacre at the Heartley property, Will had been running for his life. It had been three weeks since the brutal killings, and he still had not properly grieved. As he started the van again, tears came tumbling down his face. Slowly at first, then they began falling down in big heavy drops. In between sobs, Will looked at his reflection in the rear-view mirror. Will looked like he had aged five years in the last three weeks. He was exhausted and spiritually dead.

His eyes were bloodshot, and dark bags from lack of sleep hung heavy underneath them. His brown beard had a few gray whiskers poking out that had never been there before. His face looked gaunt; he had barely eaten anything in the three weeks since he had been on the run. He was only focused on surviving and telling his story, and then he could die. As he drove, he thought about his mom, Valerie Brakel.

She was a short, plump woman, with the same straight brown hair as Will. As a kid, they moved around a lot, usually into a home with one of his mom's boyfriends. Will had never met his biological dad, and he never wanted to. According to his mom, Will's dad Raymond Brakel had cheated on Valerie the day after their wedding. Valerie had come home one day after running errands to a note on the fridge. "Valerie… I found somebody else. I know we just got married, but I have to follow my heart. I hope you understand. Love, Raymond." That also happened to be the same day she was going to tell Raymond she was pregnant with Will. She had found out only a few weeks earlier but wanted to surprise him as a late wedding gift.

Will heard the story only once after begging his mom to tell him about his real dad. Ever since hearing that story, Will hated most men in authority, Tom being the exception. He never did well in school and ended up dropping out of high school his junior year. Being a dropout left his work options very limited. He moved to Oklahoma when he was 16 and worked for an alfalfa farmer named Bobby Miller, who eventually introduced Will to Tom Heartley at a farmer's market.

When Will first met Tom, he hated him, just like every other boss who was a man he worked for previously. When Bobby introduced them, Tom looked at Will and laughed. "This skinny little twig is working in the fields? You sure he can hold a full bag of alfalfa?" Tom cackled. Will smiled, remembering the sense of humor he eventually came to love in Tom. The moment of happiness was short-lived as he remembered what his current state of affairs was. Telling his story was not only for Will; it was for the entire Heartley lineage. He had to do this for them and for his mom.

That night Will pulled over off the side of the road just outside of Nevada to get some sleep. After several minutes, he drifted off to sleep and dreamed about the night of the crash. Buddy was barking violently as Will walked out of the house to investigate. In the next instant, Will was standing next to the metallic disc, looking at the blue lights emanating from underneath it. The mangled bodies of the little green aliens lay motionless outside the spaceship. Suddenly, one of the aliens opened its eyes and started screaming incoherent words at Will. "No! No! Get away from me!" Will said as the alien approached him. Will tried to run, but he was frozen in place. Will woke up in a cold sweat screaming. The night terrors always felt so real.

Will wiped his face and looked at the clock. It was 2:00 A.M. He had only slept for four hours, but he counted that as a win. He drank a large bottle of water and started the engine, and began driving to his final destination, Las Vegas. Will kept driving until he reached Las Vegas on January 13th, early in the morning. The city was full of life, even in the early hours. Will watched drunk men stumbling out of brothels, and women trying to seduce their next paycheck. Neon lights painted the streets and the sky a rainbow of different colors. He had never seen so many bright lights in his life. He felt out of place.

Looking at his map, he tried to locate 1108 Las Vegas Boulevard. After a minute of searching, he found it. It was right in the heart of the city. As Will drove towards his destination, he felt oddly at peace with himself. He had a purpose now, and that purpose was telling his story. He was going to tell his story to the world, even if it cost him his life. Knowing he was about to do this brought him closure. Nobody had heard his story yet, and this was his one chance to tell it. All from the newspaper he bought outside of a library in Mexico City.

As he drove to the radio station, Will winced at every large black car he saw. His brain had been changed by trauma to convince him every black vehicle posed a threat. The men in black stalked him every day for months, and now he was back in their territory.

The whole incident felt like some bad dream. On the night of the crash, Will spent hours going over the details with the Roswell police and General Ramses. Somehow, Will felt like Ramses was responsible for everything that had happened to him and the Heartley family. He would leave no stone unturned when he was telling his story. After he did this interview, he wanted one more thing: to kill Ramses. Ramses ruined his life and had taken the lives of Macey, Daisy, and Tom. Will could never forget or forgive. He missed everything about his old life.

He missed the way Buddy would wag his tail and lick his hand when he petted him. Will missed the smell of maple syrup and eggs in the morning when Macey made everyone breakfast. He missed all the questions Daisy used to ask Tom and him. He missed the conversations about politics Tomand he would have after drinking a couple of beers. Will never had a dadgrowing up, and he thought of Tom as the closest thing to a dad he ever hadin his life. That world was dead and gone now.

After driving around for thirty minutes, he spotted the radio station. The building itself was rectangular in shape and was made from red brick. A large radio tower with a white dish resting on the top of it hugged one side of the building. The entrance was two large glass doors with white lettering that read, "X-FILES RADIO STATION," on the doors. On the roof of the building directly over the front doors, was a flying saucer with a green alien sticking its head above the saucer and waving. How ironic. The hours on a sign hanging in the window said the radio station did not open up until 9:00 A.M. and he had arrived at 7:30 A.M, so he parked the van in the corner of the parking lot and decided to go for a walk to clear his head.

The radio station was close to the strip, so he walked towards it. The strip was busy with people bobbing in and out of casinos and brothels. Cigarette smoke hung heavy in the air, creating a light fog over the tops of people's heads. Will saw some men wearing suits and fedora hats puffing cigars and drinking whiskey outside of one brothel. Women in short skirts and high heels flirted and giggled at the men's jokes. All appeared to be normal, except Will stuck out of the Vegas crowd, wearing a tee-shirt and jeans.

A woman in a bright red dress and jet-black high heels made eye contact with Will. "Hey there, handsome. Let's get us a room and have some fun!"

She was a pretty black woman, full and curvy. The primal side of Will was telling him to do it, but the rational side was telling him to walk away. "I'm not interested," he said, walking away.

"Well maybe next time," the woman said with a wink.

After that interaction, Will decided it would be best if he went back to the van before he made any stupid decisions. He walked back to his van and opened the door. He sat down and looked at the clock. It was 8:00 A.M., so he still had an hour to kill before the radio station opened up. He turned on the radio and leaned the seat back, listening to the Ink Spots and the Ravens to kill time. After listening to a few songs, a small red beetle pulled into the parking lot. A blonde woman wearing a modest blue dress got out of the car and unlocked the doors to the radio station. Shortly after she entered the radio station, another car pulled into the parking lot, a 1941 Pontiac Streamliner. A man in a bright green suit hopped out of the car and walked into the radio station. Will wondered who they were. He would find out in 15 minutes. At exactly 9:00 A.M. on January 13th, 1948, Will walked into the X-Files Radio Station building.

The doors opened into a waiting lobby; a curved wooden receptionist desk sat in the middle. The blonde woman Will had seen from the parking lot was sitting behind the desk, writing something down. Behind the desk was a door that led to the studio rooms. Against three of the lobby walls were black leather couches, with magazines splayed out on tables in front of them. As Will entered the lobby, the woman looked up at him with pale blue eyes and a smile.

"Can I help you?"

"Uh, yes. My name is William Brakel. We spoke on the phone on Friday."

"Oh yes, Will! I am glad you made it here today! Please take a seat. I'll go grab George. Would you like some coffee while you wait?" she asked.

"Sure, that would be great," Will said, taking a seat on one of the leather couches. The woman nodded and walked through a door behind the receptionist desk that said, "Radio Personnel Only". After several minutes the woman returned, holding a steaming cup of coffee for Will. "George Knapp will be with you in just a moment, hun."

"Thank you," Will said while taking a sip of the coffee. It was straight black, just the way he liked it. A few sips later, George Knapp walked into the lobby. He was the man Will had seen wearing the bright green suit and driving the Pontiac. He wore brown snake leather boots and a snake leather hat to match. His tie was black, with aliens in spaceships flying around on the tie. He looked old, maybe 50 or 60 years old. Thin brown hair dangled off of his balding head.

"George Knapp, nice to meet you," he said, extending his hand. "I read all about your story as soon as my receptionist told me about you. I personally called the Roswell police department; an old friend of mine from Santa Fe works for them now. He said he was there on the night of the crash, and the government was doin fishy stuff, but wouldn't say much else. I believe your story, and I believe the world needs to hear it. Are you, William Brakel, ready to tell the world your story?"

Chapter 13

⚡

Oousma

Time. A property of the universe, unlike any other. Oousma had lived an eternity by most living organisms' standards, yet the days since Oousma's capture had felt longer than all the other previous days put together. Never had it been so mentally and physically stagnant. A being as complex as Oousma needed stimulation to match its intelligence. Oousma's will to survive was diminishing every day as its hopes of escape grew smaller and smaller. How long had it been since the crash? There was no way of knowing exactly; Ramses removed the calendars from both labs, but Oousma estimated it had been close to 7 Earth months.

Ishma's condition was now dire. Large varicose veins formed streets and highways on Ishma's head. Ishma's body was atrophying at an alarming rate; its ribs were tightly pressed to the yellowish skin of its diaphragm. Its skin was completely discolored, an almost unrecognizable yellow shade, and the bump on its head looked like a tumor. Ishma did not need to be drugged anymore; its head lay tilted to one side, spit perpetually oozing out of the side of its mouth. Each day Oousma expected Ishma to die, but death had not come yet.

It hurt Oousma deeply to see Ishma in this state, but Oousma had to be wary. After General Ramses beat Oousma the first time, more beatings had come, some for no apparent reason. Oousma was scared to advocate on Ishma's behalf. Oousma knew why Ramses was so violent. Ramses wanted to break Oousma's will to live, and Oousma could feel it slowly working.

Through the beatings, Oousma was forced to tell Ramses more information than it intended. Oousma told Ramses about Nirubu, its location in the Alpha Centauri star system, the properties of element 115 that made it special, and how the spaceship was designed to fly. Oousma was still careful not to reveal everything to Ramses. Oousma kept secret its name and

Ishma's name, and Oousma kept secret how the Annonaki had specifically modified element 115 on an atomic level to give it the properties it had. The only thing of value Oousma had to offer was knowledge. Releasing bits and pieces of information was buying valuable time: Oousma was afraid the messages it had sent to the Council of Elders would not be received before Oousma and Ishma had died, leaving Nirubu in limbo.

Oousma began to grow affectionate towards Nicolai as time passed. He was the only human who seemed to care about the aliens; all the other humans viewed them as research projects, not living beings. Nicolai would often come into the lab Oousma was held in and write Oousma questions for hours. The curiosity of Nicolai brought Oousma back to the distant past, back when humans had been more compassionate and interested. The humans Oousma saw today were unrecognizable; they were violent and cruel, uncalm and anxious.

§

Thousands of years ago, the Annonaki had tried to guide human civilization to become a more technologically advanced species. When the Annonaki arrived on Earth 12,500 years before the present, it was decided they could interact and guide the humans. The vote passed the Council of Elders by a narrow margin after days of heated debate. When it was decided that they could land on the Earth and guide human beings, Oousma championed the idea of showing humans how to build large megalithic structures that would stand the test of time. Oousma believed humans would see these enormous structures and be inspired to advance their mathematics and science to build even greater buildings. Oousma also wanted to teach humans how to farm plants, so they would have large stores of food.

"If we start with a simple design, like a pyramid, then it might spur the humans to build more complex structures advancing their math and science disciplines, and open a new stage in their evolution. They are still in the stone age in many respects, and for them to advance, they need to learn how to build cities and grow food in large quantities. If they can build something that takes thousands of them to complete, they may unify and expand under the effort, assuming they have ample food to do so."

"It also might cause them to wage war over invisible gods. We know what happened when the Annonaki of the past built temples and cities.

Other Annonaki were subjugated and killed for having different beliefs. Besides, we know little about the flora of the Earth Oousma, so what plants do you propose they domesticate?"

"Nonsense. We must not go down to the Earth and coerce them into building things and domesticating things they are not ready to build and domesticate, Oousma. We need to remember that we are encroaching on their natural evolutionary path, which could have disastrous consequences."

Thousands of years later, Oousma could still hear the words of the council echoing in its mind. The first time they decided to go to the ground, they were greeted by many confused and scared looking humans wielding spears and bows. The ship landed in what was now called North America. The people Oousma saw were short and brown-skinned, with thick black hair. Many were wearing pieces of bone as jewelry and furs to protect them from the cold.

Oousma remembered the goosebumps that dotted its flesh when it was standing only feet away from the humans. Never before had an Annonaki stood across from another living organism that was as intelligent as a human. Slowly, other humans came out of hiding from the trees and bushes surrounding the landing site. There was a noticeable tension in the air as the five little aliens looked around at the humans, who outnumbered them 10 to 1. This was their home, their world that the Annonaki had landed on: they were the aliens.

The wind rustled the pine trees' leaves, making a whooshing noise as the humans and Annonaki observed each other. One of the humans stepped in front of the rest; colorful bird feathers covered his head, and his face was painted white and red. Oousma guessed this was the leader and stepped forward to match the human being, who at 5'6 towered over Oousma.

The human bent down to be eye level with Oousma. He looked Oousma up and down, then touched Oousma's forehead with his fingers. His hand was cold and rough, and Oousma could feel the curiosity flowing from his hand. Human skin felt so different from the skin of the Annonaki. It was hard and callused, likely from years of hard work. At the contact, Oousma retreated backward towards its group, frightened by the interaction. The human opened his mouth wide and started making a strange noise with its mouth. Oousma was not sure what the human was doing, but it scared it.

"Issla, prepare the ship to fly. I do not know what this human's intentions are. They are making me nervous from all their loud noises," Oousma said to Issla as the humans started shouting around them.

"I think he is... talking Oousma. I think he is talking to us."

Oousma looked toward the leader, who bowed down on one knee. Oousma did not understand the gesture, but Oousma sensed it was not dangerous or violent. The other humans followed, and soon all of the humans had their heads down and were not looking at the Annonaki, but were instead looking at the ground. The humans started chanting in the same rhythmic pattern - like a song. The Annonaki made songs in the past, but over the millions of years they had been evolving; they gradually created less and less music and art, spending more time on mathematics and science. The humans were truly intelligent, proven by the ornaments and weapons they wielded, and Oousma stood in awe of the beings who were bowing down in front of it, chanting a song.

For 150,00 years, the Annonaki had been monitoring Earth. Until their current mission, they had only launched unmanned satellites and robotic probes, which beamed back pictures and footage of the lush planet. When the first up-close images came back to the Annonaki of the time, they were astonished that complex life had formed on the closest star to them. The Annonaki had scanned their entire solar system for life, but only on Nirubu did life exist in their solar system. The Alpha Centauri system was a barren landscape except for Nirubu, so finding and discovering life on the nearest star was a monumental discovery in the history of the Annonaki.

After discovering life on Earth, politics and civil wars overtook the inhabitants of Nirubu, and for a time, the Earth was forgotten. Most Annonaki hated the Kuhan Empire, and they fought endless battles for strategic positions and natural resource deposits against the global government. Those who rebelled against the Kuhan Empire were killed or enslaved, leading to more rebellions and wars. Asteroids with enormous amounts of plutonium and other precious metals took precedence over the Earth because they contained the elements necessary for electronic equipment and atomic bombs. They had to turn to other stellar bodies for precious metals because they had mined all the naturally occurring metals from Nirubu in years past. During the wars, plutonium was used to create immensely powerful atomic bombs, and other metals mined from the asteroids were used for supercomputers and electronics.

Oousma had been born into this state of uneasiness during the Kuhan Empire's reign of terror. Over 1,000 years, Oousma gained the respect and loyalty of the oppressed inhabitants of Nirubu, who thought of Oousma as their leader. Oousma slowly and secretly assembled a massive civilian army that would eventually challenge Kuhani Abdullah, the evil tyrant who controlled Nirubu. Kuhani Abdullah was born from the stem cells of the original Kuhani Abdullah of 500,000 years before the present, who established the Kuhan Empire. Its offspring controlled Nirubu, and remained in power until the last Kuhani Abdullah was eliminated by Oousma. Oousma ultimately led the rebellion that toppled the Kuhan Empire, and established the new world order that had remained in its place, some 15,000 years later.

The new world order Oousma established was a planet-wide government based on democratic principles, the free will of the individual, and equal voting for all Annonaki on Nirubu. Oousma was the first Annonaki to start the Council of Elders, 15,000 years before the present and was the council's first Supreme Chancellor. There were 12 members of the Council of Elders - one for each region on Nirubu, and one of them was voted the Supreme Chancellor. Elections were held every 500 years, and Oousma had been repeatedly voted in as the Supreme Chancellor since the new world order was established.

The Kuhan Empire's ideology had not been completely eradicated at the time Oousma established the new world order. Powerful individuals and military personnel from many different regions who supported the regime slowly crept into the Council of Elders, some through questionable means. These individuals wanted to see the new world order crash and burn, and made it hard for Oousma and the council to pass new laws and regulations that would help the inhabitants of Nirubu experience a greater quality of life. One of these ideas that certain council members shot down was Oousma's suggestion to explore the Earth with live Annonaki.

When Oousma first proposed the idea to the general population of Nirubu, over 85% of the inhabitants supported its idea. Some council members ran smear campaigns and produced false information stating Oousma wanted to explore the Earth only to benefit itself from the bountiful resources the Earth offered. The population of Nirubu absorbed this false information, and the approval rating gradually dropped and threatened civil war. Oousma was eventually able to convince the general public that it, in fact, did not want to benefit itself only, that it actually wanted to explore the Earth because humans lived there, and the Annonaki should be curious about its intelligent celestial neighbors. Oousma argued the Annonaki needed to explore the Earth and that it was the next stage in their evolution. 3,500 years after Oousma was born into a breeding facility controlled by the Kuhan Empire, it led the first mission to Earth with live Annonaki.

The initial first visit was supposed to be a 1-year trip to Earth and back, but Oousma ended up staying much longer out of interest. After having that first face to face interaction with the humans, Oousma was hooked. Oousma was never interested in the animals that inhabited Nirubu, but Oousma found humans and Earth to be captivating and addicting. Not all of the other four members who had come with Oousma shared Oousma's views.

"This is a pointless endeavor Oousma. These are nothing but a bunch of ugly sacks of water, no smarter than the average Annonaki infant. We can't get them to build anything, let alone understand our science," Issla had told Oousma.

Only one member of the original five decided to stay with Oousma when it was time to go back to Nirubu, and that was Vahisma.

"What do you mean you're not coming back with us? You mean to stay on this wretched planet?" – Issla.

"I want to teach humans about astronomy and math, and watch them grow and develop. Why are you disdainful of the humans, Issla?"

"I do not disdain the humans Oousma, but the Annonaki come first. You are an Annonaki. Who will lead our kind, Oousma? You are the elected Supreme Chancellor of our people. You would resign and abandon your post to live amongst these savages?"

Oousma had not just wanted to live with humans; Oousma hoped one day the Annonaki could breed with the human beings and create a new hybrid species, but Oousma kept these thoughts to itself.

"Yes, Issla, I would like to live amongst these savages. I have written a resignation letter for the council stating my reasons for staying on Earth. In the letter, I have detailed who I would like to be my successor for the remainder of my term."

"Very well, then. You know as I do that it might be thousands of years before a ship can make it back to Earth, if one arrives at all."

Oousma knew the challenges of interstellar travel and how difficult it would be to create enough element 115 again to fly back to Earth, but Oousma felt a calling to be with the humans. Dumb as they were compared to the Annonaki, Oousma had never been so intrigued by another living organism. The Annonaki had eradicated most of the life on Nirubu by overexploiting their environments and destroying their natural habitats. There had once been billions of creatures crawling and flying all over Nirubu's surface and swimming in its oceans, but most were gone now. They did not need animals for energy anymore. The Annonaki were photosynthetic. The Earth was a new world, pristine and untouched with countless creatures and plant species. Oousma feared that without its help, humans faced a similar path of destruction. Upon landing on Earth, Oousma witnessed humans hunting other animals and manipulating their environment to survive. Like the Annonaki, humans had to kill and destroy the land around them to survive: it was innate to their nature.

Oousma requested Issla to fly it and Vahisma to a different part of the Earth before they left. Oousma wanted to fly to modern-day Iraq. Oousma told Vahisma what its plan was as the ship landed near the Tigris River.

"Vahisma, we must show these humans how to domesticate the wild plants."

"Why, Oousma?"

"In order for the human population to expand, and for civilization as we know it to take root, societies must shift to farming. Hunting and gathering will only take humans so far. A surplus of food is required for the population to expand enough to create specialized, non-hunting related jobs in society. Then and only then can the humans have the time to learn advanced mathematics, astronomy, and engineering."

Vahisma understood. Oousma was attempting to mimic the history of the Annonaki they all read about. At a point, millions of years in the past, the Annonaki had been hunter-gatherers much like the humans currently were on Earth. They hunted animals, foraged for plants, and at that time, they reproduced sexually. They stayed in this state for hundreds of thousands of years until farming was invented, upon which a societal revolution occurred. The humans on Earth were still in the infancy of their evolutionary journey.

Issla stared at Oousma and Vahisma through the spaceship's glass window as it lifted off the ground. Zahmu and Mammadu were busy pushing buttons on the control panels. The ship slowly floated high into the desert air, with the Sun setting in the background. One moment the ship was there floating in the sky, the next moment, it was gone in a flash of light, and Oousma and Vahisma were all alone on Earth. The only device Oousma and Vahisma had from their home world was an emergency contact beacon that they could use to communicate with the Nirubu Space Command Center. Other than that, they were naked.

Oousma looked around the landscape for a place to shelter for the night. They needed no food - only sunlight, and water, which the Earth received plenty of. The atmosphere of the Earth was very similar to that of Nirubu, composed mostly of nitrogen and oxygen, so they could breathe, and there was enough carbon dioxide for them to photosynthesize. They did not need special space suits to survive on the planet Earth.

Vahisma spotted a small cave that they could use as shelter. The stars looked so different from Earth. Oousma was able to see and recognize stars it had seen on Nirubu in a completely different part of the sky on Earth. The Alpha Centauri system where Nirubu was located looked so far away in the night sky. The stars transfixed Oousma. They looked so beautiful on Earth. Oousma turned to Vahisma, who was also looking up at the sky.

"It is beautiful, isn't it?" Oousma asked Vahisma.

"Indeed, it is Oousma. The humans are lucky to inhabit such a majestic planet."

The first night was spent like many other nights, staring up at the stars pondering their meaning. Oousma realized the humans loved the stars as much as the Annonaki did. They created art and gods that mapped the stars, and they worshipped stellar events like eclipses. Oousma and Vahisma sat in on several rituals that were dedicated to specific stars. Oousma loved every minute of it, fascinated by the humans' ability to create and imagine things.

Oousma and Vahisma spent most of their time searching for wandering bands of humans to teach them and interact with them. Often, the humans were very interested in what Oousma and Vahisma would show them, but Oousma quickly learned that not all of the humans they encountered were open and friendly. In one particular instance, Vahisma demonstrated to a group of men the basic principles of a pulley system. Vahisma had the men tie a rope cord around a heavy boulder and lift it upwards using a series of pulleys. Two men were yanking down on the rope, which brought the large stone to a height well above their heads. Pleased with their effort, the men pulling the rope suddenly let go, dropping the boulder onto one of the men's legs, crushing them instantly. The accomplishment quickly turned to anger, and Oousma and Vahisma had to run for their lives as the men chased them off. They never saw the group again.

It was through interactions like these that Oousma hoped they could accelerate the human species technological development. The process was slow and frustrating, but over the course of several centuries, Oousma and Vahisma showed numerous groups of humans how to domesticate and farm plants, as well as how to build increasingly complex structures, some of which would last for millennia.

During these first several hundred years, Vahisma and Oousma built an airplane of their own to get around the Earth quickly. It was an electric-powered plane, drawing its energy from solar power. It was capable of flying at mach 3; much, much slower than the warp speed spaceship they had flown into Earth on, and slower than the satellites and robotic probes circling the Earth that were also solar-powered. However, it was sufficient enough to get around the Earth in a timely manner.

As the years wore on, Oousma became more weaved into the fabric of human history. Humans began building massive structures on their own, no doubt from the knowledge Oousma and Vahisma had passed on to their ancestors. Giant pyramids and obelisks were erected worldwide, and Oousma and Vahisma were featured in numerous paintings and artwork. As Oousma and Vahisma spent more time on Earth, Oousma felt its connection with the humans grow stronger to the point of compassion. Oousma had never experienced or seen what the humans called love, but it was beginning to understand it as time passed.

Oousma witnessed humans fighting and killing each other for biological mates. Oousma saw the way a mother looked at her newborn baby, and the way two humans would kiss each other and laugh. Oousma read about the Annonaki of the distant past and how they used to do similar things. They used to love, fight, and show emotions. In the current day and age, it was frowned upon for the Annonaki to show emotions, but from time to time, the primitive brain would override oneself, and an Annonaki might show its anger or dissatisfaction.

Observing and interacting with humans brought Oousma a deep sense of sorrow. Oousma wished a mother cared for it the way it saw mothers on Earth caring for their young. Oousma longed for the loving embrace of another Annonaki or human. It had lived 3,500 years of its life without experiencing love personally. Oousma wished it had been born a natural birth from a mother, instead of being born inside of a governmental laboratory. Oousma realized it wanted to be something it was not: human.

After a time, a new thought began emerging in Oousma's mind. Oousma not only wanted to live with the humans, but Oousma also wanted to sire human offspring. Oousma knew it could not share this thought with Vahisma. In the centuries they had spent on Earth, Vahisma became increasingly uninterested in humans. Vahisma told Oousma on multiple occasions that it wanted to go back to Nirubu as soon as possible, but Oousma convinced it not to contact the Space Command Center of Nirubu with the emergency beacon. Vahisma was enthusiastic about teaching the humans at first, but over time, Vahisma became disgusted with humanity.

"Our efforts are futile, Oousma. The humans will kill themselves before they have the technology to leave their planet. All of this energy we are spending teaching them is a waste of time."

Oousma understood where the disappointment was coming from. For hundreds of years, they had been traveling around the world, showing humans how to build things and work out difficult problems. Often, they would come back to a location they had visited previously, only to discover it had been deserted, with the knowledge they showed the humans lost in time.

To beings like Oousma and Vahisma, the humans seemed largely incapable of comprehending very complex subjects. Still, there were glimmers of hope Oousma found. A very small percentage of the humans they interacted with were clearly more inclined to learn about mathematics and sciences than the others. They would spend hours upon hours with the Annonaki, asking them question after question. It was these individuals who would go on to build the pyramids and other immense buildings sprouting up around Earth.

One day when Oousma and Vahisma were helping a group of humans build a dam, a message came in on the emergency receiver, the first one in 400 years. It was a message from the Council of Elders. Oousma and Vahisma dismissed themselves to hear the message uninterrupted. The emergency beacon was a small metal cube that could send signals many times faster than lightspeed. It beamed the signal to and from the Earth-orbiting satellites the Annonaki built, back to Nirubu. All Oousma and Vahisma had to do was touch it, and it would start playing the message as a hologram.

Oousma and Vahisma shared a look of concern when they looked at the cube, not knowing what to expect.

"It must be bad. Why else would the council send a message?"

Four hundred years had passed since they had contact with another Annonaki. A mere blink of an eye in the existence of an Annonaki, but dozens of generations for a human. Oousma's heart started beating faster as it reached for the cube. Upon touching the cube, it opened up like a flower, revealing a glowing green ball of energy, the message.

The glowing green sphere of energy turned into two spheres; the Earth, and the moon of the Earth. The hologram then zoomed out to the solar system, showing all eight planets, including the Sun. Soon, a small object appeared next to Neptune, and the hologram zoomed in on the object: an asteroid.

The hologram portrayed a rough size of the asteroid, 75 kilometers across and 60 kilometers in length. Its weight was estimated to be 250,000 kilograms—a truly gargantuan specimen. Green text flashed above the asteroid that read, "The Council of Elders in the highest court of Nirubu has issued this urgent message for Vahisma and Oousma, who are currently residing on Earth. A massive asteroid has been detected by our satellites at the Nirubu National Institute of Technology. Our experts believe the object has a 99.8% chance of hitting the Earth in approximately 150 Earth years. The force of the explosion is predicted to kill 75% of the land animals on Earth, including humans. A rescue ship will be sent to Earth when enough element 115 can be refined. The estimated time of arrival for the rescue ship is 125 years."

The text faded, and the hologram continued to display the graphic. The asteroid's path was heading straight for Earth. The hologram played in real-time, showing the planets' motion and the asteroid as it inched closer to Earth. When the asteroid got close to the Earth, the hologram zoomed in on the Earth, showing the continents and the seas. The asteroid made an impact in the northern hemisphere, near modern-day Greenland. A massive explosion shook the Earth, and the shock wave rippled through the mantle. After a moment, the hologram fizzled out, and the cube reformed its original shape.

Vahisma and Oousma sat beside one another silently for a time. Oousma felt a cold sensation in its heart, a feeling of despair. Oousma was not concerned for Vahisma and it; Oousma was worried for the humans. The human species was not technologically advanced enough to stop the extraterrestrial threat, let alone even know it existed. All the time, energy, and effort Oousma and Vahisma had put into helping the humans would be wasted if all the humans perished. Oousma's heart went out to Abraham; the little boy Oousma had grown fond of many years ago.

One day when Oousma and Vahisma were trying to teach a group of villagers in the Arabian Peninsula how to farm, a little boy approached them. He was only 4 or 5 years old and had big brown eyes. The other children were frightened by Oousma and Vahisma, sensing they were different, but not this little boy. When he first saw Oousma, he looked at Oousma with wide eyes, reaching to touch its face. His soft hands grabbed Oousma's small nose, and he rubbed Oousma's shiny head.

"My name is Abraham!" the little boy shouted. Oousma nodded and smiled, knowing the boy had given Oousma his name.

"He seems to be fond of you, Oousma," Vahisma said, watching the little boy.

Oousma had no vocal cords to speak, but pointed to its chest, then pointed to the stars, trying to get the message across that it was from the sky. The boy looked up at Oousma's finger, pointing to the stars. He stood up to Oousma's chest, and after a moment, he grabbed onto Oousma's torso, hugging it.

"My poppa says you two are gods. The other children are scared of you, but I'm not, even though you don't look like us."

Gods. Oousma was considered a god in many cultures around Earth, but when this little boy said it, it felt different. It felt more genuine, coming from a place of love, not fear. Oousma patted the little boy on the head, rubbing its hands through the boy's curly hair. He was such a beautiful little boy.

Oousma and Vahisma stayed in the village Abraham lived in for many years, teaching the people about mathematics and astronomy. It was the first village of humans they had encountered where the people had a written language. Oousma and Vahisma were able to decipher the language in several years' time, and as a result, they were able to directly communicate with the people of the village. Oousma was able to show them how advanced mathematics could be used to calculate accurate distances of stars in the night sky and why it was important to understand math as a language. The people worshipped Vahisma and Oousma, thinking they were the gods from the stars, who were put on Earth to teach them and show them new sciences. For hours a day, Oousma and the village leaders would write back and forth, and Abraham was always watching.

Abraham and Oousma's bond grew over time, and Oousma woke up one day, realizing it loved Abraham. The feeling was deep and powerful. A feeling of pure joy and elation would overcome Oousma when Abraham figured out a difficult problem or showed good moral character. Oousma cared for Abraham in a way that it had never experienced in all the years it had been alive. Abraham showed compassion and love for Oousma, and Oousma loved him for it.

Abraham trusted Oousma and confided in it whenever something was plaguing his mind as he got older. Oousma was always there to listen and guide him, even though he couldn't offer verbal advice. As time passed, Abraham grew and started his own family, and Oousma watched him care for his children. Observing Abraham grow from a small boy into the leader of his community gave Oousma a deep sense of accomplishment.

Abraham kept all of Oousma's writings and treated them like they were more valuable than gold. He would store them in secret places around his house, cherishing every conservation he had with Oousma. Vahisma was more interested in helping the humans of Arabia build things, but Oousma took an interest in the people, especially Abraham. Abraham was kind, smart, and compassionate. The bond between Oousma and Abraham was deeper than the connection Oousma had with any Annonaki, including Vahisma.

Oousma was present when the first of Abraham's children were born; Ishmael, and was there when his last child was born, Isaac. Abraham let Oousma hold his children when he needed rest. Oousma loved holding and playing with the babies. They were so helpless and innocent, their eyes filled with wonder. Oousma enjoyed making different facial expressions and watching the babies laugh. Their laughter was Oousma's favorite sound in the universe. It was so pure and happy.

Before Abraham died, he took Oousma aside and told Oousma he would dedicate a temple in Oousma's and Vahisma's honor. Oousma tried to refuse, but Abraham would hear none of it. He insisted time and time again that Oousma and Vahisma were gods, and a temple needed to be made in their honor. In the end, Oousma gave in and allowed Abraham to construct the first temple in Arabia. Abraham called it the Kaaba. The day Abraham died, Oousma went to the Kaaba and wept for hours. Abraham was the closest thing Oousma ever had to a son, and he had died.

It was Abraham who convinced Oousma that it wanted a child, a child of its own. The love Oousma developed for Abraham morphed into a plan. Oousma would return to the Earth and would have a child with a human. Not through sexual means, but through artificial insemination. It would take many years to gather enough element 115 to return to the Earth, but in the end, Oousma knew it would be coming back.

Exactly 25 years before the rescue ship was supposed to arrive, Vahisma and Oousma received a message on the emergency beacon. They were to meet the rescue party in the North American continent at approximately 33.3943°N and 104.5230°W. The message said the ship would arrive in the location exactly 72 hours after the beacon was received, 25 years ahead of schedule.

Vahisma and Oousma had made an unprecedented decision to stay and live on the Earth for hundreds of years. No Annonaki had ever lived on another planet away from Nirubu for this duration, but that was what compelled Oousma to do this. Oousma was a trailblazer in more ways than one. Oousma had never felt so alive as it did on Earth.

The Annonaki had been in existence for so long that life felt obsolete. Nobody had sex, and nobody loved one another - they just existed and persisted. Humans showed Oousma that the universe was full of mysteries, emotions, and life. For so long, the Annonaki separated themselves from their natural state that Oousma wondered if any remnants of the ancient Annonaki were left. Humans were in their natural state, unaltered by genetic means, and made naturally into the creatures they were.

As the hours grew closer to the rescue ship's arrival, Oousma and Vahisma huddled around a fire in the desert. The air was cold and brisk, a winter desert wind. The flickering flame illuminated the small green body of Vahisma. Large black almond eyes peered into the depths of the flames.

"What are you thinking about, Vahisma?"

"Many things, Oousma. Many things."

"I am going to miss it here on Earth. Humans have such a beautiful planet. It reminds me of what Nirubu looked like before the land was destroyed and poisoned," Oousma said, reminiscing on the past 500 years it had spent on Earth.

Nirubu, like Earth, had once been a flourishing ecosystem. Animals and plants dotted the landscape. The sky was blue, two suns hung in the heavens during the day, and three moons took their place during the night. As the Annonaki evolved, they began exploiting their environment, eventually causing the extinction of most of the animal and plant species on their planet. Through various world wars and environmental catastrophes, overpopulation included, Nirubu was now a wasteland. Oousma hoped the Earth would not suffer a similar fate. Oousma cared about the Earth and the humans living on it. Earth was Oousma's second home.

In the early hours of the morning, the time had arrived for Oousma and Vahisma to leave. A melancholic feeling passed over Oousma when it saw the metallic ship appear above it in the sky, in a brilliant flash of light.

The silver disc descended from the atmosphere, gently landing next to Vahisma and Oousma. The Sun was barely rising in the east, casting an orange-pink glow around the spaceship. The bottom opened, and a small ladder extended from the middle level, touching the ground inches in front of Oousma and Vahisma. Vahisma ascended the ladder first and disappeared into the spaceship. Before walking up the ladder, Oousma took one final look around the landscape. Cactus and weeds dotted the scenery, but it was beautiful. It was at this moment Oousma felt a deep sense of purpose it had never felt before. Oousma would return to Earth - return to the brilliant blue marble in a sea of black. Return to the humans it had come to love; return to the new planet Oousma considered home.

Chapter 14

---⋆---

Ramses

Fucking William Brakel. He had made Ramses' life a living hell since giving his interview on the X-Files Radio Station with George Knapp. The entire nation was talking about Roswell, it seemed. Every paper, every news station, and every human being was talking about it. The lid was blown off the whole thing.

To make matters worse, one of the aliens, the violent and unpredictable one, was on the brink of death. President Truman was calling him every day, questioning his judgment and decision making.

"What the hell are we going to do now, Ramses? I got the F.B.I. and the D.O.J. all over my ass. I got reporters asking me what happened in Roswell every day. I got private investigators and lawyers threatening to sue the United States government for conspiracy. How the fuck are we going to get out of this one?"

If only William Brakel had died when he was supposed to, none of this would be happening. Ramses assigned four groups of five agents to track down and capture William Brakel. His last known location was Las Vegas, Nevada, but Ramses suspected he would go back to Oklahoma at some point because his mother lived there. Ramses immediately ordered a unit to constantly surveil Valerie Brakel's house. He needed to catch the son of a bitch if he decided to pay his mom a visit.

Ramses was not sleeping at night from the sheer amount of stress he was under. Dark rings hung below his brown almond eyes. He was desperately trying to figure out how the alien spaceship worked and was slowly coming to one conclusion: he would have to let the sickly alien into the sunlight so it could stay alive and help them fix the spaceship. Ramses thought of the aliens as prisoners of war, and it made him sick bending to their requests, but he had no other choice.

It was February 14th, 1948, when Ramses called an emergency meeting with Barry and Nicolai. Ramses summoned them to his personal wartime counsel room, located directly on top of the secret underground facility. The room was gray and ovular in shape. A large circular table sat in the middle of the room. The only decoration was an American flag hung up on one of the walls.

It was 04:00 when Ramses summoned the scientists to the meeting. Barry waddled into the room wearing his spectacles and his white lab coat. Did he ever take that thing off? Ramses was not sure. Then Nicolai, long and lanky, walked in after Barry half asleep.

"Gentlemen. Please take a seat," Ramses said, pointing to two chairs directly opposite to him.

"I have arranged this meeting to discuss a change in plans. I have decided the best course of action to take with the aliens is to let them get enough sunlight to heal their injuries and come back to full health. Nicolai, I have read your reports about their ability to photosynthesize, and I am now convinced they are true. The data on the skin grafts show conclusively they rely on chlorophyll and photosynthesis to make the energy to live."

"This is not out of generosity, but out of necessity. It has been nearly eight months since they crash-landed in Roswell, and we have learned very little about the spaceship in that time. Specimen 2 has been writing to me more and explaining things in greater detail, but I still don't understand shit. If we believe what specimen 2 says, then we have to let its friend heal so it can repair the spaceship. However, in the event we let them out into the sun, and they try to escape in any fashion, using lethal force will be authorized. You two will not do anything to aid in their escape; do I make myself clear?"

Nicolai and Barry nodded in acknowledgment. With that, it was decided. The aliens would be allowed to get sunlight. The exact amount was not yet determined, but Ramses thought 15 minutes was a good number. Ramses wanted to keep the tightest lid on the existence of the aliens as possible, but the information was spreading in the facility. Since the aliens had been kept at Kirtland Air Force Base, scientists and military personnel had supposedly caught glimpses of the spaceship and perhaps the aliens themselves. Ramses heard the rumors through lieutenant colonels and first lieutenants. The only other military personnel who knew directly about the existence of the Roswell Program was Colonel Garcia.

Ramses tried to ensure Barry and Nicolai only came in at the quietest hours so as few people as possible would see them and what they were working on. Every time the conscious alien needed to be transported from lab 7 to lab 100, a heavy burlap sack was draped over the creature to conceal its identity, and armed N.S.A. agents were present. Ramses did not want any other personnel on base to know the existence of the aliens, but security forces working the camera systems had seen them taking the small alien out of the lab on a regular basis. The burlap sack helped conceal its identity, but from the cameras, you could tell the creature was much smaller than the average human. Ramses feared that the security forces – who had a reputation of tattletaling, had spilled the beans about the mysterious small person they were hiding in lab 7.

On one occasion, Ramses was walking into the main dining hall on the above-ground portion of Kirtland. He was rounding a corner into the main entryway of the hall when he overheard two men speaking.

"Yeah, I heard they got a kid from Germany as a prisoner of war in the underground base. Supposedly the kid is a super genius and is helping them build bombs."

"A kid? You're stupid as fuck Smitty. Ain't no way a damn kid can be a prisoner of war."

"Suck my balls, Sterling. You know Master Sergeant Welsh?"

"The one who operates the camera systems for the underground facility?"

"Yeah, that one."

"What about him?"

"He said that Airman Basic Salazar told him he'd seen the kid on one of the cameras that records the underground base. Apparently, only two scientists are allowed to meet with the kid. He says it's the same ones every time, and it's almost always in the middle of the night when nobody is in the facility."

"So, you're telling me he has actually seen the kid on the video playback system?"

"Well, not exactly. Salazar told Master Sergeant Welsh the kid is only moved out of its holding cell with a cloth over it."

"So how does he know it's a kid?"

"He said it's obvious from the video that whatever was under the sack was like 3 feet tall."

"No shit? That better be the kid of Jesus Christ himself, or else why would they have him?"

"Beats me."

It was at this moment Ramses walked around the corner and came into view of the two men. The two men basically fell over when Ramses walked past. They stumbled then stood at the position of attention. Ramses looked one up and down and sniffled at the other. It was not good that they knew about the existence of the alien, who they thought was a kid and that someone they knew had seen Barry and Nicolai transporting the alien. What else could they be talking about? They were not ranked officers, yet they were unknowingly talking about the most top-secret information in the United States government, even if they were misinformed. The problem was bigger than Ramses was aware of.

Eating in silence at the officer's table in the dining hall, Ramses thought over his options. He could figure out who Master Sergeant Welsh was, but that wouldn't do much; the information was already out on base. Ramses could order the security forces team to turn off the cameras to the underground facility when Nicolai and Barry needed to move the alien. That might work, but it would be a pain in the ass. The underground facility required top-secret clearance and above, so changing the security camera's operations would require a mountain of paperwork, and Ramses hated doing paperwork. The last option was to leave the aliens in lab 7 for the remainder of the Roswell Project, but that would be an extreme inconvenience and would result in the deaths of both the aliens.

Ramses instructed Nicolai and Barry to let the aliens out into the sunlight on February 26th. The plan was to fly the spaceship to a remote area in North America, where there would be nobody for miles, and let them out into the sunlight. Ramses' men from the N.S.A. would be present, as well as himself. They would all be armed, and Ramses briefed the men that if the aliens made a break for it, they should not hesitate to shoot them. It was still quite risky for them to move about during the day because the lab would be busy. They would inevitably walk past numerous scientists on the way to lab 100, increasing the chances of the secret getting out, but they had to take the risk. Another problem was one of the aliens was unconscious and could not walk, so it would need to be transported to lab 100 in some other way. It would be a pain, but if Ramses ordered all the scientists to stay on the cold side for 15 minutes, they could do it.

On February 21st, Ramses phoned Nicolai and Barry and told them to meet him in lab 100 at 12:00 sharp. Ramses made the journey from the outside world into the secret underground lab. He rode the unmarked black van into the Sandia mountainside, and navigated into the long dark tunnel. He was searched and asked to produce ID before entering the tunnel, and was cleared a few moments later. The drive was 20 minutes, with Ramses and the driver not exchanging a single word. As they approached the giant red door that protected the lab, Ramses thanked the driver who saluted him. The young driver was a slim black man, with a thick brow. Ramses saluted back as he opened the passenger door for him.

Again, Ramses was searched, and his ID was scanned under an ultraviolet flashlight.

"All clear," one of the security guards said, saluting Ramses as he walked past. The wheel and axle lock was rotated counterclockwise, and the giant red door slowly opened inwards towards the tunnel. Ramses walked into the extremely white laboratory, momentarily blinded as his eyes adjusted to the brightness. The red door closed loudly behind him as he made his way to lab 100. Only a few scientists were outside of their labs eating in the cafeteria on the cold side when Ramses walked in. Their tone quieted as they stared at the General.

Lab 100 was at the very end of the hot side, so it took Ramses a few minutes to walk the distance to the lab. He checked his watch; 11:55. He made it just in time. He slid one of the only three keys that fit into the lock on the deadbolt. He turned the handle and opened the door carefully, blocking the view of the lab from behind him, and shutting it behind himself as he walked in.

Barry and Nicolai were talking to each other when Ramses walked in.

"Gentlemen," Ramses said as he walked into the lab. "As you know, in five days' time, we will be letting the aliens out to get sunlight. I am going to brief you on the procedure we will follow and where we will be going."

"Time has run out, and the president is out of patience and is demanding new progress to be made regarding the spaceship. As such, we will be letting the aliens out into the sun. The date we have specified is February 26th, 1948. We will be departing from Kirtland Airforce Base at 13:00 local time. I have selected White Sands, New Mexico, to be the destination where we will go. Arrive at the lab at approximately 08:00 to prepare to move the aliens from lab 7 to lab 100. I will order all the scientists working in the labs to stay on the cold side from 12:45 to 13:00 on February 26th, to give us enough time to move the aliens without any peeping eyes. Two of my men will accompany us in the transport and ultimately the release of the aliens. I have contacted the local police in the area around White Sands to block the roads leading into it for several hours before and after our test. In the event that one or both of the aliens tries to escape, I have authorized my men to use lethal force on them. Any questions?"

Nicolai looked perplexed and scared at the same time. Barry nodded in stoic agreement. Neither one answered, so Ramses took that as a no.

"Good. Barry, leave us. Nicolai and I have some things to discuss."

"Yes, sir," Barry said, leaving lab 100 and shutting the door behind him.

"Do you have a girlfriend, Nicolai?"

"Uh, what?"

"I said, do you have a girlfriend? Yes or no?"

"Why do you--"

"Yes or no?"

"Yes, sir, I do."

"Very good, do you like seeing her?"

"I- I suppose I do. Yes, I like seeing her."

"And you want to see her again?"

Nicolai was silent for a moment, seeing where this was going. "Yes, sir, I would."

"Then you will do exactly as I say on this mission. No funny business, no asking questions, just obeying my orders. I am well aware you have been writing secret messages to specimen 2. If I sense that you have been compromised, I will kill you personally and blame it on an accident. No more girlfriend, no more family - no more nothing. Do I make myself clear?"

Nicolai gulped down fear before answering, "Ye- yes, sir."

"Good, you are dismissed. I will see you on the 26th."

Nicolai hurriedly left the room, almost tripping over himself to get out of the lab. Ramses didn't know if Nicolai had a girlfriend, and frankly, he didn't care. He needed Nicolai to fear him and grow uneasy in his presence, like the aliens. He had him where he wanted him. Ramses had been suspicious of Nicolai talking to the aliens when he was not authorized, and after catching him red-handed, he was on high alert. Ramses needed to make sure he was not helping the aliens forge a secret escape plan. Ramses had one of his men look through the trash cans of lab 7 after every time Nicolai or Barry were in there to make sure the secret exchanges stopped.

Ramses was alone in the lab with the metallic disc, a disc that traversed four lightyears to get to Earth. It sat in the middle of the lab, on top of the circular platform that raised it up and down. A large black tarp was draped over it, like a corpse in a mortuary.

He walked over to the ship and tore off the tarp, revealing the machine he had desperately been trying to figure out. The silver-gray disc was impeccable, not a single bolt or screw in sight, smooth as a baby's butt. How the hell did they build it? Surely they were from the same universe and had to abide by the known laws of physics, but it was such a mystery. Flying in the spaceship felt like a surreal dream. One moment you were one place, the next, you could be thousands of miles away without feeling like you moved an inch. Ramses did not believe Nicolai and Barry's hypotheses until he experienced them himself; there was nothing like the spaceship on Earth.

Thinking about the spaceship made his head spin. He sat down for a minute before exiting the lab. Many things needed to be done that day. He had to write a General's order to ensure the lab scientists would stay on the cold side of the lab for the given time period. He had to call several of his agents to inform them of what their mission would be on the 26th, and he needed to fill out top-secret paperwork to take the "prisoners of war" out of the facility. Every time they did a test flight or experiment that required the spaceship to fly out of the lab, a mountain of paperwork needed to be filed and given to the president for his ultimate approval.

Ramses knew it was risky to fly the spaceship to White Sands National Park, but there would be nobody there. The aliens had to be released soon, or else specimen 1 might die, and specimen 2 would stop cooperating if its friend died; at least that's what Ramses thought. Specimen 2 had dutifully followed the orders it was given every time after Ramses beat it into submission, but this mission was different. Its friend would be there with it. Ramses could only speculate what the temperament of specimen 1 would be if it was able to fully heal in the sunlight. This mission could either be a breakthrough in a process that had become stagnant, or it could prove to be a horrible mistake if the aliens were somehow able to escape. Dealing with one supremely intelligent being was dangerous; dealing with two was nightmarish.

Ramses wanted two of his agents from the N.S.A. to accompany them on the mission - one for each alien. He devised a plan to move the unconscious alien in the days leading up to February 26th; they would stuff it in a wooden box labeled top-secret in bright red letters, put it on a metal roller, and wheel it into lab 100. The aliens were very small, so they could easily stuff specimen 1 into a large wooden box. Specimen 1 was in a very fragile state, and Ramses hoped that the transport to lab 100 would not prove to be lethal, but he had no other choice. Wheeling the specimen on a gurney was too suspicious. Any personnel watching the video cameras would question why a dead body was being wheeled into lab 100, and an internal investigation might ensue. Ramses could not let that happen.

With the distinction top-secret on the wooden box, the video camera personnel would not be allowed to question its movement; it was above their clearance. All that was needed was an official document signed by himself, stating material had been moved from lab 7 to lab 100, and he had authorized it. Ramses already drafted the document; in the top-secret box, he said were, "parts of a German bombing plane to be transported to Los Alamos National Laboratories". Because he was the highest-ranking military official on the base, nobody would question the document's authenticity.

Ramses also needed to call president Truman to go over the plan he had. The last phone call got heated, so he tried to prepare himself. Very few men were the boss of Ramses Meddiah the III, but the President of the United States was one of them. Ramses made his way out of lab 100, out of the underground facility, through the checkpoints and guarded doors, and finally to the surface. He preferred to call the president from his private residence, away from distractions.

Ramses always had a military escort from the base to his home, both places being quite proximal to each other. He was the highest-ranking official in the United States Air Force and was an obvious target for attack. The military took every precaution to ensure his safety, even on such a short journey. Throughout the past, there were multiple assassination attempts on his life, from both Germany and Japan. One could never be too careful.

Ramses thanked the driver escorting him to his house as they arrived. He walked up to the small adobe military home, unlocked the deadbolt, and went inside. Several letters lay on the floor by the mail slot, all from the Department of Defense. The house was small and simple; Ramses never needed a mansion. His living room had a small red loveseat, two armchairs, and a radio. There were pictures of his mom and dad hanging on the walls around the house. Past the living room was a tiny kitchen with a single tubbed sink, a two-burner stove, and a refrigerator. Adjacent to the kitchen, connected by a short narrow hallway, was his room.

His room was painted a dull green color, and his king-sized bed sheets were a lighter shade of green. There was a pole extending on the bed frame, which formerly accommodated a cross, and a bible to match on the nightstand next to the bed. Both had been thrown away since the crash; Ramses was no longer a pious man.

Across from his bed was a dresser with a black rotary phone on it. Ramses sat down, then dialed the president's secretary.

A few rings went by before an answer, "Hello this is the Secretary for the President of the United States speaking. May I ask who is calling?"

"This is General Ramses. I need to speak to the president."

"Oh, yes, General Ramses. Hold for just one moment, please."

"Ramses, it's Truman here. Tell me you have good news."

"Well sir, I think it's time we take more drastic measures to get the results you are looking for."

"I don't like the sound of that. What do you mean?"

"We need to let them out, so to speak. According to the conscious alien, their species need sunlight to survive. This has also been confirmed by a skin biopsy that showed their skin cells contain chlorophyll, the pigment molecule that allows photosynthesis to occur in plants on Earth. One of them is on the brink of death and will probably die within the next week if it does not receive any sunlight."

"How can you be sure the conscious alien is not lying to you?"

"We cannot be 100% sure, sir, but it seems highly unlikely that it is. We are out of options at this point. According to the conscious alien, its friend knows how to fix the spaceship to its full capacity. Dr. Barry thinks by watching the alien fix the ship, we could get a better understanding of how it works, and possibly be able to reverse-engineer it finally."

"Didn't you say the spaceship was already better than anything on Earth?"

"Yes but--"

"Then why do we need to fix it? It doesn't sound broken to me."

"Sir, we believe the ship is able to fly from solar system to solar system and perhaps traverse the entire milky way galaxy. Possibly even between galaxies when it is fully functional."

"Hmm... I see. You are certain the ship has these capabilities?"

"The alien has not specifically stated it does, but my scientists think that it can. Based on observations and experiments, it is clear that the spaceship would be capable of faster than light travel if all three of the gravity amplifiers are in working condition. I have personally been to several of the flight tests, and believe me, sir, it is unlike anything you can imagine. The aliens have a totally different language than any on Earth, but during the flight tests, their display window appeared to show planets, solar systems, and galaxies, indicating three speeds and modes of travel."

"Yes I saw that in some of the reports you had sent me over the past eight months. Very well then, I grant you permission to take them out into the sunlight. But Ramses, I need to see some real progress after this. We need to have a working prototype by the end of the year, or else Congress will completely gut the budget for the Roswell Project."

"Yes, sir. I will take the proper precautions for the contained release of our specimens and get started on a prototype spaceship immediately. Good day to you."

Ramses hung up the phone feeling uneasy. There was no way they would have a working prototype that used the same propulsion system by the end of the year. It was too complicated and technologically advanced to be done in that time frame. According to the scientists and the alien, the engine contained an element not naturally found on Earth that was then modified on the atomic level to give it the special properties it had. Barry said it interacted with a mysterious type of energy called dark energy, something that had not even been detected by Earth scientists yet. Dark energy was only a fringe theory some theoretical physicists pontificated about. At the very least, he had presidential approval to move forward with his plans.

February 26th was still days away, so Ramses lit a cigar and retrieved the envelopes lying on his floor. There were three envelopes, all from the Department of Defense. He walked back over to his desk, where he opened the first of the envelopes and began reading the contents of the letter inside it.

The letter was from Brigadier General William Kipney out of Los Alamos, New Mexico. The letter discussed some disturbing news about the men they had assigned to watch numerous nuclear blasts at close range. Many had fallen ill from various ailments. 80% had been diagnosed with cancer, including bone, kidney, liver, and blood cancer within one year of watching the blasts. Out of 40 men who had observed a bomb blast from 2 kilometers away, 32 were either severely ill, dead, or experiencing mild symptoms like vomiting and fatigue on a regular basis. Kipney explained that the illnesses suffered by their men were irreversible and could affect their ability to have healthy kids in the future. Kipney said that some of the men were thinking of suing the United States Army if rightful damages were not paid out to them and their families. At the end of the letter, Kipney said he had sent a document containing the estimated cost of medical treatments and damages for all 32 affected by the blast.

Ramses put aside the letter and rubbed his eyes. He did not want to think about how much it would cost the Army to pay this out. He looked at the next envelope and opened it. This document was again from Brigadier General William Kipney. It was a document several pages long that listed the names of the men impacted by the radiation sickness, what their symptoms were, if they died or needed medical treatment, how many living family members they had, and finally, the estimated cost for treatment for each individual. The total cost for every person combined was almost $1,500,000, a huge sum of money to pay out to the soldiers and their families.

Ramses felt sorry for the men. They had only done what had been asked of them, and now most of them were sick or had already died. The Army was in a pickle; on the one hand, the soldiers deserved to get paid out their full amounts for the treatments they required. On the other hand, the Army would look terrible for putting their men's lives at risk when it was not necessary to do so. Ramses would have to contact the president to ask what he thought before he worked with the Generals of the Army to figure out a solution. If the press got a hold of the information, that would be a catastrophe.

Ramses moved the document out of the way and took a long puff of the cigar. Thick white smoke circled around his head as he opened the last envelope. It was his paycheck for the month. He quickly looked it over to make sure nothing appeared fishy, then set it down on top of the other documents. It was getting dark outside, and he needed to sleep. There was never a dull day as a five-star General of the United States Air Force, that was for sure.

The five days were filled with typical tedium. Ramses drafted the paperwork necessary to move the "prisoners" to lab 100, drafted the order for the entire underground lab facility to go on lockdown from 12:45 to 13:00 on February 26th, which would force the lab personnel to the cold side, and he filed the paperwork to back up another flight test. He also contacted local police agencies in the White Sands National Park area to make sure they would be prepared to close the roads leading into the park, so no unwanted visitors would see the spaceship flying around. He went into the underground facility multiple times to make sure the security forces guarding the facility knew the orders and how they were supposed to enforce them.

While he was down in the facility on one of the visits, he walked into lab 7 to find Barry and Nicolai prepping their end of the paperwork for the removal of the aliens. Nicolai was taking the daily biometric readings of the aliens, and Barry was filling out the paperwork necessary to transport the fake top-secret box that would be used to transfer the unconscious alien. They barely acknowledged Ramses as he approached the metal tables where the aliens lay strapped down.

"How do they look?" Ramses asked Nicolai.

"Not good, sir. Specimen 1 has been having erratic heartbeats all day, and it actually had a seizure of some sort today as well."

Ramses looked at the little greenish-yellow creature more closely. Its skin was now turning a deeper yellow color, and its mouth was splayed open with a blue tongue sticking out of one side. Spittle was dribbling down the side of its face. It was definitely looking worse than the last time Ramses had seen it.

"How much longer do you think it has? Will it make it to the 26th?"

"Honestly I don't know, sir. This is the first time I have seen it have a seizure, which surely is not a good sign. When they first arrived, I thought it would be dead in the first month, and here we are in month 8, with it barely clinging to life. It is still alive at the moment, so these creatures are resilient if nothing else."

That they were. They had no food the entire time they had been confined, yet here they were surviving. They only required tiny amounts of water, less than 1 liter a week. They figured this out by asking specimen 2 how much it needed to live, and whatever they gave specimen 2 they gave specimen 1 through an IV drip. There was something unnerving and unnatural about the creatures; they were able to survive in a way no animal on Earth could survive. It didn't seem possible.

Ramses woke up at 04:00 on February 26th, just like he did every day. He worked out and showered, dawned his military uniform, and made it to the dining hall before 08:00. After eating, he headed to the underground facility, where he finally arrived at lab 7 by 09:00. Nicolai was in the lab when he arrived. He was doing the daily biometric readings and closely examining specimen 1, who was still looking terrible. "Morning Nicolai. You ready for the mission today?"

"Yes, sir. I believe the aliens will be much healthier by the end of the mission. I think it was a good decision to let them out."

"We shall see. Where is Barry?"

"Lab 100, filling out some paperwork and examining the spaceship."

Ramses nodded. They still had several hours before they needed to transport the aliens. Ramses called the N.S.A. agents on the rotary phone in lab 7, and summoned them to the lab. They said they would be there by 10:00. Ramses walked out of lab 7 and walked to lab 100 to check on Barry and the spaceship before the agents arrived. Barry was going over the starting procedure when Ramses walked in.

"Good morning, sir, just prepping the necessary paperwork for the live test. Everything is looking good. We should be all ready to depart at 13:00."

"Very good, and the top-secret box we are transporting specimen 1 is where?"

"Over there in the corner," Barry said, pointing to the box off in one corner of the lab. Ramses walked over to the box and examined it to make sure there were no visible cracks or holes that somebody could peek through. Satisfied, he walked back over to Barry, holding the box.

"Barry, I'm going to wait outside of lab 7 for my agents. When they arrive, we just have to prep and check everything one more time, then wait until 12:45 to do the transfer."

"Yes, sir," Barry said as Ramses walked out of lab 7 and back down the long hallway to wait for his agents. He waited for 30 minutes and saw the two men in black enter from the cold side door and into the hot side. They walked several hundred feet and greeted Ramses by saluting him.

"Gentlemen," Ramses said, shaking their hands. They were both tall, slim, and white with shaved bald heads. They always wore the same black suits and sunglasses, to keep their identities concealed.

The group walked into lab 7 where they stayed for the next few hours, talking and filling out paperwork. At 12:30, it was time to get moving. Barry walked in right after 12:30 with the top-secret box and the metal roller, and he and Nicolai pulled the IV drip out of specimen 1. The now yellow alien lay limp on the table as they attempted to lift it up. They had the top-secret wooden box partially open, and Barry placed some soft blankets in there to make it less uncomfortable. Nicolai supported its head and shoulders, and Barry grabbed the legs. Together they gently lowered the alien into the box. Nicolai had to press its large head into its knees so it would completely fit. Barry picked up the lid and shut it.

The other alien had its head turned and was watching the ordeal. Ramses noticed this alien was starting to have a slight yellow tint to its skin as well, a bad sign.

"Unshackle that one and cover it up," Ramses ordered Nicolai and Barry. They quietly unlocked the wrist and ankle shackles. The alien blinked a few times, then looked around the room and at the top-secret box.

"Cover it," Ramses ordered again.

Nicolai fetched the heavy burlap sack they kept in lab 7. The alien knew the drill. It hopped off the metal table and stood staring up at Nicolai. They shared a glance, then Nicolai gently placed the sack over the alien. It looked like a little kid in a poorly made Halloween costume. The sack dragged on the floor, not showing the little green feet of the alien.

"All right. Is everybody ready? Let's move," Ramses said. Barry and Nicolai placed the wooden box on a metal roller, and the agents stood behind specimen 2, with Ramses guiding its path to the doorway with his hands. His hand was clasped completely around its shoulder girdle, and the tips of his fingers were touching its little chest. It never ceased to amaze Ramses just how small and delicate these creatures were.

The group walked out of lab 7, where the agents took over Ramses' role in guiding the alien down to lab 100. On the intercom system that played inside the facility, Ramses heard the security forces state his order.

"General Ramses has ordered all lab personnel to remain on the cold side of the lab from 12:45-13:00. I repeat, all personnel must remain on the cold side of the lab for 15 minutes, or they will risk punishment." Ramses saw a few scientists scurry out of their labs and walk past the group to the cold side. When Ramses was confident no other scientists were left on the hot side, they walked down to lab 100.

They made it to the lab by 12:50. Nicolai unlocked the door, and he and Barry pushed the metal roller into the lab first, before the agents followed with specimen 2 and Ramses behind them. Nicolai turned on the blinding lights and revealed the spaceship sitting on the center raising platform. The blue lights were on, indicating it was ready to be flown. Ramses locked the door behind them and ordered the sack to be removed from specimen 2.

"All right, listen up. Barry and Nicolai will go in first, followed by you guys and the aliens," Ramses said, pointing to the agents, "and finally, I will go in last."

"It is going to be extremely cramped inside the main cabin, but we can make it work. Under no circumstance should any of you press any buttons. Doing so could result in your termination."

Nicolai and Barry opened up the crate and pushed it near the spaceship. The ladder descended automatically, detecting movement, and gently touched the floor. The ladder was only 8 feet off the ground, so once Nicolai climbed up, Barry was easily able to pass him the unconscious alien who weighed 50 pounds. Nicolai reached down through the ladder opening and pulled the alien up by its shoulders. Ramses watched intensely, hoping they would not drop the alien. When all three of them disappeared into the main cabin, Ramses gave the signal for the N.S.A. agents to go up next. They ushered specimen 2 to the ladder, who climbed up rung by rung, using its little hands to do so. Ramses was last, and he was tall enough to reach straight to the top of the ladder and pull himself up into the cabin in one swift stroke.

Inside the spaceship, it was more crowded than he thought. Everybody shifted around to get as comfortable as possible in the cramped interior. Barry gave the alien the coordinates of White Sands, 32.7872° N, 106.3257° W, written on a piece of paper. The alien started punching the series of buttons that initiated the launch sequence of the spaceship.

Ramses was practically on his knees, and everyone else was huddled around the main cabin, squished and uncomfortable. Specimen 1 was splayed out on the floor, with enough space for it to lay down without touching anybody. Nicolai was looking at the alien closely.

The spaceship made a mechanical noise as the ladder ascended and folded up into the main cabin. Before they launched, Ramses thought about what was going to happen. He had no way of knowing how the aliens would react when they made it to White Sands. He was slightly fearful that they possessed secret powers like teleportation or incredible running speed. He tried hard to convince himself that this was ridiculous, but an inkling of doubt hung over his mind.

These creatures were different from any other creature that had walked the Earth. If they could truly heal and gain energy from the sun, that would make them more closely related to plants than animals. Nothing about them made sense. Ramses still had not figured out why they had come to Earth or why they crashed in New Mexico, of all places. Surely Washington D.C. was more interesting. Ramses had not been this nervous since he had watched his first atomic bomb explosion.

The spaceship turned on, and Ramses felt it leave the center platform, raising itself into the air. The bright interior white of the laboratory morphed into a sky of blue and endless amounts of white sand. They made it in less than 5 seconds by Ramses' calculations. There was nobody or anything around for miles. It was a perfectly clear February day. The local weather station forecasted the temperature would be between 55-60°F at 13:00.

"Lower the spaceship to ground level," Ramses ordered specimen 2. The alien pressed several buttons, and from the viewing window, Ramses could see the spaceship lowering itself slowly until a dull thud indicated it hit the ground. Even when it was on the ground, because of the disc shape, the ladder had to descend 6 feet from the main cabin so the occupants could safely get to the ground.

"Okay, everybody, get ready. Men, I want you to load up your pistols now and take the conscious alien outside first. One of you goes down the ladder first, followed by the alien, then the other agent." Ramses turned to Nicolai and Barry, then said, "I want you guys to come out last. I will follow my agents to the ground, and then you will pass me the alien from the cabin. You two will come out when the unconscious alien has been safely lowered to the ground."

The N.S.A. agents loaded up their guns, and one of the men started to descend the ladder. Ramses loaded his gun as the other agent descended the ladder. *The more guns, the better,* Ramses thought to himself. After the agents went down, specimen 2 descended the ladder. Ramses jumped straight through the opening and into the sand, particles of sand and dust flying everywhere as his 250-pound frame hit the earth. "Okay Barry and Nicolai, pass specimen 1 down to me," Ramses shouted as he readjusted his uniform. Barry and Nicolai grabbed the alien by each arm and slowly lowered it to the outstretched arms of Ramses, who grabbed the frail creature by the waist. When both aliens were safely on the ground, Ramses gave the go-ahead for Barry and Nicolai to come down.

The sun was high in the sky, beaming down on a cloudless day. Everyone looked ready. Ramses predicted the conscious alien would not change much, but he was not sure about specimen 1. As the group moved into the sun, Ramses watched specimen 1 intensely. Everyone in the group was silent, not sure what to expect. Specimen 1 looked weak and frail, laying on the sand. The bump on the side of its head was large and purple, with veins spreading out to the areas around it. Its skin was still a dull yellow color. For a moment, nothing happened.

Suddenly and visibly, the bump on the alien's head began to rapidly decrease in size. Its skin was slowly changing back to the light greenish-gray color it was originally when it arrived at the lab. The alien began breathing deeper, its little chest moving up and down in rhythm. The speed of change was astonishing; Ramses watched stunned. He heard Nicolai gasp as he noticed the change in the alien. Barry was busy scribbling down notes, the only one not taken aback by what he was witnessing. After 5 minutes, the bump on its head had completely disappeared, and its skin was now back to the hue it was originally. Specimen 1 made a coughing noise, then blinked its large black eyes open for the first time in months. Sunlight truly did heal the alien's wounds.

Chapter 15

Nicolai

Nicolai gazed at the alien in amazement. Moments earlier, it was on the verge of death, and here it was, silently standing 10 minutes later like nothing had happened. The alien was not aggressive, not hissing, just standing there. The biological machinery that allowed the metamorphosis was almost too perfect. A thought struck Nicolai. Did the aliens bio-engineer themselves to heal in this way? What he saw was unnatural. He could sense it. Ramses looked pale in the face like he had seen a ghost.

The two aliens were quietly looking at each other. They appeared to be communicating because, after several seconds, specimen 1 motioned for a pen and paper. The men in black had their guns drawn, pointed at the pair, one gun on each alien. Ramses looked at Barry and tersely said, "Pen and paper," pointing to his lab coat pocket.

"Yes, sir. Sorry," Barry stammered as he produced a different note pad than the one he had been taking notes on. He handed it to specimen 1.

The big black eyes of omnipotence stared down at the notepad as their creator wrote. Nicolai wanted to ask the creature so many questions when they got back to the lab. After a minute, the alien handed the tiny notepad back to Ramses.

Ramses snatched the notepad out of the alien's hands with ferocity. Both of the men in black cocked their guns, putting one in the chamber. Nicolai and Barry, along with the aliens, were looking at Ramses. Ramses scanned the notepad and finished with a frown. He ripped the piece of paper out of the notebook, then crumpled it up, and threw it at the alien's feet.

"Detain them," he growled at the men in black. The aliens turned to each other. A thought was shared, then they both got on their knees and put their hands behind their heads. The men in black tentatively put their guns away and produced plastic zip ties as they approached the aliens.

Their wrists were tied together behind their backs, and the aliens were made to walk.

The sun was higher in the sky, and the heat of the day could be felt. Nicolai wondered what the note said. He did not want to ask, so he said nothing.

"Sir, what are we going to do now?" Barry asked Ramses.

"We go back to the lab and restrain them in lab 7. We have a lot of work to do once we get back, so let's not waste any time. Men, you go into the spaceship first. When you get inside, you may undo the wrist ties around specimen 2, but not specimen 1. After they are up in the main cabin, all three of us," Ramses said, pointing to Nicolai and Barry, "will go up. We will fly straight into the lab like we always do."

The men in black immediately started walking the aliens over to the spaceship as Ramses gave the order. As they approached the spaceship, the ladder slowly extended from the main cabin to the ground. When it touched down, the agents ascended into the spaceship first, followed by the aliens who awkwardly climbed the ladder with their wrists tied, with the men in black helping them up. Ramses went up after them, then Barry, and lastly Nicolai followed. They were all squished together in the small confines of the spaceship.

"Undo the wrist ties for specimen 2," Ramses said as everyone shifted in the cabin to get more comfortable.

"Yes, sir," both men in black said robotically in unison.

The men in black scared Nicolai more than the aliens did. They seemed to not have souls, and they were all alike. They all looked the same and acted the same, and Nicolai was never briefed on what agency they came from or who they worked for. All he knew was Ramses controlled them. They only spoke when necessary; their presence was ominous.

Nicolai signed a non-disclosure agreement when he was hired by the Air Force that pertained to all his top-secret work. These men would sometimes come into the labs unannounced and want to inspect or observe what he was doing in regards to the spaceship or the aliens. He even caught them following him home on several occasions. As the spaceship started the launch sequence and the ladder folded into itself, Nicolai thought about how much he had learned in the eight months since the crash.

From a young age, Nicolai loved to learn, especially math and science. At 15, he built his own microscope to study protozoa in droplets of water. At 17, he built a telescope to watch comets and stare at the moon for countless hours at a time. He always wondered if a child on another planet was looking up at its moon, contemplating if intelligent life existed elsewhere in the universe. And now he knew; he was looking at beings far more intelligent than he could have imagined from the Alpha Centauri solar system.

Working with the aliens was surreal. It felt like a dream. When Nicolai was first briefed about the crash and the spaceship, he thought it was a joke. Reading over the briefing documents, they said things like, "faster than light spaceship, crashed from an unknown star system," he simply did not believe it. He thought it was some test the government put in place to weed out the coo coos. How wrong he had been. These creatures were from another world; their spaceship defied the laws of physics as scientists on Earth understood them. The way the alien healed from a fatal injury in a matter of minutes without any medical intervention was utterly unbelievable.

The white sand surrounding the spaceship morphed into the whiteness of lab 100 as the spaceship flew back into the lab. The lab was quiet. A dull thud indicated the spaceship had made contact with the center platform. Upon shutting down the launch sequence, the ladder door opened up, and the ladder extended 8 feet below to the floor.

"Nicolai and Barry, you go out first. Then you guys will follow with the aliens, and I will come out last," Ramses barked in the tight cabin. Nicolai was the first down the ladder, followed by Barry, the aliens, the agents, and finally Ramses. When everybody was out of the spaceship and several feet away, the ladder shortened back up, and the blue lights underneath the spaceship turned off.

"Okay, men, tie up the wrists of specimen 2 again and throw a sack over it. We need to get them to lab 7 as soon as possible." The men in black nodded, and one of them tied specimen 2's wrists behind its back for a second time. The other man in black grabbed the heavy burlap sack and threw it over specimen 2, and adjusted it so its feet would not be showing.

"As for specimen 1, it has to go back in the box," Ramses said, pointing to the top-secret box sitting on the floor. Barry lifted the box onto the metal roller and pushed it towards the group.

"Get in," Ramses said to specimen 1, who was looking at the wooden box. The alien looked back at Ramses for a moment, then calmly crouched into the open box, hugging its knees to its chest.

"Secure the lid Barry," Ramses ordered. Barry grabbed the top of the box and moved it into place. When Ramses was satisfied with everything, he gave the order for them to leave lab 100.

"I will lead the way to lab 7. Men, you will follow directly behind me with the specimens, and Barry and Nicolai will come last. Single file," Ramses ordered.

When the aliens were secured under the sacks, Ramses carefully opened up the side door to lab 100 and peered out to make sure nobody was nearby. When it was clear, he waved to his men, who quickly followed behind him, with Nicolai and Barry in tow. They walked in single file down the long hallway, one of the men in black pushing the top-secret box in front of him. Several scientists from the various labs peeked out of their labs to look at Ramses, but nobody paid much attention. They made it to lab 7 without incident, and Ramses unlocked the lab door and walked in first, followed by the rest of the entourage.

Nicolai was the last one to enter the quiet, bright lab. The bright lights took a second to get accustomed to. Nicolai realized he was sweating, despite the lab being cold. He had feared for his life the entire mission. He did not want to provoke Ramses in the slightest; Ramses was prepared to kill him if the circumstances permitted it.

Upon entering the lab, the men in black removed the sack off specimen 2. It blinked a few times, then turned to the top-secret box. "Untie its wrists and secure it," Ramses ordered the men in black. They undid the zip ties and pointed to the metal table. Specimen 2 quietly laid down on the table with its back to the metal surface in the crucifix position. The men in black shackled its wrists and ankles. When they finished and checked the shackles to make sure they were secure, one of the men said, "Specimen 2 secure, sir."

"Good. Now get specimen 1 out of the box and secure it," Ramses ordered the men in black. One of the agents opened up the box, and specimen 1 looked up with its big black eyes, like an insect in a jar. The other man in black helped it onto the ground, where he cut off the zip tie holding its wrists together. It walked over to the metal table and laid down in the crucifix position, already knowing what Ramses wanted. The agent shackled its wrists and ankles and checked to make sure they were secure.

"Specimen 1 secure, sir," one of the agents said.

"Very good. You two are dismissed," Ramses said, pointing to the agents. They nodded in acknowledgment and walked out of lab 7.

"Nicolai, will you get these creatures hooked up to a heart rate monitor and take their blood measurements? Tomorrow, if the aliens are still looking healthy and their blood work comes back normal, they will work. We will see if this alien can fix the ship."

"Yes, sir," Nicolai replied.

Barry appeared to be very excited about the prospect of fully fixing the spaceship, and he said, "We may finally be able to explore different planets in the solar system! The possibilities are endless. There are marvelous things to be discovered!"

That was a real and intriguing prospect. If the spaceship could travel outside of Earth's orbit, then Ramses would need proof. Maybe the aliens could take them to the moon or to Saturn. However, there was still a major problem.

None of their technology could be replicated. The engine, the propulsion system, the graphic displays, or the material the spaceship was made out of. The spaceship did not have any outlets or controls and no visible wiring. All the years Nicolai had spent studying and building things could never have prepared him for the spaceship. He and Barry were expected to build a working prototype in 4 months. They were about 1,000,000 years away from being able to rebuild any piece of the spaceship, by Nicolai's estimate.

"Well, gentlemen, I need to handle some different business, but I will see you two tomorrow at 05:00. Do not do anything stupid, and do not speak of what you have seen today. Before you leave for the day, give specimen 1 the math test. Understood?" And with that, Ramses left lab 7, shutting the door loudly behind him.

Nicolai turned to the aliens who were now facing each other on their respective tables. It was strange, but he could tell the difference between the two aliens. Specimen 2 was calmer and had a slower demeanor, and was several inches taller than the other. Specimen 1 made quicker movements and appeared more anxious. Maybe they did have feelings and emotions, after all.

Barry and Nicolai quietly set up the heart rate monitor machines and turned them on. The base heart rate was 115 beats per minute, and they were both sitting between 110-118, right in the normal range for their species. Nicolai took their blood pressure, and both came back at 170/130 mmHg, slightly higher than the average of 160/120. Nicolai assumed their blood pressures were higher because they were both under a high level of stress.

After checking each specimen's vital signs, Nicolai took two needles from a wall drawer and walked back to the aliens. He lightly tapped into specimen 2's forearm to reveal a vein. He stuck the needle into a vein, drawing 1 mL of blood. He repeated the process on both aliens and stored the blood samples in a box filled with dry ice, where it would stay until he processed it later.

The anatomy of the creatures was shockingly similar to humans, considering they were photosynthetic. Nicolai completely dissected the dead alien and cataloged every piece of its anatomy into a secret file archive that Ramses oversaw. They had a closed circulatory system, a four-chambered heart, and a bowl-shaped pelvis, allowing them to walk comfortably bipedally.

Ramses wanted Nicolai to perform additional mental evaluations on the newly conscious alien. One of the tests was a sheet of 20 math problems ranging from simple algebra to advanced calculus. Nicolai had given the exam to specimen 2 already, and specimen 2 aced it. Ramses wanted to know if specimen 1 stacked up to its comrade. Nicolai had an answer sheet to check the score.

"Barry, can you unshackle specimen 1's wrists? I am going to give it the mathematics exam we gave to specimen 2 all those months ago."

Barry nodded and fetched the key for the wrist shackles dangling by the lab 7 door. He came back and unshackled the wrists of specimen 1, who sat up and rubbed its wrists. "You must answer all the questions on this sheet I give you. Do you understand?" Nicolai asked the little alien. The alien nodded in response and took the sheet of paper and a pencil from Nicolai's hands.

Nicolai watched the alien scribble on the page. Its hand seemed to be moving incredibly fast, especially considering only hours before it had been comatose and near death. The little alien flew through the problems, finishing the 20-question test in 2 minutes. The same test took Nicolai, a Ph.D. holder in physics, an hour. Nicolai marked the time down at the bottom of the sheet, then looked over the answers.

The alien, like its comrade, had perfect handwriting, almost robotically good. The space in between the answers allowing room for problems to be worked out was blank. No train of thought or stepwise solving, just the answers. Normally humans, Nicolai included, had to use the empty space to write out the equations and the numbers necessary to solve the problems. The alien did not use the empty space, and had calculated the answers entirely in its head, including the advanced calculus problems. All the answers were correct. Nicolai double-checked just to make sure they were all right, and they were, in fact, all right.

"Barry, can you please restrain specimen 1 again? You're going to want to see this." Barry eyed Nicolai suspiciously, then pointed to the table, getting the alien's attention. It laid back down, spreading its arms out. Barry shackled the wrists of the alien again and turned to Nicolai. Nicolai showed Barry the page the alien had written on. Barry examined the page and then scratched his chin.

"So, it's smart. Just like the other alien."

"It's smart? Barry, it can do this complicated calculus in its head after being basically dead several hours ago. These aliens are nothing short of mathematical geniuses."

"This alien is not unique. They both have this capability. We must assume that they have a natural ability far greater than humans. It is impressive, yes, but less impressive because they both did it the same exact way."

Barry was right. They had given the other alien a similar but slightly different test and had gotten identical results. No calculations, just answers. Nicolai almost fell over when he saw specimen 2 do it the first time, but he was more prepared to handle the shock now.

"True, but the other alien had no significant brain damage. I mean, this one," Nicolai said, pointing to the newly awakened alien, "was practically a potato, and now it can do difficult math without breaking a sweat. The sun not only healed its body completely, but it also healed its brain damage too."

The more Nicolai learned about the aliens, the less he knew. Their biology didn't make any sense. Their ability to do advanced math in their heads didn't make sense. Their spaceship didn't make sense. No animal on Earth had the ability to photosynthesize for energy, but they did. No plant or tree was able to use the sun to heal a broken limb or branch in 10 minutes, but they could use the sun to heal a fatal wound in 10 minutes. To say these creatures were unique was an understatement; they were more godlike than animal-like.

"Yes, well, I will report back to Ramses that they are ready to work tomorrow. If the alien can do those problems that easily, let's hope it can fix the amplifier."

Nicolai hoped it could fix the amplifier too, otherwise, he might be fired. He had learned how to turn on the spaceship, put it into launch mode, and turn it off, but that was it. He couldn't plug in the map coordinates and fly to a destination, and he didn't know how to change its rate of speed.

Now that Specimen 1 was awake, it never took its eyes off of Nicolai, and it made him uneasy. He felt like the alien was probing him for a weakness. The other alien had a much gentler, less direct gaze that didn't bother him as much. It was impossible to tell if the aliens themselves had any weaknesses other than requiring sunlight occasionally. For the rest of the day, Nicolai did mundane tasks like cleaning the labs, checking to make sure all of his paperwork was in order, and submitting and finalizing the results of the biometric readings he had taken earlier.

The day turned to night, and Nicolai headed home at 21:00. He needed to get a good night's sleep before tomorrow; Ramses would be stressed out and anxious to see how specimen 1 would perform. He left through the massive red door protecting the secret underground facility. He rode through the dark tunnel and out of the Sandia mountains. From there, he was driven to his little apartment on Gibson Boulevard, just north of the base.

His apartment was a 200 square foot studio. The outside was painted a dark green and had a wooden front door, like all the other houses in the complex. It was a subsidized military housing, so all the houses had the same specifications and looked identical. After signing his contract with the Air Force, they had relocated him to this tiny house from his studies in California. Part of the contract he had agreed to was that he would not travel any farther than 5 miles from Kirtland Air Force Base. At the time, it seemed like not being able to go anywhere wasn't that bad; Albuquerque was boring as hell. In hindsight, he wished he would have tried to negotiate around this aspect of the contract, because in the months since working on the base, he developed a relationship with a local security forces girl named Jacqueline Chavez.

Nicolai first met her only weeks after the crash. She worked at the entrance gates of Kirtland Air Force Base, and she lived right next to him in the subsidized military homes. She was Hispanic, with beautiful black hair and brown eyes. After waving to her for many nights straight, he finally had the balls to go up to her door and ask her out to dinner. The rest was history; they had been dating ever since.

It bothered Jacqueline that Nicolai could never tell her what he was working on or why sometimes mysterious men in black suits stayed outside his home during all hours of the day and night. He wanted to tell her about the aliens, but he knew he couldn't, so he kept his work to himself. As of lately, he did not have much time for her because the work was ramping up. Especially now that specimen 1 was awake, he expected Ramses would order him to work endlessly until the spaceship was fixed. He thought about her as he walked into his house.

Inside his single-room home was a small kitchen, a bathroom, a living room, and a twin-sized bed next to a small wooden dresser. The kitchen contained a two-burner stovetop and a miniature refrigerator. A few pictures hung on the walls, all of them retired military generals, courtesy of the Air Force. Nicolai was not allowed to decorate his house because, at any moment, as stated in his contract, his position could be terminated. There was a bible sitting on the dresser next to his bed that he glanced at before brushing his teeth in the bathroom sink.

Nicolai grew up believing in God, the Christian God, but as he learned more about science, he started to question the biblical chronology and teachings. He remembered being in Sunday school, asking the teacher if Jesus knew the Earth was round and that the sun contained 99% of the mass in the solar system. Needless to say, he didn't last long in Sunday school. Now, after seeing the aliens and interacting with them, he was utterly convinced there was no god in the universe. If God had made humans in his image, then who made the aliens Nicolai was working with? He always envisioned aliens as being 7 feet tall and horribly grotesque and monstrous. These aliens were 3 feet tall and completely docile for the most part. They even looked very similar to humans in many ways.

There was a growing sense of guilt Nicolai felt since he started his work at Kirtland Air Force Base. He desperately wanted to call all of his friends and family and tell them about what he was working on, but he couldn't. He felt guilty because he thought that the general public had a right to know the human race was not alone in the universe. It was one of the most profound questions humans asked, "Are we alone?" Philosophers for thousands of years had debated and written about this very question, and Nicolai knew the answer.

Reading through the local paper, people had come up with all sorts of theories about what happened in Roswell on July 8th, 1947. People speculated about the crashed spaceship, some believing it was aliens, others believing it was a failed military experiment. The men in black drew as much attention as the crash itself. They had been seen hovering around Roswell by numerous people, but they never seemed to be part of an organization, and nobody could pin them down. Then there was the Heartley family.

Nicolai read about the murder of the Heartleys and listened to the press conference Ramses gave pertaining to the crash and their murders. It all seemed too coincidental to him. Ramses had a lie for everything. A lie for the men in black, a lie for the spaceship crash, and lies about the cover-up. When Nicolai learned of their deaths, he thought that Ramses definitely knew more about their deaths than he spoke about; he would not put it past Ramses to kill an innocent family to keep a government secret.

Nicolai contemplated quitting his job and going public about what he was working on at Kirtland, but decided against it. Ramses threatened his life on numerous occasions, so doing a public disclosure would be a death sentence. Nicolai did not trust Barry either. Barry was a man of few words, and Nicolai suspected Barry was informing Ramses about Nicolai's every move. There were times where Barry would leave the lab to "make a call," but Nicolai suspected he was reporting information to Ramses that he didn't want Nicolai to know about.

For how intimately Barry and Nicolai worked together, Nicolai knew almost nothing about him. He knew Barry had a doctorate in mechanical engineering, but other than that, he knew nothing about his personal life. Barry seemed to have deep knowledge of airplane propulsion systems and flight dynamics. Based on his extensive knowledge, he assumed Barry had been previously employed with a plane manufacturer or had been working on top-secret planes for the Air Force for some time.

Such was the nature of the job; fragmented and exclusionary. Nicolai had no friends in Albuquerque except Jacqueline, and even she didn't know what he did most hours of the week. Over the course of eight months since the spaceship crashed, Nicolai became more and more depressed. At first, his job was exciting, and Nicolai felt like he was on the cutting edge of science. But as time wore on, his days were filled with tedium and monotony, and he began to care for the aliens' wellbeing so much that it pained him to see them chained up in a lab. They were supremely intelligent beings who were treated like dogs.

That night, Nicolai went to sleep with a heavy heart. He had a dream about his work in the laboratory. In his dream, he was working in lab 100 with Ramses and the aliens. Ramses was yelling at one of the aliens to fix the spaceship faster. The alien turned to Nicolai and started hissing. The hissing alien began walking towards Nicolai, growing in size and towering over him. Suddenly the alien leaped dozens of feet and starting biting and clawing Nicolai's face. He shot up out of bed, drenched in sweat. The clock on his dresser read 03:30.

"Fuck. I guess it's time to get up," Nicolai said, rubbing the sleep from his eyes. 03:30 was only 1 hour before he was accustomed to waking up, so it wasn't that bad. The military made him wake up at all hours of the night to come into work, so he had made it a habit to wake up early every day.

He called the number of the driver who always picked him up and dropped him off on base. Ramses had given him the contact information of the driver, who was a Staff Sergeant named Larry. Any time Nicolai was summoned to work, he had to call the driver to escort him onto the base. Nicolai dialed the number on the rotary phone and heard it ring.

"Hey Larry, I'm ready to go."

"Aren't you a little early? They don't want you to be there until 05:00, or at least that's what Ramses told me yesterday."

"I know, I had trouble sleeping last night, and I'm anxious to start the day."

"Fair enough, I'm sure it won't be an issue. I'll be there in 15 minutes sharp."

Nicolai hung up the phone and headed to the kitchen. He opened up his small refrigerator and grabbed a banana. He was not hungry, but he knew it would be a long day. He might end up traveling across the universe, so the least he could do was eat something. A few minutes later, he heard honking from out front: Larry.

Nicolai dawned his lab coat, checked to make sure he had his badges and IDs in place, then headed out the front door. Outside sat the black 1943 Mercedes-Benz 770 Grober that picked him up every time. Larry was a middle-aged white man who had a receding hairline and deep blue eyes. He always wore his Air Force uniform, with the chevron of four stripes on his left arm. He had thin lips and a set of crooked teeth. He had been doing the same chauffeuring job for 20 years.

"Howdy, partner."

"Hey Larry, how are you doing today?"

"Oh, you know, same old, same old."

That was the extent of most of their conversations. Neither of them cared much for the other. They were only trying to do their jobs. For the next 15 minutes, they sat in silence as they passed through the Gibson gate and made the drive to the first security entrance to the underground laboratory. When they arrived, Larry stopped the car, got out, and opened the door for Nicolai.

"Thank you for the ride, sir," Nicolai said, shaking Larry's hand as he approached the security checkpoint.

"Not a problem. I will see you when you are out!" Larry said, driving off down the dirt road back to the main part of the base.

Nicolai walked forward where two guards stood on the outside of a metal barbed wire fence that guarded the tunnel entrance to the underground laboratory. He took his lab coat off and emptied his pockets. He was patted down by one guard while the other guard looked at his ID under an ultraviolet light. Both were young men, no older than Nicolai. After he was patted down and his ID scanned, he was cleared to proceed to the tunnel entrance.

On the other side of the metal barbed wire fence was a black van used to transport people to the inside of the mountain. A man in a military uniform, one Nicolai had not seen before, was waiting for him. His rank was Senior Master Sergeant, as indicated by the chevron of seven stripes on his left arm. The man opened the door without a word, and Nicolai said, "Thanks," as he got into the van. The driver nodded, then shut Nicolai's door.

The drive was quiet and dark. Nicolai was thinking about the aliens during the drive. Would the newly conscious alien help them fix the spaceship? Did it know anything different from the other alien, or was it all just a ploy so it could be healed? He would find out shortly. Nicolai was always more nervous and prone to mistakes when Ramses was around. Ramses watched Barry and Nicolai while they worked, like a vulture watching a dying animal.

After 20 minutes, a giant bright red door appeared around the last bend of the tunnel. They had arrived. The van stopped a few feet shy of where two armed security guards stood, both having the rank of Senior Airman. Nicolai got out of the van, walked over to the guards, and produced his ID. They made him take off his lab coat and empty his pockets, and he was patted down.

"All clear," one of the guards said, handing Nicolai his ID back. The other guard gave Nicolai his lab coat and the pencil and notebooks he stored in the lab coat pockets. They moved the giant bar into the unlocked position, and the large wheel and axle began turning, opening the door inwards towards the tunnel. A giant white laboratory greeted him, the entrance to the cold side of the laboratory. Nicolai walked past the guards and the red door, and into the open lab space on the cold side that led to the dining hall and bathrooms.

The entrance to the hot side of the facility was several dozen feet past the opening of the underground facility, near lab 2. He pushed open the large glass door to the hot side of the laboratory and walked through. He peered down the long wide hallway that led from lab 1 all the way down to lab 100, hundreds of yards away. He walked to lab 7 and unlocked the door. He was surprised to see Ramses, Barry, and two men in black standing in lab 7, hovering around the aliens strapped down on the metal tables. The two aliens lifted their large heads off the tables to look at Nicolai. "Our final guest has arrived. It looks like we will begin today's mission ahead of schedule."

Chapter 16

⌖

Will

The air was cold and pungent with the smell of pine trees. Dew had formed on the tips of plants and grass the night before. Will rolled out of his sleeping bag and headed towards the fire pit he had made. He lit a match and blew on the glowing embers until a small flame came to life. Smoke began to rise, and the fire started to grow. Birds were noisily chirping, and the sun was beginning to rise from the east, casting an orange glow on the mountain. If not for the circumstances, Will would have loved it up here.

After doing the interview with George Knapp in Las Vegas, Nevada, Will escaped to the Rocky Mountains, up near the Colorado/Wyoming border. His original plan was to live in the wilderness in Canada, but he ran out of gas, so he stopped near Wyoming instead. It was early March, and the mornings and nights were extremely cold. Before he left Las Vegas, he bought a heavy-duty tent and sleeping bag, a heavy jacket, hiking boots, several boxes of kindle, matches, a fishing rod, a collapsible pot, a compass, a map of the Rocky Mountains, and a utility knife.

After running out of gas, Will pulled over to the side of the highway in a discrete location that was hard to spot from the road. He left the stolen van and took only the back-packing gear, knowing he would never go back to the spot he left the van. He was a sitting duck driving around in that van. Ramses was looking for him, and he knew it. That was well over a month ago; Will had been back-packing in the wilderness ever since.

His beard was long and scraggly, a dark brown color. His muscles were visibly leaner from all the walking and physical labor. Each day started the same as the day before; he would wake up, make a fire, then spend most of the day foraging for food. He made snares and traps out of sticks and plants and fished whenever time allowed it. He collected water from streams and boiled it before drinking. He thought about his previous life often, and many nights he cried alone by the fire.

He knew this was a short-term solution at best. He was traveling slowly south, in search of warmer weather. There was the understanding that the authorities would find the van and conduct an investigation into its origins. It was only a matter of time before Ramses picked up on his trail and sent his men after him in the wilderness. The Rocky Mountains were huge and largely unpopulated, but occasionally Will spotted hikers and backpackers who passed by on worn trails.

Today, Will decided he would pack up his stuff and walk several miles south. He frequently changed his campsite location, so he was harder to track. This deep in the wilderness, it was almost impossible to tell if you were being followed or not, so Will's solution was to continuously move south.

Lugging around pounds of gear made you heavier and slower. It would take Will months to get far enough south to reach New Mexico. The monotony of life and lack of social interaction was wearing down his spirit. He had no one to talk to and no one to console with. Will found himself talking to himself more and more as his journey dragged on. He needed to know he still had a voice.

The mountains were a dull brown since it was winter when he arrived at the Rockies, but life still flourished around him. He came across more species of mushroom than he could count or keep track of. He avoided the most colorful mushrooms and ate the plain brown ones as he walked. Flowers of every color sprouted from fallen tree giants and bloomed in open fields, peeking out from the snow. The forest was far enough away from the highway that no cars could be heard driving past. The occasional plane would fly overhead, but other than that, Will was the only human for miles. He was walking an unbeaten path, a path that few humans had ever needed to walk on.

By midday, Will found a good spot to set up his tent. He estimated he had walked 5 miles south by the time he stopped. A sloping cave with a big enough entrance for him to stand upright in was his choice for camp. The cave was only a few hundred yards away, a dark opening quietly resting in the background of the forest. Will made it to the cave entrance and dropped his giant backpack that had all his tools. He made a makeshift torch out of sticks and used his matches to light it ablaze. He peered into the opening, making sure no bears or cougars were there waiting to eat him. The cave was small and only went back 20 feet. There were no animals except a small squirrel inside when he checked.

After checking the cave, Will set up his tent at the mouth of the cave and unrolled his sleeping bag inside of it when he was finished. Satisfied with his tent, Will took out the fishing rod he had strapped to his backpack. It was a long red pole with a spinning reel mechanism. He checked the line to make sure it was taut, then headed down the mountainside to a nearby creek.

When he got to the creek, he looked around for a good digging stick to dig up insects and worms for bait. He found a good sharp stick and started digging in the hard dirt near the creek. After digging near a dead tree, he found some maggots and two worms. He put one of the worms on the hook and cast out his line. He waited, watching the fishing line bobber travel down the ice-covered creek. He repeated the process for several minutes before he saw a fish curiously inspecting the worm under the water. Will waited until he felt the tug, then BAM, he yanked up hard on the fishing line, feeling the fish undulate to try to escape. Reeling in the line, he pulled out a sizeable brown trout. He walked over to the bank of the creek and gently undid the hook from the fish's mouth. When the hook was out, he smacked the head of the fish with a rock, killing it instantly.

He repeated the process until the sun was about to set over the western edge of the mountain ridge. By the end of the day, Will had caught four fish and thrown away a little baby. He gathered up all the fish and his fishing pole and walked back up to his campsite.

The day was near an end when Will had kindled a new fire and gutted the fish. He picked up a nearby stick and skewered the pieces of fish flesh, and held it above the flame. As the fish was cooking, the flames reminded him of Tom; Tom loved to cook pork, chicken, game meat, and fish on open fires. Will could almost hear his voice, "This here fish is the goddamn best fish in the southwest; you can put a dollar on that."

Will didn't even realize he was crying as he took the first bite of his cooked fish through tears. The warm flesh tasted amazing, but he was sad on the inside. So many memories he wished he could forget right now. "Fuck you, God," Will said through bites. Why did it have to be like this? Will never did anything wrong, so why was it fair for him to be punished? All he had now was time, time to think, and time to plot his revenge.

Will wanted nothing more than to watch Ramses suffer a painful death. He left Las Vegas for his own safety, but now it mattered little to him. He wanted to survive to see Ramses die. Heading south to New Mexico could serve a second purpose - separate from surviving the harsh mountain winter - and that was getting closer to Ramses. Will had been obsessing over Ramses since he started his journey in the wilderness. Each passing day the hate grew inside him and consumed him. Will would kill Ramses, or he would die trying. He didn't know where he was stationed, but he guessed it was Kirtland Air Force Base because it was the biggest military base in New Mexico.

With Ramses on his mind, Will put more logs on the fire and got ready for bed. At night the temperatures plummeted, so Will always kept the fire going and made sure to bundle up in his sleeping bag. Within minutes of laying down, he was fast asleep, exhausted from the 5-mile hike. He dreamed about the aliens again. He was looking out of his attic window at the Heartley's house. An ominous blue glow began filling up his room. The light became so intense that Will could barely open his eyes, then they appeared.

Three small human-like creatures were standing in the room with Will and pointing at him. "No! No! Stop! What do you want from me?" Will screamed in his dream. Will shot up in his sleeping bag, smacking his head on the top of the tent. "Fuck," he said, rubbing his eyes. He crawled to the front of the tent and unzipped it.

It was a cold and foggy morning, with the clouds blocking the light from the dawn sun. Will gathered his thoughts, then headed down to the creek to relieve himself and splash cold water on his face. He had many nightmares, and almost all of them involved the aliens. As he approached the creek, a deer drinking from the water bounded away, startled by Will's presence.

Will unzipped his pants and looked up at the sky. He wished he knew where the aliens came from. There were so many stars in the universe; it was hard to imagine that humans were alone, even before Will had seen the aliens. He often wondered what they were doing on the Heartley ranch last July. What was so interesting about a bunch of hicks trying to raise livestock and farm? There were thousands of other people doing the same thing across the country; why not them? Will had an infinite number of questions, and the only answer he knew was that he would never have any answers to his questions.

Hours turned into days in the freezing wilderness. Will was losing track of how many days had elapsed since coming into the mountains. His brown curly beard touched the middle of his chest. His eyebrows were beginning to form a unibrow; he observed this one morning while washing his face in a shallow pool of water. Worst of all, Will was horny - really fucking horny.

Wet dreams became a common occurrence, so he started masturbating to make them stop. He fantasized about girls from years past to climax, and then he would come back to his sad and lonely reality after climaxing. He did not want to admit to himself, but he had thought about catching an animal and raping it. But he decided that was madness and felt ashamed for even thinking about it. He was just so damn lonely.

The air was changing as the spring approached, and Will moved farther south. The sun was higher in the sky, and the days were warmer and drier. Will was now in mid-Colorado, indicated by a sign on a trailhead that stated he was 15 miles away from Mt. Elbert. Will was many miles away from the New Mexico border, and he guessed it was late March when he saw the sign. At this rate, Will would be back in New Mexico by May.

As Will walked farther south, he saw more and more people on trailheads. Most of the people took one look at him and hurried away. He looked dirty and homeless to those passing by, because he *was* dirty and homeless. Will was frightened by every encounter he had with another human, fearing that the next person would be one of the men in black. Despite seeing more people, the encounters were still few and far between. Will would sometimes go days without seeing or hearing another human.

The journey was slow because Will had no surplus of food. He would spend the mornings fishing and foraging and often had to stay put for several days to recover and gain enough energy to hike again. His feet had blisters that proved to be a constant annoyance. He had already hiked over 800 miles and had to walk hundreds more. As the days progressed, the blisters callused, leaving hard chunks of skin on his ankles and heels. Will also noticed the wildlife, and the scenery was gradually changing.

The mountain range was starting to thin out, and the air was becoming noticeably drier. Different species of plants and animals surrounded Will as he made his trek farther and farther south. Will was slowly closing in on New Mexico. His plan was to hike to the state line, walk to the nearest highway, and hitch-hike back to Albuquerque. Will knew that when he did cross the state line, there would be miles of desert between him and the highway. As he ventured further south, there were fewer trails to follow.

Cacti began springing up in the mountains around him. The trees were becoming less dense, and the creeks looked smaller than they did up north. The wildlife matched the desert environment; Will saw lizards and horned toads, and even spotted a pack of wolves in the distance once. Seeing the change in scenery and wildlife was invigorating for Will, but it reminded him of what lay ahead in New Mexico.

Seeing the cacti and reptiles brought Will back to Roswell, where everything started. There was blood in the Roswell soil, blood spilled by the hands of a military general and the government. Blood of the innocent who were murdered over an inconvenience. Will wanted revenge, *needed* revenge. Revenge provided the main motivation to keep walking. Will had one purpose left in his life: kill General Ramses.

After weeks of more hiking, Will was finally back in his home state. A trailhead Will had passed near Colorado and the New Mexico border indicated he had crossed over the state line several miles back. He could smell the pungent pine air. Large cumulus clouds hung in the sky around him. You could really smell the rain in New Mexico, a pleasant earthly scent. Minutes later, the rain was falling down in big hard droplets. Will found shelter underneath a tree and started setting up his tent and taking out the metal poles, when he heard a rattling noise.

He recognized the sound. It was a rattlesnake, one of the most venomous reptiles in the United States. By the sound of it, the snake was very close. He slowly scanned the ground for the snake, being careful not to move. Tangled brush and dead pine needles made the forest floor a dull brown, greenish color. Everything looked the same.

Inches away from the tent poles he had dropped, he spotted the snake, curled up rattling its tail. It was a light gray, brownish color, with visible diamond markings on its back. Its head was almost the size of his palm and had the distinctive triangular shape of a venomous snake. The rattle had at least eight rows on it, and the snake appeared to be around five feet long, indicating the snake was a mature adult.

"Easy there, girl," Will said while slowly backing away. He took two steps back, and his right foot got caught in a hole made by a tree root. His weight was already distributed to that leg, so he fell backward. The rattlesnake lunged at Will, startled by his movement. Will covered his face from instinct and adrenaline. He felt a sharp stabbing sensation in the flesh of his left forearm.

"Ah, fuck!" Will shouted as the snake slithered away into the brush. "Oh my god. Oh, Jesus. Holy shit. Ahhhh, it hurts so fucking baddd!!!" Will was gasping for breath on the cold, damp earth. Fire was emanating from his forearm, traveling up his arm through his veins. He could feel the venom working its way through his body. He broke out into a sweat despite the cold rain. His body was going into shock. Will turned his forearm over and saw two fang marks in the flesh of his forearm and a dark purple ring forming around the puncture wounds.

"I'm going to die. I'm going to die," Will began sobbing. This was it; this was the end of the road for William Brakel. Pain was coursing through his veins. He grimaced and ripped his foot out of the hole and pushed himself towards the base of the pine tree. Slumped against the tree, Will could barely think. He was feeling queasy and dizzy. The world was closing in around him. He puked, then passed out.

A bright light was shining in Will's eyes when he awoke. His jacket and jeans were covered in his dried vomit. His throat and mouth were completely parched. He needed to drink water badly. He tried to stand up but collapsed from the pain. His forearm where the snake bit him was turning a blackish-purple color. Suddenly, he had to throw up again. A nasty yellow liquid came from his mouth: stomach bile. The world started spinning around him. He frantically reached into his pack lying next to him for the canteen of water he carried. Gritting his teeth, Will grabbed the metal container, unscrewed the cap, and started drinking.

Water had never tasted so good. The can was a full liter, and Will downed the whole thing in less than a minute. After finishing the liter, he was still thirsty. The water made him feel significantly better, but he needed more. Birds were chirping in a tree nearby, oblivious to the suffering Will was enduring. "Well, I guess I better just wait it out," Will said to himself. Rattlesnakes were notorious in New Mexico. If you ever did get bit, then your best option was to go straight to the hospital. If you were stranded, you wanted to move as little as possible until help arrived, so the venom would not circulate through your body as quickly. Will knew a kid growing up named Cesar who was bitten by a rattlesnake, and three days later died from the bite.

Time was passing by agonizingly slowly. Will broke out into sweats several times and again became dehydrated. He was about 75 yards away from the creek, but it might as well have been 75 miles. He had to get more water and soon, or he would die. The sun was hanging over the western horizon, beating down on his head. Will only had a couple of hours left of sunlight before it would be pitch black again. He grabbed a nearby stick to bite down on for the pain and began crawling towards the creek. He was heavily favoring his right side; his left side was too weak. Standing and walking wasn't an option because he was too dizzy to maintain his balance.

Inch by inch, foot by foot, he came closer to the creek. The sun was now just above the mountain ridge, as the creek came into his sight. Bugs were crawling around the banks, letting off a symphony of noises. Will scooped up the creek water into his metal canister and drank. He drank a full liter, then laid down, bloated and exhausted. He forgot about the pain in his body and shut his eyes.

He felt a wet sensation on his left hand. He slowly opened his eyes and noticed his hand was in the creek. The moon and stars were out, and the night was clear. Will guessed he had passed out for a couple of hours. He couldn't see anything except for the stars and the creek, but the forest was alive with crickets and other nocturnal insects. Will did not feel so dizzy anymore. He slowly rose to his feet, tired from the effort. He needed to get back to his camp.

Step by step, he made it up the little hill where his tent and backpack were. When he reached his stuff, he slumped against the tree in exhaustion. Sleep overtook him in minutes. He woke up several hours later to a woodpecker pecking a tree nearby. Will heard his stomach grumble. It had been three days since he had last eaten, and he was ravenous. He grabbed his metal canister and fishing pole and walked back down to the creek. His left arm was still extremely sore and tender to the touch, but the pain was less excruciating than it had been. Will bent down to the stream and filled his canister. He took long, hard gulps until he was satisfied.

He had a few dead insects leftover from the days before the bite, so he carried those with him down to the creek to use for bait. He attached a dead cricket to the hook, threw out the line over the creek, and waited. The day became hot and muggy, and Will had to strip down to his underwear to remain comfortable in the sun. He caught two fish over the course of the day and planned on eating them both that night.

As the sun was setting, Will quickly snatched some branches and sticks for fire kindling and made his way back to his tent. He used several matches to get a decent flame going before he added more substantial branches to the fire. Once the flame was of adequate intensity, he quickly assembled his tent and gutted and cleaned the fish. He cooked them over the flame, his mouth watering as he smelled the cooked flesh.

Will scarfed down the fish flesh, barely breathing in between bites. Nothing had ever tasted so good in his life. A minute later, the fish was completely gone, and the bones picked clean. Will was still hungry, but he felt better. He started crying, not from sadness, but from happiness. After being bitten by the rattlesnake, Will was sure he was going to die. He was in agony for days with no one to help him. This warm food gave him comfort in a time where comfort was hard to find. Will stayed looking into the fire long after finishing the fish.

"Damn, what a life," Will said, peering into the flames. In the glow of the fire, he could see how filthy he was. Dirt and dried throw up covered his pants. Every inch of his exposed skin was a light brown from the dirt. His hair and beard were matted messes. Tomorrow he would bath in the creek. He needed it. He stripped down naked and ventured into his tent. The sleeping bag felt like a cloud as he laid down.

He slept good and hard and woke up at the first light of dawn the next day. As Will was coming to, he felt a sharp pain in his right calf. "What the fuck," Will cursed, unzipping the sleeping bag. He saw a wolf spider crawling around on the inside of his sleeping bag. "Little fucker," Will said while smashing the spider with a hammer fist. Two little red bumps protruded from the skin on his calf. At least the spider was not venomous, and the bite could do no real harm.

Will got out of his tent and grabbed his soiled clothing, then walked down to the creek. He scrubbed his pants and jacket in the water on a large rock until the dried vomit came off. After washing them, he set them out to dry in the sun. He plunged into the cold creek, fully immersing his body in the water. It was freezing cold and refreshing at the same time.

What should be his next move? Should he walk to the highway and try to hitch-hike back to Albuquerque, or should he stay a couple more days and build up his strength? He wanted to go, so hiking towards the highway seemed like the most logical plan. He was still hundreds of miles from Albuquerque, so walking there from where he was at could take several more weeks.

There was a risk of going to the highway and trying to hitch-hike. Ramses may have discovered the van and could have agents patrolling the major highways along the Rocky Mountains. Will decided he would stay one more day in the spot he was at, and then he would head southeast to the highway.

Will finished bathing, then went up to his campsite for the fishing rod. He grabbed the rod and a grasshopper he killed on his way back to his campsite. Back at the creek, he found a good digging stick and dug into the wet soil. After an hour of digging, he had five plump worms and the dead grasshopper to use for bait. He caught three fish by mid-afternoon and called it a day. The sun was still high in the sky when he made it back to his campsite.

He quickly started a fire and began cooking his catch. The smell of fish wafted in the air and brought saliva to his lips. Will took the fish off the skewer and started eating. The flesh was warm and moist, and tasted pleasant. A squirrel stood several feet away from the fire, hoping for some scraps. Will ate the fish, then used the rest of the day to prepare for his departure.

He packed up his fishing rod and his utility knife. He then wrapped the remaining meat from the fish in pine tree branches and stored it on the side of his backpack. He walked down to the river and filled his canister up, then walked back over to the fire, where he boiled the liter of water in the collapsible pan. He wanted to have clean water to walk with, so he took the extra step of boiling the creek water. The last thing he needed was to have diarrhea on the home stretch to the highway. The sun was beginning to set when he finished all his chores. Exhausted, he closed the opening to his tent and fell asleep quickly. He slept long and hard and woke up at first morning light.

Energized, Will was ready to set out for the highway. He broke down his tent and tied its storage bag to the bottom of his backpack. He compressed the sleeping bag into the size of his water canister and strapped it to the top of his backpack. He chugged some water, then began heading southeast to I-25. Will knew he would not make it there in a day, or several days, but eventually, he would run into the large interstate.

He walked and walked. By the end of the third day, his feet were sore, and his belly was empty. He had only eaten wild berries and the leftover fish since taking off for his journey, and he was too hungry to continue. He stopped for the night and planned on fishing in the morning. Will slept and woke up ravenous on the fourth day. He marched straight towards a tiny spring on the valley floor.

In the desert air, water was easy to smell and locate. The vegetation was the densest nearest to the water, and as the distance from the water increased, the plant life decreased. In 15 minutes, he reached a tiny spring, no more than 4 feet across and 3 feet deep. The water was crystal clear, and Will could see little fish swimming in it. None of the fish were big enough to eat. He scanned the river bed for movement and saw a turtle slowly moving on the bottom. It was dark green and had a light brown shell that was smooth.

Will leisurely walked closer to the turtle, being careful not to allow his shadow to be cast over it. The turtle was foraging the bottom, using its feet and head to dig up dirt and debris. Will quietly dropped the fishing rod on the side of the creek and crouched low, preparing to pounce on top of the turtle. When the moment felt right, he lunged at the turtle with his hands outstretched. His fingers grabbed the middle part of the turtle, and its legs began wildly kicking as Will pulled it out of the water. He smashed its head on a rock several times until it stopped moving. Blood and brains were leaking out into the river as Will carried the kill back to his campsite.

Back at his camp, Will used his utility knife to bash a crack into the shell, and he used his foot and hands to pull the plastron apart, revealing the fleshy belly of the turtle. He cut away as much meat as he could, leaving only the rib bones attached to the carapace and bits of the feet. He threw away the kidneys and the liver but kept the heart and brain, and the meat he was able to cut away. He started a fire, and several minutes later had a good flame. Fatty turtle meat seared on top of the flame from his collapsible pan. When the flesh was brown and crispy, he removed the pan from the flame and gorged himself on the delicacy. Within minutes all the meat had been devoured.

Will just wanted to relax the rest of the day to save up energy. He spent the day napping and collecting berries nearby. When the last light of the day was starting to fade, he prepared for bed. He was in the home stretch, according to his map. If his calculations were correct, he had to walk about 50 more miles to get to I-25. Even if he made it to the highway in one piece, there was no guarantee anybody would pick him up. Shit, he wouldn't pick himself up if he was driving by. The snake bite made him sick enough to lose several pounds he didn't need to lose. In the reflection of the creek, he looked haggard and gaunt.

Will slept through the night in dreamless slumber and awoke to the dawn light. It was a cool, crisp morning. He planned on walking nonstop for the next two days until he met up with the highway. He packed up his things and started off for the day again.

Will walked for the next two days, surviving on the berries he found and the budding fruit of cactus. As he got closer to the highway, he saw more and more trail signs, indicating he was entering a more traveled area. By the end of his twelfth day setting out for the highway, he heard the low rumbling of cars in the distance. He had made it.

He didn't reach the highway until the sun was down and the nighttime sky was out. He was exhausted and starving, but being this close to the highway gave him hope, so he persisted. Months had passed since Will talked to another human, so he was feeling apprehensive as he approached the highway.

He came down from the desert nearby and was in a shallow valley when he met up with the road. Excitement and fear gripped him as he stood on the highway holding up his thumb. Several cars passed him but paid him no mind. He stood there for several hours and was starting to lose hope. The chance of anyone giving him a ride in the middle of the night was slim to none. Just when he was about to call it quits and set up a tent for the night, a blue chevy pulled up to him, its headlights glowing brightly.

It was very dark, so Will could not see the driver from where he stood, except that it was a male with a white cowboy hat on. Will's heart skipped a beat as the driver rolled down his window and turned off his lights so that Will could fully see him. He was a middle-aged white man with white hair and brown eyes.

"Howdy, partner. Need a lift?" the man asked in a kind, rough voice.

Will tried to reply, but his voice was hoarse, and it cracked. "Yes," he finally managed to spit out.

"Where are you headed?"

"I need to go to Albuquerque."

"Well, you're in luck, partner, cause that's exactly where I'm heading right now. Throw your stuff in the back and hop in."

Will almost couldn't believe it. "Thank you, thank you so much," Will said as he threw his heavy backpack in the bed of the truck.

As Will hopped into the passenger side door, the driver looked him up and down and said, "Jesus, you look like shit. You been runnin from the cops?"

Will chuckled before replying, "Close, but not quite."

Chapter 17

Oousma

Oousma never realized how much it cared for Ishma until it woke up from its coma and recovered. The days since were filled with dialogue and planning. Connecting with another Annonaki made Oousma feel much saner and more whole. Ishma's recovery allowed them to plan their escape together.

"Oousma, we must trick Nicolai into letting us out without the armed men in black in here. You have built more trust with him than I have. We only need a few seconds."

Ishma was right. If Oousma or Ishma could manage to steal a screwdriver, they could break into any door and get to their ship. Oousma memorized the number of steps and the direction it faced when they walked to the room with their ship. With this information, Oousma would be able to tell which door they needed to break into specifically in order to fly away on the ship. The only problem was now that Ishma was awake, Ramses was taking new precautions. Any time either one of them was unshackled, an armed man in black had to be in the room.

"Our only option may be to kill the boy, or hope for a split-second lapse of judgment," Ishma said to Oousma on one occasion.

"No. I will not kill a human being, especially Nicolai. He is the only human who has shown us any type of kindness. We must wait for the humans to make a mistake."

"But Oousma, will you die like a dog? We are Annonaki. We are not human."

§

The comment brought Oousma back to the time it had first visited Earth. After fleeing the Earth to avoid the asteroid 12,500 years before the present, Oousma wanted nothing more than to return to Earth. Falling in love with the boy Abraham convinced Oousma that it was its destiny to raise a human/Annonaki child. Oousma fought with the Council of Elders to return to Earth, pleading with them that Earth was the most important planet in the universe other than Nirubu.

"Under no circumstance will we allow you to return to Earth. We have nearly exhausted our supply of element 115 rescuing you, Oousma. We must conserve it for dire circumstances, not for your own personal desires," Bousnu said. In Oousma's absence, Bousnu assumed the position of Supreme Chancellor on the Council of Elders, so it was ultimately Bousnu's decision whether or not they would vote on returning to Earth.

"But Bousnu, the Earth is greater than you could ever have imagined. There are fantastic beasts that roam the plains and jungles. The sky is blue and unpolluted. The oceans are endless and mysterious. Humans have built massive monuments and temples dedicated to their fictitious gods. They have developed sophisticated cultures and understandings of the world around them. They have the potential to be an interstellar species. They are the next Annonaki."

The great hall of the Annonaki was the chamber where the Council of Elders conversed. A perfectly flat, five-meter-long table made of black obsidian lay in the center of the room. A carving of a naked Annonaki figure decorated the table. Windows made of crystal silica, a rainbow of colors, bathed the group in a spectrum of light. Gold and amethyst bordered the windows, and the walls were made of quartz.

Bousnu shifted uncomfortably around the table and stared at Oousma. "We need to worry about our own survival. It is better to leave them alone. Maybe one day they will have the technology to visit us."

"I agree with Bousnu. You wasted 500 years on another planet. Our people were angry and worried about you, Oousma. You gave up your elected post as Supreme Chancellor to indulge in a fantasy on Earth. It appears you only want to go back for your own selfish reasons. Is visiting Earth again really beneficial for the average citizen of Nirubu?" Imaru had a point. Oousma wondered the same thing itself; was it just being selfish?

Oousma thought for a moment, then answered, "Earth has given me new hope for our universe. We are not the only intelligent beings in our star cluster, let alone our galaxy. The Annonaki have stood the test of time.

We have persisted for millions of years. For so long, we wondered if there was life elsewhere, and when we found life on Earth, we were excited. Our satellites and robots showed us a world teeming with life, much like the old Nirubu. We watched the humans evolve out of their infancy, from being cavemen to a species that could build villages and incredible monuments. I see humans as equal to us; their potential is limitless. It is the Annonaki's destiny to interact with and teach the humans what we know. There is no other way."

The council looked around at each other, contemplating Oousma's words. Bousnu was the first to break the silence. "How long will you stay this time? What tangible benefit could your visit provide? As you said, we already have satellites and robots observing the Earth as we speak. What can you see that they cannot?"

"Humans could be a new host for our DNA. Our species' survival ultimately depends upon passing our DNA down to the next generation. Since the rise of the Kuhan Empire, our numbers have decreased steadily. There used to be billions of Annonaki. Now there are only 100 million of us. We can only be created in labs now, and time is running out. There may come a time when the Annonaki ceases to exist. If we are able to form hybrids with humans, we can extend our genetic heritage for many more millennia to come. Our ultimate goal is to survive, and humans are our best chance at that."

The history of Nirubu was filled with plagues, wars, and tyrannical regimes. One plague, nicknamed the white death, killed 25% of the living population on Nirubu 580,000 years before the present, long after the backbone of modern medicine had been created. It was a bacterial agent originating from a small asteroid that impacted Nirubu near a populated city. No Annonaki had acquired immunity, and only when a powerful medicine was developed did some Annonaki live.

Tens of thousands of years later, the Kuhan Empire took over the planet, controlled by an evil Annonaki named Kuhani Abdullah. Massive world wars broke out, and some Annonaki were enslaved. Through the wars, nearly 70% of the Annonaki population was wiped out due to nuclear radiation from bombs. The Kuhan Empire controlled Nirubu in its entirety, until Oousma led a rebellion that eventually toppled the Kuhan Empire and established the current world order.

Oousma learned that life was valuable. All life. Size and intelligence did not determine the positive or negative effects a life form had on the whole.

"How do you purpose we go about creating human hybrids? We have no sex organs, and we are genetically incompatible with them," Bousnu said.

"If we are to make hybrids with the humans, there might be many problems. Meiosis leads to random combinations of genetic material. If plant DNA is allowed to recombine in a human host, it might kill them every time. We, as Annonaki, were able to splice our DNA with the DNA of local plants because we evolved from a common ancestor. Humans evolved on their own planet with their own plants, so Nirubu plant DNA and Annonaki DNA would be treated as a foreign invader and would ultimately lead to spontaneous abortion. I agree with your vision Oousma that we should find new genetic hosts for our species, but I think this will be much more complicated than you are making it out to be," Krishnu added.

"We can accomplish this through artificial insemination. We have the technology to insert some of our genetic information into a human egg. We will have to splice part of our genome with the genome of a human for it to work, but I am confident we can accomplish this. We engineered ourselves to become autotrophic, and all of our Annonaki babies are grown from stem cells. We can do it - we just need to try. I took thousands of blood and tissue samples from the humans on my first visit. This is enough DNA to run tens of thousands of genetic experiments."

Bousnu looked around the table at the other members of the council, clearly swayed by Oousma's words.

"All in favor of Oousma experimenting with human DNA, raise your hand."

The ten other members of the Council of Elders raised their hands in unison. Oousma felt triumphant. It looked like its dreams of going back to Earth were within reach.

"So, it has been decided. It will take several millennia to create sufficient element 115 to launch another mission to the Earth, but it will happen. Oousma, you and a team of our top geneticists will have to perfect your genetic hybridization procedure before I can approve of you traveling to the Earth and experimenting on humans. If you can convince the council and me that the procedure is safe, effective, and efficient, then I will approve of you going back to Earth."

Soudmo was staring at Oousma as Bousnu communicated its words. Soudmo always wore the garb of the Council of Elders - a purple hooded robe with gold and white string lacing around the waist and wrists, with a woven symbol of the new world order on its shoulder. A sword piercing a beating heart.

"Whose DNA are we going to use, Oousma? Surely not yours," Soudmo boomed.

Silence overtook the room as the council contemplated Soudmo's words. Oousma had a secret plan of using its own DNA, regardless of what the others wanted to do, but it didn't voice those thoughts out loud.

"I believe we should use a combination of all our DNA. Each council member could contribute an equal amount of genetic information." Oousma said it, but did not mean it. The statement was only meant to appease the council.

"What about the rest of the population? There is more genetic diversity in 100 million Annonaki than there is in the 12 members of the council. The DNA should come from a random selection out of the 100 million Annonaki," Arammus said, finally joining the conversation. Arammus was the youngest member of the council, born 450 years ago, while Oousma was on Earth. Arammus was elected to the council and replaced Cingua, who had died 75 years earlier, at the age of 18,590 years.

"Arammus has a point," Bousnu said.

"Indeed. My defense is this. Is the DNA in the general population distinct from our own? We all were born into the Kuhan breeding facilities, except for Arammus. The vast majority of the surviving population has the same or similar DNA to us. We all have the ability to live tens of thousands of years. We are the best of the Annonaki. We are the 12 members elected by our society to lead the Annonaki. Therefore, it should be the DNA of the council that is used," Oousma stated.

"We will put it to another vote. All in favor of using the council's DNA, raise your hands," Bousnu boomed. Six members, including Oousma and Bousnu raised their hands. "All in favor of using the DNA of the general population, chosen at random, raise your hands." Five members raised their hands.

The only member that did not raise a hand for either question was Olma, the oldest member of the council. Olma was beginning to die; its skin was saggy and wrinkled, and it slouched when it stood. Olma was

17,500 years old. The light green color of its skin was turning into a paler, more yellowish tone.

"Why have you chosen to abstain from voting, Olma?" Bousnu asked.

"I am not sure there is a correct answer. I agree with Oousma that we must ensure our species' survival, and humans could be the vessel that allows us to survive. Whose DNA we should use is not a question of biology; it is a question of politics. If we chose the DNA from the council, then are we saying our DNA is better or more exceptional than the DNA of the general population? The common folk may not take kindly to such a sentiment."

"Wise words as always, Olma. I cannot provide you with an answer that is satisfactory. I believe we should use our DNA, but that is my personal opinion," Oousma responded.

Olma scratched its chin and looked up to the sky, the two suns shining their light into the room. "Aye. I share your thoughts Oousma, but I don't know if that makes me cruel or unjust for my decision. I am as old as dirt, and pontificating on the possibilities hurts my head too much. I vote we use the DNA of the council members."

"Then it has been decided. We will use the DNA from the Council of Elders. Each of us will be required to provide 1/12th of our genome for the hybridization testing and experiments. Oousma will lead the research efforts," Bousnu declared.

Oousma was pleased with the votes, even if others in the council were not. Oousma's 500-year dream was one step closer to coming to life. Soon Ooumsa may have its own offspring, a genetic link to another living organism. Oousma was excited about the prospect of the future, a future with children from the Earth.

§

Ramses was getting more desperate to fix the spaceship. Day and night, he watched Ishma try to fix the central gravity amplifier with the tools available in the lab.

"I can't fix the amplifier with these tools, Oousma. I need a magnet powerful enough to move the gravitons in the gravity amplifier. The gravity wave's shape will be imperfect if we go faster than lightspeed, and that could be disastrous. The wave will collapse, leaving us stranded."

When Oousma wrote to Ramses about what Ishma told it, he ripped up the note violently. "You little bastards think you can fool me? I know you can fix it and operate it. It flies good enough around Earth even though it is broken. Why can't it leave Earth as is? Never mind that, just fucking fix the ship before I kill you both." Ramses seemed impossibly wide and tall as he stormed out of lab 100, leaving the aliens with Nicolai, Barry, and an armed man in black.

Ishma stopped its work and looked at Oousma. "I do not trust him, Oousma. He is not mentally stable; he could harm us at any given moment."

"That is why we must tread carefully, Ishma. One false step could mean death for the both of us."

The situation had only deteriorated since Ishma became conscious again. Ramses beat Ishma several times for failing to fix the spaceship immediately. Bruises and bumps dotted its flesh from the beatings. Ishma knew how to fix the spaceship, but it needed a large number of materials to construct a machine that could fix the ship's gravity amplifier. Ramses refused to buy the materials Ishma said they needed, and they ended up in this stalemate. Ramses kept claiming they had all the tools necessary to fix the spaceship, which was true if they were building or fixing a human-made airplane, but Sirius was not made by humans. Annonaki did not use nuts and bolts. Sirius was 3-D printed in a special laboratory on Nirubu, giving it the completed structure without having any visible earthly mechanical parts.

The exact specifications for every part were put into an advanced computer system capable of translating the codes into a physical object. Due to the lack of materials, the Nirubu world government could only produce one of the spaceships. The main source of power for the spaceship, element 115, had to be created separately.

Element 115 was a naturally occurring element on Nirubu, but when it was mined from deep within the ground, it was unstable. Nirubu's total mass was 1.25 times the mass of Earth, but despite its large size, only .0000000000001% of its total mass was the unstable element 115. To make it stable and usable, it needed to be reorganized from the atomic level by lasers. It was an extremely difficult and time-consuming process. Hundreds of thousands of years ago, the Annonaki discovered the useful properties of stable element 115, and since then, it had been mined extensively, leaving very little element 115 remaining in the current age. This was why missions to Earth and other interstellar missions were so few and far between. Special, powerful magnetic equipment built on Nirubu was required to fix the spaceships, and the Earth had no such equipment.

Time was running out for Ishma and Oousma. With each passing day, Ramses grew more volatile. Oousma and Ishma concluded they only had several more months to live before Ramses killed them. When would be the best time to attempt an escape? In the months since they had been at the facility, not a single second went by where they could have escaped. They were monitored like hawks, and now more so. Ramses was always lurking in the shadows, showing up to the labs at random times, questioning Oousma and Ishma, and beating Oousma and Ishma when he didn't like the answers they gave.

His men in black were ominously present in the labs at most times. Oousma sensed negative energy, almost unnatural energy from them - they did not feel entirely human. Oousma learned from his previous encounters with humans that all of them had strong emotions. It was a human characteristic. The men in black were so emotionless that they walked and breathed like robots. Oousma was certain they would kill Oousma and Ishma if Ramses ordered it. They were like his hunting dogs, except even hunting dogs had emotions and feelings.

After a long day trying to build a strong magnet out of the tools Ramses had given them, Ishma turned to Oousma.

"This will never work, Oousma. We need a magnet that is 100 million times stronger than this to move the gravitons into the correct alignment in the gravity amplifier. Building a magnet that strong from these materials is futile. I have been drawing the propulsion schematics for Barry to try to show him why we need much more powerful magnets. I think I can convince him to pressure Ramses into buying the materials we need to fix Sirius."

"And if Ramses keeps refusing to buy the materials you need to construct a magnet powerful enough to fix the spaceship?"

"Then we will die, Oousma. We need to fix the spaceship before we can escape. Right now, we can only go 10 percent the speed of light. It would take us hundreds of years to reach Nirubu, assuming we can successfully escape alive."

Oousma had been avoiding the idea of death since Ishma went into a coma. Thinking of death gave Oousma anxiety, preventing it from thinking clearly. Avoiding it became increasingly impossible, as the threats and beatings from Ramses loomed over them. Oousma had lived for so many years, it felt like time and life were infinite. Oousma was ancient by human and Annonaki standards, but it was not ready to die. Death was so final and absolute, it scared Oousma. Death brought pain; Oousma had lived long enough to experience eons of pain, especially after the humans killed its only son 1,916 years ago.

§

"Oousma, do you have the vials of the hybrid DNA?"

"Yes, Veezma. All 10,000 of them have been checked, labeled, and put into the system."

"Excellent. Vahisma, do our power levels look good from ground control?"

"Yes. The core is operating at 99.99%."

"We are prepped and ready for launch to Earth. All clear in hangar bay 1."

"All clear from ground control. Have a safe journey to Earth, Oousma, and Veezma."

"Thank you, Vahisma. We will see you in 50 years' time."

And with that, Oousma and Veezma were off. The hangar doors opened wide to reveal the light of the two suns in the Alpha Centauri star system. Veezma powered up Sirius and selected the interstellar setting. The control panel lit up as Veezma and Oousma selected the coordinates for Earth. The mission was simple; produce a viable Annonaki/human hybrid in the 50-year timespan the Council of Elders granted Oousma and Veezma. They had been trying for the past several millennia to create a living hybrid, but nearly all the attempts ended in failure, up until recently. Most of the inseminations resulted in genetic mutants that didn't survive long.

Slowly over the millennia, Oousma and Veezma and their team of molecular geneticists perfected the hybridization process. Embryos began to emerge with both human-like and Annonaki-like qualities. They were eventually able to produce hybrids that lived past the first trimester, then the second, and finally the third. The Annonaki genetically engineered themselves to develop at a greatly accelerated rate hundreds of thousands of years ago, so the most difficult part of the process was honing in on the life history of the hybrids. They wanted to produce a hybrid that looked and grew up like a human, but had the Annonaki DNA in its genome. They needed it to look and develop like a human so other humans would not grow suspicious, and still go on to mate with the hybrids to pass on its genetic information.

Finally, after countless years of research and development, they were able to produce offspring that looked and grew like humans, but still had some of the capabilities of the Annonaki, such as telekinesis and superior intelligence. One such hybrid named 4267 was able to solve calculus problems at the age of four years. Another hybrid named 6784 was able to communicate telekinetically with other Annonaki from a very young age.

When Oousma proved to the council they could produce viable offspring that met their specifications, the council approved the second live mission to Earth. That was where Oousma and Veezma were now. The journey to Earth was instantaneous. The hangar surroundings melted away into a giant blue ball in front of their display window. It had been 12,000 years since Oousma last visited the Earth. It was as Oousma remembered it. Oousma hoped some of the humans survived the asteroid impact that forced them to flee the Earth on the first mission.

"This is a beautiful planet, isn't it?" Oousma asked Veezma, who was staring at the Earth wide-eyed.

"It is Oousma. It looks so much more beautiful up close. The textbooks don't do it justice. There is so much blue and green. Earth is lush and teeming with life. What are they like, Oousma? I have only read about them from the studies you and Vahisma authored after your return to Nirubu."

"They are amazing and complex creatures. They are tall, some standing over 2 meters," Oousma could see the excitement in Veezma's young eyes. Veezma was young by Annonaki standards, only 9,550 years old, but it was very talented with genetic work. Oousma personally selected Veezma to lead the human hybridization trials on Earth.

"2 meters tall?! That's huge! Do they really believe that gods created the universe?"

"Some of them do, and others do not. Different peoples believe in different creation myths, but most of them do have a creation story. Some have many gods to explain the universe, and others only have one god."

"When Vahisma and I first visited the Earth 12,500 years ago, some of the humans thought we were gods. They saw us building flying machines and instruments to track the stars; it was beyond their comprehension.

They could not explain our presence, so some thought we were there to save them. Others thought we were enemies and attacked us every chance they got. We are approaching the ionosphere. Prepare for the landing sequence."

"Landing sequence engaged. Mediterranean Sea in view. Descent velocity is 2,000 kilometers per second. Coordinates 34.5531° N, 18.0480° E enabled. Making contact with the water in 5 seconds. 4 seconds. 3 seconds. 2 seconds. Landing successful, hover mode enabled."

Oousma felt the spaceship gently touch down on the surface of the sea, swaying back and forth with the current. The sun was high in the sky, casting a shimmer upon the water's surface. From where they landed, several people could be seen staring at them. There were fishermen fishing on the sea, clearly stunned by their presence.

"Veezma, enable the invisibility shield. We have company," Oousma said excitedly, realizing that humanity had not been completely wiped out by the asteroid.

"Invisibility shield enabled. When should we start the mission, Oousma?"

"We can start right away. We will need to fly around the settlements near here to pick out a good first host. We need a strong, healthy woman to increase the chance of survival. We will fly around and scan all the inhabitants of the area to see who is a good genetic match for us and who is the healthiest. If we detect a human with a genetic disorder or some other anomaly, then we must not use them."

"I see. So how will we know which specimen to use when the bad ones have been discarded?"

"There will be no perfect specimen; this is an imperfect world. We may need to choose several, but we will start with just one. Prepare to fly the spaceship to the east. Our radar has picked up a large active settlement, so we will head there first."

Veezma activated the control panel and selected the planetary speed setting. The spaceship rose in the air with a whooshing sound as it lifted from the water's surface. Veezma pressed in the coordinates of the settlement, 31.7683° N, 35.2137° E. In a few seconds, the settlement came rushing into view.

They were several hundred feet above the village, so they could easily observe the people going about their daily lives. It was cold out, evident by the clothing the humans were wearing. Most were wearing goat fur, and some were wearing hats as well. Shepherds walked through the streets, herding their flocks of sheep around people and buildings. Merchants were yelling at people passing by, trying to sell their spices and clothes. The village was alive and healthy, a good sign that they would find a specimen to inseminate.

Oousma was looking at the people below with wonder. Did they tell stories about the asteroid that smashed into the Earth all those years ago? Did they even know about it? This particular village had obviously survived the impact, and had even developed agriculture and the domestication of animals. A river from the sea ran through the small farming village where people could be seen bathing and drinking. Oousma directed the spaceship towards a small stable built of wood, with a yellow star painted on the roof.

"What do you think that building is Oousma?" Veezma asked excitedly.

"It is hard to say. It might be a structure related to one of their gods. Humans often associate astronomical events with a divine deity. A long time ago, our species thought the very same thing."

"I know, I have read about that in my history classes, but it is fascinating to see how these humans build and live and worship."

"Humans have an extraordinary ability to conceive abstract thoughts that hold their societies together."

"I cannot wait to meet them, Oousma. They are so intriguing!"

"We must be careful, Veezma. Humans are unpredictable and can turn violent when they feel threatened or frightened. They are physically much stronger than us Annonaki, so avoid physical confrontation at all costs. We are here to run our experiments, nothing more. It is hard not to get attached to them. Some of them love without restraint, so be cautious," Oousma finished, thinking about the little boy Abraham.

"We will need to get closer to the ground for our biometric tool to scan the inhabitants properly. I estimate there are 17,000 people at this settlement in total. We need to scan all of them for genetic abnormalities - their body fat, their age, and the amount of lean muscle mass they possess. Approximately 800-1,000 will be women of reproductive age. We will screen all the women more extensively and chose the best specimens to start our experiments. From those women we do choose, we need to select 1 to start with, and then move on from there."

Veezma nodded its head and pressed a series of buttons on the control panel, then responded, "Sirius is lowering to 10 meters above the ground surface. Turning on the 500-kilometer biometric scan tool."

A few moments later, a 3-D model of the surrounding area began to appear on the display window of the spaceship. With each second that passed, the image grew in detail, showing all the plants and their root systems, trees, bacteria, and fungi in the soil, the fish swimming in the river running through the village, and the people walking around the village. The image grew and grew until the entire local ecosystem and all the life contained in it appeared on the glass in front of them.

"Isolate the humans from the rest of the web," Oousma said to Veezma.

"Humans isolated," Veezma responded. The dense picture filled with the different species of plants and animals disappeared to a living image of the humans in the area. They were walking, talking, and going about their activities.

"Show the biometric values for all the female humans between the ages of 17-28," Oousma ordered. On the side of the moving images of the humans, a picture of their faces appeared in a different part of the window, with a description of their biomedical information, including their body fat, height, weight, age, and genetic abnormalities if they had any.

"Discard women above 30% body fat and below 18% body fat," Oousma ordered Veezma. Veezma pressed several buttons on the control panel, and more women disappeared from the side of the window. "Discard any women with a genetic abnormality or disease." Pictures of more women disappeared. They now had 250 women left, from the original 987 they had started with.

"Eliminate ages 18-21, and 25-28." The specimen pool dropped to only 75 women.

"What should we do now Oousma? The potential pool of specimens is dwindling."

"Sort the specimens by the number of recessive alleles. We want an individual who is as heterozygous as possible. We will eliminate the bottom 50% of the specimens."

Veezma punched in the parameters Oousma ordered, and 33 more women were eliminated. Only 34 women remained on the window. These were the best specimens to choose from. All they had to do was look at the pictures of the women and choose which one to start the artificial insemination process with.

Oousma was scanning the images until it found a woman near the top of the panel, indicating she had very high allelic diversity. She was 23 years old with a body fat of 22.8%. Her genetic profile indicated one of her parents was from Africa, and the other parent was from near where she was currently living. She had olive-colored skin with thick black hair. Her eyes looked hazel on the window. Oousma knew she would be the one to bear its child.

"Okay, specimen #3 is my choice for our first experiment. We need to find her and impregnate her with the sperm we have. We will use vial #1 for the procedure." They were supposed to choose a vial at random to make the experiment more valid, but Oousma did not care. Oousma had secretly inserted all of its DNA into vial #1, excluding the DNA of the council members. The rest of the vials contained Oousma's DNA, along with the 11 other council members. Oousma wanted the first hybrid to bear its DNA, and only its DNA.

"We are supposed to use a random vial Oousma. It is against protocol to select a specific vial," Veezma said, looking questioningly at Oousma.

"Yes, we are, but it will be easier if we go in numerical order."

Veezma looked at Oousma suspiciously, then nodded. Oousma outranked Veezma in the council, so he had no choice but to oblige. Oousma was reelected to the Supreme Chancellor position only 50 years before they departed to Earth for the second time, winning the popular election by a landslide. The Annonaki of Nirubu wanted Oousma to lead the next mission to Earth, and Oousma had campaigned on this specific promise. It reenergized the interest of the Annonaki in the Earth and the humans.

Veezma stood up and walked down to the lower level of the spaceship, where the vials were stored. There was an ultracold freezer next to the gravity amplifiers that housed the vials of human sperm, spliced with Annonaki DNA.

In the ultracold freezer were 10,000 1 milliliter vials of the human/ Annonaki sperm. Each vial was labeled with a number corresponding to its production. Vial #1 was produced first, vial #2 second, and so on. Oousma heard Veezma open up the freezer and take out the vial. Veezma walked back up the ladder and handed Oousma vial #1, with ice still sticking to the outside of the small tube.

Oousma's excitement was palpable. Oousma had not felt so alive for thousands of years.

"Excellent. Prepare the vial for the reverse tractor beam."

Sirius could do almost anything imaginable, including beaming up objects and beaming out objects from near the bottom of the ship. The power came from the power core. The spaceship was equipped with laser weapons and magnetic shield capabilities, and a tractor beam that could be operated in the forward or reverse direction.

The tractor beam required negative matter to be generated to create a pushing out effect. The effect allowed them to beam objects from the ship to a location of choice. To create the negative matter, a complex reaction was programmed through the computer that diverted the power from the power core to a small device at the bottom of the ship that could separate matter from negative matter. A substantial amount of element 115 was required to start the reverse tractor beam; 0.1% of the supply of element 115 was used every time the reverse tractor beam was started.

Veezma opened up the program on the ship's interface that could divert power to the reverse tractor beam. "Wait before you fully start the program, Veezma. We will need to fly directly over our target at a distance of fewer than 50 meters for the beam to work. We also need to disable the invisibility cloak because the beam cannot function if the invisibility cloak is on."

"So, the humans will be able to see what we are doing?"

"See? Yes. Understand and comprehend what is going on? No. Theoretically, they will be able to see our ship and a beam of light coming from it. The procedure itself will only last a few seconds. After we have confirmed one of her eggs has been inseminated, then we can turn the invisibility cloak back on. It is unlikely very many people will see our ship, and if they do, we will be out of sight within seconds. Locate the target, and plot the course for us to fly to her."

Veezma pressed the image of the young woman on the window and opened the ship's target tracking program. The three-dimensional view of the humans collapsed and showed only one blinking red light. "Target acquired. Target is 8.5 kilometers away. Estimated time of arrival is .00001 seconds."

Oousma gave Veezma the go-ahead to fly the ship to the target's location. The scene flashed from the village to a small wooden house, with no one around. Surrounding the small wooden house was open land filled with grazing sheep. Oousma looked down at the ground below but could not see any humans.

"Are you sure we are in the right spot?" Oousma asked Veezma.

"I think so. She is probably inside the house." This made things more difficult. Thick walls caused the tractor beam to suck up more energy from the power core.

"We have to wait until she comes outside. The tractor beam is less effective when it has to travel through walls. We want to make sure we have plenty of energy left to get back to Nirubu."

So, they waited, floating invisibly in the sky above the house. They waited several hours; the sun was beginning to hang low on the western horizon. With the light of the day nearly gone, the woman finally emerged from the house, completely oblivious to the spaceship floating silently above her. Oousma quickly grabbed the vial from where Veezma had set it down and placed it in a hole near the power core that led to the tractor beam machine.

"Drop the invisibility cloak and prepare to fire the beam," Oousma ordered Veezma. Oousma felt its hands get clammy as it nervously heard Veezma punching in the commands. Oousma would be the first Annonaki to have a child in 2,000,000 years. The moment was immense.

A shepherd with a cane in his hand, attending to the sheep in the field, walked towards the woman as she walked out of the house.

"Invisibility cloak disabled. Power successfully transferred to the tractor beam in the reverse direction. Vial 1 loaded and ready to be fired," Veezma said nervously.

At first, the pair of humans did not see the spaceship, but after a few seconds, the man pointed up, and the woman looked up startled. "Fire the tractor beam," Oousma said, staring at the pair of humans. Veezma pressed a red button on the control panel, and a green circular light appeared on the woman's belly.

"Sperm has entered the host and is successfully implanted into a healthy egg," Veezma said. The woman was slapping her stomach, clearly alarmed by the beam of light. The man was shouting and shaking his cane at the ship.

"Turn the tractor beam off, and turn on the invisibility cloak again," Oousma ordered. The woman was now running back inside her wooden house, scared by the ordeal. The man fell to his knees and raised his hands to the sky, dropping his cane.

"Tractor beam disabled, and invisibility cloak has been turned on. Fuel at 75%," Veezma said.

"Excellent, now we wait and watch."

"How long do we have to wait before we know if the fertilization was successful?"

"Nine Earth months. That is the standard gestation time period for humans."

"What will we do during that time?"

"We will wait and observe. We have 50 years before we need to head back to Nirubu. This is our first live experiment with a human being. We can mimic the fetal environment in the laboratory as best we can, but it is still is not the real thing. We do not want to start inseminating other females until we know how the first hybrid turns out. If all goes according to plan, we can use all 10,000 of our vials within one Earth year, then head back to Nirubu."

"Understood. Can we go down to the ground and interact with the humans to pass the time? I am very curious, and I want to meet them."

"Not at this time. Let us see how this village responds to our presence since it has now become known. I am assuming a few other humans saw the spaceship during the insemination process. We will see how they react, then we may go down and interact with the humans if I deem it safe."

For the remainder of the day, Oousma and Veezma talked about Nirubu, Earth, the Annonaki, and humans. By nightfall, something strange started happening at the small wooden house below. Villagers started congregating at the house and dropping off gifts. Some of the gifts were not very valuable, like food and clothes, but some of the villagers were bringing jewelry made of gold and silver and beautiful pieces of art. Veezma was typing a message to the Council of Elders, updating them on the mission, when it noticed the large group of people below.

"What are all those people doing at the house, Oousma?"

"I do not know Veezma. Your guess is as good as mine," but Oousma had an idea. When Oousma visited Earth 12,500 years before, the humans would often bring luxurious gifts to Oousma and Vahisma. The humans did this because they thought Oousma and Vahisma were gods incarnate. They tried to convince the humans that they were not gods, and they were biological organisms similar to them, but it never worked. Those who believed they were gods could not be convinced otherwise. In India, the peoples called the ship they built a Vehmana and formed a religion based on their visits. Abraham had constructed the first temple in Arabia in honor of Oousma and Vahisma. Oousma had a hunch that word spread through the village of a visitation by God.

§

"Can you pass me the plasma cutter, Oousma?" Ishma asked.

Oousma passed Ishma the device it built from spare parts around the lab. Ishma was attempting to build a housing chamber where giant superconducting magnets would be placed. The metal was from old plane parts that Ramses had allowed them to use. Ishma needed to build a donut-shaped housing to amplify the magnetic fields generated from the magnets. The idea was to remove the broken gravity amplifier and place it in the center of the doughnut, where the magnetic fields would converge and be the strongest. They needed a super-strong magnetic field to properly align the gravitons inside of the middle amplifier, so it would be in synchronization with the other two amplifiers. Ramses stood by in his Air Force uniform, closely watching Ishma's and Oousma's every move.

After several months of no substantial progress and convincing by Barry, Ramses finally agreed to purchase the materials necessary to fix the spaceship. The superconducting magnets had to be made at Los Alamos National Laboratories before they could be shipped. Ishma wrote instructions on how a lab with their capabilities could build the magnets, and drew the blueprints and diagrams for Ramses' workers to work on the metal housing for the magnets when Oousma and Ishma were not working on it. Oousma and Ishma were playing a deadly waiting game, and numerous times Ramses grew impatient and threw a temper tantrum.

Ramses understood the science on a basic level, but not on the intimate level Oousma and Ishma did. He did not have the foresight or understanding as to why Ishma was doing what it was doing, or why the incredibly expensive magnets needed to be built to fix the gravity amplifier. All he could see was Ishma not fixing Sirius.

The process of fixing the broken gravity amplifier was painstaking and slow. Ishma and Oousma had been building the doughnut-shaped housing for the superconductors for weeks, but only at night. They could not lift much weight on their own, so only small bits of the structure could be built at any one time. Whilst Oousma and Ishma were working on the doughnut structure; they were being tested physically as well.

Each day Nicolai and Barry would draw their blood and take their weights. They would then do some type of physical test in regards to their strength and conditioning. Some days they were made to lift weights. Other days they were made to do endurance runs on treadmills. The exercise and work were exhausting and demanding. Oousma remembered one particular exercise called the squat. Nicolai demonstrated how to perform the movement and asked Oousma to do the same. Oousma was so much weaker than Nicolai it was laughable. The Annonaki had deteriorated for millions of years due to their reliance on machines.

Long ago, like humans, the Annonaki used to build with their bodies. As their technology became more sophisticated, they used their bodies less and less, causing their muscles to shrink over generations. From skeletal specimens kept in museums, the trend was obvious. Taking these physical tests was a reminder that Oousma and Ishma were constrained by their biology like humans. If Oousma and Ishma were strong enough, they could fight their way to escape, but they were not.

After failing miserably during one strength assessment, Ishma sat down in disappointment.

"What is the point of traveling through the stars if we are so weak? We are helpless without our machines. We have doomed ourselves to be forever dependent on the machines that we have built."

As the days dragged on, Nicolai paid more interest in their health. "Are you feeling well? Are we working you too hard? Are you happy?"

The last question shocked Oousma. Why would this human care if Ishma or it was happy? Oousma had a eureka moment. The fact that Nicolai was even asking such questions spoke volumes. Nicolai genuinely cared about their wellbeing. Humans of the past showed compassion to Oousma, sometimes too much compassion. But this was the first indication that a human in the present day was capable of such feelings. This made the chance of escape more likely; the more emotionally involved humans were in something, the more likely they were to have a lapse in judgment. Ishma took notice of the questions as well.

"I can sense the boy's feelings are growing towards us, along with his trust. It is only a matter of time before he makes a mistake."

"Indeed. We need to be ready to capitalize on an opportunity when it presents itself. We will have only one chance of escape, and if we fail, we die."

§

"Veezma, it is almost time. Our specimen has been pregnant for 8 months and 20 days. She will deliver the baby any day now."

"Can we finally go down and meet the humans when the baby is born?"

"Yes. We need to be cautious however."

Oousma had been nervous for months. The baby was gestating normally according to their biometric readings. It had a healthy heart and lungs and was 7 pounds, just about the optimal size for delivery. Oousma and Veezma were keeping constant tabs on the mother. Every day they got new readings on her health and the health of the child. After a few months, they were able to determine the child would be a boy. Oousma had been alive for 14,053 years and had never been a parent. Oousma itself did not have parents. Oousma was born in a laboratory -like every other Annonaki of its time.

Oousma felt an enormous amount of responsibility to ensure the safety of the child, its child. It was developing deep feelings of affection for the unborn baby, despite not knowing it or meeting it yet. The baby and the mother were on Oousma's mind constantly. As the sun was setting on the 25th day of the 8th month of their specimen's pregnancy, she went into labor.

"Oousma, our biometric scanning tool is indicating her cervix is opening, and her water broke. Her heart rate is currently 110 beats per minute. The time is upon us."

"Fly the ship closer to the ground so we can see what happens more clearly. Prepare the medical instruments in case of emergency. Turn on the microphone as well so we can hear what is happening outside the ship."

Veezma followed the orders and flew the ship close to the wooden manger, where the woman and her male companion were. As the ship flew closer, Oousma could see more people huddled around the woman. In the manger next to her was a lamb resting its head on a stack of hay. The woman had sweat dripping from her face, and she was breathing heavily.

"Turn on the microphone," Oousma ordered Veezma.

Veezma pressed a button on the control panel, and abruptly the ship was flooded with noise.

"AHH!!! Ohhh, ohh!!! It hurts Joseph!!!"

"Keep breathing, Mary. Take my hand and squeeze it. Push! That's it! I can see its head!"

"Errrahhh!!!! Ohhhh!!! Ohhh!!!"

"Ahhhhh!!!!" and with a final push, the baby came out with a rush of blood and the placenta. One of the women assisting the birth cut the umbilical cord with a knife and smacked the baby's back.

"Waaaa!!!!" the baby screamed. It was the greatest sound Oousma had ever heard. Oousma's stomach began to feel light and fluttery, a feeling it had never felt before.

"Oh, Mary, look how beautiful he is! Bless this child, for he is the son of our Lord! He is the light of the world! What will you name this king of kings?"

"His name will be Jesus."

§

The day of the repair was upon them, and everybody was tense. Weeks of preparation led to this pivotal day when the gravity amplifier would be finally fixed. General Ramses was smoking cigarette after cigarette as men in military uniforms double-checked the transformers, wires, and superconducting magnets. "Right there. No, you idiot, lower it the other direction."

Oousma and Ishma could hear the men working from a walkie talkie Nicolai had placed in lab 7. They could hear the sound of a lighter lighting every 10 minutes; Ramses smoking another cigarette.

"When we fix the gravity amplifier, we can make it to Nirubu instantly with our current amount of element 115. We shouldn't get stuck in hyperspace, and if we do, we will be close enough to Nirubu for a rescue ship to come to save us."

"Then we may have to try to escape sooner than we planned. We will be of no use to Ramses once the ship is completely fixed. He might kill us immediately after it is fixed."

"I do not think so, Oousma. We are too valuable to be killed like animals. Ramses has already talked to us about working on secret military projects once our spaceship is fixed. If we try to run and escape, we will surely be killed. We must be patient. A mistake will come."

Oousma knew Ishma was right. Oousma was just scared because it didn't know what Ramses would do once the spaceship was fixed. All they could do was fix the spaceship and hope for the best. Oousma noticed Nicolai furiously scribbling down notes on a note pad as he listened to Ramses shouting commands at his men through the walkie talkie.

Sweat was dripping down his face onto the pen. He was concentrating intensely. Barry was running back and forth, gathering material that they needed in lab 100. The two humans were very preoccupied and stressed from the look of it.

Oousma was fully shackled while Ishma only had its ankles shackled. Ishma was helping Barry direct the movement of the magnets and their placement, even though Ishma was not in the lab where they were doing the repair. Ishma was also helping Barry finalize any last-minute adjustments that needed to be made to the wiring and the transformers. When Ishma told Barry they were ready for the repair, Barry called Ramses on the walkie talkie.

"Specimen 1 says we are ready, sir."

"Good. Everything appears to be ready to go in lab 100. The wires and transformers are good, and the superconducting magnets are all in place. Barry, I want you to come to lab 100 now. Tell Nicolai to run a biometric diagnostic on the specimens before he comes in."

"Roger that," Barry said, lowering the volume of the device. He turned to Nicolai, "I'll go into lab 100 right now."

"Make sure both the specimens are secure before you leave," Barry said, pointing to Oousma and Ishma. Barry shackled down Ishma's wrists before he left, leaving Nicolai alone with Ishma and Oousma.

"If I am killed, you must leave me and rescue yourself, Oousma. I am not 100% certain this will repair the spaceship."

"I trust your judgment Ishma. This is only a minor fix. You have done it many times before, with different equipment. I have confidence in you," Oousma responded, trying to quell the doubt in Ishma's mind.

Nicolai looked at Oousma and retrieved a note pad to write on. He unshackled Oousma's wrists and started writing. He finished quickly and passed the note pad back to Oousma.

"Are you happy?" the question asked.

Nicolai was looking at Oousma intensely as it responded with a one-word answer, "No."

"No," Nicolai said out loud. Nicolai scratched his chin, then wrote another question. "Do you wish to be free and leave this place?"

Why was Nicolai asking such questions? Oousma knew he could get in trouble for this. The questions Nicolai usually asked were related to science - hardly were any of them personal up until recently, but this felt different. Oousma was not sure how to respond immediately. Could Nicolai be trying to trick Oousma in some unforeseen way? This seemed unlikely, because Nicolai would gain little value from the question. Oousma decided to answer the question truthfully.

"Yes, I would like to be free."

Oousma passed the paper to Nicolai, who nodded. For an instant, the two looked at each other; one in a lab coat, the other naked on the table. Nicolai wrote down another response and passed the note pad back to Oousma.

"I care about you and your friend, and I would like to see you two free. I wanted to tell you, but it has been hard since Ramses has been monitoring us so closely. What he is doing to you two is not right, and it pains me to watch it."

Oousma's heart was pounding. Was this real? Oousma looked deep into the tired young face of Nicolai. Oousma sensed sincerity and urgency emanating from Nicolai. If he was deceiving Oousma, he was uncanny in his skill. Oousma picked up the notepad and wrote its response.

"You have been kind and compassionate to us from the beginning, and we are grateful for that. Thank you, Nicolai. My friend's name is Ishma, and my name is Oousma. Nice to meet you."

Chapter 18

---✦---

Ramses

Ramses was monitoring the activity of his scientists and specimens closely. The alien who had been revived two months before was now requesting 100,000 kilograms of superconducting magnets to fix the gravity amplifier.

"You have to be fucking kidding me. Barry estimates the cost could be as high as $50 million dollars. I have to go through congress to get approval on this," he told Nicolai, who passed on the alien's message to Ramses. That was four weeks ago. Ramses eventually caved from the pressure and asked congress for the money, who gave it to him reluctantly.

"Goddamn it, Ramses. This has already cost taxpayers $100 million dollars. Now you want $50 million more? This spaceship prototype of yours better suck my dick too," Senator Taft said during the budget hearing.

Another senator chimed in, "So you mean to tell me that we should give you $50 million dollars for a spaceship we can't even see? You blacked out all the relevant information. I need to know if this is worth the taxpayers' money or not."

"I can't disclose classified information to you, senator, you know that. What I can tell you is that the United States military is in possession of a spaceship with flying capabilities far beyond that of any other spaceship on Earth. My scientists have informed me this is the only way we can get the engine to its fullest capacity."

"What kind of engine do you fix with magnets, General? I know I fix my ford engine with oil, just like every other engine on the planet."

"This engine is unlike any other engine, Senator Stennis."

"Well, that's just great, isn't it, General? If you can't tell me what we are looking at, then I cannot give you my vote for the money. This money could be used to build schools, repair roadways, or provide electricity to rural America. For all I know, you could take this money and use it for a different purpose. I know how the military likes to use taxpayer money on black-box projects. We give you guys $10 million, and it vanishes into thin air without a trace."

The tone of his voice made Ramses angry. "Listen here, dumb fuck; I'm telling you we have advanced technology on our hands that could potentially dismantle the entire German and Japanese fleet with one ship. Have faith in the military - the same military that saved you from being a slave to the Nazi regime."

The hearings and budget committee meetings lasted for days, but congress eventually approved the $50 million-dollar budget expansion when the president joined the chorus with Ramses. Construction began immediately upon the Air Force receiving the money. Nearly one year after the spaceship crashed into Roswell, New Mexico, they were on the verge of fixing it. It was May 1st, 1948, when the construction officially began. Ramses ordered an entire squadron of men under his control to stop their current jobs and help build the huge structure. With guidance from the aliens, they were making slow progress.

Part of the issue was that Ramses did not allow the aliens to work alongside his men. During the day, his men worked based on the diagrams and blueprints the aliens had drawn. At night, Ramses, Nicolai, Barry, and the aliens went into lab 100 to check on the progress made that day and corrected any errors. According to the aliens, the placement and alignment of the magnets needed to be exactly precise; any small deviation would mean the repair would be impossible.

Ramses was coping with the stress of it all by smoking cigarettes and abusing the aliens. Any time he felt the aliens were not obeying his commands, or if they showed any slight confidence around him, he beat them within an inch of death. Sometimes he used his fists; other times, he would use a whip or some other form of torture. Inflicting pain on the aliens brought a sense of relief and satisfaction to him. Ramses read the medical notes from Nicolai on a daily basis: "Bruised right eye, swollen upper lip, shallow cuts to the back." All inflicted by Ramses to instill fear into the aliens.

Ramses began to resent the creatures more and more. They ruined his sense of self and destroyed his belief in God, and he blamed them for it. These aliens, these creatures were the closest things to God he knew, so he wanted to make them suffer. He felt immensely powerful whilst he was beating these gods into submission. In a way, it made him feel like a god.

While the construction of the giant superconducting magnets' housing was underway, Ramses was still trying to track down William Brakel. He had received word from a sheriff in Colorado that the van he had stolen was found near the highway on the Colorado/Wyoming border, close to the Rocky Mountains.

Ramses sent one of his secret agents and two Senior Airmen to try and find Will, but so far, they had no luck. Will might be somewhere in the wilderness, but Ramses had a hunch he was out, trying to find a place to live and hide. Ramses knew Will had not gone back to his home in Roswell, because he had a group of his men watching the Heartley house, and they had not seen him.

Ramses received calls and letters weekly from other military officers asking about the George Knapp interview Will had given. Ramses became so tired of the constant bombardment that he stopped responding to all of them, even inquiries from other generals. Will was as good as dead to Ramses, and if he was able to find him and capture him, he would be dead.

Ramses was also keeping a more watchful eye on Nicolai. He was certain Nicolai and the aliens had exchanged information they were not telling him. The thought of Nicolai helping the aliens escape kept Ramses up at night. On one occasion recently, Nicolai almost called one of the aliens by its name after Ramses asked him a question about it.

"Yes, sir, Oous-, uh specimen 2 has been securely locked down." Ramses pressed Nicolai for answers, but he wouldn't budge. "A slip of the tongue," was what Nicolai said that was. Ramses thought otherwise.

The aliens would not give Ramses their names to this day, even when they were being beaten. The defiance infuriated Ramses until one day, he finally gave up asking them for their names. In the end, it made little difference to Ramses other than he couldn't impose his will on them to change their minds.

Ramses was giving daily briefings to Truman since the second alien had woken up. He got chewed out by the president for the $50 million it would cost to build the superconducting magnets, even though he backed Ramses up against congress.

"$50 million dollars Ramses? Is this a fucking joke? What am I supposed to tell the American people? That we need $50 million dollars for you to play with magnets?"

"Mr. President, it is not just for show and tell. Believe me, we exhausted every other option regarding the repair of the spaceship. If we want that spaceship to function properly, we need to build these magnets."

"Jesus Ramses. $50 million dollars better get the job done, or else I'll be having a very different conversation with you in the next couple of months."

Lack of progress was frustrating for Ramses too, but he had a sliver of hope the aliens could repair the ship. Nicolai and Barry only knew how the ship worked theoretically, but they could not build it and repair it themselves. Many times, Ramses thought about firing one or both of them, but it would make everything more complicated. They had been with the spaceship and the aliens since the beginning. Training another team from scratch would take time and money, both of which Ramses did not have.

The aliens predicted the superconducting magnetic structure would be completed by the end of May. All other work and research on the ship were to be halted until the structure was fully built. It was assembled piece by piece in lab 100, the largest room in the underground facility. Forklifts and cranes were moving the pieces to and from the outside world, all while the spaceship was stored in the very corner of the lab, tucked under two security cloths to hide its appearance.

The giant superconducting magnets were another set of problems by themselves. They had to be stored in special metal containers so they wouldn't impact any of the electronics in the facility. One test ran by Nicolai indicated each magnet produced 100,000 Teslas worth of magnetism. They also needed to be kept at the coldest temperature possible, so their magnetic properties were at their peak strength. The aliens formulated a special liquid that kept the magnets at absolute zero. This liquid was part of the $50 million cost. Every week Ramses filled out purchase orders for scores of reagents the aliens requested.

How the aliens knew what to build, what to buy, and what to do was a complete mystery. Ramses never saw them doing any calculations by hand. They may as well have been pulling answers out of their asses. Ramses pressed them on everything, but they had an answer for it all, explaining in a detail that was nauseating. He also understood almost nothing about their technology, so he was completely reliant on them for accurate information. He witnessed the advanced capabilities of the spaceship firsthand, but he couldn't explain what he experienced.

Ramses had a secret plan that he told nobody about, including the president. He wanted to fix the spaceship, so he could visit the world the aliens came from. God had a house, and he wanted to go to the front door. Specimen 2 told Ramses that its home planet was in the Alpha Centauri solar system, the closest solar system to Earth. The spaceship was capable of going a significant percentage of the speed of light already, but it would take many years to get there with that rate of speed. With the spaceship fixed, Ramses believed it could travel faster than the speed of light at an almost unlimited speed, and get anywhere in the universe instantaneously. The clock was ticking.

The doughnut-shaped structure the aliens proposed was coming into its final form. You could tell what the final shape would be even though it was still missing several large pieces. Thick silver wires ringed around the structure. The aliens told Ramses they needed to generate a massive amount of electricity to create a strong enough magnetic field to fix the gravity amplifier. According to them, the machine needed two gigawatts of electrical power to achieve the magnetic field strength necessary to fix the amplifier.

"You're fucking kidding me. We'll black out three-fourths of the base once we turn the machine on," Ramses had argued to the aliens. But it was what it was. Ramses needed to make plans and notify personnel that a "planned" power outage would happen on May 31st, 1948, at 00:01.

"How long do we need to sustain the power?" Ramses asked the aliens. In their response, they estimated it would take 30 seconds. The procedure would take so much power that Ramses would have to force the Public Service Company of New Mexico to divert a large portion of the state's electrical output to Kirtland Air Force Base for 30 seconds. One good thing about being a five-star General was that actions like this were possible. The only person who had any type of authority over Ramses was the President of the United States. With his approval, Ramses was essentially immune from criminal charges. On May 15th, 1948, at 13:00, Ramses placed a call to the state's Director of Operations for the Public Service Company of New Mexico.

"Hello, this is Timothy Chavez, Director of Operations at PNM. May I ask who is calling?"

"Ramses Meddiah the III, General of the Air Force."

"Oh, uh, hello. How can I help you?"

"I need you to redirect two gigawatts of electrical power to Kirtland Air Force Base on May 31st, at 00:01 for 30 seconds."

"Is this a prank call? That is the power we distribute to all of Albuquerque, Santa Fe, and Las Cruces for an entire week. I can't do that; the board of directors would never approve. The power from our plants goes to hospitals, schools, and residential homes. Taking power away from this many people, even for a short time, would be catastrophic."

"You misunderstood me, Tim. I did not ask a question. I am speaking on behalf of the federal government. You will divert the power at the specified time with the amount I requested."

"And how will I explain the statewide power outage when it occurs?"

"Get creative."

"What if I deny your request?"

"I'll show up to your biggest power plant with 50 armed men. Do you understand?"

There was a long pause.

"I'll see what I can do."

Ramses was really prepared to raid the main power plant outside of Albuquerque if he had to. Fear of an orchestrated attack would probably persuade Timothy Chavez to divert the power, even if the board of directors did not want to.

The immense amount of power was only a small barrier to achieve a much bigger goal. The day after his call with Tim Chavez, he received a letter from the director, stating PNM would divert the power to Kirtland Air Force Base at the requested time. All the stars were lining up the way Ramses wanted them to. The giant doughnut cylinder was nearly complete. The magnets had been built and were ready to be shipped. The wiring for the cylinder had been laid out. For the first time in a long time, Ramses thought they were close to making actual progress, the progress that could help them decipher the secrets of the alien spaceship.

On May 27th, 1948, the doughnut structure's construction was completed. Ramses personally thanked all the men who helped build the structure. None of them knew why they built what they did, only that they were ordered to build it. The night the structure was completed, Ramses, Nicolai, and Barry looked over it.

It took up a substantial portion of lab 100, measuring 100 meters in diameter. Nicolai and Barry were in their lab coats, checking wires, bolts, and welds. The magnets were all set in place and ready for operation. Gaseous fog was slowly building up on the floor and dissipating as the machines the aliens designed to keep the magnets cool worked around the clock.

"Everything looks good to me, sir. No open wires, no partially welded plates. All the bolts are tight. I believe we are ready," Barry said while pushing his spectacles up his chubby face.

"Excellent. And Nicolai, what is your assessment?"

"Everything is in good condition. My only question is, where will we get the power necessary to operate the machine? The generator on base can only supply 750 megawatts of power."

Nicolai always had a fucking question. "Do not worry about that. I have it covered."

Nicolai looked like he wanted to ask another question, but thought otherwise.

"Now, we must prepare the structure to plug into the main power supply of the underground facility. Nicolai, you will be in charge of checking the wire set up. I have granted your card temporary access to the power module control panel."

Nicolai nodded and walked out of the room. "Barry, I want you to monitor the aliens closely for the next couple of days. Inform them that we are prepared to start the repair on schedule. And make sure you watch Nicolai closely; he's been acting fishy lately."

"Will do, sir," And with that, Barry left lab 100. Ramses was alone in the cavernous laboratory. The spaceship lay in the corner, covered by two tarps to disguise its shape and design. Ramses tore off both of the tarps, revealing the large silvery disc. He ran his hand along the perfectly smooth surface, imagining he was flying through space. Stars were flying by faster than he could count. A moment later, he was in the Alpha Centauri system, heading towards Nirubu.

He imagined the surface of Nirubu covered with great skyscrapers and huge buildings. Silver, gold, and diamonds lining the roadways and the building tops. This was the home of the gods. Goosebumps dotted his flesh as he let the images flood his mind. He never believed a world like this could exist, but the possibilities were endless, now that he knew humans were not alone. Only ten months ago, he thought the God of Abraham created the human race. Now he was three days away from being able to traverse the galaxy.

Ramses had to fill out an enormous amount of paperwork over the next three days. Some of it pertained to special permits he obtained from PNM; others were waivers for his workers moving the superconductors from Los Alamos to Kirtland Air Force Base. He was also keeping a close tab on Will.

He received a tip from a police chief in Albuquerque that Will or someone who matched his description was staying at a local motel. Ramses dispatched two crews to investigate the motel, but he knew it was too late. By the time they got there, he was nowhere to be found. Clearly, Will was on the move, but Ramses did not know where he was going.

News stations were asking Ramses to do interviews nonstop since Will's radio appearance. He either flat out ignored the requests or declined them, but the information was catching up to him. On May 28th, a story was published in the Albuquerque Journal about Ramses. It talked about the Roswell crash, the killings of the Heartley family, and eyewitness reports of strange men in black suits appearing around numerous parts of Roswell, immediately after the crash. The author of the article was a woman named Ann Reid. Ramses was infuriated after reading the article.

He picked up his phone in his above-ground office and dialed Colonel Garcia.

"Hello, this is Colonel Garcia speaking. May I ask who is calling?"

"Ramses."

"Oh, hello, sir. What are you calling about?"

"Did you read the article about me in the Albuquerque Journal?"

"Uh, yes, I did, sir."

"I need you to find the author who wrote that article and bring her to me today. That's an order."

"I, uh… yes, sir. I will call you when she has been located."

"Good. Tell nobody about my order, only the men you need to pick her up from wherever she is. Do not let them abuse her in any way while they deliver her to me, or I will have their asses."

"Yes, sir."

Ramses was sitting in his office, filling out paperwork. The office was on the third story of the Kirtland Air Force Command Center. He had a large oak desk that he filled out his paperwork on. His windows were big, and they opened up to the east, showcasing the Sandia Mountains. Pictures of Ramses shaking hands with world leaders and military generals hung on the walls. After several minutes, his phone rang.

"Ramses speaking, who is this?"

"Colonel Garcia, sir. My men have located Ann Reid. She will be on base in approximately 20 minutes. Security arrangements have been made to escort her directly to your office."

"Perfect. Thank you, Garcia. We will be in touch," Ramses said, hanging up the phone.

This meeting was different than any Ramses had ever had. He rarely met with the heads of media empires, let alone random journalists. He wanted to probe Ann Reid for information. Who were her informants? Where did she meet them? Her story was astonishingly detailed. She had eyewitness accounts that accurately described the blue light underneath the spaceship and the dimensions of the spaceship itself. One account came from someone who either witnessed the crash from a distance, or was on the scene right after it happened. Ramses needed to know who wasn't keeping their mouth shut.

Ramses had never met the woman, so he did not know what to expect. If he tried to dominate her, she might lock up into a shell and tell him nothing. If he was too gentle, she might think she could lie to him. Ramses decided he would have to play it by ear. He was pacing up and down in his office when he heard three knocks at his door.

"Come in," he said while standing straight up. The door opened, and two young security airmen and the reporter walked into the room. He towered over them. The men popped to attention, and one of them said, "Ms. Reid, sir."

"Thank you, gentlemen. You two are dismissed," Ramses said to the airmen as they shut the door.

"Good to meet you, Ms. Reid. Please take a seat," Ramses said, pointing to a black metal chair that sat across from his desk. The woman was short and fit. Her hair was jet black and pinned tightly into a bun. She looked Korean, with high cheekbones and light brown skin. Her mouth was small and delicate.

"Do you know why you are here, Ms. Reid?"

"I'm guessing it has to do with the article I wrote about in the Albuquerque Journal." Her voice was sharp and precise.

"Let me be frank, Ms. Reid. You need to tell me who your sources were. Some of the information in your article was top-secret. Releasing that information to the public is dangerous and felonious. Who were your main sources?"

"That is private information I cannot release to you, sir. I am legally allowed to keep my sources hidden for their own safety."

"Do you know who you are talking to?" Ramses asked, frustrated. The conversation was beginning to go south, and it just started. He needed to use a different tactic. Before she could respond, he said, "Look, I'm sorry. I'm just stressed out. How much are they paying you over at the Journal?"

She looked a little bewildered. "Umm, I'm not comfortable talking about how much I make. What does that have to do with what we are talking about?"

"Nothing really, I'm just curious. Have you ever seen $50,000 cash in person?"

"I- I never have, no. Where are you going with this?"

"I will give you $50,000 in cash if you give me your sources." Her eyes lit up at the idea of money.

"I can't do that. I told you, all the eyewitnesses' information is private. I will not disclose their information."

"$50,000 is more than you will make in 10 years, that's what I'll bet. You may never have to write another article again if you invest it properly." Ramses had seen money corrupt the greatest of men. Nobody was immune to its clinching grip; everybody had a price. He just had to find hers.

She looked down at her feet, then said, "Okay, but I'm not signing any contract, right? When will I get the money?"

"No, this is under the table. I can have it delivered to your front door tomorrow. Now, what are their names?"

She thought about it again, then asked, "Isn't this illegal?"

"Oh, it is. But this is the military, sweetie. We can do whatever the fuck we want when we want. All you have to do is tell me their names."

She nodded in agreement, then began spilling the beans. After half an hour, Ramses had the names of eight of her sources. Five of them were men in the Roswell police department, and the other three were neighbors who lived close to the Heartleys. Once the ship was repaired, Ramses would pay every one of the informants a visit. Ramses had $500,000 cash stowed away under his bed, so paying the journalist would not be a problem. After she had given the names of all her informants, Ramses thanked her and called the Colonel again.

"Colonel Garcia here."

"Garcia, it's Ramses. Ms. Reid is ready to be escorted off the base. She did a wonderful job today. Tell your men to buy her some lunch."

"Yes, sir, I will send my men to pick her up right away."

Ten minutes later, the same two men who had dropped her off earlier came by again and escorted her out of Ramses' office. Ramses lit a cigar and prepared to go meet Nicolai and Barry in the underground facility after finishing his paperwork for the day.

Ramses met up with Barry and Nicolai in lab 100 later that evening for final preparations. All the giant superconducting magnets sat in their metal housing containers. Ice crystals covered the surface of the magnets that were being cooled from the special liquid the aliens designed to coat them. Gas was dripping off the sides of the liquid storage containers, creating an eerie fog in lab 100. They were checking the gravity amplifier with one of the aliens. The creature's little hands moved up and down the object, checking for defects.

The alien looked to Nicolai and nodded.

"Is everything ready?" Ramses asked the little alien. It looked up at him with big black eyes, then nodded again.

"Very good." Ramses walked slowly around the structure, touching his hand to the freezing magnets. "Did you check all the wiring, Nicolai?"

"Yes, sir. Four times. I have already coordinated with the electricians on base, and they are prepared for the power surge. It will be completely dark for 30 seconds, but we should be able to manage."

They had to build dozens of large transformers on the outside and inside of the facility to handle the power surge. The machine would only be used once, but it would cost the base an estimated $75,000 in expenses for the 30 seconds that the base would be non-operational. The original budget of $100 million dollars for the Roswell Project had been surpassed long ago. The president made it clear to Ramses that failure was not an option. This operation alone cost more than all other Air Force operations combined. Ramses had to succeed.

He was meticulous about everything from the moment they retrieved the ship from Roswell up until the present. It all led up to the next 48 hours. The disabled ship was superior to any spaceship on Earth, but Ramses had since shifted his ambitions. The Earth was finite; space was infinite. The United States of America could tap into resources anywhere in the galaxy with this ship fully functioning, and his name would be attached to the technological advancement that would come with it.

Ramses did not like Nicolai, but he was a good scientist. His paperwork was thorough, his handwriting was neat, and he always did what he was asked to do. Ramses double-checked all his paperwork as a military standard, but he could never find any errors. Nicolai's paperwork regarding the wiring was thorough, and Ramses was sure he had adequately checked all the wiring components of the large doughnut.

By May 29th, 1948, everything was ready to go. The magnetic structure passed all the final inspections, and the power from the PNM power plants was ready to be used. Ramses had organized several teams to monitor the power output from the transformers on the outside of the facility, built above ground. They would communicate to Ramses via landline if anything appeared bad, or if one of the transformers started to fail. During the actual repair process, only Ramses, Nicolai, Barry, and two men in black would be allowed in lab 100. Ramses didn't want to risk another information leak, so letting anybody else see even the gravity amplifier was out of the question.

People were running around the outside of the underground facility coordinating how to safely deliver the absurdly large amount of electrical power at one time. Wires lay strewn about in jumbled messes near the entrance to the mountain base. Electricians and engineers were busy labeling and testing the wires one final time, with their ammeters and voltmeters. Ramses mailed out a letter to every person living on Kirtland Air Force Base, notifying them that a massive power outage would occur at 00:01 on May 31st. If all went according to plan, the outage would last no longer than 30 seconds. Even the emergency power supplies had to be switched off to prevent them from drawing in too much power and overheating.

The day passed by quickly, and soon Ramses was in his bed trying to sleep. He would wake up at 04:00 on May 30th the next morning, just like he did every morning. He laid in his bed for several hours, but sleep wouldn't come. He was too anxious. He was dreading the consequences of a botched repair. The military was now $150 million dollars in the hole, and this was their last hope at fixing the ship; there was no turning back.

Ramses thought about his parents as he stared up at his ceiling. They were both very religious like he had been; he wondered how they would have felt about an alien presence. He thought his dad might attribute them to God, or would refuse to believe it. His mom would probably try to have a conversation with the aliens and make them some tea. Ramses missed his parents. He wished he could speak to them right now. Maybe they could help him make sense of all this madness. He eventually drifted off to sleep and was awakened by his alarm at 04:00.

He walked into the bathroom and splashed cold water on his face after turning off the alarm. He looked at himself in the mirror and stared at his reflection. In his entire military career, he had never been so nervous as he was this morning. Not even when he flew over Germany during World War II with a bombing squadron. His 20-year career depended on what happened today. Failure was not an option. He quickly got dressed and was escorted by his personal driver to the base at 04:45.

He went through the Gibson gate, the outer gate guarding the underground mountain facility, and finally through the checkpoint by the giant red metal door. At the giant red door guarding the underground facility, the guards checked his badge and saluted him, waving him through. Men were checking amp and voltmeters on a transformer that had recently been built for the power surge, right outside the main entrance to the laboratory.

None of the men working on the project knew the true purpose of it, they only knew Ramses had ordered the construction of the doughnut-shaped structure and the 75 transformers necessary to handle the power surge. The word around the base was that the Air Force was testing out a new secret weapon. One of Ramses' subordinates overheard several airmen talking about why they were ordered to lay all the wires and build the transformers. Ramses was fine with that, as long as they did not know the truth.

Ramses made it inside the facility at 05:30. It was buzzing with scientists, engineers, and electricians frantically moving about. Young soldiers were aiding in the process, helping make last-minute adjustments to important things, moving wires, and screwing in bolts. Ramses had never seen the facility so alive.

At the very end of the hot side was lab 100, with both of its doors closed. Ramses headed toward the lab and opened the smaller door when he got there, carefully blocking the entrance from the workers checking wires nearby.

Barry and Nicolai were checking all the equipment one last time. Two men in black stood by the door, armed with guns. They greeted Ramses as he walked over to the scientists. Nicolai looked up momentarily from his notepad as Ramses approached.

"Everything looks good?" Ramses asked the pair of scientists.

Through his goggles, Barry responded, "Yes. We are ready for the final authorization to turn on the machine." Ramses was the final authorization. All he had to do was place a call to Timothy Chavez and let him know he was ready, and he would divert the power from his power plants to Kirtland Air Force Base. It was now a waiting game. They had approximately 18 hours until the power surge would occur.

Ramses spent the rest of the day going back and forth from lab 7 to lab 100, seeking advice from the aliens, his scientists, and his engineers and electricians. He was running on autopilot, double-checking almost every square inch of the doughnut structure himself. Completely built, the structure had a diameter of 100 meters. The housing was 10 feet wide and 4 feet high. Each of the magnets weighed 1,000 kilograms, and there were 100 magnets that fit perfectly into the metal housing. It was a magnificent feat of engineering, even though the blueprints and a large part of the construction were carried out by the aliens.

At 23:58, Ramses was back in lab 100. The facility had been nearly emptied out. Only a few scientists remained working late in the laboratories. Inside lab 100, two men in black and Nicolai and Barry were waiting for the machine to be turned on. The gravity amplifier, which looked like a trashcan stuck to the top of a pole, was sitting on the ground in the middle of the machine. The aliens had marked an X in the exact center where the amplifier needed to rest.

Ramses scanned the lab bench for the rotary phone in lab 100. He located it and picked it up, dialing the phone that was just outside of the massive red door. It rang once, then one of his men picked up.

"Sergeant First Class Ramirez."

"Sergeant, this is General Ramses. Call our boys on the outside and make sure everything is ready."

"Yes, sir, I will call you back shortly."

Ramses hung up the phone and dialed Timothy Chavez. The phone rang twice.

"Hello, Ramses. Are you ready for me to switch the power to the base?"

"Yes, sir, I am. Wait until exactly 00:01, then divert the power. We will be waiting."

"Sounds good. I will let my power plant lead operators know you are ready."

"Excellent. Thank you," Ramses said, hanging up the phone again. He turned around to look at the huge structure sitting in the middle of lab 100. The giant superconducting magnets encircled the amplifier as the Roman colosseum did around its gladiators. The stage was set. Everything was in place. The phone inside the lab rang again.

"Hello?" Ramses answered.

"Hi, sir, they are ready up there when you are."

Ramses looked at Barry and Nicolai as they stared at him, waiting for his command. "Are we ready?" Ramses asked the scientists. They both nodded at the same time.

"Okay, Ramirez, we are ready. Start the power transfer to laboratory 100."

Ramses hung up the phone and walked over to the scientists. "Turn on the machine," Ramses ordered the scientists. They walked over to the side of the machine that contained the on and off levers. Barry pulled down the on lever, turning on the massive machine. For a second, nothing happened, then a loud hissing noise could be heard as the incredible amount of electrical power started being directed into the machine.

The lights in lab 100 began to flicker. The superconducting magnets changed from a dull white color to a piercing blue color. Suddenly, the lab went pitch black as the machine fully turned on. Arcs of blue lighting began zapping the amplifier as it started to float in midair. The amplifier began spinning wildly as more lighting started hitting it. Ramses' hair was standing straight up on the back of his neck as he watched the machine in awe. After a couple of dozen seconds, the amplifier's spinning slowed down, and it dropped to the ground with a thud. The lighting ceased, and the glowing blue magnets changed back to their dull white color.

Lights came flickering back on, and Ramses was momentarily blinded by the brightness. Nicolai had turned the machine off, evident by the lever resting in the upward position. Barry was the first to break the silence in the lab.

"So, did it work?" he asked the room.

"There is only one way to find out," Ramses responded while walking towards the amplifier, hopping over the short structure. "Let's take the spaceship for a spin."

Chapter 19

⚓

Nicolai

The lights to the lab came back on, and everything appeared to be normal. All the miscellaneous equipment Nicolai and Barry had plugged into the wall turned back on. Ramses was talking on the phone with Timothy Chavez from PNM. Ramses hung up the phone then turned to Nicolai and Barry.

"Nicolai, Barry, put the amplifier back into place in the ship. I need to question the aliens," Ramses ordered while motioning his men in black to follow him. The agents followed Ramses as he walked out of lab 100. Nicolai moved towards the amplifier where Ramses had placed it.

Before he picked up the amplifier, Barry stopped him. "Wait. We need to check it for radiation." He was right. The aliens told them after the repair that the amplifier would be ready for immediate use in the spaceship, but they had to be cautious.

"You're right. I'll get the radiation scan tool and the electricians' heavy-duty gloves."

On the far side of the large lab was a wall that had drawers full of tools and lab supplies. Nicolai opened a drawer labeled "radiation" and pulled out the yellow scan tool. The scan tool could detect alpha, beta or gamma radiation from an object of choice. It looked like a yellow brick phone with a glass half-sphere on top. The glass half sphere absorbed the radiation, which told a sensor in the tool if the object of choice was radioactive for an alpha, beta, or gamma radiation. Nicolai then opened a drawer close by labeled "gloves" and sifted through a couple of pairs until he found the thick rubber gloves he was looking for.

Barry watched Nicolai as he dawned the gloves, turned the scanner on, and walked towards the amplifier. No beeping was heard at any of the three radiation settings; the object was not emitting any detectable radiation.

"All clear. No alpha, beta, or gamma radiation detected," Nicolai said to Barry. Barry nodded in acknowledgment and scribbled down something on a notepad he had grabbed.

Nicolai then attached the positive and negative terminals of an ammeter. The meter read 0 amps. There was no electrical current running through the amplifier. Nicolai was astounded, considering huge magnetic and electrical fields were generated inside of the doughnut. Not to mention bolts of electricity with millions of volts had struck the amplifier repeatedly.

"No electrical current detected," Nicolai said as Barry looked at the ammeter.

"Nicolai, bring a compass close to it. I want to see if a strong magnetic field is still present within the amplifier." Nicolai walked over to Barry, who pulled out a compass from his lab coat pocket.

It was copper along the outside, with the inside covered by a circular glass piece. An eight-pointed star was painted on the back, with each point pointing to 0°, 45°, 90°, 135°, 180°, 225°, 270°, and 315°, respectively. An iron needle with an N painted on one end dissected the circle across its diameter. It reminded Nicolai of an old nautical compass.

Nicolai walked closer to the amplifier while holding the compass out in front of him. As he approached the amplifier, the needle began to bob back and forth, signifying a magnetic field was still present in the object.

"Barry, the compass is picking up a magnetic field. I'm going to walk closer."

Nicolai inched forward, now only 5 feet from the amplifier. With each step, the needle moved more and more. From 3 feet away, the needle in the compass was spinning wildly inside the glass.

"Barry, come look at this," Nicolai said while motioning Barry to observe the compass. Barry pushed his spectacles up on his nose and waddled over to where Nicolai was standing.

"Hmm... interesting. The object's magnetic field is oscillating many times a second. And it is not generating an electrical current. This is very strange."

Nicolai could feel the invisible tug of the amplifier on the compass. It seemed to want to pull him towards it and every other direction simultaneously. It was a bizarre sensation.

"What do you think will happen if we put it into the spaceship right now as Ramses wants?" Nicolai asked Barry with his eyes transfixed on the spinning needle.

"I'm not sure. There is no electronic wiring, so to speak, so we won't have an issue with anything short-circuiting. I say we put it in and turn on the power."

"Don't we need Ramses' approval for that?"

"We are already supposed to be installing it into the spaceship. That's an order. If we turn on the spaceship, it may indicate whether or not it is fixed. If the spaceship doesn't turn on at all, then we can assume it's because the amplifier is now completely broken." Barry had a thirsty look in his eyes, like a mad scientist.

"Yeah, I agree. Go get the core. I'll put the amplifier back into place," Nicolai said. He picked up the amplifier, which weighed only 10 kilograms. He walked over to where the spaceship lay covered in the corner of the room. He tore off the tarps concealing its identity. The shiny metallic disc lay in front of Nicolai, perfectly balanced on its bottom center. As he walked around the side, the mechanism for opening the ladder started, and a small 6-foot ladder descended to the ground.

Nicolai climbed up the ladder, crouching as he stepped into the main cabin. Below him was the bottom level where the amplifiers were placed. He lowered himself through the hatch, opening down to the amplifiers. He could stand straight up on the bottom level. Two of the amplifiers sat on either side of the empty slot where the center amplifier was placed. The amplifiers snapped into clamp rings at the top and bottom. Nicolai made sure to line up the amplifier in the correct orientation, with the trash can lid facing down, and snapped the bottom and top part of the amplifier into place. Nicolai used a small tightening device to tighten the bottom and top clamps until he was satisfied.

Barry nosily crawled into the main cabin a few moments later. Nicolai looked through the hatch, climbed back up to the main level, and saw Barry taking the core and the metallic ring it sat on out from underneath his heavy arms. He placed the metallic ring gently on the spire that held the power core. He then placed the silver metallic core onto the metal ring. The interior lights turned on, detecting the power core was in place. Nicolai sat down at one of the childlike chairs in front of the control panel as it lit up, detecting the power core.

With the ship turned on, Nicolai wanted to check the power levels of the power core. He knew the correct sequence of buttons to push to make the power level graphs display on the viewing window if he had his notebook; he had watched the aliens do it many times and had recorded it down in his notes. He did not understand their written language, but Oousma and Ishma showed him how to interpret the basic graphs, such as the fuel level and power level graphs.

"I need to get my notes, Barry. I can't remember the exact sequence to display the power levels and fuel levels. I'm going to look for them really quick."

Half crouching, half walking, he squeezed his way out of the ship as the ladder automatically descended to the ground. He looked for the lab notebook that contained all his notes on the spaceship operating systems. Sleep-deprived and anxious, he finally spotted it lying under some papers on a lab bench. He moved the papers out of the way and picked up the notebook that read "Sequences."

There were hundreds of pages of button sequences that led to specific outcomes. He flipped to a tab labeled "power levels."

"Okay, I found the notebook. I'm heading back into the spaceship now."

Nicolai walked to the spaceship, and the ladder to the main cabin detected his movement and extended downwards to his feet. He walked up the small ladder and into the cabin where Barry was waiting.

Nicolai looked down at his notebook and started pressing the sequence of buttons to display the power levels. The control panel would often change colors, and the size and number of buttons would change, making it almost impossible to work without notes. Nicolai carefully input the command to display the power levels and fuel levels.

Two bar graphs appeared showing both the fuel levels and power levels. "Power levels back up to 99% Barry. The last time we checked it, the power levels were hovering around 30%. I think the middle amplifier is back up to full capacity. Element 115 stores are down to 20%. We have used quite a bit of the fuel during our experiments."

"Very good. That's all we needed. Turn off the ship's interface, and I will remove the power core."

Nicolai nodded and pressed the buttons on the control panel to turn off the ship's interface. The graphs displaying the element 115 fuel levels and power levels disappeared, and the window went black, showing the white lab 100 walls in front of it. Barry took the power core off the metallic disk, and the ship's main cabin ladder opened up and extended to the ground below.

Both scientists squirmed their way out of the small main cabin and onto the lab floor. After they walked back to the lab benches, Nicolai heard the mechanical noise of the ladder shortening back up and folding into the spaceship, creating a perfectly smooth exterior again.

"Well, the spaceship turns on, and the power levels have risen dramatically, but we still don't know how it will fly. We will need the aliens to run diagnostics before we can test its flight."

"Hopefully, we can conduct flight tests later tonight," Barry said to Nicolai.

Nicolai was exhausted, but he wanted to see if the ship's flight capabilities were greatly enhanced as well. He hoped they were, otherwise the money put into the spaceship for all those months was a complete waste. For the alien's sake, Nicolai hoped it would be fixed.

"Yes, hopefully. It all depends on when Ramses decides he wants to run more tests. He told us he wanted to test it tonight, but you never know with him."

Just then, the telephone in lab 100 started ringing. Barry looked at Nicolai and answered the phone, almost expecting an order from Ramses.

"Yes. Yes, okay. We will be right there."

"Nicolai, Ramses wants us to meet him in lab 7. He says he has a new important mission for us."

Nicolai wondered what the mission was, but realized he would soon find out. The two scientists quickly cleaned up lab 100 and put the tarps back over the spaceship. Barry went out of the lab before Nicolai, and Nicolai shut and locked the door behind him. There was nobody else on the hot side as they walked down the long hallway to lab 7.

As they walked down to lab 7, Nicolai thought about the aliens. Every time he worked on the spaceship or with the aliens, he was reminded of how minuscule his intelligence was. It was scary and awesome at the same time to be in their presence. Their technology was so incredibly advanced, Nicolai still had a hard time convincing himself it was all real. Flying across the globe in the blink of an eye was a life-altering experience. These thoughts flooded his mind as he unlocked the door to lab 7, with Barry in tow.

Ramses was standing over the two metal tables where the aliens were shackled. He was writing messages back and forth with Oousma, who looked up at Nicolai as he entered. Ishma was chained down completely on the table. The two men in black who had been present for the repair 30 minutes earlier were standing behind the aliens. Ramses barely noticed Nicolai and Barry as they walked in. Without looking up from what he was writing, Ramses asked, "So does the ship work?"

Nicolai was bewildered. "Uh, yes. It can turn on at least, and the power levels jumped back up from 33% to 99%."

"Good enough for me. We fly to the Martian moon Phobos at 01:00 sharp. I need both of you to accompany me on the trip."

Nicolai stood there in disbelief. Why Phobos? Phobos was an insignificant moon that orbited Mars. Nicolai didn't understand why it was of such interest to Ramses and why their first interplanetary test would be to Phobos. Did the ship have enough element 115 to make it there and back? There was no way of knowing. At least if they flew around Earth and something catastrophic happened on the spaceship, they could get out and survive. But Phobos would be different.

"Okay. Why are we going to Phobos?" Nicolai asked.

"There is an object of interest there that the military has wanted to investigate for some time," Ramses replied.

"What is this object of interest?"

"You will see when we get there. We leave in 30 minutes."

And with that, Nicolai and Barry were dismissed to lab 100. Nicolai had so many questions that needed answering, but the decision to go was Ramses'. Nicolai and Barry walked out of lab 7, and started making the journey back to lab 100. There were still dozens of wires sticking out of the lab 100 door that led to a transformer on the hot side. As they walked, Nicolai thought about Mars.

He had seen blurry images taken by telescopes from Earth, and he had looked at it many times through his own telescopes. It was a desolate, cold world, but beautiful none the less. Nicolai remembered hearing his astronomy teachers postulate about life on Mars and how a small microbial colony may live in one of the volcanic tunnels, shielded from the radiation by the ground.

As a kid, he imagined there were aliens on Mars who watched Earth, flying futuristic cars and shooting futuristic weapons. In the past ten months, he realized they weren't from Mars at all, but from the nearest star to the Earth's sun. They had futuristic technology, far beyond what Nicolai could conceive as a kid, and even as an adult. Now, he was minutes away from flying to the tiny red dot in the sky.

Nobody had photographed Phobos clearly before. It regularly appeared blurry in every picture he had seen. It was estimated that its dimensions were 17 x 14 x 11 miles, a tiny spec of an object in the solar system. That's what made the mission so precarious. Phobos was one of the smallest moons in the solar system and posed no real interest in the astronomy community. Nicolai could only speculate what Ramses' object of interest was. Clearly, Ramses knew more than what he was letting on.

As Nicolai and Barry entered lab 100, the phone was ringing. Nicolai picked it up.

"Hello?"

"Nicolai, it's Ramses. Come back to lab 7 immediately. I need your help."

Nicolai hung up the phone and looked at Barry. "Ramses wants me back in lab 7. I'll see you in a little bit."

Nicolai walked back to lab 7, and approached the door. As he opened the door, he heard Ramses talking loudly.

"Bullshit we don't have enough fuel. Just yesterday, you were saying it would take 2% of our fuel to travel to Phobos and back. We have 20% of our fuel left, so how does it make sense that we don't have enough?" Ramses asked Oousma.

Nicolai walked into the lab, and Ramses turned around.

"Nicolai. Can you explain to these idiots that 20 minus 2 is 18, not 0?"

Nicolai looked at Oousma, who looked at him with big black eyes.

"Can I see the notepad?" he asked Ramses, pointing to the one in his hand. Ramses flipped to a blank page, then handed the pad and pen to Nicolai. Nicolai could see on the previous page that Ramses had asked the aliens numerous times how much element 115 it would take to get to Phobos, and they kept repeating the same answer. It appeared they were lying, but Nicolai couldn't figure out why.

"18% should be plenty of fuel left over. There is no logical reason why a malfunction should happen at that level," Nicolai told Ramses before he wrote anything down.

"That is what I thought. Okay, it has been settled. Unchain specimens 1 and 2, and tell them they are going on a mission to Phobos. Men, grab the burlap sacks," Ramses finished. Nicolai looked at Oousma, then back at

Ramses. "Wait, let me ask specimen 2 some questions," Nicolai said as the men in black started to unchain Oousma.

Ramses nodded in approval. Nicolai wrote down his first question on the note pad. "Why do you not want us to travel to Phobos?"

He passed the notepad back to Oousma, who looked over the question. Its little hands wrote the response and passed the note pad back to Nicolai.

"There are some things humans should not know."

What was Oousma talking about? Nicolai wrote his response, "What do you mean? Why can't we know what is on Phobos?"

The alien read the message and shook its head. It wrote its response. "The secret on Phobos could destroy human civilization. Humans must not find out. I told Ramses we built a structure on Phobos, so now he is curious about what we built, but humans cannot see it at the present time. They cannot comprehend the reality of the object."

Nicolai stared at the note pad, shocked. These aliens had built an object on Phobos that could destroy civilization? The answer was making Nicolai's head spin. Oousma noticed the distress on Nicolai's face and motioned for the note pad. Nicolai passed back the note pad, and Oousma wrote another response.

"Fear not, Nicolai. It is not a weapon we built on Phobos. It is a picture, a description of events that happened thousands of years ago on Earth. We placed it there to guide humanity in the distant future when they became advanced enough to find it themselves. The human species is currently too young and volatile to comprehend the knowledge contained on it."

The phone in lab 7 started ringing as Nicolai tried to think about the words Oousma had written to him. Ramses walked over to the phone and answered. He spoke quietly on the phone, then hung up a few seconds later.

"Nicolai, we are ready. Wait for my men to transfer the aliens out of lab 7, then you and I will follow behind them. Our first interplanetary test begins in 5 minutes," Ramses said, watching his men in black cover the aliens in the burlap sacks.

There was no stopping the test, despite the warnings from Oousma. Nicolai nervously paced around while he waited for the men in black to walk out of the lab. They unshackled Oousma, and Nicolai solemnly followed behind the agents as they walked out of lab 7, guiding both aliens. Ramses towered over him from behind, shutting and locking the door to lab 7 as they left.

Barry was standing next to the metallic disc as Nicolai walked into the cavernous lab 100.

"Men, you can take the sacks off the aliens. Barry, is everything on the ship ready to go?"

"Yes, sir. The power core is in place, and the ship is turned on," Barry said.

Nicolai could see the blue lights glowing from underneath the spaceship.

"Are you ready, Nicolai?" Ramses asked as the party got ready to enter the spaceship.

"Yes, but the alien was telling me we should not go. It said-"

"I don't give a fuck what your little friend said to you. We are going, that's final." The tone in Ramses' voice was serious, desperate even. The argument ended there.

Barry was the first to walk up the ladder to the main cabin, followed by Ramses, the aliens, the two men in black, and finally Nicolai. They were packed like sardines in the main cabin as they all clambered their way into any available free space. Ramses was practically in a deep squatting position to keep his head from hitting the ceiling. As Nicolai made his way up, the aliens took their seats at the control panel. The ladder shortened, and the opening to the spaceship closed.

Ramses passed a sheet of paper that contained the desired coordinates to one of the aliens and said, "Here." The alien nodded and started pressing the now-familiar sequence of buttons to initiate the launch sequence. The diagram of a planet, a solar system, and a galaxy appeared on the display window. The alien pressed another series of buttons, and the solar system image was selected. The coordinates were input, and a picture of Mars appeared on the window. Nicolai could see the fissures and craters more clearly than he had ever seen them. After several more buttons were pressed, the image of Mars was replaced by a picture of Phobos. Nicolai could see its uneven surface in amazing detail.

"Put us directly in front of the obelisk," Ramses said to the aliens. Before Nicolai could ask what the obelisk was, he heard the humming noise that indicated the spaceship was about to fly. The bright white surroundings of the lab melted away. There was blackness and stars in the background. They were in space.

Several moments later, they were on a rocky surface. An enormously tall, upright tower stood in front of them. It took Nicolai several seconds to realize what he was looking at. The tower was rectangular and made of a different material than the surrounding dull brown rock. It was a bright white color and was clearly artificially made, evident by the sharp 90-degree angles that formed its squarish base and cuboid appearance.

There were pictures and symbols carved into every inch of the side they were looking at. Everyone in the spaceship stared at the obelisk in disbelief. The only words Nicolai could say were, "Oh my god."

One picture showed two winged beasts carrying a box in their talons. Another showed the scene of the birth of a human child. The mother was holding the baby in her arms, the umbilical cord still attached. The baby had what appeared to be a halo around its head. Nicolai's mind was racing.

"Fly around it. I want to see the whole structure," Ramses boomed. He was perspiring profusely; big droplets of sweat dripping down his face and onto his uniform. The aliens acknowledged his command and flew around the obelisk. More images and symbols appeared on the other sides of the obelisk. Some of the symbols looked identical to the symbols that were on the side of the spire that held up the power core inside the spaceship.

"Fly up. Let's see what is on the top."

The aliens obliged, and the ship slowly rose to the top of the obelisk. The symbols and images became more dispersed as the ship quietly ascended. Nicolai estimated they were at least 200 feet off the surface of Phobos and still were not at the top. The symbols and images stopped abruptly, and soon a double helix pattern could be seen that wrapped around all four sides of the obelisk. Dozens of feet before the top, they all flowed to one side of the obelisk. Finally, they were at the top, and the image in front of them was unmistakable.

Jesus Christ was being crucified, with the double helix pattern flowing into each foot. The face was the face Nicolai had seen in countless paintings. His hair was curly and long, coming down to his shoulders. A crown of thorns sat atop his head, and a ragged cloth draped across his groin. Blood was running down his face and wrists, with the red color of the blood being the only color on the obelisk. The carving of Jesus was far more sophisticated and intricate than the rest of the images on the obelisk.

"No, no, no, no!" Ramses screamed as he looked at the carving of Jesus. He was weeping as he shouted.

"What the fuck is this?" he shouted at the aliens. It seemed like everybody's heads were spinning. The men in black looked at each other with a stunned expression, and Barry had dropped his spectacles to the ground, not caring to pick them up. Now Nicolai understood why this could destroy human civilization.

Jesus was perhaps the most important historical figure of all time, certainly to the western world. If Jesus was, in fact, created by these aliens and not by God, billions of people would lose their minds. World wars would be started over information this sensitive and revealing. Nicolai was never religious, but his mom was a roman catholic, so he grew up thinking Jesus was a real person and the son of God.

"Take us back to Earth now. Nobody will speak of this, or I will kill you personally. Now go!" Ramses shouted to everyone in the main cabin.

The aliens started quickly pressing buttons, and soon the tower faded behind an image of the Earth. The barren moon and the space behind it morphed into the blinding white lights from the lab. The aliens turned the ship off, the ladder extended, and the opening widened. Ramses stormed off the spaceship, with Barry following closely behind him. What happened next happened so fast that Nicolai almost didn't see it.

He saw a blur of movement, and abruptly, the two aliens had the guns of the men in black. It was like they had slowed down time and grabbed the guns. Ishma fired its gun into the head of one of the confused men in black, who fell to the cabin floor dead. Oousma shot the other man in black in the head before he had time to react. Pools of blood started collecting under their heads, with pieces of brain leaking out. Stunned, Nicolai looked at the aliens who were now pointing the guns at him.

"No, don't! Please don't shoot me!" Nicolai pleaded as he backed away towards the exit. Ramses had heard the shots and was running back to the ship with his gun drawn. As Nicolai descended the ladder, shaking uncontrollably, Ramses cocked his gun. Nicolai scrambled to get out of the way as Ramses started firing blindly up into the cabin of the spaceship.

Nicolai watched three bullets hit Ramses in the stomach before he dropped to his knees, the gun falling out of his right hand.

The aliens wasted no time as they saw Ramses had been hit. The ladder opening closed, and the blue lights from underneath the spaceship started spinning in a circle. Nicolai heard a buzzing sound, and an instant later, the spaceship disappeared with a whooshing noise. They were gone. Nicolai squatted next to Ramses, who was bleeding heavily.

"Call for help," he gasped as he passed out on the floor. Dark red blood oozed onto the perfectly clean lab floor.

Chapter 20

⚶

Will

The driver who helped Will get back to Albuquerque was a man named Billy. On their drive back from the mountains, Will explained his predicament. Billy sat there quietly and listened to the whole story. By the end of it, he had offered Will a place to sleep for a few weeks.

"That's the craziest shit I ever heard, but I've read about you in the papers. You can stay with me, man. I live by myself on the far west side of the city."

It was May 15th, 1948, when Will had come out of the mountains and found Billy. Recovering to full strength took several days for him. Billy had picked him up emaciated and dehydrated. He rested on the couch of Billy's studio apartment until he felt like he had regained enough strength to go out.

Billy worked at a local gun shop and got Will a job working there under the alias Bobby. Will learned about building and repairing firearms. He worked 20 hours a week and helped Billy pay the rent on his studio apartment. Working at the gun shop provided Will the opportunity to purchase a firearm, a Colt revolver.

After work, Will would go out to the mesa near Billy's studio apartment and practiced shooting until it got too dark to see. He wanted to be ready when he faced Ramses again. Will never told Billy of his true purpose in Albuquerque. He kept his hatred of Ramses quiet. When he practiced shooting, he imagined Ramses' face on all the bottles and cans he shot. Will just needed to find him.

Every day Will was reading the local newspapers, hoping to find an article that could somehow lead him to Ramses. Occasionally, an article about Kirtland Air Force Base or operations going on pertaining to the military would show up, but most of them helped little. He was searching for Ramses. Ramses had not had another public appearance after his first address where he talked about Will, the crash, and the Heartleys. He read the lies Ramses spewed in an old article he found in the Albuquerque Journal about the press conference. Will also managed to get a videotape that KRQE had of the conference. A copy of the tape was in the local library. Will checked it out and watched it dozens of times on Billy's old, grainy television.

"You watch that damn recording all the time," Billy told him once.

"Yeah, I do," was all Will said in response. Billy got weirded out and didn't question Will about it after that. Will accumulated baskets of newspaper clippings and miscellaneous notes he had taken in the weeks since living at Billy's apartment. The living room in Billy's apartment was crowded with his junk.

Little was said in the city about the crash in Roswell. Will never heard it discussed in the coffee shops or the barbershops. It was like nobody knew or cared about what had happened there. The military had not put out an issue of its magazine in two months, which struck Will as odd. Normally, they published a new issue at the first of every month, talking about new big promotions and things they were working on at Kirtland, but they stopped cold. Just as Will was losing hope in finding Ramses, he heard an enticing story on a local news station, 89.9 FM.

"A general at Kirtland Air Force Base was shot in a suspected terror attack on June 1st. He is currently in critical condition at the V.A. Hospital." Will was writing down the message frantically. The radio in the gun shop was old, and there was always static, but he knew what he heard. A general had been shot on Kirtland Air Force Base. The only general Will knew of in Albuquerque was Ramses.

The reporter on the station explained that the military was not releasing the name of the general. He then said Kirtland Security Forces would be opening an investigation into the shooting, but would not publicly disclose information until the investigation was complete. There was only one V.A. hospital in Albuquerque, so Will knew where to go.

Getting into the hospital would be easy. There was public access from an entrance on Gibson Boulevard. Security officers were stationed outside, but they only had two on the clock at any one time. Will visited a dying cousin at the V.A. a few years back, so he knew the entire layout of the building and grounds.

It was June 20th, 1948, when Will finally had the courage to go to the hospital. He was hyper-alert for the men in black, weary that they would be lurking around the hospital. In the weeks since he had been living in Albuquerque, he had not seen them. He never let his guard down for fear of being recognized. He wore a hat and sunglasses everywhere and kept his thick brown beard long to conceal his facial structure.

Will was too nervous to eat in the morning, so he went straight to the bus stop on Central, checking to make sure he had his colt revolver in his jacket pocket. He walked to the bus stop and waited for the bus to arrive at 7:00 A.M. Billy asked Will where he was going that morning, and Will responded with, "On a mission."

"Why are you loading up the gun, Will?" Billy asked, eyeing him.

"Billy, I don't think you are going to see me again after today. I want to thank you for everything you have done for me. From picking me up on the side of the road, to giving me a place to live. I will forever be in your debt."

"Will, you're freaking me out. Are you leaving, or are the feds on to you?"

"Don't worry. I'm only doing what I need to do. They won't be after you. They have no idea you allowed me to live with you." Will could tell Billy wanted to ask more questions, but he didn't. Billy shook his head and walked away.

Will left the apartment without telling Billy goodbye. It was easier that way. He walked to Central, where he would catch the earliest Central bus. The turquoise bus stop stood out from the dull, brown surroundings. Will sat quietly, watching the sunrise over the Sandias. Today might be the last day he saw the sunrise. He accepted the idea of death and breathed in the fresh Albuquerque morning air.

Will's plan was to go to Gibson Boulevard, walk in through the public entrance, and ask someone at the reception desk for a map of the building. He didn't know where Ramses was, but he bet he could figure it out by looking at a map. If he was stopped or questioned, he would lie and say he was visiting one of his cousins. If worse came to worst, he would force his way in and hope for the best.

After what seemed like an eternity, the 40-foot-long city bus pulled up, with an advertisement for the Albuquerque Journal painted on the side. Will got on to a mostly empty bus and took his seat. An old Native American woman sat next to him, and she eyed him suspiciously as he sat down. Will was careful not to reveal his gun.

It took the bus almost an hour to get to Central and San Mateo, the closest cross streets to the V.A. Will tugged on the wire when they neared his stop, letting the driver know he wanted to get off. As he got off, he turned around and saw the Native American woman kissing a piece of jewelry she had on while staring at Will. Unnerved but not undeterred, Will began the walk to the V.A. hospital.

At 8:00 A.M., it was already 85°F, and Will had on a denim jacket, with pockets on the inside to conceal the gun, and blue jeans to hide his legs. He walked the 1.3 miles to the V.A. hospital, sweating badly by the time he arrived at the public entrance. There were four armed guards surrounding the entrance, twice the usual amount. Something was up.

Will wiped the sweat from his brow and walked towards the hospital, crossing Gibson. The hospital was five stories high and painted a dull brown color with windows that had blue trim. Adobe was the material used to construct the hospital, indicated by the texture of the building. Surrounding the hospital was a grass courtyard that had benches for people to sit at. A long concrete walkway led from Gibson to the public entrance.

As Will tried to enter through the public entrance, he was stopped by a guard.

"What is your business here?"

"I am visiting a sick relative."

"What part of the hospital are they in?"

"He is in the I.C.U."

"No visitors are allowed to visits guests in the I.C.U. at the moment."

"Why not?"

"Orders from my boss. Now get out of here," the guard said angrily. He looked like a big white toe, with a wrinkly forehead and a burly body.

"Look, I just need to go in and visit him quickly. He has nobody else. He's a dying man!"

"I said no."

"Please, sir, please. I walked miles in the heat to see him. I'm dripping in sweat and half-delirious, for God's sake."

The guard scrunched his face and looked at the other guards. They looked at him and shrugged.

"Fine, go ahead," he said, stepping aside.

Will thanked him and pushed open the double metal doors. Nurses and doctors were running around, wheeling patients, and doing paperwork as they went. Nobody noticed Will.

After walking down the entrance hallway for a minute, it opened up to a large waiting room. In the middle of the room was a reception desk, evident by the phones and women working there. They all seemed to be on the phone at once. Will walked up to a pretty Hispanic girl talking on the phone. She looked up and said, "Please hold," then put down the phone. She looked up at Will and asked, "How may I help you, sir?"

"Hi, can you hand me a map of the building?"

"Yes, sure, here you go," she said while passing Will a map. Will thanked her and walked around to a staircase near the western side of the building. A fire exit was placed by the stairwell, and Will could see no security personnel on this side of the building. He noted that in his head, marking a possible escape route.

Will looked at the map and could tell that the I.C.U. units were on the fifth floor. Based on the guard's reaction, Will guessed Ramses was in the I.C.U. It was the smallest floor according to the map, so it was easier to protect. Before walking up the stairs, he checked his revolver and made sure there were seven rounds in it. He spun the barrel in his fingers, watching the hollow points rotate in the light.

The five flights of stairs had him winded by the time he made it to the fifth floor. A green door labeled "Floor 5" was the only barrier between him and Ramses. He composed himself as he took a deep breath and put his hand around the gun. He opened the door to the fifth floor quietly, slowly peeking around the doorway for dangers.

One man in a black suit and sunglasses was standing outside a room on the far side of the fifth floor. Bingo. Will stuck out, considering few people were in the hallway at that time. He quickly ducked into the nearest room before the man in black noticed his presence. A surprised elderly man was resting on a hospital bed, with a ventilator attached to him. Will put his finger to his lips and showed him the gun. He had to think fast. The only way to get to Ramses' room was from the front. He would have to face the man in black with a head-on firefight, but he had one advantage: the element of surprise.

Because the room he was standing in was closest to the fire exit stairs, it had a fire alarm on the wall outside of it. Will could see the fire alarm from where he was standing but couldn't reach it. He inched closer to the doorway until he was close enough to pull it. Will pulled down the fire alarm from behind the door, and a loud wee-woo, wee-woo sound began playing on speakers in the hospital. Ink splattered onto his hand, and the sprinkler system in the hallway turned on. He heard a thunder of footsteps and voices outside of the room. He slipped out and hung low between the sea of doctors and nurses who were trying to get the I.C.U. patients out of the building. He slowly made his way closer to the man in black guarding the door.

20 feet. 15 feet. 10 feet. He could make out the bone structure in his face from here. He grabbed his gun from his jacket pocket, and in one swift motion, let out six rounds into the man in black before he even knew what happened.

"He has a gun, run!" someone screamed from behind Will. People started frantically running and shouting, alarmed by the gunshots.

Blood poured out of the man in black, and his mouth lay open, spit oozing from the side. Will stepped over the body of the man in black and heard labored breathing from behind a curtain. Will peeled back the curtain and saw Ramses propped up in a pillow, drooling. He smelled like death; clearly, an infection had developed around his abdomen. Will could see yellow pus from underneath the bandage.

"Hey Ramses," Will said while shaking the massive general awake.

"Ahhhh," Ramses blurted out as he came to and realized who was in front of him.

"Fuck you!"

BANG!

Epilogue

I was devastated when they killed you. You were such a beautiful boy, my boy. You were filled with joy and laughter, bringing wonder into the world. You could talk to the animals, and they hated you for that. You spoke of loving your enemies, and they hated you for that too. Such a beautiful child you were. Oh, why did they take you from me? I watched as they nailed your wrists and ankles to the cross. I watched you plead for me to spare your life, but I could do nothing. I loved you like a father loves his proudest son. You showed me the joy that I never knew was possible. I wish you were here now, but you are not. I built this monument so your memory will live on forever in the cosmos. I will always love you, my son, Jesus.

Annonaki Timeline

- **5,000,000 years before present-** Anatomically modern Annonaki arise on Nirubu.

- **2,000,000 years before present** -Annonaki change their DNA to make every individual autotrophic. Annonaki also alter their DNA to reproduce asexually. They reproduce new babies through stem cells.

- **750,000 years before present** -Annonaki no longer speak verbally, only telepathically, through natural evolution.

- **500,000 years before present-** Annonaki change their DNA to make them live tens of thousands of years.

- **500,000 years before present-** massive world war kills 70% of the living population on Nirubu as result of the decision to alter their genome for longer life.

- **500,000 years before present- 485,000 years before present -** Kuhan Empire establishes power on Nirubu, created by Kuhani Abdullah, and implements the policy that every new Annonaki baby have its genome altered to make it live longer.

- **250,000 years before present** – Annonaki begin to develop warp drive engines, using atomically engineered element 115.

- **150,0000 years before present-** Annonaki launch first unmanned satellites and robotic probes to Earth.

- **16,000 years before present-** Oousma is born into a breeding facility.

- **15,000 years before present-** Oousma topples the Kuhan Empire and establishes the Council of Elders.

- **15,000 years before the present-** Oousma is elected the first Supreme Chancellor of the Council of Elders.

- **13,000 years before present-** Warp drive technology is advanced enough to send live Annonaki to Earth.

- **12,500 years before present-** Oousma leads the first expedition to earth and abdicates the Supreme Chancellor position to stay on Earth. Zahmu, Mammadu, Issla and Vahisma accompany Oousma on the first trip to Earth.

- **12,000 years before present-** Oousma leaves earth because of an impending asteroid impact.

- **2,000 years before present-** Oousma is reelected to be the Supreme Chancellor of the Council of Elders.

- **1,947 years before present-** Oousma comes back to earth on the second live mission, in an attempt to create the first human/ Annonaki hybrids. Veezma accompanies Oousma.

- **1,000 years before the present-** Ishma is born.

www.ingramcontent.com/pod-product-compliance
Lightning Source LLC
Chambersburg PA
CBHW020245180626
46810CB00006B/2376